# King of Egypt, King of Dreams

Other books in the Insomniac Library Series:
Gwendolyn MacEwen, *Julian the Magician*

# Gwendolyn MacEwen

## King of Egypt, King of Dreams

INSOMNIAC PRESS

Text copyright © 2004 by the Estate of Gwendolyn MacEwen
Afterword copyright © 2004 by Carol Wilson
First published by Macmillan (Toronto) in 1971.
Insomniac Library edition 2004.

Series editor Richard Almonte
Interior design by Marijke Friesen

All rights reserved. No part of this publication may be reproduced, stored in a retrieval system or transmitted, in any form or by any means, without the prior written permission of the publisher or, in case of photocopying or other reprographic copying, a license from Access Copyright, 1 Yonge Street, Suite 1900, Toronto, Ontario, Canada, M5E 1E5.

National Library of Canada Cataloguing in Publication Data

MacEwen, Gwendolyn, 1941-1987.
    King of Egypt, king of dreams / Gwendolyn MacEwen.

(Insomniac library ; 2)
First published: Toronto: Macmillan of Canada, 1971.
ISBN 1-894663-60-8

    I. Title. II. Series.

PS8525.E84K55 2004          C813'.54          C2003-907381-5

The publisher gratefully acknowledges the support of the Canada Council, the Ontario Arts Council and the Department of Canadian Heritage through the Book Publishing Industry Development Program. We acknowledge the support of the Government of Ontario through the Ontario Media Development Corporation's Ontario Book Initiative.

Printed and bound in Canada
Insomniac Press
192 Spadina Avenue, Suite 403
Toronto, Ontario, Canada, M5T 2C2
www.insomniacpress.com

*It is a very common belief that the further man is separated from the present in time, the more he differs from us in his thoughts and feelings; that the psychology of humanity changes from century to century like fashions or literature. Therefore no sooner do we find in past history an institution, a custom, a law or belief a little different from those with which we are familiar, than we immediately search for all manner of complicated explanations, which more often than not resolve themselves into phrases of no very precise significance. And indeed, man does not change so quickly; his psychology at bottom remains the same, and even if his culture varies much from one epoch to another, it does not change the functioning of his mind. The fundamental laws of the mind remain the same, at least during the short historical periods of which we have knowledge; and nearly all the phenomena, even the most strange, must be capable of explanation by those common laws of the mind which we can recognize in ourselves.*

Ferrero: *Les Lois Psychologiques*

# INTRODUCTORY HISTORICAL NOTE

In 1575 B.C. the Pharaoh Ahmose I of Thebes freed Egypt from the rule of the "foreign chiefs," the Semitic Hyksos kings, pursuing them from their capital at Tanis to the southern frontiers of Palestine. The period known as the New Kingdom opened up with the 18th Egyptian Dynasty—a dynasty whose rulers included the "Pharaoh with breasts," Queen Hatshepsut, and the famous conqueror Thutmose III who carved out an empire in Syria and Palestine. During the reign of Amenhotep III (1405-1367 B.C.) Egypt was at the height of her glory, and foreign tribute poured in from the conquered nations of north and south. No less abundant than the wealth of Amenhotep was the wealth of the ruling priesthood of Amon in the capital city of Thebes, for Amon-Ra was supreme deity of king and state. The ancient capital of On (Heliopolis) which had flourished in former days, and its sun-priests of Ra, had long since been eclipsed.

The empire extended from Kush (Ethiopia) in the south, ruled by a viceroy of Pharaoh, to Naharin, the northernmost frontier province on the southern border of Mitanni. Mitanni, a kingdom populated by a Hurrian people from the region of what is now Armenia, and ruled by an Indo-Aryan royal house, played an important role in Egyptian politics, for it lay between the Hittite territories in the north and Pharaoh's possessions in Syria, forming a kind of buffer state between the two powers. Some areas of Syria were dependent on Mitanni, while others (mainly the coastal areas) and Palestine, were divided into principalities with fortified cities presided over by local kings. Often Egyptian regents or "Watchers" were placed at the side of these vassals to ensure fidelity and the paying of tribute.

During Amenhotep III's latter years the Habiru tribes were attacking the eastern fringes of Palestine and causing havoc within the country, and the Hittites had begun to gain a hold in northern Mitanni. But the son of Amenhotep who inherited the throne and the empire of his forefathers was not a warrior but a priest. He ruled from 1367 to 1350 B.C. Later generations were to mutilate his monuments, strike off his name from the list of kings, and refer to him under their breaths as "the Criminal." His name was Akhenaton.

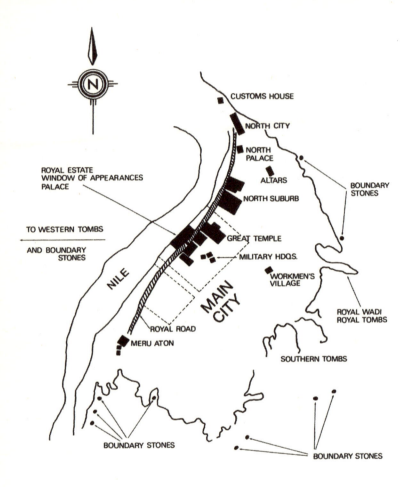

Akhetaton
(Tel-El-Amarna)

# King of Egypt, King of Dreams

morning         the sun rises

As a child in the palace of his father he spent a great deal of his time in a dark room, lying naked between thin sheets, and there was a narrow sliver of light from a niche in the wall which at certain times of the day drew a band of fire across his belly, dividing him in two. His skull was so long one would swear some barbarian had shaped it while it was still soft after birth. He claimed that a demon resided in his head, fighting to be born. His grotesque fleshy flanks enlarged with the years, while his chest remained narrow and nervous as though refusing to acknowledge the alarming little mounds of flesh beneath the nipples. Then there were his eyes—one blue and one brown, one strong and one weak like the two eyes of Heaven—the sun and the moon—neither of which could bear bright light though they hungered for it endlessly. But these were only his shapes and colours—his illnesses were something else. One mysterious ailment followed another—the falling sickness, the shivering and vomiting disease, the noise in his head which only he could hear, the wild pulsating of his heart, a long series of drumbeats which distorted his thinking. He was a living archive, a walking medical library of arcane illnesses.

He used to actually *smell* the sun in that dark room; Ra in his absence was wholly present, and that painful sliver of light was a dividing knife of fire across his flesh (cutting him up, he claimed, for sacrifice). The sickness was broken by short periods of health when he would return to the court and gaze wildly and uncomprehendingly at the activity around him. Then his vision would gradually be assailed again by strange bands of moving light, and the familiar dizziness would overtake him for days. His skull would crawl with a thousand unseen creatures, and he swore that fingers and needles and feathers were tickling and pricking him to distraction.

Many times he dreamed of a vicious winged sphinx which descended upon him while he slept, changing in her descent into a hideous vulture whose wings stank of salt and death; she would squeeze his frail ribs as a whirlpool might surround a child's boat and then she would embrace him finally in the coffin which was her body. For hours he would struggle to escape her claws and the beating wings, for he knew he was not dead and the vulture had no claim upon him.

Finding him tangled up in the linen sheets after such a session, his nurse would try to soothe him by saying, "Have no fear, prince—it is the Lady of Dread who assails you. She is Nekhbet, a goddess of the Upper Land, and she protects a royal person; why, she's even worn on the crown as the Right Eye of the king to watch over him."

"She doesn't protect me!" the boy would protest. "She smothers me with her wings, and her wings are death . . . and she has great hanging breasts. . . ."

"Then," the nurse would sigh, "she is also Mut, the Divine Mother who first suckles the royal child—and her wings embrace a royal person in his coffin when he dies. You know the word for 'mother' is written with the sign of the vulture."

The dream had started when his mother Tiy gave him a medallion to play with. It was part of a bracelet engraved with an image of herself in the form of a winged sphinx. Tiy, being a basically tasteless woman, had imagined the thing to be a fanciful depiction of her strength and beauty, and even had copies of the medallion circulated throughout the empire—but it was a hideous piece of work. It presented Tiy crouched low on lion's paws, Tiy with a ghastly piled-up coiffure topped with one of the abominable floral headdresses she always used to wear, Tiy with the name of Tiy between her paws, and a smile on her mouth like the smile of a lioness who had just eaten her fill of delicate gazelles.

Sometimes he lost track of how long he had been in bed. Months, years? He passed the time studying the painful little slit of sunlight across his belly, until he decided his body was a broken, alien thing, and he cursed Amon, Lord of the gods, for creating him. When servants came to ask him if he wanted anything he used to cry, "Light, give me light!" as a man lost for days in the desert might plead for water. And when his mother visited him, the double plumes of her crown would dive menacingly towards his face as she bent over him to ask how her young prince was, her "poor bird burning with fever in his nest of fire." She would whisper his private name "Neferkheprure," "Beautiful Are the Creations of Ra"—and her salt-sweet breath was the burning nest of spices in which the bird of Ra was consumed, and the syllables would fall like petals of flowers onto his eyes, his ears ... but then the plumes would start to change into wings and he would turn away and seek the darkness. And the darkness he encountered was a tangible thing, it was Apop the snake, the enemy of Ra whose black coils strangled the sun and brought night to the earth.

Occasionally his father the living god Amenhotep would come, but his visits were short and furtive and he barged into the room as though someone outside had given him a stiff kick. He resented losing time from his various sports to visit the sickroom of his son. Always the breath of the god was heavy, reeking with wine, and he would stand over the bed looking embarrassed and put out, and mumble meaningless but appropriate sentiments. He never touched the body of the prince and all that the boy remembered of his visits was the ludicrous shape of the god's nose. That and the foul breath, for the royal teeth were rapidly decaying. But mostly the nose, that over-large, outcurving nose of Amenhotep III, Lord of the Two Lands and Ruler of the World, single-handed slayer of one hundred and two wild lions. Nose in the darkness, foul breath inquiring after his health, blue gleam of helmet, rapidly closing door....

It was a favourite pastime of the young men of the capital to imagine what might have happened in the royal bedroom on the holy night when the seed of Pharaoh's monstrous offspring had been sown. The king had to do everything at an appointed time, and the very hour at which he might father a royal child was fixed. The wisest temple seers studied the constellations and determined the time at which the seed of the god Amon would enter Pharaoh's loins, and when the divine fluid flowed within him he went into his Chief Wife. As for her, the moment she felt the holy seed burst within her, she cried aloud the name, sex and physical attributes of her desired offspring so that the great Potter would hear and shape his *ka* in the womb of heaven accordingly. But what weird sounds must Tiy have uttered to produce this misfit when her husband as incarnate Amon entered her?

The monstrous tales of his conception never ended. *("Tiy lay, legs apart, under the body of the god and cried out, A son! Hear me, Great One! Give him a swollen head and narrow chest, great ugly thighs and slanting eyes, a long face, face of a sick horse, O Potter!")*

There were also rumours that the placenta which Tiy had kept in the customary manner, it being the twin brother of the child, had rotted within a day.

Since no one could diagnose the nature of the diseases which afflicted him, therefore it was argued the gods were punishing him for an evil only they understood. And who knew about his private parts? Perhaps he was a woman, another Hatshepsut! (But then Hatshepsut might have been a man.) Or perhaps he was the sorry offspring of the lesser gods. The Snake of the Granaries might have slithered out of the grain one day with him on her back, or the crocodile Subek might have spat him forth during the flood.

But all those stories were far more unflattering to Tiy than to her son. She was closer to the people than any queen before her had been; in fact she was one of them for her mother had been a commoner. Such sarcasm was finally a measure of affection, for nothing was more dear to the people of Keme than their wit; foreigners found them the most humour-stricken people in the world. Tiy was the victim of parody, which only meant she had a special place in their hearts.

The boy never wrestled, swam or hunted gazelle and hare. One might have knocked him over with a breath, or—as people often imagined—a thought. Someone did blow on him once, a boy at least five years his junior, a dark-skinned son of one of the nobles of Kush who was being educated with other boys of high blood at Amenhotep's court; he let out a great gust of air and the prince fluttered to the ground like a wounded bird.

But he was very good at his lessons; he mastered the problem of the area of a triangle at a very early age; later he could calculate the number of men needed to transport an obelisk of given dimensions, and the proportions of the ramp needed to lift it, with amazing speed. Still, mathematics bored him. He longed for knowledge of another kind. "You carry a palette," his teachers would say. "That is what makes the difference between you and one who wields an oar. Plunge into a book as one plunges into water; poverty awaits him who does not go there!"

"But I want to plunge to a depth beyond books and words!" he would protest, as his teachers raised their patient heads to heaven.

He was an everlasting embarrassment to his father Amenhotep, for no sooner was he allowed freedom at court after some illness or another, than he would commit a gross blunder—express his ignorance of court affairs or ask wild and annoying questions about irrelevant things. Once during an important reception, he approached his father's throne to stroke the head of the gorgeous leopard reclining beneath it, but stumbled over his own clumsy feet and fell flat on his face in sight of ten visiting ambassadors from Karaduniash. The prince lacked sophistication. He simply couldn't navigate in public, and carried himself like a frail boat caught in an eddy during floodtime.

It was in an effort to help him gain some knowledge of the world that Tiy assigned to him a special tutor, a man who was to remain at his side for life and who knew the boy and later the man as no one else knew him. Parennufer was old even then, one of those people who seemed to have been born old, and he pitched the prince headlong into the mysteries of men and gods, thrusting his mind into darkness in order that he find his own way back to light. In the end the boy was frighteningly precocious. Better he had been left to thrash about in the dark sands of doubt, complained Amenhotep. He was tutored well, too well in the opinion of the king, who had instructed Parennufer not to feed too many of the ripe fruits of wisdom to a boy who would never reach the throne.

Violent arguments went on between Tiy and Amenhotep whenever the issue of Pharaoh's successor was raised. Amenhotep was in a tight position, for Tiy was his Chief Wife, and the boy recovering from mind sickness, eye sickness, falling sickness and belly sickness was her only son... and as such was entitled to greater consideration than his casual harem offspring.

"I will never allow this Accident to mount the throne of the Two Lands!" he would cry.

And Tiy upbraided him for the fact that he never even acknowledged his son's existence by including his name on his monuments.

"I am assuming that what is not written does not exist," was the answer.

It was his wish to choose a son of one of his lesser wives and marry him to the first royal daughter and heiress Sitamon. But Tiy fought for her own claims and vowed up and down the palace that she would put *her* son on the throne and marry him to his sister, so that her only two offspring would be the rulers of Keme. She would storm through the palace, which was known as the House of Rejoicing, in a spitting rage, cursing the world and everyone in it, mistreating her handmaidens, insulting the noblemen, and finally fall into a long deep sleep from which she would awake clear and calm with a new plan.

This was the main struggle within the palace, but there was another greater struggle going on outside, one for which old Parennufer tried to prepare the prince, and which he swore would one day tear the land apart.

"Child, gird yourself for war," he told the boy.

"I will never take up arms in any battle," he replied.

"I am speaking of another battle, my prince, a battle of the mind. There is a war even now. You cannot see it, it is invisible, but it goes on...."

Once they walked together along the banks of the Nile and Parennufer said, "Cast your eye to the great temple of Opet across the river!"

"I cannot see it, it's too far!"

"I meant you to cast your *inner eye*, my prince. Now—there is the war, between the royal house and the House of Amon. The power and wealth of the ruling priests is as great as that of your father. The servants of the god dictate to the throne by means of oracles which always favour the ambitions of the High Priest over those of the royal house...."

And he leaned over his young pupil and said in a whisper among the quivering waterplants, "Beware the parasites of the temple— even the scribes and cattle-slayers! I tell you the men who serve Amon are fleas on the body of the god. Always remember this night, remember that I told you that when the affairs of state and temple are closely joined, their union is an abomination. In the old days the priests were mere delegates of the royal house, performing their services in the king's name...."

"But now?"

"Now they grow fat and ugly preying upon men's fears—not their love, little prince, but their *fears*. They are many, but they are corrupt, and their god is a piece of wood chewed up by termites, dry and full of holes...."

To have spoken such words on the other side of the river would have been to invite death, but no one in the royal house persecuted the old tutor for his beliefs. Since the days of the prince's grandfather Thutmose, the royal family had sought to reduce the power of the temple of Opet. As for Parennufer, some guessed where his true devotion lay. He was probably a secret initiate in the mysteries of On, the ancient capital of the land and the seat of the worship of Ra. He'd been born in the Land of the Papyrus, and there was a period of a few years in his youth which he'd never convincingly accounted for. But he kept his past a secret out of simple fear; the Purifiers of Amon would scarcely have tolerated the fact that an initiate of the ancient mysteries of Ra was tutoring the crown prince.

Long before when On shone like a sun among cities, and Ra in his many forms was the supreme god of king and state, Amon had been a local deity worshipped by the people in the city of No. But when later the princes of No had risen up and claimed the throne of the Two Lands, their deity was raised to supreme Lord of the gods. He was known as Amon-Ra, borrowing the majesty of the old god by means of his name—and the capital city became No Amon. The ruling priests then melted the old into the new, and subordinated the worship of Ra and all other gods to the worship of theirs; all deities became mere aspects of him, and the great temple of Opet enclosed many sub-shrines devoted to the worship of these lesser gods. So the worship of Ra was never forbidden, but his forms became the forms of Amon, and his priests were placed under the jurisdiction of Opet.

But there had always been some, like Parennufer, for whom the almighty Ra in his original forms was still the Lord of the gods, and in some of his sessions with the prince, he talked of the Creation as it was understood in On, and the ancient legends of Ra.

"In the beginning, my prince, were the waters of Nun, the Great Nowhere. Then the Creator, the Complete One, created Himself from Himself by joining His seed with His secret self or by uttering His own name. He was Ra in His form as Atum, and He appeared as a *benu* bird on the primeval mound. Later, He spat out Shu, Lord of the Atmosphere, and Tefnut, whom some say is Maat, the goddess of Truth and Order. And from *their* union came forth Geb the earth and Nut the sky...."

"Last week," the boy whispered, "my uncle Ineni told me the Creator appeared as a child in the midst of a lotus on the waters of Nun... and before that he said the god was a great wind that stirred the primordial waters...."

"Your uncle," put in Parennufer patiently, "is a prophet of *Amon*, did you forget that?" He paused a moment as his young pupil frowned darkly, then he went on. "From the union of Geb and Nut came forth Osiris, Isis, Set and Nebhet. Horus was the son of Osiris and Isis; every Pharaoh is living Horus, and Son of the Sun..."

"Then Horus must be the direct son of Ra!" broke in the prince.

"Well He is as well!" Seeing another frown come over the boy's face, Parennufer leaned forward seriously and added, "You must understand that there are many accounts of such matters and the heart must try to support them all."

"Well my heart can't! How can many things exist all at once, all being the same thing?"

"Little prince," sighed the tutor, "you *must* understand. In the Nile there are a million droplets but there is only one river. Truth takes many forms, but there is only one truth."

"Then why not just *say* there is one?"

*"No one knows how, my child."*

They both lapsed into silence for a time, after which Parennufer took up the thread of his tale. "Now the Eye of Ra had a mind of its own, and one day it went off looking for Shu and Tefnut; when it got back Ra had replaced it with a brighter one, but so as the first Eye wouldn't feel abandoned, He placed it on His brow as the *Wedjet* eye to rule the world. The royal cobra your father wears on his crown is the *Wedjet*; it is the Left Eye of the king and it defends him. It has the power of giving immediate death. Now the Right Eye of the king—"

"—I know what it is, the Vulture," said the boy.

"Very good. Now another time, the Eye of Ra fell to earth; it didn't want to go back to heaven so it cried, and its tears created man. *Remyet, romyet, tears, mankind*... you see how similar the two words sound? Perhaps it means that man was born to weep.

"Now Ra was King of the Universe and also King of the World. The Morning Star brought Him His breakfast every morning. But when He began to get old the other gods wanted to do away with Him, and Isis, with her devious trickery, tried to discover His *secret name* to gain power over Him. She made a snake out of His spittle which poisoned Him. Then Ra cried, *I am son of Myself, I am Ra! I was wounded by a serpent I couldn't see. It's not fire and it's not water, but I'm hotter than fire and colder than water!* Then Isis asked, *What is it, Divine Father? Behold, a worm has done Thee this wrong! Tell me Thy name, Divine Father, for he whose name is spoken shall live.* And the almighty Ra replied, *I am He who created heaven and earth and piled up the mountains and made all living things.* But He didn't reveal what Isis wanted to know. Later, however, He did. Now my prince, what is the lesson contained in this tale?"

And in a frightened whisper the boy replied, "Let no man know your secret name."

Parennufer smiled. He hadn't expected quite that answer. "Now when Ra was very old and weary the gods said of Him, *'His majesty has grown old, and His bones are of silver and His flesh is of gold, and His hair is pure lapis lazuli.'* He became so weary in fact that He left the earth and went to heaven forever, so man and the gods were separated."

Then Parennufer's words took a more practical turn. "Yesterday we were talking of how the ruling king receives the state to deliver it to the god in the form of Crown land which is donated to the temple...."

But the boy's voice interrupting was urgent and high-pitched. "If the land is *already* the god's, why should the king deliver it back to him?"

"A good question. But doesn't a son often buy a present for his father with money that he got from him in the first place? Such matters are complicated, but we must dwell on them until they become as clear as the waterbeads on the back of a duck, whence they will flow off and rejoin the great river of mysteries and paradoxes which leads to the sea of Truth...."

But the boy was silent. He disliked mysteries and paradoxes; he even disliked simple diversities in food. (He once ate nothing but goose meat for a solid year, and when asked about it he replied that if something was good, then it was good *enough*.) Eventually his attention returned to the last part of the lesson, the part he disliked, the part that nevertheless fascinated him.

"All night Ra sails through the terrible darkness of the Underworld, and Wisdom and Magic are with Him. As He passes through the Twelve Cities and Fields and Gates and Circles of the night, He battles hundreds of demons and almost dies...."

Parennufer noticed that the prince was absently tracing the twelve circles in the air.

Pa-Opet was a month of oracles, and in the prince's fourteenth year the seers of the temple were more busy with their visions than usual. They'd been alarmed at the rumours of the boy's progress towards health, and began to see him as a potential threat. If Tiy had her way, a virtual idiot would sit on the throne—which in itself was not so bad (one could always make terms with an idiot), but this idiot was rumoured to be stubborn, and clever, in a frightening sort of way, and liable to upset their administration.

As the time for the great yearly festival of Opet approached and the flood reached its height and overflowed the banks of the river, the offering trays in the temple burned with a hundred resins and gums. The voices of the evening singers rose out of the temple on the smoky incense, while inside the High Priest's chamber a secret council was in progress, which lasted a full night. The First Prophet of the god had decided to review all the wrongs committed by the royal house during the previous two generations, and fan the old fires of resentment, to create the proper atmosphere for an oracle to be received.

"Who among us has forgotten the foul deeds of Thutmose?" he cried, clutching the paw of the panther skin he wore and gesticulating with it as though it were his own hand.

*"None of us, none,"* chanted the priests.

"Thutmose who freed the great Sphinx from the sand and tried to support the priests of On who in turn called him 'Protector of Horakhte' in defiance of our god? Or his son Amenhotep who sits on the throne of the Two Lands by *our* grace and *our* intervention . . . who dared appoint his own Grand Vizier, thereby insulting us and mocking the tradition which demands that *I* serve as Pharaoh's Vizier?"

"*We remember, we remember,*" they chanted.

"—Amenhotep who only two years ago appointed his own Master of Ceremonies in the feast of Opet, a man who for years had slandered us and called us stinking scum who infested the capital? Do you remember?"

"*We remember.*"

"And now—Amenhotep's son! From the beginning hasn't the god frowned upon him? On the very night of his birth didn't He cast down a rain of thunderbolts into the eastern desert? And wasn't there, on the second night of his life, a fire in the sanctuary when a nervous priest dropped a tray of burning holy oil? And on the third day of his life wasn't the liver of a freshly killed goat found to be hideously diseased?"

"*It was!*"

"Then is it not true that the prince embodies all the evils of the house of Thutmose and the house of Amenhotep?"

"*True, true!*" all cried.

"And how does the oracle speak?"

In the innermost recesses of the temple a creature of indeterminate sex, who wore the mask of the Ram, clutched the curling horns about its head as though they were ears it wanted to tear off, and cried, "I who am Amon, Lord of the Silent, condemn and abhor the son of Amenhotep! *The sun of him who knows Thee not will set!*"

It was dawn by the time the council broke up its meeting, and the sun bathed the colossal pillars of the temple in splashes of pink and gold light. The High Priest performed his morning lustration and went forth to attend the god in his shrine. He loosened the sacred cord which sealed the chapel of the divine statue, chanting, "The cord is loosened, the seal is broken, I come to bring to Thee Thy gifts, the Horus Eye!" Then he approached Amon the Potent, whose phallus was great with life, and pampered the Divine One, washing him and offering him the four ritual strips of linen, the

## Gwendolyn MacEwen

necklaces, the oil. He painted the divine stone face and offered salt, resin, natron, food and flowers. And after the sanctuary was fumigated and the footsteps of the High Priest swept away, the ecstatic singers in the outer courts sang, "Thy beauty snares our hearts, our love for Thee enfeebles our arms and Thy beautiful countenance causes the hands to fall, the heart to forget...."

For the first time in his life the prince was allowed to attend the festival of Opet. He was carried on a litter to the canal, which in floodtime connected the palace with the Nile. The late afternoon light stung his eyes, and at the quay he could scarcely absorb the frantic activity going on around him. His hurting eyes were following Ra, who was about to dip His fiery red day boat into the horizon; the sight filled him with joy and terror and made the blood pulse wildly in his wrists and temples. It was a glory sensed but uncaptured—a glory related to other times, the times he lay on his dark bed between sheets of thoughts and listened to the sound of a double pipe outside in the night, the times he twisted about in a fever of desire, trying vaguely, darkly, to create himself, his hands grasping the swollen organ between his thighs and feeling it beat and pulse until it gave forth an awful beautiful wetness like long pent-up tears. All this he felt in the red orb which was Ra—the secret times of his solitude, the compelling voices in the night which was always night, the throb of the double pipes, the burning of his body, the waiting.

At the quay he whispered to his teacher, "Who is mightier than Ra, Wise One?" And Parennufer answered quietly so that none might hear, "Ra is the beginning and the end of the gods, but it is well to remember there is room for all."

Throngs of officials and merrymakers lined the canal banks, and he stared at them with a curious mixture of interest and apprehension. But when they began to stare back he avoided their eyes and scanned the harbour, counting the boats with their checkered sails. Parennufer pointed out Tiy's pleasure boat, the one she called "Brightness of Aton," and added that Amenhotep had built a quaint little shrine for Aton on the east bank of the river, and another in the land of Kush. He often referred to his own palace as "Aton's splendour."

"But Aton is simply the name of Ra's disc, isn't it?" protested the prince.

"In the old days," Parennufer sighed, "no aspect of Ra was *simply* anything. Your grandfather Thutmose once tried to excite a new interest in the Aton. He was recalling the ancient worship of the Disc when he said that all mankind was subservient to it. For a while the Aton was quite fashionable among those at court close to Thutmose, and your father, I imagine, built the shrines more as a whimsical gesture of respect for his father than anything else. He also erected sanctuaries for heaven knows what lesser gods. It annoys the servants of Amon, you see."

"I've heard," the boy said, "that he's even built temples to *himself*... am I right?"

Parennufer smiled. "There are a few places, yes, where Amenhotep is worshipped as a god."

The boy fell to silence. When Amenhotep and Tiy boarded the royal barge, he seemed not at all hurt by the fact that he was not going to sail with them. Rather he seemed to be studying the stranger who was his father, whose life and character he knew from a great distance, as objectively as he knew his history lessons. Foreigners imagined Amenhotep, Lord of the World, to be almost as colossal as the statues of himself he had erected in the desert, but in fact he was heavy and ungraceful—tall to be sure, but inclined to fatness. He had a head which was just a little too large for his body and which made him look off-balance and top-heavy. There was a coarse impatience about his speech and bearing. It had been rumoured for some time that he was in ill health, but the boy had the impression that he was more the carrier of a disease than its victim—like the Nile, which seethed with parasites and abominations yet appeared on the surface cool and clean.

It was the opinion of the priests that bad blood, foreign blood, polluted the veins of the royal family. Amenhotep's father, Thutmose, had taken a princess of Mitanni as his Chief Wife, but worse still, he'd brought back from one of his foreign campaigns a tall hook-nosed Khorian upon whom he'd lavished honours and affection. Some said it was because the foreigner had once saved his life. He gave him the title of Master of Horse in the military and finally appointed him Chief Adviser to the throne. Then the foreigner—Yuyu was his name—married a dark-skinned commoner whose mother had been a native of Kush, and by her had three children who were favoured above the children of the other nobles in Thutmose's court. One of those children was Queen Tiy.

Yuyu was a man of new ideas and the priests of Amon had always seen in him a dangerous new personality which threatened tradition, an individual who wielded altogether too much power from behind the throne. Bad blood, said the priests, was in the line of Yuyu. It flowed through the veins of Tiy, and now through the veins of her son, whose body, crawling with a hundred alien diseases, was its proof. The boy in the litter was already marked out for death. People were seized with a sort of disgusted pity for his ugliness. It was in his limbs, it was on his pale bony face.

They sailed across the swollen river towards the Northern Sanctuary, Opet Risut. Ahead of them the royal couple in their private barge was obscured by ornaments and drapes, though from time to time they caught glimpses of Tiy's red sash against the changing sky beyond the boat. The river was alive with pipes and harps.

"Teacher, I'm cold," the prince said, pulling a blanket up to his chin and shivering. "I hear voices in the river, voices of creatures who live deep deep down—listen!"

"It's only the splashing of the oars."

"No. There are things down there with a hundred tongues and ears!" Then he clutched Parennufer's arm. "Why are you taking me to Opet? You told me to beware the priests of Amon!"

"One must face what one fears. Your mother and father face it—look, they're not afraid. Your father was always a brave man. He was betrothed to your mother when they were both still children, for your grandfather wished to honour his favourite, Yuyu, by marrying his daughter into the royal house. The priests were appalled, for Tiy was the seed of a commoner and a foreigner...."

"Why does this make him brave?" the boy exclaimed. "Everybody tells me how brave he is, the number of lions he's killed, the wars he's fought! Now you tell me he's brave because he dared to marry my mother!" He buried his chin in the thick blanket and the rest of his words were a muffled comment on lions and soldiers.

"The priests," went on Parennufer, as though he hadn't heard him, "swore that the future offspring of such a union would be little better than—excuse me—bastards. Nevertheless, when Amenhotep married her he made her his Chief Wife, and when he was crowned he issued a marriage scarab throughout the empire which bravely proclaimed her humble parentage...I remember the exact words.... *The name of her father is Yuyu and the name of her mother is Tuyu; she is the wife of a mighty king whose southern boundary is Karoy and whose northern boundary is as far as Naharin.* You see, the clever composition of the words reminded people that Tiy had acquired nobility from *his* glory...."

"He was brave," admitted the prince, then looked for a moment towards the royal barge and added under his breath, "but I don't think he's so brave now."

Parennufer fell into an uneasy silence as the barges on the dark water approached the east bank. The riverbank was lined with villagers holding torches and bouquets of flowers whose petals burst like blood in the light of the flames. Oxen with dummy heads between their horns murmured across the water.

Now the ceremonies began, and the sacred statues of Amon and his divine family were removed from their shrines and placed upon their ceremonial barques for their journey to the Southern Sanctuary. Parennufer and the boy followed the long procession that escorted the Divine Ones up the river. Once they had landed at Opet Isut, Amenhotep led the procession into the temple of Mut, for tonight he was the incarnate god, and his divine consort awaited him in the form of the Chief Votaress of Amon. He went forth to celebrate the mysteries of the holy union of Amon with Mut, and there was a great hush behind him as the gates of the sanctuary closed. There were many who mused on how he would fare in the arms of that insatiable priestess. In the old days her forebears had had intimate dealings with the sacred rams bred for the god. And Thutmose had once claimed that her voluptuous predecessor almost tore him limb from limb.

But while they waited in one of the outer offering courts for the conclusion of a ceremony they could not witness, something happened which later gave the prince chills and feverish nightmares. Even as a man he was to wake up time and time again in the blackness and plead for the light which he felt would one day fail him.

A man with a cane who had once been a temple scribe, and who, after going blind, took to wandering about as a Seer and Healer— (the blind were often Seers)—approached the prince's litter and stood above him. His sightless head appeared to be encircled by the two great horns of the Ram which stood in stone behind him. He stretched out a gnarled hand to touch the prince, but the boy recoiled like a snake.

"Come no closer, mole!" he cried. "Blind bat, come no closer!"

"But my young lord, I meant only to touch your face, for all my fingers are like eyes," the seer pleaded. But the prince held back, cowering among a myriad cushions, his teeth chattering from cold.

Then the blind one smiled, and it was an idiot smile like the one on the stone lips of the Ram.

"So!" he whispered, and the spirit of the god entered his mouth, and he flung his cane away and staggered back until he was at the feet of the Ram. Its face was lit by a torch, the shadows thrusting upwards into the night, the thick horns curling around the terrible head. And there among the offering tables the seer fell down and spoke and his words were the words of the god.

*The sun of him who knows Thee not will set, O Amon!*
*The forecourt of him who assails Thee*
*Shall be in darkness*
*While the whole earth is in light!*
*Thou will find him who transgresses against Thee.*
*Woe to him who assails Thee!*
*Thy city shall endure*
*But he who assails Thee shall fail!*

Then his lips were flecked with froth and he spoke no more, for the name of Amon meant "That Which Is Hidden" and Amon never revealed more than was necessary. But how obvious it was to all who heard that the damning words referred to the son of Amenhotep! The boy's face was carved from stone. He knew that to be damned meant that one was feared. He also sensed the great secret of the priests—that in predicting the future they helped to bring it about. The three figures were suspended in time—the Ram with its idiot grin, the blind one thrashing about beneath it, and the boy, motionless and frozen among the cushions.

At last Amenhotep emerged—dishevelled and a little drunk—from the sanctuary. Around his shoulders he wore the skin of a freshly killed ram. Acrobats tumbled and twirled around him and the people showered him with flowers, crying, "Strong Bull Appearing in Truth, Horus of Gold who Smites the Nine Bows!" And as the procession passed by the prince he heard the words *"Ka Mut Ef"*—*"Bull of His Mother."*

Gwendolyn MacEwen

"The god has re-created Himself, He has come forth from His own seed," explained Parennufer. "Ra as a bull fertilized His mother Nut in the form of the heavenly cow, and is reborn from her loins each morning. . . . It's one of the more primitive descriptions, very colourful, I think. Another example of what the priests of Amon have incorporated from the past. Of course we know Ra has no mother. . . ."

The festivities would continue for many days but the two went back to the palace at dawn, leaving Opet with the hysterical shouts of the crowds ringing in their ears. "Sun of Rulers, Fierce-Eyed Lion!" On the way back the boy sat awkwardly in the boat, his knees drawn up to his chin. Suddenly he blurted out, "Is my father a puppet whose strings are in the hand of the High Priest of Opet?"

"Remember," Parennufer replied, "it is by *their* grace that he is on the throne!"

The boy shivered and stared hard into the black depths of the eastern horizon until at last Ra rose in his boat of the morning, and then the early rays outlined the dim peaks of the West. Soothed by the sight he dozed; the morning river was silent, yet alive. He thought of a poem of the Nile which ran, "a secret of movement, a darkness in daytime. . . ." Now the peaks of the West grew bright and the demon who dwelled on the highest peak awoke—she who was known as the Lover of Silence, and who struck instantly and without warning, as all lovers of silence. Parennufer remembered that when he looked into the pale, intense face of the son of Amenhotep.

"Parennufer, what did it mean when the Blind One held up five fingers to my face, then closed them into a fist?"

"The five fingers were five regnal years. The fist meant . . . that you will not endure past the fifth."

"And what does *that* mean?"

"It means, among other things, that you will rule!"

# King of Egypt, King of Dreams

When he came of age he was told to conduct himself silently and demurely around the palace, and in this as in everything else he went to an extreme, and became so silent and demure that no one ever knew where he was. Sometimes he could be seen sitting with his little sister Sitamon beside the river, talking quietly, with his legs dangling limply in the water, while she absently wove collars from the little flowers that grew all around them. The two were very close, and never had there been such melancholy, quiet children. Some who passed the spot where they sat thought they heard the sound of weeping—whether his or hers, they could not tell. But no one gave it much thought.

The rest of the time he was busy absorbing the new world around him. Kept from light for a long time, his vision was sharper and clearer than that of most and he developed certain terrifying insights often found in very young children. He saw how the Two Lands was still trembling from the shock of its expansion into an empire, but he was unmoved by the fashionable, timely cynicism which infected his father's court—the self-conscious turns of speech, the glib expressions borrowed from looser-tongued nations than his. No Amon was called "The Mistress of Every City," and it had never seen such opulence. Spices, metalwork and bronze daggers and swords flowed in as tribute from the conquered nations of the world. But he felt an uneasy foreignness about things. Aristocrats adopted the new elaborate empire styles in clothing, and wandered about (as he put it) like dolls, in robes adorned with meaningless fringes and pleats. He had the gall to tell one of his father's chief advisers that he both looked and thought like a woman, and that that was a dangerous state of affairs. Indignantly the man replied that the court was not "frivolous," it was "cosmopolitan."

"Then the empire itself is frivolous," replied the prince.

That remark swiftly found its way to Amenhotep, who could think of nothing better to do with it than to turn it into a joke which would further prove the idiocy of his son. For some weeks the court amused itself tossing the statement back and forth until it got so revised in the process that its final form was *"The prince has said that the land of Khor is full of women. He thinks there are no men there!"* The joke circulated in the banquet halls, which were filled every night with effeminate young nobles lolling about while eunuchs poured wine for them, and dancers of every nation trailed long feathers and silks over their perfumed bodies.

Foreign gods and foreign customs had shattered the stability of the Two Lands—a stability which permitted no change but the predictable change of the seasons. Any alteration in Maat, the order of the universe, was a catastrophe. The land was not ready to absorb anything new; the people merely made fools of themselves trying. The land was eternal; it did not change. The prince grew impatient and restless, and tried to cast his vision outwards towards the huge complex of provinces which made up the empire, whose endless quarrels and petty disputes were constantly erupting into full-scale rebellions. The slackening of power had already begun, and small city-states had begun to drift away from Amenhotep's rule, like boats whose mooring stakes had been uprooted and freed. The deputies or "Watchers" of Pharaoh who ruled beside the vassal kings of the subject nations possessed none of the loyalty their predecessors had when the empire was first won. The Two Lands was far away to them; Pharaoh's court was upset and involved in internal problems. The troops of Keme stationed in Khor and Retenu grew lazy and disillusioned. Amenhotep was growing old, and there had been no glorious victories for some years.

Parennufer countless times tried to talk with the prince about the current political issues, but the boy showed little or no concern for the topic. What fascinated him from the start was the diversity of peoples and gods in the empire, the differences of skin and tongue and creed. He was bored with discussions of foreign tribute, foreign diplomacy, the thousand and one political manoeuvrings which somehow held the empire together. He was angered and appalled to learn that the empire was not a friendly organization of different peoples with similar interests, but a vast network of jealous and warring states with rulers always ready for the merest excuse to start another battle. He thought that the empire should have one goal, one purpose, even one god. And Parennufer smiled sadly and muttered something about how nice it would be to be young again and have such dreams.

But his own land obsessed him before anything else. He saw most clearly what was immediately around him, and, like a harp whose strings were vibrated by the merest breath, he felt all the complex palpitations of a royal house which had only recently learned it was not the only royal house in the world. Even the divinity of Pharaoh, that most fundamental axiom, had been attacked when the great *Sar* of Karaduniash had asked Amenhotep for one of his daughters as a gift and the girl had written back haughtily, "Since time immemorial, a daughter of the king of Keme has been given to no one!" How the *Sar* mocked him after that! "You're a king," he wrote once. "Surely you can do what you like!"

Although Pharaoh's offspring were divine and not to be touched by foreign hands, he himself could bed foreign princesses by the handful. Amenhotep had a harem the size of which was legendary throughout the world. It was crammed to overflowing. But that harem, at first a lush jungle of thighs and breasts smelling of the east and the north, gradually degenerated into an old rotting vegetable garden, for he didn't have the time (or the strength) to explore a tenth of it. When the beautiful Mitannian princess Tadukhipa arrived, he was furious because he'd worn himself out in his vegetable dump and couldn't even begin to consider how he might enjoy her. He tired of his women once he deflowered them; he claimed he got no pleasure unless the creatures were in paroxysms of fear. In the end, he could scarcely give away the rest of his untouched concubines to his noblemen (who shuddered to think of the ones they were offered—some of them the oldest virgins in the world).

No one could help noticing that the prince was making a startling recovery. He often disappeared for days at a stretch—no one knew where and few cared to ask. Several times he went disguised into the capital and mingled with the cabbage-sellers and fishmongers, listening, as he put it, "to their thoughts." He heard incredible stories about himself—stories of how he was kept locked in a room in the palace, living under the shadow of an ancient curse, waiting to die. Stories of how palace servants had accidentally looked into his crazy eyes and gone mad or blind. People imagined that if he ever took the throne, the sun would disappear immediately— for that was the way they interpreted the words of the oracle. A little old woman who sold rugs kept her customers enthralled by telling them that the prince had no sex. Hearing this, he smiled and stepped into the booth where she sold her wares, gained the attention of the listeners by raising his hands for silence, and said in a loud voice, "My friends, *I* have heard he is both man *and* woman!"

"Really?" asked the old woman. "How did you find this out?"

"I have it from the coppersmith down the street, who has it from the tanner on the next block," he replied.

"Well then! What's all this about his eyes striking men blind?" said a wealthy young man who was fingering the corner of an expensive carpet from Amor.

The prince couldn't resist going over to the man, and gazing deeply into his eyes from a distance of not more than two or three inches. "My friend, I really don't know about that!" he said.

"Oh. Too bad," said the buyer, and turned away.

On other occasions he dressed up like a peasant and went wandering in the fields and farms north of the capital. He'd have a servant take him a few miles downstream in a little boat; then, while the vessel lay hidden in a bed of tall reeds, he'd go ashore and walk through the cultivated areas broken by little networks of irrigation channels, until he found someone to talk to. Once he made his way to someone's well, and found an old farmer sitting on the ground eating some raw carrots and leeks and staring at the lean ox that was circling round and round the well, turning the water wheel. A boy not more than eight years old thrashed the poor beast with a stick to keep him moving.

Amenhotep the younger sat down beside the peasant, who immediately offered him a withered half of a carrot and began to speak. "My ox is dying," he announced. "See the way he stalls every second turn? A bad sign. I've had him fifteen years. If he dies this week I'm in a spot. I'll have to requisition another ox, and that takes weeks. Meanwhile, who's going to turn the wheel, I ask you—eh?" He glanced sidelong at his companion. "Where are you from anyway?"

The prince nodded his head vaguely to the south.

"Ah—oh well, you're better off down there. Less taxes on that land, I hear—eh?"

Another vague nod of the head sufficed to keep the old man talking. "Yes, less taxes alright. You wouldn't believe what I had to pay this year! The collectors from Opet came out last month and carted away a good two-thirds of my grain crop. *Two-thirds!* The measly bit I had left will scarcely see us through the winter. Then—who knows?" He gave a short ugly chuckle and heaved the green ends of the leeks onto the ground.

"How much land have you got?" asked the prince casually.

"Ha! Well, my friend, in my youth I had a fair-sized plot—enough for me and my family; we managed. Then the land surveyors of the temple came out and decided to seize my neighbour's farm for temple land. He was completely dispossessed, and now he and his family are working as serfs—on their own farm! Me, I guess I was luckier. They only took half of my land—but the best half, of course—and left me with this." He swung an arm around to indicate the boundaries of his poor farm. "They decided to let me manage it myself, so long as I paid my taxes. Then the taxes went up—and up, and up. So I'm left with a dying ox and a few grains of chaff. Funny, isn't it? They know, they *know* what I'll have to do. In order to make a living I'll have to sign over to them the rest of the land, and me and my family will be serfs like the others. At least when you're a serf you're guaranteed the clothes on your back and food on your table. That's more than I've got right now."

The boy at the well thrashed the ox and the thing suddenly fell to its knees and refused to get up.

"Oh damn!" cried the peasant. "Not today!" He rushed to his feet and joined his son at the well, and the two of them stood over the collapsed ox, thrashing it and pulling its ears. Hearing the commotion, a woman came out of the hut nearby, followed by five or six grubby little children. Then everybody was at the well, shrieking and squealing and thrashing and pulling and pushing, until finally they quietened down and drew back, leaving the beast on the ground. The peasant slowly disconnected the wooden yoke from its collar. "He's dead," he said, his voice a monotone. "He's better off. What a life, to have to walk round and round day in and day out, round and round. Only he never knew he was going round and round, because there was always something covering his eyes to make him blind so he'd think he was going straight and getting somewhere. . . ."

The prince wandered over to the well. He kicked the carcass of the ox gently, then shuffled his foot in the dirt. "Maybe," he said, keeping his eyes away from the others, "when Amenhotep dies things will change. I've heard his son has dedicated himself to breaking the power of Opet."

"That idiot?" laughed the peasant. "Listen, my friend, don't believe it! They say he's so feeble-minded he doesn't even know his own name. How will *he* stand up to Opet, how will anyone?"

"You'll see," whispered the prince.

"Hey—who are you anyway? You caught me at such a bad time I didn't bother asking what you were doing here." The eyes of the man and the woman and the grubby little children turned on him, suddenly hostile.

He drew himself up to his full height and said, *"I'm the idiot."*

Everyone broke out into gales of laughter. The woman clutched her stomach, which was huge with another child, and laughed until tears rolled down her cheeks. The dirty, wide-eyed children rolled on the ground, and the man leaned feebly against the edge of the well, where, according to popular belief, the primordial waters of Chaos still churned. His whole body was shaking with mirth.

Amenhotep the younger slipped away and ran through the fields back to the boat which lay hidden in the tall reeds.

He grew strong. He attributed his recovery to a force manifest through Ra—in the rays that streamed from the secret centre of the sun and penetrated his body and revived the chilled bones and the blood—a healing force within the Aton. The court physicians were flabbergasted by his progress and some even dared admit that the sickroom and spells and charms had not been the answer after all. The more conservative among them, however, stuck stubbornly to the opinion that he still needed darkness to rest his eyes, and were appalled when they saw him staring into the very Eye of Heaven for a longer time than they themselves could have done without going quite blind from the light. He began to be treated with a kind of awkward awe; men kept their distance from him as they would from a timid horse, which, in the act of shying away from danger, might well trample them under its delicate, unpredictable hooves....

And as he watched the line of shadow move around the *tekhen* which marked the hours, gaining strength in time, his father weakened. Time was Amenhotep's killer, and each new rising of Ra only brought him closer to the sickness which was death. He groaned with bellyache from his endless banquets; the passions of war and sport abandoned him; he led no more troops and slew no more beasts but continued to depict himself on monuments at the head of mighty campaigns in which he never participated. He began to worry about posterity, and grew to worship the stones he constructed as he had once revered his own body. He feverishly continued construction of his fantastic court in the Southern Sanctuary of Opet, with silver and gold columns thicker than trees in the forest of Khor, tearing down old chapels and shrines to get the necessary blocks of stone. But while he built, he himself decayed, and as the stones of eternity were erected, his body and spirit fell away like old neglected temples.

What had once been strength in him was now a frivolous mockery of strength. He was fat and horrible; his mouth decayed and he gave himself over to the courting of young boys (another foreign custom). He looked upon his son, during those rare occasions when he dined with him, with an expression so close to outright disgust that it was embarrassing for all present. He considered the boy an utter idiot and was indiscreet enough to make his opinion known. To make matters worse, the pressure on the prince produced by his father's presence only served to make him sweat and stammer, and his nervous face would search that of his father and his mouth would twist spasmodically until the god would lean forward, cruelly mimicking his stutter and say, "Y-y-y-yes, you want to s-s-s-say something?" But whatever it was the boy wanted to say, it was never said; he couldn't train his mouth to shape it. He would bow his head, his brow dripping with sweat, fumble the food in his fingers, and make a poor mess of everything. His father, heaving a long disgusted sigh, would ask, "How does your mother imagine you would fare on the throne, carrying on my struggles, when you can't even chew your food properly?"

As Amenhotep aged, Tiy youthened, as though seizing the strength that he lost. Her strong dusky features, so unlike the features of a queen, grew more determined and more ruthless. She was beautiful but it was the tough unyielding beauty of a sphinx.

Her plans for her daughter's marriage were crushed when Amenhotep, to consolidate his position on the throne in the customary manner, himself married the royal heiress. The little Sitamon awaited with disgust the entrance of her aging father into her bedroom. Four teeth had recently been pulled from his lower jaw and he suffered excruciating toothaches in his upper jaw—toothaches which he swore extended right up into his skull. His maladies gave him the temperament of a crocodile, but Tiy's temperament at the time was no better, for in snatching up the royal heiress for himself, he had succeeded in severely weakening her plans for her son.

After Sitamon's marriage to her father, she and the prince still met secretly in the northern palace. She told her brother how she was pampered and perfumed for the pleasure of the king, whose horrid breath kept her awake until dawn. The prince held her small shaking hand in his and they wept together; both of them were alone, both of them were hated, and both were instruments in the hands of their elders. They loved with sorrow as though to heal each other's wounds; the very bed beneath them smelled of their father.

Tiy rather hoped that Sitamon would bear no children, and in fact expected that she couldn't—for Amenhotep's loins were as parched as the desert and his divine organ withered and fainted like a flower whenever he approached *her*. Tiy was sure that with Sitamon he would fall asleep at the crucial moment, after another drunken night surrounded by little brown dancers of both sexes, himself dressed in female clothes—one of his stranger amusements—and leave his child-wife still a child. But after some time passed Sitamon bore a son, Smenkhare, so Tiy had to conclude that the god's power must have returned to him at some point.

The child was a child of sorrow from the moment he first opened his eyes.

Later Sitamon bore another child called Tutankhaton, but on the birth-stool, when the head of the boy broke from her loins, she screamed and died.

The prince disappeared for two weeks. When he returned his face had changed—or so people said. The features were the same, but they fitted together differently. He made a cryptic remark to Parennufer, to which the old tutor gracefully listened, without understanding.

"There was a night," he said, "when the seed of my dark years was wrung from me, old man. And my weeping ceased, it ceased from that moment."

And late that same night someone passed by a storage room for old furniture, and saw him sitting on a tiny chair which had been his sister's when she was a child. It was more of a toy than a chair and it had pictures of funny little animals in wood and gold. He could scarcely fit; his hips were jammed into it, and no one knew how long he sat there in the darkness. He took away two such chairs of hers from the storage room and hid them in his apartments... but when later his venerable grandparents Yuyu and Tuyu died, a servant found the chairs and took them away to be used as funerary furniture in their tombs. Seeing the chairs being moved, the prince covered his eyes and fled down the hall.

Tiy later arranged for Sitamon's two sons, Smenkhare and Tutankhaton, to be reared in the harem along with the other offspring of Amenhotep's secondary wives, where they were to remain in obscurity for some time.

To assure himself and his people that he was still vigorous, Amenhotep held a traditional Heb Sed jubilee, and ran the required four laps around the huge jubilee field to symbolize his traversing of the whole earth. The thousands of spectators hailed him as the "swift jackal who circles the land in the twinkling of an eye"—but there were times when he could scarcely circle his bed in the twinkling of an eye, let alone a field. If anyone might have represented the mysterious renewal of strength, it would have been the prince, who sat silently taking in the ceremony.

Amenhotep returned to the royal canopy with sweat streaming down his face. His breathing was tortured, but he'd proven he was still a god. The crowd went wild as the sacred Djed pillar was raised in the field like the great erect organ of Osiris, Lord of the cycles of death and rebirth. Later that night there were dances in the Festival Hall, but Amenhotep sat all alone, crumpled up inside his pleated gown, his floral necklace, and his very fashionable double wig, exhausted from his lonely race about the whole earth.

He fell desperately ill and the king of Mitanni sent him a statue of the goddess Ishtar to help speed his recovery, for when a man's own gods failed, he wasn't adverse to seeking the aid of foreign deities. (Amenhotep had often called upon countless alien creatures, only to find them as impotent as himself. Once he'd gone so far as to invoke the weather god of Kheta, although heaven knows his last concern was the weather.) But Ishtar didn't help and the royal doctors invoked the spirit of Imhotep the Healer and consulted the sacred books day and night—however, once out of the king's hearing they shook their heads and muttered that what was decayed couldn't be made whole.

The infection spread from the royal mouth to the royal body, and Amenhotep suffered extreme stomach cramps and attacks of nausea. The god felt himself crumbling away like an old sandstone statue. He lay on his bed staring at a great fresco of a leaping bull which was painted onto his wardrobe cabinet. He thought about his days of bull-hunting and became utterly depressed. He recalled his prowess as an archer and how people had called him "the star of fine gold circling on his horse." Then the magnificent Amenhotep was dead, gone at last to meet his heavenly *ka*, and Tiy was left pregnant with his last fierce seed.

The capital wept crocodile tears into the Nile and the streets were jammed with professional mourners beating their breasts and tearing out their hair by the roots as though they personally were responsible for the death of the king. A very thin line separated mourning from rejoicing. They rejoiced that they were not among the dead; they mourned out of fear of the jealousy of the dead towards the living. All the prayers and food offerings in the world couldn't compensate for one hour of a lost life, and the living knew it.

At Amenhotep's funeral they chanted the ancient formulas to ensure his admittance into heaven.

*In heaven his servants cook the gods*
*And he devours*
*The great gods for breakfast*
*The middle gods for dinner*
*The little gods for supper.*
*He becomes the Lord of Heaven,*
*He eats all the crowns and bracelets,*
*He eats the wisdom of all the gods!*

Tiy demanded that her son make the required offerings in his father's mortuary temple in the desert. He refused, shouting, "What offering did he ever make *me*!" and then refused to eat for four days, which put Tiy in an agony of fear that he too might die.

Meanwhile the people wondered what would become of the Cursed One, for that was how they referred to him. Would he come out of his locked room and strike dead with his ugliness anyone who looked at him? Would he dare to mount the throne despite the oracle which had condemned him to an early death?

One day the Cursed One rode out to his father's great mansion of death in the desert, and stood in front of the two giant statues which stared out across the sand. One of them gave off horrible hollow sounds at dawn; it had something to do with the heat and air rising through the stone, but the peasants thought it was the voice of Amenhotep. When the prince arrived it had just begun to give off its eerie music. He listened a moment to the maddening hum, then in a fit of anger tore off the thin circle of gold which was his crown and threw it onto the sand beneath the giant's feet. He ripped open his tunic and stood stark naked in front of the terrible twin effigies of his father. He lifted up his arms to Ra and let the rays of the god caress his chest and loins. Two temple servants stood nearby and watched him, awed.

One whispered, "It is the dead king, it is his *ka*!"

But the other laid a hand on his arm and said, "No, it's his son—look!"

There was a smile on the prince's face, the smile of a dreamer freshly awakened. He looked up into the faces of his father towering above him and spoke in a loud ringing voice: *"As my father Ra lives, the divine Youth who came into being out of Himself, joining His seed with His body to create His egg within His secret self... I tell you this is how I came to be!"*

And he stared hard into the giants' eyes, daring them to reply, but they were silent, and the awful hum had ceased.

"Father, I will chew my food well! Father, I will carry on your struggles!" he cried. Then he broke into a string of curses which would have jarred the ears of a latrine keeper; these were followed by peals of wild laughter which continued long after he mounted his chariot to ride back to the palace.

The two dumbfounded temple servants stepped forward and stood transfixed between Amenhotep's huge stone feet, gazing after the disappearing chariot.

## Gwendolyn MacEwen

"It was a mirage," said the first.
"I wish it were," replied the second.
"He is mad," said the first.
*"He'd better be,"* came the reply.

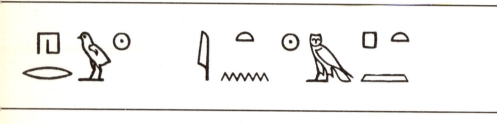

daytime         Aton is in the sky

By means of lavish promises to donate a vast amount of wealth to the temple of Opet from her dead husband's treasury, Tiy obtained the reluctant consent of the High Priest for her son's coronation to be blessed in the House of Amon. To have opposed the coronation would have been folly, for too much of the temple's income still depended on the throne, and after all, hadn't the oracle implied that the son of Amenhotep would not endure beyond the fifth year of his reign? He was not likely to do or think anything out of the ordinary in a mere five years.

He was married to his cousin Nefertiti, the daughter of Tiy's brother Ay. Now both king and queen would be grandchildren of the despised Yuyu, and the throne, in the opinion of the priests, would be utterly polluted.

And so he was crowned, but on the day of his coronation a great flock of ibises, frightened by some disturbance on the shore, rushed up from their reedy marshland, and the sound of their ascent was like a long sigh from the throat of the Nile god. As they levelled out, their wings darkened the sun for the briefest of instants.

He was greeted by Purifiers wearing grotesque masks to emulate the gods; he was given the ritual bathing by what seemed to him to be a pack of beasts. In a side chapel a woman wearing the huge broad head of a cobra leapt upon him and he felt terrified and disgusted by the embrace of her cold coiling limbs. Then in a special shrine a priest wearing the ceremonial leopard skin touched the Blue Crown to his head, giving him sway over all the domains of the sun. He knelt in the customary manner, with his back to an image of Amon, and felt cold ghastly hands touch the nape of his neck. The Hidden Wind of the god was all around him, the Wind that in the beginning aroused the dormant primordial waters of Nun, and the eyes of the priests who blessed him were dark with anger. They were recalling how only the previous night the oracle had spoken again in a voice as hollow as the desert wind, of a time of darkness which was to come masqueraded as light. . . .

But when at last he sat enthroned in the holy-sounding silence of the Coronation Hall and received the Double Crown of the Two Lands on his head, the watchers hailed him as "Mighty Bull, Lofty of Plumes, Golden Hawk, Lord of Diadems"—and his face wore an expression of purity and utter relief. In accepting the weight of the Red and White Crowns, another weight had been lifted from him, and he shone with a secret triumph—whether over the forces within or without, no one could say. His first official act as Pharaoh was to stand before the throne, let his gaze single out the High Priest MeryPtah, and make an announcement which everyone in the hall immediately recognized to be a daring rewording of the oracle's warning.

"The sun of him who knows Thee not will *rise*, O Amon!"

He was Neferkheprure Wanre Amenhotep IV—"Beautiful Are the Creations of Ra, Son of the Sun, Amon Rests."


He shocked everyone by assuming, from the very first day of his reign, an air of command which he couldn't possibly have learned, an authority which radiated from deep within him. It was not merely the presence of the crown which caused those at court to treat him somewhat more seriously than they had when he was the butt of his father's jokes; nor was it Tiy's ever-watchful eye (she accompanied him almost everywhere). There was something in his own eyes—a kind of anger, a kind of certainty. His nervousness had become intensity of purpose, his impatience had become determination. He often recalled the crazy stories he heard in the marketplace—about how people went mad or blind when they looked into his eyes—so he became aware of his eyes and used them to punctuate his commands.

One day he stood over Tiy's bed—(she had just given birth to the daughter of her late husband, and was such a systematic woman that it was entirely possible that she delayed the event until after the coronation), and free now of her cumbersome pregnancy she proceeded to lecture him on how to deal with foreign powers. She produced letters of congratulation on his coronation from a dozen different rulers of foreign nations.

"Look," she said, resting herself heavily on one elbow. "Our golden-tongued messenger from Mitanni brought this only this morning. King Tushratta greets you and says: *Amenhotep is not dead, for now you, his son, rule, and I know you will not make any changes in the affectionate relations between the house of Keme and the house of Mitanni. Your mother Tiy knows all the words your father and I shared in the past; ask her, let her tell you how your father was on excellent terms with me.*"

He looked puzzled and asked, "What's he so worried about? Does he think I plan to be unfriendly? I've never even met him!"

"My son," Tiy replied patiently, "must I remind you that the kingdom of Mitanni lies at the outposts of our empire and borders on the lands of Kheta? Kheta has already occupied part of northern Mitanni and Tushratta's lands are in danger. Our relations with the house of Mitanni are of prime importance, for it is Tushratta alone who stops our enemies from moving southward. In fact, I've been meaning to tell you—you'll have to perform a marriage of state with his daughter Tadukhipa; it's the best way we can cement our relations with him."

"No, absolutely not! She was sent here as your husband's bride!"

"Your *father* is dead. As far as foreign nations are concerned, *you* are he."

"No! Must I do what he did, be friendly with whomever he was friendly, sleep with the women he slept with? What else, wear his clothes? Acquire his disgusting tastes? Walk like him, talk like him, make his mistakes?"

Tiy raised herself higher and her face turned a shade paler than it already was. "Yes!" she warned, "if you don't want to hear the worst curse of all—from your own mother's tongue!"

At length he gave in and there was a hasty marriage with Tadukhipa, but he never consummated the union, and she was put back into the vast neglected harem where she soon faded into obscurity. (It was rumoured that he was impotent, until Nefertiti bore him her first child.) Meanwhile, Tiy took over his foreign correspondence and sent carefully worded dispatches to foreign rulers to the effect that they handle him carefully, or better still—address him through her. But when the king of Mitanni began to beg for some of the gold that was "common as dust" in the land, the king, in a moment of sarcastic caprice, sent off some wooden statues which were only very thinly overlaid with gold. The house of Mitanni was profoundly insulted, and the incident gave rise to several years of strained relations between the two countries—not to mention those between Tiy and her son.

"Whatever did you think you were doing!" she cried, storming across the palace floors, her double plumes quivering with fury, her finely plucked eyebrows arched in indignation. "Now look what's happened! The court of Mitanni is detaining our messengers; Tushratta begins to distrust us—do you realize where all this can lead?"

"Well, I'm sick of this endless game of foreign diplomacy," he replied. "I'm tired of letters full of high-flown, meaningless endearments from people who've never laid eyes on me. I'm sick of the whining and niggling of kings who act like spoilt children! And I'm sick to death of politics, which is nothing more than the petty haggling of merchants on a grand scale! Look at this list of silly complaints from the *Sar* of Karaduniash—he sounds like a spinster crying in her beer!"

"Karaduniash," she reminded him, "is a very powerful kingdom. Trifle with it, and you have a formidable enemy."

"But listen to him! You sent him so many gifts the inventory alone filled fifty tablets, but he cries, *The gold didn't come out full weight on delivery.* Also, *Would you please make no alliance with the nation of Ashur*—which recently had the gall to approach him on friendly terms! And *this* I can't believe—listen! *I have nothing valuable to send if you have nothing valuable to send. For the mistress of your house I sent only thirty rings of lapis lazuli because she didn't do anything I asked.* Are those the words of a *king*?"

"They most certainly are; and you'd better remember it."

"I want to be alone," he said. "I've got to think."

"Nonsense! I haven't been alone for thirty years; a king has no right to solitude. All around you are the noises of the empire—the voices of ambitious princes and persecuted vassals—and they demonstrate that you are very much *not* alone. Or do your ears simply ring with the noises of a world you don't care to understand?"

"I understand too well," was the reply.

"Do you? You don't even take advantage of the benefits of your power. Your father, dearest and most virile of men, used to demand anything he wanted from foreign nations. *Send me forty beautiful women and no slanderers,* he used to write."

"I don't want forty beautiful women who aren't slanderers."

"Then what *do* you want, my impossible one?"

"Peace. Time. Something's growing in me, waiting to see the light...."

"You're pregnant!" she shrieked.

He ignored her. "I see it, I know it, I can't name it yet."

"Why do you always answer questions which aren't the ones people ask?"

"Another voice in me is asking."

When Tiy was a child she used to spit when she got angry, but now she couldn't do it without a great loss of dignity, so she compensated for it by going through all the facial motions, then swallowing the saliva furiously. Afterwards she circled around her son, picking away at him for his indiscretions, closing in on him like a great bird and tightening her circle until her breath was hot on his face—sweet breath which grew very sour in her wrath.

"You must dispel these rumours of your madness! Fantastic stories are circulating about you! You turn up in strange places and do *strange things*. You must start making a monthly appearance at Opet and offering gifts to Amon."

"Never. You're paying them off, aren't you? That's your affair."

"Be thankful your mother lives to guide you through these terrible times," said her brilliant red sash, said her arched eyebrows, said her double plumes. And as he crossed his legs and studied his fingernails, she went on to remind him how she had fought for him, fought for Nefertiti, fought the priests, fought his father (dearest and most virile of men)—and what had he shown her for her troubles but the behaviour of a village idiot? Then she collected herself and assumed her motherly (and even more powerful) air and told him that of course the years of illness had not equipped him for the responsibilities to come, and not to fear—for *she* would be the anchor, the oars, the very sails of the frail little boat which was her son, and guide him through the dark torrents of the years to come.

He turned his back on the empire and left the hundreds of voices to babble on without him. He concentrated on the vision taking shape within his own mind, and began to build a great new temple for Ra-Horakhte, a little to the southeast of the northern temple of Amon. On the first day after its completion he conducted the dawn services, and as the last note of the hymn still hovered in the air, he declared himself "Great One of Visions of Ra" after the manner of the priests of On.

In the past, all kings of Keme were officially represented by the priests in their temples, but never themselves assumed the High Priesthood; they were themselves the offspring of Ra and were required only to offer to their divine father as dutiful sons. For Wanre to set himself up as First Prophet of Ra-Horakhte was an uncomfortable breach of tradition, and his advisers looked on askance, afraid to criticize his move lest, like a pregnant woman given a scare, he might let loose some dreadful hysteria.

When his artists asked him how he wished to be depicted on the great statues which were to be raised in the new temple, he smiled a moment as though recalling a private joke, and whispered, "Make one of them nude. And without genitals. Sculpt me as neither man nor woman; it's rumoured I have no sex." And so he was cut into stone, tall and bony with bulging thighs between which there was—nothing. Every day he went to his temple and gazed at his one naked sexless self. Twenty-seven other selves gazed back, and on all the thick lips were secret smiles.

Not long afterward he journeyed to the holy city of On to consult with the priests of Ra—(this against the advice of Parennufer, who warned him that such a move might have dire consequences)—and they, profoundly flattered, greeted him as Son of Ra and Great One of Visions and introduced him to the ancient mysteries of their temple. It was built on the site of the primeval mound where Ra as a bird first alighted after Creation (a geographical honour also claimed by No Amon and Men Nofer and the other main cities which were centres of the worship of the predominant gods). They presented him with one of the sparrow-hawks symbolic of Horus, which they kept in a special courtyard; the image of Horus with the sun on its head was the emblem of Ra in his form as Horakhte. They taught him the inner meaning of the words "Living Horus" which always designated Pharaoh. Then they showed him the great purple heron, which represented the *benu* bird, the *ba* of the sun; it was burned alive every year in a nest of spices and gums, to be succeeded by a younger bird said to come from an egg of myrrh left in the ashes. The true *benu* bird, they told him, was a fabulous red and gold hawk with a heron's head, who was reborn thus every five hundred years, for he was the recurring Ra who created and recreated himself eternally.

"There are many mysteries," said one old astrologer, leaning forward and speaking in an excited whisper, "which the servants of Amon long ago stole from us and applied to the worship of their god. But remember—the recurrence of Ra is the world-year in the mastery of the sun; while Amon, My Sun, is only the principle of Ra in His time of the Ram."

He asked them of the Aton, and they told him that in ancient times Aton was the name for the true and outward form of Ra, the disc of the sun itself. He gazed behind their words and saw something faintly luminous in the distance, a shimmering circle like the circle of delicate light around a candle's flame.

"You mean," he asked, "the form which *contains* Ra like a vessel containing fluid. The circle which *surrounds* the god, but is not in itself the god . . . ?"

"My Sun, the Aton is the Disc, that is all we can tell you."

"My body," he murmured, more to himself than to them, "contains me, but is not me. . . ."

By the end of the night he felt overpowered by the many names and aspects of Ra. There was Ra-Khepri of the morning, Ra of the day, Ra-Atum of the dusk, Af of the Underworld, Aton the Disc....

There were many who dreamed by night, but he was a dreamer of the day as well, and when he returned to the capital he went to his secret spot on the riverbank and lay face up among the thick plants under the beams of the god. A large swaying leaf moved rhythmically against the sun, creating alternating bands of light which arrested his vision and sent him into a trance (pulsing, alternating light always had this effect on him, rows of torches in a corridor, files of lighted ships on the river at night). Awake, he dreamed that the twin giants of his father in the desert came striding across the sands towards him, but melted into two puddles of yellow water before they reached him. He dreamed that his other Father, the divine and blinding one, touched his mouth with fingers of fire and bade him speak. And the words he spoke, haltingly, clumsily, were to form the title of a new god.

"Ra-Horakhte Who rejoices in the horizon in His name Shu which is in Aton."

The long epithet puzzled him for a while, but the next day in his temple he announced it and explained its meaning. The god was not the mere disc of the sun, but the mysterious power which emanated through it in the form of intense heat, Shu. And this intangible force manifest from within the Aton was in fact the essence of Ra.

It was a long time before he could successfully explain the inexplicable or speak the unspeakable. The very nature of his vision was such that mere words could not convey it. For some months people were baffled by his meaning, and there were some around him who would never quite grasp what he was trying to say—except for the few times when they could sense something behind his words, something subtle and strong as the light within an alabaster lamp. What confounded them always was the fact that finally the god had no *form*. The Disc contained the god but was not in itself the god. He tried to explain that the god was *"Lord of all that the Disc surrounds."* He asked of his pupils that they see the Invisible and became impatient with them when they could not.

But the young men of the court flocked around him to hear what later became known as the Teaching. Most of the followers were sons of the nobles of Amenhotep, and they sat for hours listening to his maddening, yet strangely compelling incoherencies. Most were more anxious to win his approval and favour than to be enlightened by knowledge of his god. He knew this; it did not distress him.

"My lord Amenhotep," queried one of the more eager pupils, "you say the Disc contains the god, but is not in itself the god—how so?"

"My body," explained the king, "contains me, but is not me. Until now all have believed that the shape of a thing is the content of that thing, whereas it is only the boundary lines drawn around its force, that that force or that spirit might not spill out over the universe...."

"But," the student insisted, "you have said that the force within the Aton *does* manifest itself everywhere!"

"That is because the Aton is a circle," he replied. "And a circle is a perfect form without beginning or end, it is one unbroken line. Therefore the force within the Aton is both contained and uncontained. This is the mystery."

"My lord Amenhotep!" remarked another. "You said that the body is but a shape. Do you mean to tell us then that the body is not the vessel wherein we enter eternity? Do you say the *ka* of a man is not the shape of the man?"

He hesitated, for he knew he was treading on dangerous ground. He had not been prepared for this. The logical outcome of his argument had to be that the invisible man, a shapeless *ka*, would endure for eternity, while the body, being an imperfect form, would not. He had not realized he would be called upon to apply his theories to this most delicate and vital issue of human life. For the briefest of moments he had the distinct sensation of being disembodied, of watching his flesh being chewed up and torn away, his bones crushed, his spirit flying away from his heart like a ray of sunlight.

His silence lengthened, and the pupils began to murmur disapprovingly, casting quick glances at him and making low remarks to their neighbours. Then he blurted out, "I will wait and see how the god shapes my death! Perhaps this body will be crushed or devoured... but meanwhile, I will wear it well!"

He knew he had not really answered the question.

The great heresy began in his own court, although the common man concerned him more than the nobility. To make himself somehow more real and accessible to his people, he dispensed with formalities of titles and announced one day that he was to be addressed by his simple solar name—the name which proclaimed every Pharaoh to be Son of the Sun—*Wanre*. And his new temple came to be known, almost without his consciously willing it, as the House of Aton.

He was so preoccupied with the Teaching that he slipped from Tiy's hands like an elusive fish. To lure him back she often tried to use Nefertiti, but the queen wisely enough never allowed herself to become overly friendly with her aunt. She cultivated the delicate arts of courtesy and pleaded ignorance of those matters into which, as she told Tiy, "it was not feminine to inquire." So Tiy lost another link to the throne.

Nefertiti, however, was not so unaware of things as she appeared. She understood much but bore it silently. Her aloof, finely chiselled features, her calm lucid eyes, often wore an expression which faintly resembled pain—an inner secret pain which she herself could never quite define. Yet she would break out into gay laughter at a moment's notice and it was a laughter which softened her husband's austerity, took the edge from his intensity, and even at times allowed him to chuckle at himself. In a hundred unseen ways she tamed the Great One of Visions and saved him from falling blind and babbling into the sheer gulf of his own mind. When she was pregnant with her second daughter he composed a long hymn to the Aton which celebrated the chick in the egg, the child in the woman, the small and large animals of earth gathered under the beneficial beams of the god. He learned more from her about the vast quietness of love than he had learned from the complex mysteries of the priests of On. She purified and simplified the final image of the god which took shape in his imagination. Eventually he needed one all-embracing symbol for the Aton, and one day as he watched her long slender arms reach down to lift the child from its crib, that image came to him. Later, the walls of his temples were decorated with the sign of the god—the gold disc from which many blessing arms stretched, their hands holding the *ankhs* of life to the earth. Nothing more.

On the first day of his third regnal year he went off on a pleasure cruise looking for a site to build a new city. He went downriver with a brilliant designer known as Hatiay and a host of attendants and scribes, and when the royal boat rounded a certain bend in the river his inner eye looked outward and saw to the east a span of land bounded by the Nile and the Orient Cliffs. Mad with excitement, he spent three days walking up and down the land, his god telling him that here was the place to build a new capital, far from civilization and insulated by a wilderness, where He might be worshipped in peace.

    The child was conceived, and its name was to be Akhetaton, "the Horizon of the Aton." A team of surveyors measured the boundaries of the site and began drawing up plans for the construction of the city. He walked about carrying the city within him, bloated with it to the point where his advisers gave up trying to turn his attention elsewhere and instead laid their ears, so to speak, next to his belly and listened to the great rumblings within. Some felt the city was not a child; it was a parasite burrowing and multiplying— a thing which once embedded, like a dangerous idea in the mind of a madman, would never leave its host.

During this period Tiy's brother, Ay, had just returned from a depressing trip to Retenu and Khor, where he had been reviewing the political and military situation in the various outposts of the empire. He had witnessed the beginnings of an alarming rebellion among certain vassal kings, and tried desperately to gain Wanre's attention, but to no avail. Tiy gave him an ear, then told him to send word to General Haremhab, who had recently been appointed Governor of the Lower Land in Men Nofer. But the general replied that although he would like nothing better than to lead troops into Khor to relieve the various besieged cities, he had in fact no troops to lead. Wanre locked up his treasury when it came to military requisitions. So Ay inwardly mumbled his apologies to the northern rulers whom he had vowed to assist, and politely bowed his head away from the empire and down to his son-in-law's belly, where he too listened to the pregnant murmurings within.

It was going to take some time for the city to be ready for occupation, but Wanre couldn't endure the waiting. He spent all his time in long consultations with his designers, frequently sailing downriver to watch the construction of his vision. He couldn't see how the city of No Amon rocked with the insult he was dealing it, for his new city would reduce it to the status of a mere provincial town. Blind, he couldn't see the obnoxious cloud which gathered over the capital, its origin in the burning offering trays of Opet. He saw nothing. "The sun," mused Parennufer, "is in his eyes."

# Gwendolyn MacEwen

For some years the main link between the royal house and the House of Amon had been Tiy's other brother Ineni, who sat at the right hand of the High Priest MeryPtah, and who had more than once intervened with him on behalf of the royal family. Ineni served both as Second Prophet of Amon and as First Priest of Ra-Atum in Opet; for generations it had been the custom to keep the shrines of other gods under the administration of the House of Amon by having one priest serve in a double capacity. But when Wanre declared himself Great One of Visions of Ra, he began to criticize the administration of all the shrines of Ra, in any of his forms. A situation arose which was very uncomfortable for Ineni, for, like an island left high and dry in the Nile after floodtime, he had more than one man trying to claim him for cultivation. MeryPtah on the one hand demanded that he continue serving both gods, for only thus could the shrine of Ra-Atum remain under the complete jurisdiction of Opet. The king, on the other hand, would not tolerate the "double dealings"—as he put it—which insulted his god.

Tiy begged her son to keep peace with the House of Amon by permitting Ineni to continue in both of his roles. He alone, she told him, could reconcile palace with temple as he had done in years past. Who else but her own brother could appease the insulted servants of Amon and help to soften the hatred that crackled throughout Opet? But Wanre ground his teeth for hours and a muscle which Tiy had never seen before kept twitching in his cheek, and finally he arose and said, *"This is total war!"* and went off without another word to spend the day at the small shrine of Ra-Atum across the river. There Ineni, who was in the act of offering to the god, found the offering tray fairly stolen from his hands as the Great One of Visions himself conducted the rituals and gave up the abundant fruits into the arms of the sun. Then he waited bewildered as his nephew the king bathed himself at least three times in the sacred waters of the scarab pool and disappeared for two full hours into the sanctuary, to emerge at dusk glowing and smiling and blind to Ineni's wrath. Wanre graciously accepted an invitation to dine in the priest's private quarters, and over the beef and wine plied him with questions about the upkeep of the shrine, expressed his disappointment with its administrative staff, and then flung down his napkin and stared at Ineni furiously, pleading, and asked:

"How do you survive as two men in one body? Do you possess two skins, shedding one and donning the other for each temple you worship in? Your double function doesn't *distress* you? You devote yourself to two gods at once; you're worse than a whore with a different man in every bedroom. Who appointed you First Servant of Ra-Atum?"

"Your father, Wanre, whose spirit is among the Imperishable Stars."

"And did he do it to make you a whore-priest embracing two gods?"

"But of course. It is the custom." He thrust about for something else to say, something withering, something insulting, as Wanre twirled a wine goblet between his fingers and concentrated on the ceiling.

But very quickly the king's mood grew turbulent, as though someone had cast a pebble into the still pool of his mind, and he leaned forward and whispered, "Ineni, brother of my mother—you will abandon the House of Amon forever!"

"Wanre . . . what?"

"No priest of Amon shall pollute the sanctuaries of Ra. I will not tolerate the stink of the ram's skin within Ra's shrines! Tomorrow you will go to MeryPtah and tell him what I have said. Tell him

Wanre spoke, *Wanre who has no sex, Wanre who won't endure beyond the fifth year on the throne!*"

"My Sun . . . no!"

"Then, Ineni," he went on, holding his wine glass high as though to toast his own words, "you are no more a priest of Ra-Atum. I bar you from this shrine."

Now Ineni, torn between the king and MeryPtah, who threatened to remove him from the House of Amon if he surrendered to Wanre's wishes, went whining to his brother Ay to help him out of his predicament. After all, wasn't Ay "It Neter," father-in-law of the king, as well as his uncle? Surely he could exercise an influence over him. But Ay replied drily that he had *no* influence over his son-in-law, no one did. The brothers glared at each other in silence. They'd never been too fond of each other. Ay could never stomach priests and was almost glad that Ineni had for once in his life been crossed by somebody. Ineni, on the other hand, had loathed Ay since the day years back when Ay had served him a particularly appetizing and highly spiced dish, then said to him after he'd eaten his fill, "O Seer! O Great One who can see the god! You've eaten Amon stew tonight, for my cooks cooked a ram!" Ay had only been pulling his leg, of course; he had no wish to blaspheme the gods, but Ineni never forgave him his harmless trick, especially when he piled insult upon injury by adding, "Lucky for you I didn't serve fish! Who knows which Nile creature swims around to this day with the phallus of Osiris in his belly?"

Ineni was finally driven out of Opet, to be succeeded by the former Third Prophet of the god. And in the shrine of Ra-Atum he was replaced by a new priest appointed by Wanre. The schism had begun.

Ineni went into early "retirement" seething with hatred for everything living, and making no secret of the fact that he sought revenge. He died, though, shortly afterwards, from a viper bite he got on his heel while walking in the desert and shouting curses on the royal house.

As the fifth regnal year advanced towards its close, the servants of Amon shook their bald heads in unison. Bad days had come, bad days brought about by the bad blood in the line of Yuyu. Despite the prophecy that the king would die, he was still alive. Certain of the priests began to worry about the fact that the oracle had not yet been realized, and held numerous divination ceremonies by night to try to determine the exact date and manner of his death. A child looked into a jar of oil and water and saw the surface dance with moving light; then she saw the light take many forms, and one of them was the body of the king slain upon the altar of the sun, his blood running moist among the sacrifices. At the same moment the Lord of the Silent spoke through the lips of MeryPtah and revealed that on exactly the last day of the fifth year Wanre would die from a heavy blow on the head in his sun sanctuary. To demonstrate his profound "dismay" MeryPtah fasted for a full afternoon. This sarcasm was not lost on the king, for he immediately sank into a depression which lasted over a week, locking himself up in the dark little sickroom he had lived in as a child.

But when he finally came out again he had undergone a frightening transformation. When a man lived beneath the shadow of a prophecy he had two choices—he could either wilt like a flower and humbly await his death; or, he could fight the god by calling up some inner power and drawing upon a hitherto unused source of energy. Wanre twisted the secret threads of his will into a thick strand; he turned about and discovered a power in himself which most men did not *need* to find.

*Does not the thought of death make us giants?* he mused. *I swear I will be He Who Lives To Live Long—didn't I write that very phrase in my hymn?*

He looked down at his body and found it still grotesque and deformed—but in health. It was almost as though the limbs, having accepted their ugliness, now created their own peculiar invulnerability—as though his very sickness was his unique strength. What had been disgust at his body suddenly became pride. He would not hide it—he would flaunt it to the world! It would not be his shame, but his tool.

As the days wore on and the year drew to an end, a wild elation possessed him. *Aton*, he told himself, *will determine the length of my days.*

At midday on the last day of his fifth regnal year, he went to his temple and walked down the stifling courts towards the sanctuary. His body was afire and the thin garments clung to his skin, forming another layer of flesh above his own. A disc of pure heat encircled everything—the gates, the offering tables—and he felt suspended in time like the sun itself, should it one day stop and rest in its journey across the sky. At the high point of noon, on the day he was destined to die.

When he stepped into the roofless sanctuary the god hung throbbing directly above his head like a great golden gong.

"*Supreme Child, Who creates Himself from Himself...*" he began, but he couldn't finish the recitation, for strange broken phrases kept disturbing his tongue, and his thoughts wheeled around each other like a flight of wild birds.

"*Lord of all that the Disc surrounds!*" said his mouth.

"*No one knows You save Your son who lives to live long,*" said the secret voice within his skull.

Then the sun beat down upon his naked head and beneath the layer of his skull and touched with fingers of fire the soft tissues of his brain. He covered his head and bent forward under a crown of pure light, and at that moment the god entered him. Something crashed against the wall of his vision and he felt he would faint. Just as he was about to fall, he saw it. Not the light, not even the

Disc, but something within his own sense. A force terrible and miraculously silent.

It was the living centre of all things.

*"The sun of him who knows Thee not will set, O Amon!"*

The voice came from somewhere behind him and he wheeled around just in time to avoid the blow of the blunt instrument the man was carrying. The thing crashed into the surface of the altar, and fruits and flowers fell to the ground. He caught the man's wrist in a vise and cried, "Who are you, assassin?"

"A student in the college of Amon," came the reply. "I serve my lord MeryPtah."

"And your business here?"

"I come to fulfill the prophecy that the Great One of Visions shall die from a heavy blow on the head in the sanctuary of the sun."

Wanre burst out laughing. No one had ever heard him laugh like that before. Was *this* the fear he had entertained for years?—this incredibly silly and abortive attempt at murder? He laughed and leaned back against the altar, his shoulders shaking and his head flung back. "Your name?" he managed to ask.

"Merire."

"*Merire* . . . Beloved of Ra! Why, you're an instrument of my father the Aton, and you'll remain with me, for I think you'll be good luck!" Then he picked up the heavy club and handed it back to the unsuccessful killer. "No, Beloved, don't try to run away now. Look at me, and you'll see that you cannot!" For many moments he held Merire's rapt gaze, then left him standing alone beside the altar of the sun. He wondered why he suddenly loved the man who had come to kill him.

A temple servant saw him emerge from the sanctuary with a hesitant step like that of a man walking after a long illness or a child walking for the first time. He rushed forward to give him aid, but he was repelled by a kind of shield which surrounded the king's body—a layer of pure heat or light, forbidding and untouchable. Wanre held out his hand to him, saying, "There's a man inside who came to destroy me. Have him escorted to the palace. His name is Beloved of Ra; he shall be one of the first to understand the Teaching."

His father-in-law Ay held his chariot that day and as he approached him he smiled and said something which at the time made no sense at all, *"And you, It Neter Ay, shall be the last!"*

Ay gazed into the crazy eyes seeking an explanation, but the blue one told him nothing and the brown one less—and anyway it was bad luck to stare into his eyes, for the brown one was a closed door and the blue one was an open door with the sky beyond it, and a man might lose himself in the coming and going.

They started to drive towards the river, but the king laid a hand across Ay's forearm and said, "No, I want to go to the House of Amon. Drive straight to the gates. I want to see MeryPtah!"

Ay dreaded the thought but drove the horses at top speed down the avenue of smiling ram-headed statues which led into the temple of Amon. When they arrived at the gates, Ay was loath to let Wanre enter the temple unescorted, but he broke away telling Ay to remain outside. Then he entered the gates on foot, and the hundreds of temple servants and worshippers parted like waves to let him pass.

MeryPtah was attending to a new band of voluntary temple recluses—criminals seeking sanctuary from the law, repentant fanatics flagellating each other, wandering seers and waifs. Curious at the sudden hush which had come over the courtyard, he turned to see the king striding towards him.

"Why . . . am I honoured with your presence, my lord Wanre?" he asked, trying to keep the surprise from his voice.

## King of Egypt, King of Dreams

The king stared at him a long time. "Because I'm alive, priest! You're trembling—why? Are you worried about the thug you sent to kill me? Don't worry—I'm going to make him my prize disciple."

"Son of evil, son of Set!" MeryPtah cried.

But the expression in Wanre's eyes was full of pity. "You Who Can See the God, hear me! Hear me, circumcised little priest with your white sandals and panther's skin, wretched little parasite with your mouth stuffed with natron to cleanse its filth. I am the king! Today the words of Ra are before me, my august Father taught me their essence. *It was known in my heart, revealed to my face, and I understood.* If I endure beyond this day—and I shall—then beware! I am *He Who Lives to Live Long.* Guard well the possessions of the House of Amon, the boats and gardens and fields and work-yards and towns and beasts and servants—for I shall destroy you, I shall destroy your god, I shall destroy all that went before! From this moment Opet receives no subsidy from the throne. I do not know you and you do not know me. The seat of my government will be elsewhere, far from the capital you and your servants have defiled!"

"But you will not endure, son of Set!" cried the High Priest. "Amon has condemned you to an early death; you have less than a day to live—beware!"

"I have more than an eternity to live, MeryPtah, for I am my own oracle!" And turning to the hundreds of stunned watchers he cried, "Hear me—no god can dictate to the life of a man! All gods which rule by fear are false!"

MeryPtah did not like the effect those words had on the people, and muttered under his breath so only Wanre would hear, "When you die, king, and try to enter the boat of Ra, you will drop off and never sail through the heavens with your god! Your death will be shameful and ugly—dogs will tear your flesh!"

But he was not listening. "I will make my Father supreme in this land," he announced to all. "I will make of the whole land one great roofless temple to Him. *It was known in my heart, revealed to my face, I understood.* Amon is dead, priest—clothe him in obscene wool!"

Wanre turned to leave but MeryPtah shrieked, "Criminal!" and the king wheeled about, his face drained with wrath.

"You dare address me to my back? Your breath stinks of leeks, I can smell it from where I stand."

"Do you really think you can leave the House of Amon alive?" MeryPtah challenged.

Wanre smiled. "I know it," he said, and walked away.

MeryPtah called one of his servants to go after him, and the man drew a dagger from his belt and sprang forward. But his hand froze in the air and sweat poured down his face and he was unable to move. The dagger dropped onto the sand. Dumbfounded, MeryPtah watched the king move away towards the gates, his path once again clear, for the crowds fell aside silently to let him pass. He carried his body skilfully, proudly, the long head held high, the great thighs moving slowly, the narrow chest taut. And as the High Priest's fist clenched and unclenched over the panther's paw, a low groan broke the silence, for in the cattle pen another beast was being sacrificed to the god.

Outside the gates Wanre gave a single cry and fell to the ground, his lips speckled with foam. Ay ran forward and, having nothing to place between his teeth to stop the king from biting through his own tongue, thrust his own hard hand into the gaping mouth and felt the teeth sink into the leather of his riding glove.

It was said some time later that inside the temple Wanre stripped off all his clothes to stand stark naked before MeryPtah. But that was legend. The day became known as the Day of Revelation.

MeryPtah himself died shortly afterwards, and there were many who believed that Wanre's curses brought about his end. But those who were close to him knew that he had been suffering for years from an awful disease very common in the land, which caused the victim's penis to itch and prick unendurably when it brought forth blood with its water. The peasants called it the Curse—and foreigners imagined that in Keme the men menstruated like women.

As the last hour of the last day of the fifth year drew to a close, there was a triumphant smile on Wanre's face.

"I am not dead," he informed his mother, who was pacing back and forth beneath a rich frieze of purple grapes.

"You would be, if there wasn't someone sane enough to answer for your follies!"

"What do you mean exactly?"

"Today I donated Crown Land to the House of Amon in your name."

He sprang forward and grabbed her arm. "You *what*?"

"Just what I said. It appeased them. That's no doubt why you are still alive."

"Don't ever do that again! I'm my own apologist, I'll answer for whatever I do. I am alive because I *willed* it!"

Tiy smiled indulgently.

"I don't care what you give them from your dead husband's treasury, but they will get no more from my throne—do you understand?"

"Too well! You have destroyed the capital; we are losing an empire—which, in case you are interested, is more important than that silly poem of yours about a chick coming out of an egg. Your indifference to it has invited treason. Has it occurred to you that Mitanni is falling and Kheta advances to *our* borders? You should have been a leader, a general!"

"I am a general. I hold complete power."

"With what!" she sneered.

"With love, with light. My god will unite the empire."

"Well then do it, build temples in foreign lands, do *something*!"

He returned to his chair and sat silent for a long while. His eyes looked feverish but his face wore all the calmness of sleep. He rested his chin in one cupped hand and the royal cobra on his brow tilted lazily to one side.

"I *am* going to do something," he said at last. "The fifth year is over. I will speak with Hatiay about the immediate removal of the court to the Horizon of Aton."

"I forbid it!" cried Tiy. "There's a world outside that city of yours! Besides, it's not even finished."

"There's another world within it. I'm going now, *He* has told me."

"You know I will never join you in the city!"

"I know it and I'm going."

*"Amenhotep!"*

"Mother," he whispered. "My name is no longer Amenhotep. From this day my name is *Spirit of Aton*. Neferkheprure Wanre *Akhenaton*, Who Lives to Live Long."

night          the land is in darkness

the first hour of the night

Akhenaton was almost naked. He stepped down from his silver-gold *merkebet* chariot and saw that the pastel reins had left blue and pink stripes on his palms where his sweat had mingled with the colours. He rubbed his palms together and they went purple. It was the sixth year of his reign.

Almost naked, although he was adequately garbed. He wore a tight linen kilt with an alarming slit down the front where the ends parted company after their futile attempt to embrace those enormous thighs, his favourite Blue Crown with streamers floating out behind his neck, and the double insignias bearing his name and the name of his god strapped to his forearms and upper arms.

Almost naked, for now they judged him not in terms of his dress but of his flesh, and his nakedness was a matter of degree. Since they had come to Akhetaton he had gradually stripped himself of the elaborations of a king and made it known that he preferred to wear his own flesh like an extraordinary costume. He flaunted its outrageous contours, its insane symmetry, and everyone became fascinated with his body. It seemed to be in many places at once. It sprawled all over, yet it contained itself, like the city. Only a month ago he had driven down the Royal Road with Nefertiti and the child Meritaton; they'd all been stark naked and lost in laughter and he and Nefertiti enjoyed one long public kiss in the rattling chariot whose sides just barely hid their private parts. One might often see him leaning from the royal balcony in early morning, apparently quite nude, but then again the edge of the railing came up to his belly, so one could not say for sure. It depended on his mood, on how much he cared to reveal, in any sense, at any given time.

But his anatomy was a sacred matter and no one dared joke about it, save perhaps the bored sentinels far away upon the cliffs. On the contrary, anyone within earshot of him seized the opportunity to rhyme off some rehearsed flattery, for Akhenaton was known to raise a man's rank overnight on the basis of the slightest indication that he was attuned to the Teaching. Such a man was Suti, a standard-bearer, very proud of bearing his standard—(he'd once borne baskets of cauliflowers in the kitchens of Amenhotep)—who turned as the king passed and remarked so that all the world might hear: "See, my lord Ay, how he depends only upon his own body to garb his soul in Truth! He is surely 'Ankh-em-Maat,' he is surely 'Living in Truth.' One lives, one is in health when one sees him...."

Immediately Ay, who was standing beside Suti, disliked the man. He was sick of the business of "Living in Truth," which Wanre took so seriously he had made it part of his name. Ay recalled wryly how Amenhotep had been "Lord of Truth"—and it angered him to realize that the secret name he loved to apply to *himself* was "Ir Maat," "Lover of Truth"—and he blurted out, "That he lives in Truth, Suti, I have no doubt. It all depends," he added wearily, "on what Truth is!"

The king heard the last remark, turned, and smiled disarmingly, still trying to rub the purple stain from his palms. "Still the unhappy philosopher, Ay?" He made a half turn and allowed his profile to address him. "And what *is* Truth, Ay?"

"It is harmony. It is the feather in the hand of Maat. It is the order of the universe."

"And do you think then it is blown to and fro in the breeze like any feather? Never mind, you are progressing. But your thinking is so dreary, so painful. Leave off, why don't you? Witness the sun." He stepped away.

The standard-bearer watched from the corners of his eyes. "Don't worry," Ay told him. "He hears everything, he remembers everything. You'll receive your due." Then, looking up to the sky, to the dizzy sun, to the circling hawks above the cliffs, he added under his breath, "We all will. . . ." and thought that the sky was full of flying truths and feathers and he for one couldn't count them, not for anything.

A group of worshippers formed a semi-circle around the king to prostrate themselves before the Father, the Giver of Life, whose rays beat down cruelly on their naked backs. Wanre stood in rapt adoration, half aware of the fact that most of those present did not care to understand the real nature of the god. Most were paying lip-service to the Teaching; a few were obviously parrots with good memories. Yet he loved them. He *had* to love them—hadn't the god revealed Love? Ay was probably the only one who didn't pretend. He was the most honest man there, and Wanre loved him too—because he had to. Or was it more than that, he wondered, gazing sidelong at his inscrutable father-in-law. Was it possible It Neter Ay was in fact "Living in Truth" although he didn't *profess* to? Through the haze of the heat their eyes met for a brief moment. Ay was smiling, and his dark mocking face was half turned towards the sun.

Wanre was a little envious of the fact that Ay's skin was so brown. His own was dead-white. He never tanned: the god's beams penetrated him to the core, burning his heart and liver, but left his skin untouched. Aton, on the other hand, turned Ay a healthy nut-brown on the outside but never got beyond the surface of his flesh.

A small commotion in the background made him turn to see Nefertiti arriving in a little cloud of golden dust thrown up by the wheels of her own chariot. She had been laughing, and the laughter still hovered about her mouth as the horses snorted and coughed. She looked wild and fresh from her ride, but by the end of the day she would be as weary as the rest. It was three miles from the core of the city to the Orient Cliffs, and they would have to visit the other boundary stones of Akhetaton, located far to the south and north, and across the river to the west—all in the next two days, for he was fixing the limits of the city and swearing never to pass beyond them. For the next two nights the royal tent would be pitched in the desert.

Now he was bathed in sweat. He did not enjoy the desert. It was mean, it taught him that the god could be ruthless as well as merciful, and the rays which gave tremulous life to green and growing things were the same rays which scorched human flesh and shrivelled the eyes. He stood before a huge stone slab set high in the walls of the Orient Cliffs. Carved upon it was a long text, and as he began to read from it there were tears in Parennufer's eyes. His voice mingled with the heat, the light, and the great stone shimmered as in a mirage.

"Year Six, fourth month of the second season, thirteenth day. This is the oath pronounced by the king. As my Father Ra-Horakhte lives, as my heart is happy in the queen and her children ... this is my oath of Truth which I wish to announce, and of which I will never for all eternity say 'It is false.' The southern boundary stone which is on the eastern hills is the boundary stone of the City of the Horizon of Aton, namely this one by which I have halted. I will not pass beyond it southwards forever and ever."

He repeated the same oath regarding the southwestern stone, and the northeastern stone.

"And the area within these four boundary stones from the eastern hills to the western hills is the City of the Horizon of the Aton proper. It belongs to my Father Ra-Aton—mountains, deserts, meadows, islands, high ground, low ground, water, land, villages, embankments, men, beasts, groves and all the things which my Father the Aton shall bring into existence forever and ever.

"I will not neglect this oath which I have made to the Aton my Father. It shall not be erased, it shall not be washed out, it shall not be kicked, it shall not be struck with stones, its spoiling shall not be brought about. If it be missing, if it be spoilt, if the tablet on which it is shall fall, I shall renew it again afresh in the place where it was."

He had commanded that all his officials memorize those words so none might forget that this natural sanctuary bounded by the river and the cliffs was wholly owned by the god whose rays claimed every corner of the land. Finding it absurd that he as king should donate the land to the god as was the custom, he had decreed that the City of the Horizon had in fact been donated by the Aton to *him*. The words carved on some of the other boundary stones were even more fervent:

*As my Father Ra lives, the great and living Aton, ordaining life, vigorous in life, my Father, my rampart of a million cubits, my remembrance of eternity, my reminder of the things of eternity, Who formed Himself with His own hands, Whom no artificer knew ... my eyes are satisfied every day when they see Him rise in the temple of Aton in the City of the Horizon, filling it with His beams, beautiful in love, and laying them upon me in life and length of days forever....*

*If I die in any town of the north, south, west or east, I will be brought here and buried in the City of the Horizon.*

*Evil were those things which I heard until Year Four, evil were those things which Amenhotep heard, evil were those things which Thutmose heard.*

Ay accompanied the king and Nefertiti back to their chariots, carefully manoeuvring himself close to the queen to take advantage of the breeze from the fanbearers' fans. When his shoulder accidentally brushed hers he felt obliged to give her a broad smile which scarcely reflected his true disposition. He eyed her sideways, surprised as always that she was a woman now, not the little daughter he remembered. She had grown straight and slender as a pillar in a temple; she wore an elongated crown which made her seem taller than the king, and the exaggerated curve of her slim neck bore witness to its weight. A hot wind whipped against her dress and pressed it to the contours of her body. She was only half as naked as her husband, but being a woman she was in fact twice as naked, or so Ay mused. The flimsy tunic was really more of an excuse for clothes than an actual covering, joined as it was just below her breasts and dropping loosely to the ground. Her manner of dress, or undress, was the height of fashion, and Ay tried not to wonder too often where the line should be drawn between "Living in Truth" and outright nudity. It only bothered him when applied to her, the Thrice Beautiful, and whenever he was with her in a crowd he found himself anxiously scanning the faces surrounding them for signs of an admiration based on something other than her royal position. Who for instance, was that young man whose eyes were just then devouring her? *He* saw the woman beneath the queen, Ay was sure of it. He shot the fellow a scathing look. The fellow shot him one back, and he realized a little belatedly that it was Thutmose, one of the most talented royal portraitists, brilliant with his hands. Artists make it their business to stare, thought Ay, and if he was going to be bothered by something like that, then surely he was becoming as outdated as someone's old sandals. Still, he had seen foreign harlots more modestly dressed than the queen of the Two Lands. Dark ones from the islands to the north, brown ones from Kush, white ones from . . .

His thoughts were interrupted when the king and queen stepped into their chariots. They seemed to be sharing some private joke, for Nefertiti's hand was raised for a moment to hide a wide smile. Then there were two consecutive snaps of the reins and the horses bounded forward.

That night they went out of the royal tent to breathe the chill air of the desert.

"Will it be a son?" she cried, her hand on his arm. "Tell me, Wanre—predict it! I've given you four daughters...."

"You know how I abhor any kind of prophecy," he told her. "The sex of the child is being shaped in heaven, and I will *not* tamper with heaven, I will *not* look into the future."

She walked as though in a dream, her head thrust back to study the burning, uncountable stars. "When you are upon me I cry out for a son ... but somehow it seems impossible you and I will ever have a male child. It will be another girl, I know, I *know*. You're destined to sire—to be surrounded by women!" She gave a short little laugh but it ended abruptly. "But without a male heir, my husband, what will become of all this?" And she swept an arm about to indicate the city, the boundary stones, the holy land of the god. "I'm uneasy...." she whispered.

He slowed down and coughed nervously in an attempt to hide his embarrassment. He was never at home in such discussions. Somewhere in the night a jackal barked, and then all was silent.

"What sort of woman am I?" she challenged.

Taken aback, he muttered, "An ideal one, of course! Whatever made you ask such a foolish question?"

"I don't know myself."

"Does anyone?" he countered.

"I mean, sometimes I have an awful cold feeling. When I'm not pregnant. It grows within me, into those spaces which are otherwise filled with your seed. I'm like the river, rising and falling, ebbing and flooding."

"You're fortunate then. I can't imagine a greater peace than to have the same rhythms as the seasons and the Nile. You're at one with everything. I'm not."

"—But then I ask, where is my *self*, what do I really want? There's something else, something I can't name...."

He listened but he didn't really understand. He was too sure that his world, his god, was also hers; he was too sure she was somehow the female equivalent of himself.

"Isn't it strange to be a woman?" she asked suddenly.

"It certainly is," he said with authority, then realized how odd that must have sounded.

"Look at Nut," she said, tilting back her head. "With her body of stars, the silver moon in her belly!"

"You know I don't like to hear you speaking of Nut."

"But she's my sister, that great woman of stars!" and she laughed again, lightly, but her laughter was stilled by the barking of jackals beside the cliffs. "Besides," she teased him, "haven't you yourself told me that you rise in the morning like the sun out of her thighs, and my body is the starry heaven through which you've passed?"

He didn't answer. He had told her that, some years ago when they awoke to a flaming dawn when the sky was crimson with the blood Nut shed for the daily birth of Ra. He had emerged from the loins of night refreshed, reborn . . . but that seemed long ago now.

When they returned, the air was chill as death, and just outside the tent a blind parade of scorpions was marching down a line of water from a bucket someone had overturned—the largest in front, the smallest behind, their stingers poised like swords.

Although the City of the Horizon had been occupied by a number of citizens since the fifth regnal year, it was still undergoing construction. Sentries were posted high on the Orient Cliffs to keep watch over the desert—red-brown men from the desert tribes who made excellent policemen not to mention spies and mercenaries, so excellent in fact that the entire police force was named after them—the Medjay. But the task of these particular city guards was almost ludicrous, for although Akhetaton was not impregnable, it was a most inconvenient place for anyone to consider attacking. So the patrol troops spent a good deal of their time playing knuckle-bones and exchanging ribald jokes, many of which had their origin in the anatomy of the king. But on a day when the wind blew from east to west no such jokes were circulated, for then they believed that the slightest breeze would carry the words three miles away to the palace, and he would hear.

The city was well planned, but some sensed a terrible urgency about its design; it was being built against time, torn out of space with fervent, multi-coloured shapes, a beginning. Yet there were times when its very incompletion seemed complete, and that temporary state became somehow its eternal character. A hawk, cruising eastward from the river, would first have seen the great Royal Road which ran north and south, connecting the two extremes of the city. The royal palace and the Great Temple lay in the city's core, on opposite sides of the road. Close by were the villas of the noblemen and a little eastward lay the main city. On the easterly fringe were the military and police headquarters and beyond that the desert, broken by rows of radiating chariot-wheel tracks left by the city patrol. Beyond the desert were the cliffs, and cut into them were the tombs Wanre built for his nobles. And in the royal wadi were his family tombs, beautifully made, empty as skulls. He deliberately made the homes of the dead lie east, towards the Rising.

He had brought with him the best scribes and artisans of the old capital, so the city was full of young men eager to abandon the old ways and follow him who promised them unlimited glories if they would hear the Teaching. He ordered trees from Khor to make Akhetaton green, for he loathed the desert. The general populace was composed of workmen and their families, some of them foreigners from Khor or the islands of Hau Nebet.

Everyone moved towards the vision of the final city, and it was common knowledge that it was unethical to refer openly to the break from the old capital. It was a closed issue. One might at best delicately allude to the event, for the king would not hear the name of that hated city spoken without a terrible pallor creeping across his face and a nervous quivering about the nostrils. He never punished anyone who let the name slip; he had something worse than punishment, he had a *look*.

During the first year in Akhetaton he woke every morning before dawn, for he was unable to control his excitement at the completion of a new building or the breaking of trenches for another. In his favourite light chariot with its bright red leather tires, he'd go to watch the sun rise over a construction site, personally turning the first shovelful of sand for a trench or even "instructing" his architect Hatiay in some of his own obscure mathematics, a square rule in one hand and a hunk of bread for breakfast in the other. He wanted to be in on everything; he tried, sometimes successfully, to be in a hundred places at once. He'd often turn up unannounced at a site, grab a guide-line from the hands of a startled worker, and stand proudly pulling the string taut to mark the line of the wall. Several times he'd been seen elbow-deep in wet gypsum, grinning sheepishly when the workers arrived half an hour later at sun-up, explaining to them how he just wanted to feel the city "when it was in its fluid state."

Often in those morning excursions he was in such a rush that he was fairly flung out of the chariot as the wheels hit loose stones on the road. He steadied himself by kicking off his sandals and digging his toes into the leather meshwork on the floor, which, although designed to allow for the vehicle's bouncing, was equally good for keeping one's balance in this manner. Once, though, the chariot was completely overturned, for he drove the horses too fast, and an extra large stone knocked it completely off balance. He'd been unable to free himself, because his toes had remained caught in the leather strips. He thrashed around like a fly trapped in a honey pot, immensely glad that there had been no escort to witness the humiliating scene.

Another time, he tripped over a guide-line and stepped knee-high into a pot of paint. He hid himself behind a wall, and a workman, thinking he had seen an apparition, went to his foreman and whispered, "I saw the king close by me wearing a great scarlet boot on his right leg." The overseer shouted that the place for such visions was in the temple, and told the man to prepare him twice his quota of gypsum for the day. But the unfortunate worker went home on the pretence that he shouldn't have reported to work at all that day because his wife was having her monthly bleeding and he'd quite forgotten.

The first ring of a hammer or the sight of pure white lime flowing freely into a fresh trench became as much a herald of the day for him as the first rays of the Aton which darted over the Orient Cliffs. It was said he was Lord of the Morning, like the god. He might be anywhere at any time, and many a careless joke among the workers was silenced by someone whispering, "Sssh, he's watching!"

But Nefertiti began to fear for his safety on those solitary journeys and begged him to take an escort. One day, she told him, they would start to call him fool. One day—when they were tired of the novelty of seeing him alone. "You mean someone might kill me?" he laughed. "Who among my people would kill me?" But he secured a bodyguard of five soldiers who, for appearance's sake, were armed with axes and spears, and whose job it was to run beside the royal chariot. Wanre would often take his eldest daughter Meritaton for a ride, drive out leisurely past the city limits, and then, giving the child a secret smile, allow the horses free rein. They'd bound ahead into the desert, leaving the escort, who until that point had been running at top speed, far behind them.

the second hour of the night

When the time came for Nefertiti to bear her fifth child, the king pleaded with her to let him be present in the birth-chamber to witness the alarming spectacle. "I must learn all things, I must *see*!" he said, and she agreed. He sat in a corner of the room during the long hours of her labour, occasionally cracking his knuckles and lifting his eyes to the ceiling as though the god would intervene. When, towards the end, Nefertiti began to cry out particularly loudly, he rushed to her side and glared at the midwives and accused them of ill-treating her. Then he bent over her and asked, "Does it *hurt*?" In a few moments' respite from the pangs, she managed a wan smile and said, "Yes, my husband, that's the first thing you must learn." Then she crouched upon the birth-stool for the delivery and at last, after one long wail from her lips, the red head of the child appeared like that of a blind swimmer surfacing. Its first salt scream broke the silence of the room.

Akhenaton fainted dead away. Two of the nurses rushed to give him aid and he lay for almost an hour, prone upon a couch, his eyes rolled up into their sockets, his face dripping with sweat. Meanwhile Nefertiti too faded away into another sort of slumber, and as the royal pair slept their separate sleeps, the midwives carrying buckets of water to and fro from one to the other could scarcely contain their snorts and giggles at the ridiculous scene.

"Another girl, Great Lady," they told her when she awoke.

"There's nothing in my whole city which smells so foul as the Records Office," Wanre said, then seeing the hurt look on his Foreign Minister's face hastily added, "—No offence to *you*, dear Tutu. It's only that—how I loathe history! Shelves full of dusty rolls of papyri, cabinets full of tablets I can't even read. It turns my stomach—oh, no offence to *you*, dear Tutu! But why do men spend days recording their pitiful little problems, when they need only look up and witness the very majesty of creation?"

"But my Sun," Tutu ventured, "permit me. Isn't history creating itself every day? Today is the history of tomorrow, therefore..."

"I prefer to word that differently. *Today is the future of yesterday.* Yes... I like that phrase!"

"As you say, my Sun, today is the future of yesterday."

"Aton," the king went on, leaning his elbow against a dusty shelf labelled *Replies to Mitanni, Year 6,* "is not concerned with His previous risings. No, He is concerned with His present shining-forth. *Neferu, Setut, Merut—beauty, beams and love.* Memorize these, Tutu; I have noticed your temple duties are lagging. The words will aid you in your long office hours."

"Beauty, beams and love, I hear," said Tutu. But when the king left he returned to the maddening chicken-foot scratch of imperial correspondence; beauty, beams and love had nothing—or everything—to do with the fact that Keme was losing control of the empire. By the end of the day Tutu felt like a peasant who had spent ten hours driving his team around a threshing floor, but for him the grain escaped through holes in the floor, and he was left with no simple reward for his labours. At almost any time of the day, and occasionally night, he could be found behind his desk studying the latest dispatches from foreign kings or enraged vassals. He had a flawless command of the script of Akkad in which most of the diplomatic correspondence was written, and it had been a nightmare to learn. But in all things he had persevered, and now his authority was beyond dispute. Every letter written to the king and every reply to it had to pass through his hands, and he employed a huge staff to draw up copies and translations of royal correspondence. His background had equipped him for his monumental task; he was born in Amor and had come to the Two Lands as a young man. He had served under Amenhotep in the same capacity in which he now served Wanre. He was Chief Mouthpiece of the Whole Land, Chief Minister, Chamberlain of the King, Chief Servitor in the Temple of Aton and in the Barge, Overseer of all the Commissions of the Lord of the Two Lands, Overseer of all the Silver and Gold in the Treasury—he was, in short, the most indispensable man in the kingdom. Also, unfortunately, the least persuasive. He once presented himself at the quay when he knew Wanre was taking a pleasure cruise and the king consented to have Tutu fan him ten miles downstream and shade him ten miles back. While fanning and shading, Tutu delivered a long report on foreign politics, accompanied by a flute and the swishing of the oars. His words had no effect whatsoever, and he returned with his first suntan in years and a multitude of blisters on his fat white palms.

 He was a short man, completely bald (not merely shaven), with a certain air of agelessness which made him not so much a figure as a presence, the type seldom remarked upon, like a wall or a door or the eastern cliffs. There they were, there he was. He, like them, might only be noticed should he one day disappear. He lacked a sense of humour, which meant he endeared himself to no one, save perhaps the small pearl-grey cat which hung around the Bureau of Correspondence and which also lacked a sense of humour. The two understood each other very well; together they pondered the problems of life and politics. He poured out his troubles to the little beast, for he was the sort of man who felt he was constantly persecuted—by the world in general and certain people in particular. He walked about with an air of haughty, offended dignity; one had only to bid him a pleasant good morning and Tutu was cut to the quick. And woe to the man who mispronounced his name—*Duut, Tuut* or *Dudu*! His bald head was the roundest, shiniest head in the city, and it was said that if one night all the flares went out, Tutu could be stuck up on a pole as a beacon for travellers. He had a strange little dip in his skull bone, just behind the left ear, and when he was troubled his fingers would fly back and find the soothing little valley and caress it like a rare fingering-stone of alabaster, hollow and comforting as the contours of a mother. But few ever caught him in this attitude, for as soon as anyone entered the office his fingers would race back to the papyrus and he would assume once more his sensitive, eternally offended air.

Wanre scarcely saw his own correspondence. Not wanting to be disturbed by what he called "petty" petitions or complaints, he had given Tutu authority to answer some of the dispatches without even consulting him. "Tutu," he had said, "if the Aton fails to rise in Khor, if the sea swallows the land, if the heavens break and fall, tell me. Consult me on any complaint of that order. But meanwhile, reply to the usual letters in your own subtle manner. Besides," he had added, "I can't read the script, and if we spend hours laboriously having *every* letter translated, we shan't have time for anything else." Then he had gone off and taken some of the scribes who were employed in drawing up translations, and put them to work copying hymns.

Tutu almost wished that the enemies of the empire would speed up its destruction and leave him at peace. When Ay dropped into the Records Office he always made a point of chiding Tutu about it. Was he, in the deepest recesses of his mind, a potential traitor?—Ay would ask in some obscure, roundabout way, and Tutu would reply wryly that he was a passionately loyal man, and couldn't Ay see it just oozing from his pores? Once Tutu looked quizzically at him, and added, "Don't you realize, Ay, that all passionately loyal men are would-be traitors?"

Ay, who was now Master of Horse, Master of Chariots, and Chief of Bowmen, was planning a second journey to the provinces of Khor and Retenu, where he intended to convey messages to the vassal kings of the northern cities, inspect their troops, and determine what reinforcements they required. Meanwhile he planned to keep an eye open for signs of treachery, for while Wanre was praying to the god whose beams blessed every living thing, the empire was being threatened on two fronts—in the north by the partisans of Kheta, dispossessed local princes trying to extend their lands, and elsewhere by the desert barbarians, the cut-throat Habiru who struck into Retenu.

He asked for the latest news and Tutu sat for a long time as though the simple question needed a hundred translations before it could be answered. "First I have to separate the facts from the lies. I know what's imminent, and I wish I were blind." He sucked the end of a reed pen and gazed up mournfully. "One has always to read between the lines, you see, and that's no fun for there's hardly any space between the *words*, let alone the lines, in the script of Akkad...."

"Tutu, let's not be academic, I've got to get away tomorrow."

"Even *I* have to draw an occasional red guide-line to read a single sentence coherently, and *then* I might worry about the lies and ambiguities contained in the crowded messages. Take the letters from Kheta, for instance—have you seen any recently? There's one on the shelf behind you with more lies than fleas on a horse once you get past the surface meaning. It's a clumsily cordial thing from Shubiluliama; he writes while his warmonger friend Itakama is busy attacking the fringes of the empire between the lines. His grammar is inexcusable! His scribes are abominable spellers; do you know they call the king *Hurria?*"

"Their spelling doesn't matter a hoot on the battlefield!" cried Ay, annoyed with him. "I asked what was *happening.*"

"Well, the balance of power is shifting almost daily. The provinces have become small turbulent seas; city states rebel or sell out to the enemy. Kheta has annexed the whole of northern Mitanni, plus a few areas in Khor which were under Tushratta's rule. Dumaska and Kadesh fell to Itakama ... and many of the coastal cities have crumbled or are holding out against endless siege by the rebels of Amor. Loud protests of loyalty break out from princes who are proven traitors. There are the usual lies, slanders, secret coalitions, all the diseases which infect—if you'll pardon me—a dying empire. What else would you like to know?"

"Who remains loyal?" Ay asked, his skin creeping from a sudden chill, his nose itchy from the dust which settled on the grey shelves.

"In cabinet 129," said Tutu, "you will find a letter from some southern prince who swore he would drive a sword of bronze through his heart for love of Wanre. One month ago he openly attacked Megiddo. Does that answer your question?"

"Rib-Addi of Gubla ... what of him?"

"Oh, Rib-Addi," sighed Tutu wearily. "His letters are the most numerous, the most depressing. Wanre won't listen to him, he doesn't realize he's the only faithful vassal he has left. Gubla is besieged—everybody knows. So Wanre once told him, *Defend yourself and you shall be defended!* And Rib-Addi answered, *Against whom shall I defend myself—my enemies or my own people?* And running through all his letters there's that old refrain of his. *Like a bird in a net, so am I in Gubla.* Cabinets 130 to 137, if you care to look him up."

Ay sneezed from the dust and a piece of papyrus fell to the floor like a wounded bird. "What of Aziru?" he asked, pausing a moment to recall what he knew of the rebel prince of Amor who was growing rich on the gold of Kheta, in return for his invaluable services in creating chaos and confusion in the provinces. It was not known how many vassal kings and army leaders he in turn was paying off to desert their loyalty to the house of Keme. He was an elusive devil, protesting his love for the king while he burned the king's cities, always eloquently explaining how he did it to defend the royal strongholds and keep them from falling into enemy hands. Meanwhile the territories of Amor expanded.

"Ha!" said Tutu, banging his fat little fist on the desk. "You know what I have to show you, It Neter—a traitor's *dream*!" And he led him through several narrow aisles to a cabinet marked *Amor, Year 1 to Year 7*, and pulled out a tablet which he gazed at with glee. "This man has the most gall of anyone in the world. Listen to this! He writes me under the guise of 'friendship' because we once met for five minutes some years ago in Amor. Now I tell you never was an invitation to treason couched in more subtle terms. Listen! *Whatever is the wish of Tutu, write it and I will surely grant it. Look—the lands of Amor are your lands and my house is your house. Now you sit before the king my lord and my enemies have spoken slanders against me in front of him. Do not allow it to be so!*"

"And how much will he pay you if you 'do not allow it to be so'?" asked Ay.

"*Very* much," Tutu smiled, "but I am not ambitious."


Ay set out on his mission, sailed the Great Green, and landed on the coast of Retenu in high spirits. But when later he encountered the distraught deputy of Ursalim his mood rapidly changed. The deputy was a huge man with little watery eyes, who, on learning who Ay was, smothered him with the embraces of a long lost friend and poured out his city's tale of woe. Ay immediately struck him off his list of potential traitors, for never was a man so anxious to show him the lamentable state of his troops and shower him with blessings if he'd only tell the king how many men and supplies he needed to ward off the onslaughts of the *Sa Gaz Mesh* pillagers. Later, as Ay lay pampered and petted by three of Abdi-Khiba's female slaves, word arrived that trouble was brewing in the plain of Amki in the north—beyond the river Aranti. One of the partisans of Kheta was preparing to occupy the region, which was part of Pharaoh's northernmost border territories. Ay quickly took leave of his host, who fell upon him once more and crushed him as a boa might a rabbit, begging him to convey his eternal devotion to Wanre on his return home.

He took the fastest overland route to the north—the sea road along the shore of Amor, but underestimated the dangers of the unguarded highway, and learned only much later that the garrisons stationed on the main roads had been deserted for months. A gang of bandits fell upon him and his four escorts and stripped them of their possessions. The others refused to continue and Ay was left alone. When he finally reached the river Aranti he paid the boatman with promises that in future he would get some of the gold which was "common as dust" in his land. The old fellow ferried him across the western bend of the river and said that three local princes had gathered all available men at the southern end of the plain to meet the invader. He himself, he added, was not going to set foot out of the boat when they hit shore.

Ay arrived on the plain looking like some wretched messenger—but then, he thought, what better disguise? He'd learn more about what was going on as a messenger than he would as the king's father-in-law. As he drew nearer to the big tent at the southern end of the plain he was sure he smelled treachery; the princes were probably making a great show of defending the territory while in fact they merely waited to embrace the army of Kheta.

But when he presented himself at the tent the three vassals (he forgot their names after that nightmarish day) were engaged in intense debate around a makeshift table; maps were stretched out before them and they looked as though they were peering over the bloody landscapes of the whole world. Their faces were drawn and weary; they had been there for days. Behind them in the flickering shadows a short squat fellow was being beaten black and blue, and Ay heard his assailant muttering over and over, "Where is your chief camped? At which end of the plain? Where is Kheta camped, scum, *where*?"

"A Beduwi scout," murmured the guard who had led Ay into the tent. "We picked him up this afternoon. He plays us for fools; his tribe was with Kheta, which is why they're so far north, but now he tells us his *sheikh* longs to join us and become a subject of Pharaoh. He lies, they all lie...."

"I'll pluck out all your teeth from your head save one for the sake of toothache!" cried his assailant. "Speak!"

The Bedu sank to his knees and wrung his hands. "Kheta," he began, and the heads of the three princes shot up in attention. "They are stationed with the many countries they have brought with them. Behind the first hill they wait, the one shaped like a crouching lion. Itakama leads the troops."

There was silence. Presently one of the princes spoke up. "If you lie, tribesman, it will not be your mere teeth that we pluck out of your head. You will *have* no head, do you understand?"

"By the gods, I do not lie! By the breasts of my mother I do not lie! By him who sits on the throne of *Misrii* I lie not!!"

The three princes noticed Ay only then and motioned for him to speak.

"I bear a message from the Two Lands," he announced, his voice sounding very flat to his ears.

"Whatever it is, it's too late!" said one prince. "We don't need messages, we need men. What are you anyway—a tax collector?"

He told them angrily that he'd just arrived after a long and arduous trip, and started to go into detail about his misfortunes on the sea road but was cut off with, "Messenger from *Misrii*, what's-your-name, we are *invaded*! Three days ago the troops of Itakama moved in. I am not interested in messages. Have a seat."

Ay sat down hard on a nearby crate, suddenly weary. There seemed little point in striking up another conversation, but he couldn't resist asking, "What happened to the treaty between Kheta and the Two Lands?"

"Ha! *Treaty?* You must be joking! The great Shubiluliama pays Aziru and Itakama to attack Pharaoh's territory, while he himself concentrates on the lands of Mitanni. Akhenaton, I understand, still believes he's friendly."

"So you're planning a counterattack?" Ay put in.

"You think perhaps we're standing here planning how to kill an ass and seal a treaty with *Kheta*!" he roared. "Of course we attack. At dawn. They haven't attacked, they've just moved in like tenants taking possession of an old house. Shubiluliama can't forget that hundreds of years ago Kheta once ruled these lands. Anyway, this invasion is most unorthodox for him; usually he has the grace to send people a polite letter of warning before he declares war; this time he didn't bother." He passed a hand over his brow and said in the most carefully planned tones of sarcasm, "You see, messenger, we need *men*. We need *provisions*. We need a miracle. The Aton, so I hear, makes miracles. Is that your message?"

Ay struck off the three princes from his list of possible traitors. He felt almost disappointed.

The huge plain was a death trap. The only way to combat the chariots of Kheta was by guerrilla attack, which was all very well in mountainous country, but this place afforded no way of surrounding and surprising the enemy; it was an open palm offering up its armies for sacrifice. Even troops of light cavalry which were employed for swift stinging attacks would have been totally ineffective. No choice remained for the vassals but to march their armies head on into the enemy camp.

Incredibly, Ay slept. The night was silent, yet alive with the sound of the slow, bloodthirsty gurgling of the river at his back. At dawn someone woke him and pushed a mug of water and a loaf of bread into his hands. Outside were sounds of muffled activity—clanking of armour in the morning mist, snorting of tired horses.

"Eat this, messenger from *Misrii*. What's your name?"

"Ay."

"Can you by any chance handle a chariot or use a bow?"

He forgot himself and somewhat rudely told him that back home he was Chief of Bowmen. At this the man guffawed and congratulated him on his sense of humour. He could *handle* a bow, yes, that was all he needed to know. He ate and stepped outside the tent into the grey light of morning. The sight that met his eyes made him stagger; confronting him were hundreds of the most disorderly soldiers his eyes had ever seen. It was obviously a pooled army, a good half of which was a contingent of Beduwi mercenaries, their faces flinty, their eyes sharp as those of hawks. In front of the infantry was an assortment of feeble, tragic old chariots which looked to Ay like veritable relics from the days of Thutmose. He looked about for the three vassals but they were somewhere up front; the captured scout was hoisted into one of their chariots to lead the way to the enemy camp. Then the "army"—a great chaotic mass of underfed men and rusty chariots and unpredictable desert warriors—started to move. Ay's imagination carved out an insane monument to commemorate the day. *O valiant defenders, O mighty warriors, Wanre is with you! Your king dances in your midst clutching daisies and forget-me-nots, therefore be brave!* He thought of the glorious battles which had won the empire, and his stomach turned over with fear and revulsion. He almost turned tail and ran, but someone caught him by the shoulder in a comradely way and led him to a chariot. He found himself beside the driver, a man whose eyes were slightly but noticeably crossed, and who asked, gazing at the bridge of his nose, "You can handle a bow?"

Ay started into a lengthy discussion about how back home he was such and such, but there was no time to finish. There came a tremendous clamour as the men beat their battered shields and cries of "Itakama! Ten gold pieces for the head of Itakama!" filled the air. Then they bounded forward in the most haphazard formation the mind could conceive, and more shouts went up about how there would be *twenty* gold pieces for another, more delicate part of the unfortunate Itakama.

As the sun rose the plain opened out before them, flat as a fallen shield. *Did Wanre ever see his glorious god rising under these circumstances?* Ay thought. Far ahead the first beneficial beams of the god pinkened the Hill of the Crouched Lion; in his imagination he thought he could already see the glinting of the armour of Kheta. He picked up his weapon—a badly made bow, and not the type he was accustomed to—and thought that Itakama's head or private parts would be hard to locate, for he had heard that the Chiefs of Kheta protected themselves in the midst of their infantry, disdaining to lead their troops like men.

But there came from his right a tremendous clattering and screaming, and they swung around in time to encounter the enemy. They were nowhere near the Hill of the Crouched Lion; they came out of the east with the rising sun. Ay turned to the princes' chariots and saw one of them in a fit of fury strike off the head of the Beduwi scout who had misinformed them of the enemy's position. As the smiling head fell to the ground—a signal unplanned but understood by all—the entire contingent of Beduwi mercenaries let up a great roar and charged to the east to sell themselves out to Kheta.

They were left with half an army. They roughly assembled themselves in a position of hasty defence, and waited. Two great horns, the lines of the enemy chariots reached out to embrace them. Their chariots were heavier and more massive than those the defenders drove. Each was manned with a driver, a bowman and a shield-bearer, while the defenders fought with two men apiece, knowing full well their disadvantage. Ay's own chariot seemed to him suddenly an insanely delicate thing, almost a showpiece, and as the enemy drivers bore down hard, their chariots creaking and clattering with sheer mass, he wouldn't have been surprised to see a winged bull charging out from their ranks, or a lion-drawn vehicle come roaring out of the midst of them.

But they were slow; this he learned quickly enough. His driver, an experienced man, waited till the last minute before slapping the reins and sending them darting off to one side. Ay sent an arrow singing into the vulnerable slit between the front and back of an enemy's armour, and half heard his driver cry, "Messenger, you really *can* handle a bow!" As the enemy fell, Ay's vision clouded with red and for a moment he thought, *The sun is bleeding*, for it was as though a curtain of blood coloured the morning light.

For what seemed like an eternity they held them off, though Kheta had long since broken their lines. When Ay saw the enemy chariots drawing back at one point, he had the absurd idea that they'd been repulsed. But Kheta had punctured their lines and were now withdrawing to allow the infantry to plough through the hole they had left in their ranks. The defenders' chariots, or what was left of them, drew back and all but the drivers leapt to the ground to join in the hand-to-hand combat which was to come.

The enemy was armed with everything from iron swords to battle axes with hideous curved blades which glinted grey in the light. Beneath some of the plumed helmets the hawk-eyes of the treacherous Beduwi mercenaries gleamed. The enemy was pressed together in close formation; they were a wall—and the defenders a chaotic flight of birds dashing their brains against it.

"Itakama, Itakama!" the wild curse still sounded, but it was more like a prayer than a battle cry.

The remainder of the day receded into a dark red place in Ay's memory; he never spoke of it later, when he returned to Keme. He tried to forget the dark red gardens on the plain of Amki, horrible gardens of blood, of twisted limbs and scattered shields and fallen helmets like skulls, incomplete bodies and wounded horses. And finally, the murderous echo in his ear which was the order to retreat. The left wing of the Kheta chariots had thinned out enough to permit a few defenders to escape. *Escape,* because those gardens were theirs, their blood flowers, their fallen horses. Escape, like wounded dogs with dusty tongues flapping in the dirt.

A very few chariots, including those of the vassals, broke through the thin enemy lines; Itakama did not bother giving pursuit.

As a token of that day Ay received a flesh wound in his left thigh carved out by a curved blade. Later it developed into a dainty white scar shaped, oddly enough, rather like the royal flail.

If it hadn't been for the tremendous skill of his driver he too would have been buried in Amki. Later he expressed his admiration for the man's performance and invited him back to Keme, where he promised to see to it that he was given a high military appointment. But to his amazement the driver laughed in his face. "I should come to *Misrii,* the land of the sun king, the poet prince? Thanks, but no. I'd rather stay here and die an honourable death!"

Ay felt personally insulted and told him so. He remarked inwardly that the words had been treasonable, but somehow it didn't seem to matter anymore.

"No offence to you, Ay. You fight well, you amaze me. I thought no soldier came out of *Misrii* nowadays with an inch of guts. What does the army do back home, tell me—besides drinking beer and sleeping with all those fat white creatures you have there? Do they fight? Does Pharaoh send aid to us? You've seen! You are a messenger, you say—then go back with *this* little note to our precious king!"— and he made an obscene gesture with one hand to indicate the message.

At that point Ay could easily have revealed who he was, but it was an absurd situation and his pride was at stake. He could not blame the driver for his bitterness, for he'd been too appalled at what he'd seen riding on that tragic sea of rusty chariots. Maybe the man was an ex-prisoner given his freedom for joining the army, just another reluctant defender of Pharaoh's rapidly waning territories in the north. He thought of the well-fed young soldiers in Keme, and of Wanre wandering through his beloved gardens—not the gardens of blood he'd seen.

One of the three vassals together with his men planned to seek refuge in one of the coastal cities and build up another army. They parted that same night in a cold, black wind. Ay asked him if he might convey from him a message to the king; the prince burst out laughing and Ay thought for a moment he had gone quite mad.

"Ay, what's-your-name, messenger from *Misrii* . . . go back and ask him *politely* if we might in future get a few *men* up here. Politely, mind you! I hear he has big ears at least, though he lacks certain other attributes. But then I gather he doesn't like war. Well, everyone to his taste! Dead men with their hands or their sex cut off are not the most pleasant of sights. I heard he fainted once years ago at one of his father's tribute festivals when they brought in a group of captives from Kush. Perhaps you will forgive us if we are reluctant to defend the lands of the Fainter. He does think of his empire, though, doesn't he? Why, he wrote a poem and said there was a Nile in the sky for foreigners. Isn't that a stimulating thought! I have an idea—what if we compose a poem for him requesting troops? Maybe he'll listen. Hey! Can anyone in this cursed crew write *poetry*?"

Then his swarthy features softened and he looked at Ay sorrowfully. "Go back to *Misrii*," he said, "and in the name of all the gods tell Pharaoh what you have seen today." Then he looked him up and down a while, and his voice was suddenly curious and cautious as he asked, "Who *are* you, exactly and what is your station in the house of Pharaoh?"

It Neter Ay bowed his head before that insignificant vassal feeling lower than he had ever felt in his life, and murmured almost apologetically, "I am the brother of Tiy."

He made his way to Ugarit, where he thought he would take a ship back home, but it was a long wait, for Aziru and his men had recently marched down the coast and taken three cities with incredible ease, slaying their kings and looting their treasuries—no doubt another act of "protection." Ugarit was a city gone mad, for now Aziru was virtually at its gates. The harbour was jammed with hordes of screaming women clutching children to their breasts, giving away their jewels and savings to boatmen to carry them safely down the coast.

Some had no jewels or savings; they paid in other ways. Ay caught a grim scene taking place behind a huge bale of grain where one woman, clutching a small girl to her side, was arguing violently with one of the boatmen. Eventually it seemed they settled on a price—for, still keeping the child's hand locked in hers, the woman drew up her skirts and leaned back against the bale and closed her eyes as the boatman hastily collected his due. The child let out a piercing series of shrieks, for she thought her mother was being killed, but the woman held her firm all the while and murmured broken, soothing words.

He decided it was madness to stay in Ugarit and quickly took off overland down the coast to Gubla. On arriving he presented himself to Rib-Addi, the famous vassal king of the city, and requested safe passage back to the Two Lands. Meanwhile he found himself sizing up Rib-Addi and crossing *him* off his list of possible traitors. Others might hand over their cities for a palmful of gold, but men like this one, who had absolutely no secret dealings with Aziru, were few enough to count on the fingers of one hand. He had grown lean and ill in the service of Pharaoh, and Ay confessed he thought him a fool for it.

Rib-Addi leaned back in a chair and made a kind of pyramid with his fingers, delicately placing the tips together and studying the effect as he spoke. "Ugarit is taken. Tunip, Simyra, Biruta, Saru and Sidon are holding out. Gubla is holding out. When Aziru moves into Simyra, we are doomed. I need archers, chariots, everything! I have nothing. It's a matter of months, maybe weeks. Our supplies are completely cut off. Aziru has been harassing me since the days of Amenhotep. Akhenaton refuses to send aid. That is that. Like a bird in a net, It Neter Ay, so am I in Gubla."

The quiet restraint of his speech was terrifying.

"Already the troops desert us and join Aziru. Those 'captured' cities—how many of them were taken and how many gave themselves away? Their cries remind me of the deceitful whimperings of a voluptuous young girl who claims she is being raped while her own hand helps loosen the clasp of her dress. How long, Ay, before those three brave princes you met give up their struggle and open their hands for enemy gold? Treachery? You might call it that. I have no intentions of selling the city of Gubla, don't misunderstand me. But how in the name of Baal can a man remain loyal to a king who will not hear him!"

He offered Ay some wine; he took it but the taste was sour on his tongue. Rib-Addi leaned back and broke the pyramid; his fingers clenched up into little fists. "Tomorrow I'll get you a boat out of Gubla. May Baal give you a safe journey home. Oh, I'm sorry! I shouldn't swear by Baal, for you may be a religious fanatic like your king. Once I congratulated him on his coronation and made the profound mistake of adding that the god of our city decreed he should sit upon his throne. He never wrote back. No doubt that's why I'm not getting any troops up here!"

Ay started to protest that Baal would do as well as any god, but Rib-Addi was becoming tired.

"I ask only that you convey to Wanre my enduring devotion to his house. Tell him I will hold out until my hair falls out strand by strand from my head. Tell him Simyra will hold out, but it will fall. Tunip is holding out but it will fall also. Saru and Sidon are holding out, but how *long* they can last is another matter. Zimrida of Sidon is weak, I don't doubt he'll eventually make terms with Aziru. Abdi-Milki of Saru is strong. I am strong. But tell Wanre to send *archers*!"

Ay left for home the next morning in an old boat which stank of fish. On the way back he rehearsed what he would tell the king. Everyone he met was a traitor, and yet no one was. He would plead the case of the northern vassals, he would beg him to send troops out of Keme. He would be forceful, eloquent, poetic, brutal, utterly convincing.

But when he got back, he went to the Great Temple at dawn and entered one of the small chapels which lined the walls. He saw Wanre climbing the ramp which led to the great altar, his arms laden with baskets of fruits and flowers and bread; he was dressed in a pure and awful white. He piled the altar high with the offerings, then sprinkled them with holy water which sparkled as it flowed. The temple singers intoned the morning hymns.

Ay felt something catch in his throat. He stared, fascinated with Wanre's whiteness, the early sunlight on the crown, the long white arms outstretched to embrace the very substance of the light, the white body poised on the high white ramp, absorbing the sacred rays. He covered his face and for a brief instant had a sensation of such sweetness and warmth that it made him ashamed. Perhaps this was the way things should be, he thought . . . quiet, bright, reverent.

Later he followed Wanre outside the temple walls and, seeing him, the king stopped in surprise. "Ay—*you* in the temple? What's come over you? Have you seen the light at last . . . has the Aton warmed you, coldest of men?"

He couldn't speak. Wanre's head was in front of the sun and the White Crown was outlined in a hazy film of gold. The light made his eyes smart with pain. "My Sun, I can't see you—the light's in my eyes!"

"Then speak to me without looking at the light."

*"You, king, come away from the sun,"* he wanted to cry, but lowered his head in shame.

"It's a rare day for you, Ay!" Wanre laughed, and a moment later was gone. When Ay raised his head he saw the bright red banners on the masts of the temple flapping easily in the breeze. And where Wanre's face had been, only the disc remained.

Once or twice later on, he tried to engage the king in a discussion of northern affairs, but Wanre was busy designing a new temple, and wouldn't take time off for politics.

One day some time afterwards a letter arrived from Rib-Addi of Gubla. Its brevity was frightening. Tutu sat staring at it, blinking, and brushing the sweat from his forehead.

*The king my lord should be advised that Kheta has taken over all the countries affiliated with Tushratta.*

The house of Mitanni had fallen.

**the third hour of the night**

Every month Wanre held a Meswet Aton banquet for a small group of his favourites. He loathed large ceremonies and preferred to discuss state matters in casual intimacy (which usually meant that nothing of any importance got discussed). One month there was Ay, Tutu, Nakht the Vizier (who so lacked character that all anybody could remember about him was that his villa had the reddest pillars in the land)—and the Chief Architect and city designer, Hatiay. Hatiay had a gorgeous greyhound which he insisted on taking everywhere with him (he had no wife)—and in fact he resembled his sleek pet, with his lean and dignified manner, the slender tension in his body which made him ready to act on the merest suggestion, the merest flicker of the king's eyelid.

During dinner they all sat and listened politely while the eldest princess Meritaton, still a child not quite nine years old, told them that the boy Smenkhare from the harem had visited her that day and told her when she had breasts he would come and *touch* them. Everyone was long past the point of being embarrassed by such intimate family matters, for Wanre's Truth was something like nakedness.

"And when he comes, Beloved of Aton," asked the king, "will you *let* him? That's the point!"

The child was given a big slice of melon and taken to bed by her nurse Benremut, who left the banquet with a sour face, for she'd been flirting with Hatiay, one of the few eligible bachelors left in the city, and at one point he'd actually looked at her. So, however, had the dog which lay drowsing at his feet.

The Chief Mouthpiece of the Land couldn't get a word in edgewise. He was cultivating a nervous ulcer from the pressure he experienced at these banquets, the horror of having to sit speechless and polite over the date wine and palmsap, cakes and honey. Goose leg in one hand and wine goblet in the other, he desperately awaited an opportunity to speak. Now a chance came and he leaned forward with grease dripping down his fingers and announced (casually and conversationally as he knew he must), "By the way, my Sun, the vandals have sacked another of your coastal cities in Khor."

A flute and harp drowned out the last part of his sentence and a dancing girl from Mitanni twirled around him and shook a spangled ankle in his face.

"So what do you think, Hatiay, of the new sanctuary to be called Gem Aton built within the confines of the Great Temple, with great wooden pillars?"

"Wanre, there's no wood forthcoming as long as the coastal cities lie under siege," put in Nakht.

"What? Oh. Oh, yes." said the king, and fell into a distracted silence.

Tutu pressed forward and started to sweat. "Gubla needs archers, Wanre, for it can't hold out any longer...."

Wanre dangled from his fingers a few freshly picked flowers; his long legs were languidly stretched out, his long face attentive—not to Tutu's voice, but to another, inner one. Then he said "Yes, yes, Tutu ..." soothingly, as to a child, and then he said nothing at all. He was lost in thought a moment, then turned suddenly to face the Master of Horse.

"To live in Truth, Ay, has its disadvantages. What would you say to that?"

Ay squirmed; the king had been reading his thoughts again. "Wanre, surely *everything* at one time or another has its disadvantages."

"You're a cautious man. As always." He smiled and studied the long stem of the alabaster goblet.

"Caution," put in Ay, "has even greater disadvantages than Truth."

They enjoyed each other in an odd, incomplete sort of way. They seldom conversed in the real sense of the word, but challenged each other instead. It never occurred to the cynical Master of Horse that Wanre might have wanted to learn something from him. He merely recognized his role and played it well. Today, though, Ay was in short temper, for his favourite horse had died, and he was pondering over whether or not he should have him mummified and buried in a special tomb.

"You looked so at home today in the parade grounds," Wanre told him. "But why do you fool around with such games? It's a clumsy, ignoble task for a man of your calibre."

Ay smiled. "I love horses, I love them to distraction. They're so glamorous, so sensitive, so utterly unconcerned. They can be trained to strut their magnificence and go through all the required motions without a single serious thought as to what they do. They perform to perfection—they're kings of ritual!" He saw Wanre frown at that and the frown excited him so he pressed on. "I love parades! I make of my beasts a kind of lyrical display and use them to express my thoughts. I garb their heads in those multi-coloured feathers and watch their gorgeous eyes grow angry with the nuisance of the plumes. Then I drive them forth in rows, snorting and tossing, and I stand at the edge of the parade ground, my hands clenched behind my back for joy, watching the reds pass through the greens, the yellows lining up to approach the blues...."

Wanre laughed but it was a hollow laughter. "People tell me you've even gotten into the habit of riding alone on horseback. How barbaric!"

"But I love to feel the animal beneath me," Ay put in.

*"Animals,"* whispered the king. "They affect you more than men, don't they? You sit here wondering what to do about your *dead horse* when the souls of men are at stake. I know what I'll do—I'll call you *Father of the Horse*—how's that?" Then he leaned forward, his eyes bright with wine. He was no longer amused. "I heard you had some new words inscribed in your cliff tomb this week. *The king put Truth in my body and my abomination is lying. I know that Wanre rejoices in Truth.*" He smiled to see Ay's face grow beet-red with embarrassment. "What are you really thinking, Father of the Horse? What do you love, what do you fear? But you're a stranger to fear, aren't you? You answer doubt and terror with that gentle devastating irony of yours. *That* is your core—not Truth! I told you some years ago—do you remember?—that you'd be the last man to understand the Teaching. You're not ignorant, and therefore consistent—no, you're cursed, or blessed, with a sensitivity of spirit which causes you more pain than joy. In me it glows white; in you it burns black. I hate black. Does your gentle horrible irony keep you sane?"

Ay sliced a cucumber, lost for an answer. He knew the king was not playing now, and he was interested. The others were confounded by such moments of caprice and anger; they found it out of keeping with what they thought was Wanre's real nature—but then no one had been able to decide on his "real nature." Ay believed that he alone, of all of them, understood what it meant to be dual-natured. For him Wanre was the Serpent of the Lower Land and the Falcon of the Upper Land, slithering, soaring, through his own mind. His moods made him appear uncanny; but in being their victim he was more his own master than others. Ay always preferred the serpent over the hawk.

"Yes," he answered, snipping off the head of the cucumber. "I guess it does keep me sane."

Wanre draped an arm loosely around his wife's pale shoulders, his hand playing idly with one breast. Then he remembered that it was night, and darkness fell over him like a cloak. His hand left Nefertiti's breast to pass over his brow, soothing the noise in his head. They needed no other dismissal.

Tutu was the first to leave. Ay followed him out to the gates of the royal estate and asked what troubled him.

"A very trivial matter," Tutu snapped back. "The last of the coastal cities—with the exception of Gubla." He glared at him and cried, "Ay—do something!"

"Do what?"

"Oh I know, I know. You won't discuss it, will you? The war, I mean."

"I gave you my report when I got back; that was all I could do. Anyway, what happened?"

"Shall I give you a neat, dispassionate list of the towns which fell since your return? All right. Sidon made terms with Aziru, then turned on Saru. That was months ago. Then I started getting desperate letters from the elders of Tunip when Aziru moved on Simyra. *Who formerly could have plundered Tunip without being plundered by Thutmose? When Aziru enters Simyra he'll do as he pleases in the territory of our lord the king—and on account of this our lord will have to weep. Now Tunip your city weeps, and her tears are falling, and there is no help for us. For twenty years we have been asking for help but there has come to us not one word—not one!!*

"So a while ago Aziru burned Simyra. I told Wanre, and in a rare moment of clarity he ordered him to rebuild it. The man's positively sarcastic! He wrote back saying he was sorry but he was too busy being the 'Protector' elsewhere! Then Wanre demanded that he explain himself in person, but the wily prince avoided the letter and it was returned undelivered. Wanre has given him a year to show up here in the Horizon. Ha! Does he seriously think he'll come? I ask you—explain me this man! He claims Tunip 'slandered' him when they wrote those fiery notes. And one of his recent weepy dispatches reads, *'If the king does not love me but hates me, what can I say?'* Really!"

The Foreign Minister gave a short, ugly little laugh and stumbled away, the ulcer in his gut gnawing away at him like a live thing. "An empire crumbles away piece by piece," he muttered, "and a king sits playing with his wife's teats. He tells me to recite *beauty, beams and love* five hundred times a day because my temple duties are lagging. Tell the empire about beauty, beams and love! It's the vogue to fondle your wife in public. Well, he may get me to recite something five hundred times but he won't catch me playing with my wife's teats. I don't have time."

Ay said nothing.

"I'm not just a foreign minister," he went on, "I'm also a *foreigner*, and I thank heaven for that. I can see everything more clearly than you children of Keme."

He must have seen Ay stiffen at that, for he added, "Now mark you, foreign father or not, you were born in this land and like it or not you're a native, you share all its graces and deceptions. Keme is your mother, not reason or 'Truth' as you care to think. Everything must conform to her needs, her seasons; you live within her or you die thirsting in some desert beyond the limits of her favour...."

"Tutu, whatever are you trying to say?"

"That nowhere in the world might one find such niggling, silly, lying, fooling children as one finds here in Keme. And the king—how well he represents them! He opens his mouth, words come out, he believes the words and tries to shape a nation after them—and when things go wrong he cries *Mistake, mistake!*, totally forgetting that mistakes have causes and a man's actions determine their own results...."

"You have said too much," Ay warned, but Tutu only gazed up at him with large liquid eyes and smiled.

"And you have *thought* too much, have you not, It Neter Ay?"

"I *never* think."

They had stopped, and Ay shifted about uneasily; Tutu's words had a bad effect on him. He felt not so much stung by them as cruelly tormented by a thousand crawling insects.

"Of course you know the joke—everybody does—about the man sitting in the marketplace at a loss as to how to amuse himself? The idea occurred to him to create a sensation by telling all the passersby that something interesting was going on over in the next street. He told a few people, the few told another few, till finally hordes of them were running off to the scene of the excitement. Watching the crowds running past him, the man said to himself, 'My God, something must be going on! I'd better take a look!' and ran out to join them."

"Tutu, is this quite necessary, at this hour of the night?"

"Quite, quite! We are losing an empire because we (I should say you) are a race of children living in dreams and fantasies. Once the Hyksos walked all over you; in future someone else will do the same. Mark my words—again and again Keme will be overrun by foreigners who will take advantage of your games and dreams to lead you as they wish."

"You're being ridiculous."

But Tutu didn't listen. "Once as a young man," he went on, "I got into a scrape over a lady; someone's honour was at stake. I forget the exact circumstances. But the one thing I remember is my rival looking at me with wild eyes and saying with utter frankness, *The least you might have done was lie.*"

"What has that silly story got to do with anything!" Ay cried, utterly provoked and growing angrier by the minute.

"It's all about 'Living in Truth,'" mumbled Tutu. "Words, words, I'm so sick of words. Here I am, the Chief Mouthpiece of the Land;

it's my job to apologize for you, explain you to the rest of the world, turn your disorder into order, rewrite the words of your king until they sound half reasonable. You depend on me, a foreigner, to clear the way for you with foreign nations. Akhenaton depends on me; Amenhotep depended on me. *Everybody depends on me!* And who was *your* illustrious father, the conscience of the court, adviser to the king? A *Khorian*. The sanest man in the land when Amenhotep ruled, the only man around whose actions were consistent with his *words*, right?"

He glared at Ay, implying that his were not. Ay started to say something but Tutu stumbled away to his litter mumbling, "Words, words, words. A third of them puns, another third jokes, and the last third, lies...."

On his way home Ay made a detour and passed by the parade grounds; he went eastward across the Royal Road, and the great arched bridge which connected the palace with the king's estate seemed suspended in air above him. The Window of Appearances was dark. He walked alone down the passage separating the north and south harems, and then into the great gates of the parade grounds. The moon was full and he was thrilled by the sight before him; the court was empty of horses, nothing lived there, but everywhere his eye fell there was the colossal king on stone pedestals, the cold beams of moonlight playing upon his repeated bodies, silvering the features, striking the eyelids, the hands, the broad thighs, just as it struck and silvered the cobra cornices which leered down from the top of the gates. The court smelled of horses and old sunlight.

Ay did not like the monstrous statues which lined the walls, those vast images of him who believed everything. They were always there, behind the parades and plumes, austere yet smiling. He often felt they were a joke at his expense, for by day when he watched his beautiful beasts heave their angry heads, the eyes of the Believer watched him.

"Don't you feel uncomfortable in the moonlight?" he asked the statues; but they didn't reply. "You look so temporary in this half-light, Wanre!" Then his voice grew harsh. "Don't you fear its fickleness, its way of playing upon your bodies, never actually illuminating them—always lending light and then withdrawing, implying and never stating? Moonlight casts a silver shroud over all of you!" he told the endless faces. But the faces smiled, and Ay whispered under his breath, *"In the name of heaven, who are you?... Tell me before I go quite mad...."*

"Who has ever seen you outside at night?" he cried. "No one. Ra is in the Underworld battling the demons of the darkness. Some say you fear blindness but I know it's more than that! Why have you avoided moonlight for so many years, why do you fear the dark? Speak!"

And a voice from nowhere answered, *"Once as a boy I fell down beneath these silver beams and froth came on my mouth and I spoke strange words which later I could not recall...."*

"Who speaks!" he gasped. *"Who speaks?"* He wheeled about and his eye caught a flicker of movement behind one of the statues.

*"I am only eternal in the light of Ra; by day it seems I will endure forever, my fixed eyes will stare forever into that secret place only I can see...."*

"Come forth, name yourself!" The blood chilled in his veins. Then a small figure, a boy, stepped out from behind the stone. He was laughing gently at some obscure joke. He stood a while, watching. *"Name yourself first,"* he said.

"The snake Apop," Ay said. "And you?"

"Smenkhare," came the voice. "So I am called, Smenkhare."

Then he ran from the court and disappeared into the darkness.

Ay stood a moment, trying to understand. He knew who the boy was well enough—he was the first son of Amenhotep by his daughter Sitamon, born three years before Wanre took the throne. When his mother died bearing her second son Tutankhaton, the brothers were deposited in the vast royal harem, there to be reared by Amenhotep's concubines. They'd later been brought to the Horizon.

113

Now that he thought of it, the boy was something of a mystery at court. Wanre allowed him freedoms and privileges almost equal to those of his own children. He had full run of the palace; he could go where he pleased when he pleased, and people were often baffled by this favour which Wanre granted his young half-brother. It even baffled the boy himself. The king often raised unlikely people to staggering heights, but why this almost forgotten son of Amenhotep? He had many enemies at court, the greatest being his own brother Tutankhaton, whom everybody hated because he was such a pest. The north harem where the two boys lived was the scene of frequent fist fights, for Tutankhaton bullied everybody out of jealousy of his favoured older brother. It was often wondered how the two boys, so utterly different, could both have sprung from the loins of Amenhotep.

There were many, including Ay (although he didn't admit it), who were jealous of the fact that Smenkhare was known rather intimately as "Mer Wanre," Beloved of the King.

Silver light played upon the thighs of the colossi. From the harem came the shiver of a late flute and cymbal, and the laughter of a dancing girl who twirled and spun about the pools and fountains—her body naked save for a single band about the hips, her long hair held back by a heavy ball which dipped and swayed in time to the music.

The statues brooded beneath the scary rays. *Since the Aton determines the duration of day,* Ay pondered, *will it also determine the duration of Wanre's life?* But his musings were absorbed into the darkness and the late music faded away until it too was gone. "Who is he?" he asked aloud, and an owl in a tree nearby asked back, "Who is *who*?"

Before the banquet Ay had bathed to remove the sweet reek of horses from his body. Now, on returning home, he bathed again to remove the odour of the king.

Wanre's times were the times of the sun; in the morning he was the Lord of Glorious Appearings, glowing with the god, waking with music in the palace at the same instant as the temple singers woke the sun. But as the day wore on he became increasingly uneasy, and at dusk the temple was fearful to him; it brooded, shot full of awful purple shadows, and the altars were bathed in a sad grey light. The priests swore that the king of the morning and the king of the evening were two different men, just as his right eye was different from his left.

One day his eyes bothered him more than usual—was the god punishing their boldness by burning out their very fibre?—yet he refused to tear them away from the disc which was slowly descending into the river. He was terrified that everything would disappear—light, disc, world, life—if he only once relaxed his gaze. The *tekhen* in the garden cast a hard disturbing shadow, and he thought he saw it move back and forth in a mad, frightening dance of time. It was a small needle, a mere time-marker, for he abhorred the monstrous structures others kings had erected, just as he abhorred the great pyramids in the north—the mere thought of which gave him gooseflesh on his back as he imagined their awful mass crushing his bones to sand. Size was for him a clumsy attempt to rival the majesties of Creation—for what were those giant structures but oversized *ben-bens*—the sacred pyramid of land on which Ra as a great bird first alighted at the beginning of the world? He felt the ancient kings had traded Truth for size. Yet wasn't Truth as implicit in a fly's wing as in the whole breadth of the heavens?

Female musicians had gathered outside the gates of his private temple, Hat Aton. They beat tambourines and waved palm leaves, and some had children with them who played hide-and-seek among the trees. It was time for the evening services, and the offering tables—one for each day of the year—stood naked now in the dusky light.

This night was not like other nights. The fine linen robe with its fiery red sash caressed his tingling, shaven body; his papyrus shoes felt soft and yielding as he walked down the sloping mud floor and through the gates of the second court. The music of the women receded, to be replaced by the evening choruses of the blind singers who chanted in their small court just outside the sanctuary. He wanted to see them and turned off the sunken path. Tonight he didn't want to go directly to the god—it was as though something waited for him inside the sanctuary, something fearful.

A hush fell over the singers and one by one their blank eyes and faces turned towards him. He took a torch and dipped it into a tray of incense. Astringent smoke, sweet and sour, burst upwards and filled the night. Now the light was purple, and the singers (did they know it was he?) resumed their chanting until the smoke and the music merged and became the great prayer to the Aton. Tonight his own beautiful hymn disturbed him, and the blank awful eyes of the singers filled him with fear. The lining of his nose and mouth stung with the fumes of the burning resin, and he felt suddenly unreal—as though he himself were no more than a disembodied note of the hymn rising up into the purple sky. He approached one of the singers and breathed on his neck.

"Singer, why do you sing so sweetly?"

"O Priest, I sing for the light I cannot see."

"Have you ever seen Akhenaton, singer?"

"Never, O Priest, never."

"How do you imagine him then?"

"White, O Priest, white like the space behind my eyes! White as light. His eyes are the eyes of Ra and when he looks upon you they burn holes in your body!"

"But now you feel nothing burning you, singer?"

"Nothing, Priest. I will know it when Akhenaton looks upon me."

He shivered, and when he heard a faint rattle of far-off tambourines he spoke again, this time to himself. "It has happened before," he said. *"It has all happened before . . ."* and he was frightened—for whenever he had had the strange feeling in the past that what he was doing he did for the second time, it always culminated in some blinding vision or command which he was compelled to obey.

He passed down the line of singers, threw more incense onto the burning tray, and took the complicated circuitous route which led to the sanctuary. He felt like a child trying to return home by an unknown path; that maze had not been designed for him, and he had never entered the holy place this way before. And when he found himself at last in the sanctuary he stood a long while as though struck dumb and blind. Here was emptiness broken by no holy image, a holy house without an occupant, a sacred place without a single statue. Not even the ancient *ben-ben* was housed here, for in his austerity he had rejected that too. Only a few small offering tables graced the void.

Then the tambourines, the incense, the blind song fell back behind him until every image and every symbol had vanished save his own self, and he was struck with a sudden terror that in the absence of an image the people might begin to regard him as the tangible form of the god. The words of the singer had frightened him more than he could tell. The night frightened him; the god was preparing some vision for him at the end of his fear. He forced himself to listen to the great hymn whose words in his ears sounded natural as the rippling of the river.

*Living Aton, Disc of the Daytime, Lord of Life—*
*Rise in heaven's horizon and fill*
*The whole world with Your beauty!*
*Enfold the earth to the limits of all You made*

# Gwendolyn MacEwen

*And deliver it to Your beloved son.*
*You are before us, but Your movements are unknown.*

*When You set, dark as death is the land,*
*And men pass the night in bedrooms, blind.*
*Thieves steal their wealth from under their heads,*
*Lions creep from their lairs, snakes bite*
*And utter darkness is the only light.*

*But You banish darkness with brilliant rays,*
*The Two Lands rejoice and men arise*
*For You lift them out of their beds*
*To wash themselves and eat and dress,*
*And raise their hands to Your mightiness!*

*The whole land labours, the cattle low,*
*Trees and pastures grow to living green.*
*The wings of birds lift prayers to Your spirit*
*And all things fly and walk when You shine!*
*Fish in the rivers leap towards Your face,*
*The highways of the world are open; ships sail free*
*And Your rays illumine the very surface of the sea.*

*You make the male seed grow in woman,*
*And cause the son in the body of his mother*
*To descend and breathe on the day of his birth,*
*And the chick in the egg protests and beats*
*His shell, to come forth walking on his own two feet.*

*O sole God, Your works are mysterious to men,*
*For You made the world after Your own heart—*
*The countries of Khor and Kush and Keme—*
*And gave each man his place, his food,*

*His term of life, his tongue,*
*And separated mind, and speech, and skin*
*That we might distinguish man from man.*

*You make a Nile-flood in the Netherworld*
*To give life to the poor, and another in the sky*
*To descend and drench their thirsty fields.*
*How perfect are Your plans, Lord of Eternity!*
*You separate the seasons so we can forget*
*In the cool of winter, the summer's heat.*

*You set Yourself far away from us to see*
*The vastness of all You made, above*
*The towns and fields and roads and rivers,*
*Distant from them, yet at the same time near.*
*All eyes are upon you, Disc of the Day,*
*For when You shine we live, and when You set we die.*

*No one knows You except Your son*
*Who came forth from Your body into life,*
*The Lord of the Two Lands, Living in Truth,*
*Neferkheprure Wanre of Glorious Appearings,*
*Akhenaton, who lives to live long,*
*And his great wife whom he adores,*
*The Lady of the Two Lands Nefer Nefruaton Nefertiti—*
*May she live and flourish forevermore!*

A solitary wreath of burning incense climbed and lost itself among the stars. The melody which had put the god to sleep wove round and round him. Now there was almost total darkness, broken only by a single torch and the smoky light of the incense which the night winds wafted into the sanctuary. His mind drifted upwards with the smoke, up and over the walls of the temple, to a place without sun—an endless and enduring night. Hating it, he was nevertheless fascinated by it, drawn like a child or a lover to his own deepest fear.

He took the winding path out of the holy place back to the singers. Would they know him this time—would they recognize the footsteps of their king? Approaching one, he laid a forefinger over the man's left eyelid. "Is it," he asked again, "because you are blind that you sing so sweetly?"

At first the singer could not speak for he had felt the touch to be the touch of the Great Seer. Then he stammered, "My Sun, I sing for the light I cannot see."

"But the arms of the Aton embrace you also," he said. "His burning fingers reach down to your mouth, your eyes—they hold the *ankh* at your nostrils and your lips. No one is excluded from His sight, not even the blind. Heed my Teaching, singer! Can't you feel His rays touch your eyelids just now as my fingers touch them?"

"I feel them, yet it is night."

*"There is no night."*

"I feel them."

"You feel them, Aton has gone down yet you feel them! Lions come forth from their lairs and thieves flourish, yet you feel the burning fingers of the Sun."

"*You* are the Great Seer, *you are He!*"

He felt his fingertips melt and tingle with a strange new power. Just as he moved to place them all upon the singer's stricken eyes, his own eye caught a glitter of gold about the other's neck. Sweat clouded his vision and his hand trembled as he reached beneath the singer's robes and yanked out something that glittered in the moonlight. He examined it as though it were a slimy fish caught in a murky pool. *"But what is this?"* he cried, giving the thing a great tug until it came free in his hand.

The hateful pendant swung before his eyes, and as it swung, wave upon wave of nauseating light made his vision blur.

*Amon*—dangling from a golden cord, *Amon* with a carnelian phallus and turquoise eyes. He flung it to the ground, and at the sound, the sightless heads of all the singers turned down.

"My Sun, it is a simple trinket, a gift from my dead mother...." stammered the owner. But it was well he was blind and could not see the king's face at that moment.

When Wanre spoke again it was with an awful hoarse whisper. "Sing on," he said, "sing long into the night, long past your time, for I'm not yet finished here!"

When he returned to the sanctuary the silver moon rose remote and cold above the temple—moonchild of Amon. The Obscene. The Unspeakable. He abhorred the shimmering rays; they were devious, unclean.

As the tired voices of the singers rode in on the burning perfume he felt his reason slip and the gates of his consciousness give way to allow a commanding inner voice to be heard. He knew he should not stay, he knew what was happening, but the voice took hold of him and he could not shake it off.

The god was calling him to war. *"I will never take up arms in any battle,"* he had once told Parennufer. *"But I swore to MeryPtah on the Day of Revelation that I would destroy his god and all that went before."* Until now he had destroyed nothing; Amon might hang from a hundred necks of worshippers in his own temples. He felt for the first time in years an exultant surge of hatred, and was ashamed and surprised to discover how it burned his blood more strongly than love. In the sanctuary which had no roof to stop the awful streaming beams he let the voice possess him. It broke through the black soil of his thoughts like some plant sprung up overnight, and he found himself whispering over and over, "Beside Whom there can be no other, beside Whom I will *permit* no other!" and the plant turned to poison within him.

The sanctuary became oppressive with the squeezing black fumes from the burnt-out resin in the censers. Lost in time, he stepped out once more. The singers still sang, their voices cracking with fatigue. Had he not then told them to stop they would have gone on all night until dawn found them strewn sightless and speechless on the ground.

He asked the time from the temple timekeeper and the old man replied that the constellations were in the position of the third hour of the night. Tomorrow would be the last day of the eighth regnal year. He was to remember that day and that hour; they never should have come.

In the third hour of the night, according to the ancient books which told of Ra's voyage through the Underworld, five gods waited with knives; it was their business to hack living souls to shreds.

the fourth hour of the night

The star Septet rose at the same time as the sun, and it was the beginning of a new year, the first of the month of Thoth. He decided it was time to announce his new plan, and summoned Ay into the chamber where he reclined on a long couch supported by the legs of two golden jackals. It seemed to Ay when he entered that their heads rose alertly to warn him of something, and down their faces dripped what looked to him like great turquoise tears. Jackals, he mused, preferred to be in perpetual movement, circling, hunting, while these two were mere sticks of furniture supporting the king and keeping a vigil over his body.

He ignored Ay for a while and lay motionless, staring at the ceiling. He looked melancholy and lean as the gilded beasts and Ay wouldn't have been surprised to see blue tears falling from his eyes. It seemed like hours before he raised himself up onto his elbows and then it was only to murmur, "Ay, I love my city."

Ay nodded vaguely and feverishly asked himself if the remark were meant as a statement or as a challenge.

"I tell you I love it! It's clean, it gleams in the morning, it's new. It has no history, that's the point. No rubble buried beneath it to contaminate its foundations. It has only its own history. Do you understand? I too have only my own history. Nothing *preceded* me! *Amenhotep was not my father!*"

Ay felt a chill creep through his spine; he wasn't too sure why.

"Ra is my father. I have no earthly begetter.... In the sky there is only Ra-Aton; in the daytime no other orb or star can be seen to rival His brightness. Hawks alone are visible, sometimes I see them fly across the disc. Only Horus exists beside the Aton." He gave Ay a long impenetrable gaze. "Do you know what this means?"

Without thinking, Ay answered, "Of course."

"*Of course!* It has taken me nine years to understand a truth which you take so lightly!"

"Wanre, I'm sure you've discovered a deeper truth than I."

"Yes. I am Horus, I alone might fly across the disc."

"Yes, Horus," he replied. But he was thinking that even the hawk didn't approach Ra; it was an illusion when its wings caressed the light.

Now the king ran long fingers down one of the jackals' faces and whispered, "*The hour has come. I will erase the name of Amon from the land.*"

Ay felt his legs give way and was sure he'd faint from sheer horror. Somehow, though, he managed to stand upright, his face cocked at a stiff unnatural angle, his mouth wide open like that of an idiot, as Wanre went on.

"*Amon, I utter your name for the last time.* And that false deity whom you supplanted, *Min*—I erase you, you are no more, you never were. I expunge you, I strike you out, I cancel you, I remove you from the world and from the heavens...."

Ay had a sudden image of a venerable old man falling, falling. His own father, who'd once served as a priest of Min at Ipu when Ay was still a child. Min the Thunderbolt One, a form of Amon.... Min whom he'd imagined as a child to have his father's stern face and shock of blazing white hair....

There was a water clock in the room, and only then did Ay become aware of its dribbling. *Time*, he thought, *dribbling like saliva down the chin of a madman.* The jackals stared at him with mournful eyes. He couldn't close his gaping mouth.

Wanre's voice grew more brittle.

"First. All monuments bearing the Name of the Unmentionable One shall be defaced, especially in the old capital."

Ay listened, horrified. Pharaoh offered him a pear.

"Second. Are you listening? All inscriptions bearing the Name, whether they be in temples or tombs or carved upon amulets or written in sand, are to be likewise expunged. *Throughout the land.*"

For a wild moment Ay thought he was joking; he had the insane conviction that the terrible hour would pass, and they would collapse into each other's arms and scream with laughter at the marvellous joke they had played. But Wanre was pacing the floor, and his eyes were narrow and severe.

"Wanre, may I speak?" ventured Ay.

"Not too much."

"If this is done . . . the wrath of the priests . . . the anger of the people, the disorder . . . we can't calculate. . . ."

"*Disorder,*" whispered Wanre, "is what we have now. I will create order. I will erase false names, I will close false temples. That's neater. That's order."

He paced the floor with his hands clenched behind his back, a most uncharacteristic attitude. In that moment he looked more masculine than anyone had ever seen him. He was a general—but in what war? For years Ay had wondered what battle he was waging when he wore the Blue Crown.

"It mocks me. It mocks my god that *his* Name appears thousands of times carved throughout the land and that there are hundreds of temples serving *him.* Why? Men carved them. Men shall erase them!" His voice softened. "Then it is done. How many men are available from your troops?"

*Surely he would not employ the army.* "Some . . . a fair number, but . . ."

"Good. Then select from them a work team and call them the *Chisellers*, and send them to the old capital. Where's Haremhab, is he still in Men Nofer?"

"As far as I know, yes." *Where else would he expect to find the man he appointed Governor of the Lower Land?*

"Then get a message to him. Tell him I want him to do likewise with his men in the north. I charge them to disperse themselves throughout the Lower Land in groups of ten, seeking out and destroying all inscriptions which bear the Name."

This was not the first time he'd used Ay to intervene between him and the General. Ay dreaded another encounter with Haremhab, for they liked each other not at all, and every time he became a go-between between him and the king, they liked each other less.

"But Wanre . . . such an enormous undertaking, the land is large. . . ."

"I know it is large. It is my land."

"I mean only to suggest that such a project would occupy the men for *years*. Haremhab will protest. You know what he's like when he protests!"

"Let them be occupied many years. As it is they do nothing of use anyway. They ride about in chariots, they shoot arrows like children, they consume vast amounts of my grain and beer and corn. I pay for their maintenance and they're useless. A few are needed for patrol. What else?"

"My Sun, this is the army of the Two Lands!"

"My land," said Wanre very softly, "does not *need* an army."

"Couldn't we use some of the state labour corps as well as full-time soldiers?" pleaded the Master of Horse.

"Fine! Farmers, veterans, old convicts, Medjay—that's your problem. Give them papers of state authority in case they're delayed anywhere; get them off immediately. But get in touch with Haremhab at the first opportunity and convey my wishes to him."

Further protests were useless. Ay took his leave, wondering how he managed to get out of the room in one piece, or leave Wanre there in one piece for that matter. The last thing he remembered was the slow sarcastic gurgling of the water clock, a kind of horrible laughter. *Why couldn't Wanre be a serpent instead of a high-flown fanatical hawk? That wild bird could create more havoc in the land than the lowest and evilest of snakes.*

To his horror the General arrived in the city on some business or other, and Ay had no choice but to confront him directly with the royal command. He went wild. Ay spent five agonizing days with him while he sought audience with Wanre but was put off so often it became obvious the king had no intentions of seeing him. The truth was Wanre was terrified of Haremhab. Ay never forgot those awful days; the General was in one of his most obnoxious moods, and pulled him here and there inspecting troops and magazines as though he were conducting a last-minute examination preparatory to war. A flood of relief swept over him when on the fifth day Haremhab made to depart. He looked down from his chariot as though he intended to shoot his way out of the city and down to the river where his boat awaited him.

"I am forced to maintain," he remarked, continuing a conversation begun five days before, "the entire army of Keme within Keme. Half of it should be in the north keeping border revolts down. But where is my army?" he asked one of the horses, and when the beast didn't answer, he gave him a swift clip with his whip. "In *Keme* drinking beer and soaking up the treasury! I've got two divisions of troops stationed on shepherds' land—useless, part-time farmer-soldiers! All this is harming the lower classes, the backbone of the land."

He turned away from the horses, perhaps realizing that they were not listening to him. Ay started to speak, but he was not finished complaining.

"I can't lead an army north because Wanre hates *war*. Naharin is no more his frontier. What do I do? Inspect 'troops,' train 'men,' and listen day after day to endless complaints from the peasants about soldiers hiring boats they don't need for trips they don't need to make and interfering with the normal prosperity of the civilians! Unoccupied, the army is ruining the land. And now!" he exploded. "Now I have to use my men for scratching out names on stone because Wanre hates the *gods*. Ah! Where are the days when Pharaoh used to capture rebel kings and hang them upside down from the prow of his galley! Where are the days of *men*, It Neter?"

His horses danced about, eager to be off. "The only place nowadays where there are no revolts is Kush. Kush isn't revolting, it's too hot."

Ay spoke at last and reminded himself of one old woman comforting another. "Things are bad all around, General. How many people will be out of work once the shrines close down? Amulet makers, singers, scribes...."

"*Amulet makers!* I wish to heaven I were an amulet maker! Come, why don't you and I go into business; you can bake holy loaves and I'll make pendants and we'll forget all this other nonsense, eh?"

Ay thought the idea not at all a bad one. "General," he said, gazing down fondly at his own old worn-out leather gloves, "your hands are chaffed from the reins. Why not buy leather gloves like mine?" and held them out for his inspection. Haremhab grabbed them impatiently, grunting with approval.

"Better still," he said, "I'll trade you!" and in a moment he flung down his whip. The handle was elaborately carved in ivory in the shape of a galloping horse. It was a fine piece of work, but Ay loved his gloves and fumbled about, trying to dissuade Haremhab from the barter, yet unwilling to insult him. But already the General was putting them on, and Ay could see by his face that he'd dismissed the whole matter as done. He coughed impatiently; he was a big man, and a powerful one. It occurred to Ay for an instant that if

Haremhab really wanted, he could rule the land himself. But he doubted that the day would ever come, for the army was disunited and fat from long inactivity. Yet the General was a man to look out for. The way he held the reins told much; he had a tight grip on them, but it was himself, not the horses, that he kept in check.

"Tell Wanre," Haremhab said bitterly, "*if* you can tear him away from his flower gardens and fish pools, that the government of the Lower Land is in order. Tell him I will select 'men' from my troops and make them Chisellers. But by heaven they'll be only those dolts and pretty boys that I can well afford to do without. Meanwhile," he snapped the reins, "enjoy yourself, my good It Neter Ay, in this beautiful city of yours!"

The horses bounded forward and Haremhab was lost in a cloud of dust. A moment later Ay heard his voice once more. "My thanks for the gloves!" Ay stood silently seething and turning his naked hands over and over.

Names of gods and kings had been erased before; no one could count the number of souls which had been doomed to eternal nothingness by the destruction of their names—but never had the Two Lands seen anything like the mad campaign of the Chisellers. After a time, to be sure, their presence in the land was so common as to be scarcely noticed—but when in the beginning they first appeared in No Amon they looked like some ghostly army of the Underworld, something one might find drawn in the pages of *Am Duat*, armed with their weird assortment of picks and chisels and hammers. There were so many protests and riots in the streets of the old city that the king had to send out an armed division of troops under Ay's command to keep order. What they witnessed there in the streets filled them with shame, and fear. The people were fighting fist to fist in the marketplaces; the followers of Aton turned upon their own brothers or fathers who were pummelling the Chisellers with stones and eggs and tomatoes. Women hid their smallest children beneath their skirts, as much to free their own arms to fight, as to protect them. Everywhere the air rang with vilifications and obscenities and screams of protest, while the warm beams of the god rained down upon all.

An old man, half blind, tried to climb up over the railing of Ay's chariot, which was stalled in the thronging streets. He lost his balance and fell, with his arms flailing in all directions, and a friend picked him up.

"The king who hates war makes war in his own land!" he screamed. "He who swore to uphold the rights of the common folk sends troops through our streets! He who Lives in Truth overthrows Maat!"

Very gently Ay leaned over the railing and said, "Look, old man, it is not upon you that Akhenaton makes war!"

But the man laughed. "Isn't it?" he cried. "Doesn't he know that by attacking Opet he is attacking us? Me and my entire family owe our very existence to the House of Amon. I'm a baker myself—my sons are field labourers and cattle-keepers. We serve the temple because we have no other livelihood!"

Ay was very patient with him. "Old man, don't you recall that it was *because* of the House of Amon that your ancestors lost their land and their livelihood? A few years ago you were complaining because you had to work as serfs under Opet...."

"That's not the point!" the man exclaimed. "The point is now, today, this hour, this minute! If Akhenaton makes war upon the god, and if the god's house falls, we fall—all of us here in the streets ... and thousands more in the villages scattered around!"

"This is a religious war," said Ay, stiffening, aware that he should maintain some degree of authority. "It is not a war against the people."

"Religious wars!" snorted the baker, turning to his friends who had gathered around to listen in. "What have religious wars got to do with the *gods*, I ask you! They've got to do with the bread and meat we eat, the houses we live in, the education of our children! Because of my labours, my sons have a chance to enter the college of Amon. I care nothing for the *gods*—do you really suppose any one of us here cares for the *gods*? We're thinking of how many of us will become beggars in the streets when the House of Amon can no longer support us!"

His speech was met with cheers by all those gathered around. A few people were arguing at the fringes of the crowd, and one man managed to make his voice heard above the racket. "Well, *I* care about the gods!" he cried. "If Wanre intends to erase the name of Amon in tombs as well as temples, who will protect our dead? I ask you, who will protect my dead son who even now lies in the Valley? Who will guide his *ka* to heaven when Amon's name is erased from the walls of his tomb?"

More shouting and arguing followed; then suddenly without warning, the men and women and children who lined the avenue grew still as sentinels. A small boy had been trampled in the riots; the mother came walking towards Ay's chariot, carrying the limp body on two outstretched arms. She said nothing; her huge and uncomprehending eyes stared at Ay. For a sickening instant, Ay remembered something, he remembered his father, in the town of Ipu, who had once told him, "Kings and rich men, my son, possess the gods as luxuries. But for the poor, the gods are friendly helpers who cure sick children or make the crops abundant. Amon of the rich and Amon of the poor are different deities."

Ay felt his eyes clouding over and, scarcely aware of what he was doing, he threw out his arms and cried, "Leave this place—all of you! Come to the Horizon where there is work and wealth for everyone!"

But his offer fell on deaf ears and he even heard a few low snickers from the crowd. The baker stepped forward once again with a sad broad smile on his face. "My dear sir," he bowed sarcastically, "and just how do you expect us to *get* to the Horizon? Unfortunately we don't have private pleasure boats to take us there. Also, I forgot to mention, none of us had the money to order *villas* built for us in the place!"

A few laughed softly, but the rest were silent. Crimson with shame, Ay drove his horses through the crowd. Later the troops escorted the Chisellers down the long avenue of sphinxes and up to the gates of the Northern Sanctuary of Amon.

They met with no resistance but a cold stony silence that hung in the air like a shroud. To his amazement the gates were not closed, but had been flung open in ironic welcome. He hesitated just outside, not sure whether to remain or proceed. High above him some nameless birds were circling and screeching. A small grass snake slithered into a hole beneath the stone wall. The sun was so strong that day it might have melted the great pylons inside the temple.

A solitary priest stepped out of the gates and addressed him through the haze of heat. "You must be It Neter Ay," he said. "You resemble your brother who once was Second Prophet of our god. I remember him well...." He paused to allow his words their full measure of meaning. Then, as though in answer to Ay's unvoiced question, he added, "No, we're not going to resist you and your men. We admit we cannot. We have towns and fields and wealth but we have no army. My Lord the First Prophet of the God bids me welcome you and advises you to go about your business quickly."

Ay started forward but not quickly enough to avoid hearing the last words.

"He also says: *'Tell the Criminal, whose name I will not utter, that his sun will set!'*"

Then the Chisellers entered the gates.

Ay appointed one of his best officers to take charge of the troops who were to be stationed in the old capital, and went to visit his sister Tiy who was in her holiday retreat at Miwer. He found her dictating a letter. The four years which had passed had changed her much; she had become thin, but it was the sinewy leanness of a cat. Her eyes were cold, yet disturbingly bright. After some stiff, embarrassing greetings she showed him a letter she'd just written to her son:

*Neferkheprure, for four years I've occupied myself with the upkeep of your dead father's mortuary temple. I've apologized for you and kept a certain peace with the House of Amon. Now I have learned of your latest insane scheme to deface the House of Amon and destroy the god. When will you learn that one cannot justify one's beliefs by force? You who loathe and abhor violence have stooped to sending a military force into the capital of your fathers. How thankful I am that I vowed never to join you in your city! I tell you now that I rue the day I bore you—or did I bear you? I would have preferred a water rat or a turtle to creep out of my loins. Neferkheprure, I disown you, I disavow any recollection of your birth. For all I know the old tales are true, and the crocodile Subek spat you up from the Nile during floodtime.*

Reading the scathing little note Ay couldn't help smiling, for it was so characteristic of Tiy—so colourful and melodramatic.

"Well, it's all I can do!" she exclaimed. "It's all I *will* do. I'm powerless to stop him, you know that. I lost my hold on him long ago.... I refused to join him in the Horizon. I still refuse. Nothing could make me go there ... *nothing*."

But when Ay looked around her residence and saw the gardens and pools and maidservants, he knew one thing for sure and it disturbed him to know it. The Great Mother Tiy was bored.


Throughout the land the smaller temples of Amon closed down quickly, for Wanre cut off every source of their income. The great House of Amon had been existing for some years without direct subsidy from the throne—consuming, so to speak, its own fat. But now Wanre's soldiers drove the priests from Opet and closed the great, reluctant gates of the sanctuaries. The sacred statues of the god were left unattended and defaced in the darkness of their shrines; no longer did the god's servants paint the god's face in the morning or place wreaths of fresh flowers at the cold stone feet. The defacers returned again and again to mutilate the pillars and inscriptions. The dispossessed priests met in secret, by night, to conduct forbidden ceremonies and plan revenge. Thousands of innocent men were suddenly out of work—farmers, bakers, latrine keepers.

At first there was some confusion as to what to destroy and what to leave intact. The name of Amon, for instance, was found in the name of Amenhotep. Must they then strike out the name of Wanre's own father, the very name he himself bore before the Day of Revelation? Must he chisel himself out to remove the offensive name, like a man cutting off a forearm to be rid of one poisoned finger?

He was vastly confused, and Parennufer made matters worse by reminding him that an act of destruction was also an act of acknowledgement. He told him that by attempting to remove all knowledge of the god he was in truth admitting that he *did* exist. Only Parennufer could get away with such criticism. He begged his prince to stop the chiselling, but Wanre cried, "Does a man stop halfway through the act of love? What I start, I finish! I must purify the land!"

The Chisellers sent a message one day from the old capital to ask what to do about the two colossal statues of Amenhotep in the desert, for although they contained abundant references to Amon, they were in fact the very effigies of Wanre's father, the god Amenhotep. The fact that in the message Amenhotep had himself been referred to as a "god" was the last straw. Furious, he screamed, "*That* is the supreme blasphemy!" and immediately ordered the

Chisellers to hack away the name of the man who was *not*, he emphasized, his father.

No one saw Tiy's face when the Chisellers went to work on the statues of her husband. She sent another letter to her son; the contents of it were never known, for when he read it his face turned pale as death and he threw it into a fire.

As time wore on he began to realize that it was not enough to make war against Amon alone. In the other main cities of the land the cults of Ptah, of Osiris and of the Lords of the Underworld flourished as they had flourished for generations. For a long time he had been *saying* there was no Judgment after death, no ovens of hell, no lakes of fire, no scales upon which the heart of the deceased was weighed against the feather of Truth. He had thought he could overcome such primitive beliefs by careful argument, by the logic and beauty of the Teaching—but it was not so. If the people refused to understand his Truth, he had no choice but to suppress the worship of the other main gods.

"My prince," warned Parennufer, "you have thrust a single pebble into a pool, and now the rings are widening and widening and soon the whole pool will be churned. Do you not see it's not a matter of a few *main* gods? The gods have families, relatives—in erasing Amon you had to include Min, his consort Mut, his son Khonsu. If you suppress Osiris you must also suppress Isis, Anupew, Thoth . . . where will it all end?"

"In Truth." Wanre replied. *"Osiris, Isis, Anupew, Thoth, I utter your names for the last time!"* And yet, noticed Parennufer, how deliciously, how sensuously he rolled his tongue over the forbidden words.

Later, he extended his campaign to Men Nofer, the seat of the worship of Ptah. General Haremhab, who was very much in favour with the priests of that god, sent furious messages to the effect that

Men Nofer was in a state of utter disorder and chaos. To this Wanre replied that in the Beginning was Chaos; then the Creator appeared on the waters and Truth was born.

Special troops were stationed in the main cities to keep order, and eventually the people settled down into a dark sleep and there was relative silence. He interpreted this as victory. But Parennufer, who was the only man close to him who still dared speak his mind, whispered, "It's dangerous sleep, little prince, and the silence more dangerous still."

the fifth hour of the night

The chief sculptor Thutmose was doing new portraits of the royal family, and Nefertiti's face was turned from him in silent, weary profile, the proud lines hiding the dark thoughts which troubled her. She had recently borne her sixth daughter; she felt drained of her strength and was sure she had conceived for the last time. Wanre wept now when he came to her, she did not know why, and she felt him failing, weakening. He was more, and yet less, than a man. She had heard herself whisper, "Who is he, who is he?" when the midwife delivered the last ball of blood and fire from her loins. She remembered seeing a handmaiden in the room clutching an image of the hippopotamus Teweret to her breast to assist the birth, and the grotesque face and giant bosom of the beast had filled her with revulsion.

Now she remembered a day over four years ago when she and her husband had ridden in the chariot down the Royal Road, their arms about each other's waists, the ribbons from their crowns streaming red and blue in the wind, their bodies naked as children, their mouths wide with laughter. Meritaton between them, poking the rumps of the horses with a little stick. The wind whipping the banners of the temple. The people lined up along the road, laughing. The drunken flowers strewn in their path. . . .

When the sixth daughter of the Aton had been brought to her she had turned on her side and refused to look at its writhing body. When her husband came and stood over the bed she had not been able to look at his face, only at the huge unreal thighs like pillars of a temple she did not want to enter.

The wet splashing of the clay was the only sound in the studio as Thutmose worked. He was the hero of all the young men who flocked to the sculptor's training school to enroll as students. A generation before, they would have idolized a general or a prince and looked upon a mere artist as some sort of effeminate craftsman . . . but portraitists and carvers of stone reliefs on tombs and temple walls had been given absolute freedom by the king and, as a result, a man might prove himself by the sheer power of his artistic expression as well or even better than he could on a battlefield. Wanre had encouraged his artists to depict everything "in Truth," and to break from the artistic traditions of the past, which demanded that certain figures always be depicted with conventional emblematic gestures frozen for all eternity. Whereas the sculptors of former kings had had to consider the royal body as a stately, rectangular symbol whose limbs might bend at sharp, given angles, Wanre's artists were allowed to depict him or any member of his family in any pose, however casual, limp or asymmetrical. And the flaws of the body were not to be overlooked; on the contrary, they had to be emphasized, even magnified, for he believed that an abnormality was not a shame, but a divine sign.

It was a far cry from the art of the past, and in the beginning the results had been astoundingly beautiful. But as time went on Truth became its own formula and artistic freedom set into another exact style. Thutmose, for example, had sculpted the king so many times he could do it blindfold. Realism had begun to border on caricature and student sculptors were like scribes memorizing the fixed characters of Wanre's face and body. Some artists had even started to give his anatomy to other persons—so on the walls of some tombs, noblemen and courtiers acquired drooping bellies and swollen legs.

Nefertiti noticed a student's model of her husband on a shelf nearby. She smiled, and remembered the day she had told him how she loved the breath of horses, hot and smelling of oats, and how sometimes she dreamed of him as a great white horse. He had replied that her musings smacked of some kind of obscure paganism, but she knew he'd been over-sensitive about it for he was well aware that his profile was not unlike that of a nervous skittish stallion. The sculptors had seen the similarity long ago, and when he instructed them to depict him "in Truth," the result was sometimes a long, leering, large-nostrilled, definitely horse-faced king.

Thutmose for his part was remembering a small pair of statues the king had ordered made early in his reign; they depicted him with two feet together, which everyone knew was the standard female stance in art, and Nefertiti with one foot ahead of the other like a king. There'd been some cruel jokes about that. "What do they do in bed?" people had laughed. Thutmose confessed he'd wondered about it himself at times.

He was a strong youth, dark and muscular, applying himself to his work with quiet, tight-lipped determination. Nefertiti kept her eyelids lowered so as not to encounter his disquieting, insolent stare. It was his business to stare, of course, but it made her uneasy. It wasn't that he looked, she thought, but that he *saw*. When she noticed him making many false starts on her portrait and staring gloomily at the shapeless hunks of clay, she asked what troubled him, and he replied that hers was the most difficult head in the world. She chided him about it—was there then something wrong with it? He said no, it was worse than that; there was altogether too much *right* with it, and he could find no flaw on which to build. Did he then seek a *flaw*, she asked, and why? He answered that in every face there had to be some detail, however slight, which was out of keeping with the whole face, which interrupted its symmetry—a small nose, a round chin, or something more elusive like a slight difference between the eyes. The flaw was for him a point of reference which gave a face form and meaning. He wanted to create living portraits, not—he hesitated—not mere caricatures.

"What is human is flawed," he went on, "and in the flaw we understand perfection!" At that point her eyes strayed around the room, and her husband's flawless, delicate world seemed to her a child's pitiful dream in contrast to the disorderly studio with its living imperfect forms. "Do you find no flaw in me?" she asked suddenly, realizing too late that she had meant to say *my head*. And he flung up his hands in vexation and for a moment forgot he was addressing a queen. "Your right and left profile are identical—what can I do with them?" he complained, as though the symmetry of her features were a crude insult to his sensitivities, and then his hand guided her chin this way and that and a moment later he remembered to add, "My Lady."

She told him he needed only to copy her, to create a likeness, and she could not explain to herself the reason for the thrill which she felt when he answered, "Lady, I don't want to *copy* you." She wanted to tell him that she had a hundred flaws inside, but her face, so long accustomed to its cool sculptured impassivity, gave no indication of them. It had been a long time since that face had laughed well or crumpled up into a sweet, severe mask of sorrow. She had become an ornament in Wanre's temple. Each night she sent the god to rest with her sweet music—her voice, her sistrums. Each night she sent *him* to rest with sweet words or sweet silence or the sweet limbs which now ceased to feel him as a man but enclosed him in a ceremony whose origins she had somehow forgotten.

She listened to the soft splash of the clay in Thutmose's hands. Strong hands, explorers. Strong body poised like that of an athlete for some unknown contest to come. Suddenly she laughed, and her laughter surprised her like the arrival of an old unexpected friend.

"Thutmose, I just had a very funny thought—I thought if you needed a flaw badly enough, why not create one? You could omit my nose, for instance, or leave out an eye!"

He seemed not to have heard her, or if he had he was not going to acknowledge it. She was stunned by the insolence of his silence. But later when he came to her to adjust the angle of her face, his strong fingers guided her chin to one side and his elbow brushed for a moment against her breast. He pretended not to notice, but all the while his dark eyes were upon her, and they acknowledged.

Later, whenever she went for a sitting, she wore a robe so fine it was a mere whisper; beneath it the tips of her breasts were painted a deep carnelian red.

"*Nefer Nefruaton Nefertiti, Beautiful Are the Beauties of the Aton, the Beautiful One has come, the Great Lady who fills the palace with her beauty, may she live and flourish forevermore....*"

Those words no longer moved her when recited by chancellors and priests; she had ceased to believe the hymns to her enduring beauty after her body bore its sixth child. But from his mouth they were different; he lingered over the names and breathed new life into them. His voice was the wind brushing the sand from her names. *Nefer Nefer Nefer, Thrice Beautiful....* And three blue flowers grew where the sand had buried them.

He brought a brown quartzite bust to the palace and unveiled it. The guidelines were still visibly drawn from brow to chin. The eyes were blank and the features unpainted. The whole face had merely been mapped out, then left like an abandoned landscape. "It's unfinished!" she cried, not understanding why the blankness disturbed her, why the blank eyes stared into her own asking, *"Where is your self, Nefertiti?"* And his hands caressed the stone cheeks, the stone mouth, the stone brow, and she felt a moment's mad envy that this blind sister should feel his touch. She passed her own hands over the parts caressed by his. "It pleases me," she lied. "It's accurate. Finish it."

"Great Lady," he said, "it's obscene. Look at it—it's a piece of geometry! It insults the marvellous disproportion of nature. When one has missed the point one knows. I've missed it." He glared at the bust as though accusing it; it gazed back with a maddening calm.

"There's nothing wrong with it," she remarked, thrilled that her words made him tremble ever so slightly.

"Nothing—everything!" he cried. "I'm looking for the imperfection, the *surprise*, and I encounter this calm pool. I feel like a warrior battling a dove. You know," he added, gazing into the eyes he'd drawn in the stone, "not once in a lifetime can one's eyes look upon one's own face. That which sees is forbidden sight of itself. Isn't it frightening?" And as her hands again allowed themselves the sensual liberty of trailing over the stone flesh he whispered, "Your eyes, Great Lady, when they look upon me, for instance—what do they see?"

"A warrior battling a dove! Try again, Thutmose, and this time let the Aton guide your hands."

"I have no god, Nefruaton," he confessed and his words shocked her. Was he so bold as not to claim, like Bek and the other artists, that the king and his god had "taught" him? "In my youth I loved Khnum, lord of potters, and in my adolescence I favoured Ptah who made the universe come into being by uttering a single word. Then I grew weary of pots and words and as a man I worship the power in my hands, the force in me yet not in me. I am its tool just as the chisels are mine. It's raw, impersonal, and it belongs to me alone."

"But," she whispered, half afraid to speak her thoughts aloud, "where does it come from?"

"If I asked that, Lady, it would no more be mine."

"But then you *have* a god," she said. "He doesn't differ from the Aton. The words differ. Men make words."

He laughed then and in a lighter mood began to model her a second time. His hands worked more swiftly with the clay, and whereas before it had seemed to her that he was the elusive one, now it was the portrait itself which struck her as inaccessible, unreal. He fought to make it real but the shape which grew beneath his fingers remained a mystery. She imagined that her thoughts entered his hands and from there seeped into the clay where he moulded them, grasped and wrestled them, removing some of them in strips which he dropped into the bucket at his feet.

"The art," he said, as his hands worked to shape his speech, "lies in what is skilfully left out, not in what is stated. Yes . . ." he went on, and then slowed down a moment as a second thought reached him, ". . . the unanswerable, the unattainable!" And once again his eyes were upon her steadily, candidly, and she did not move, but let herself be given up into their gaze. When his fingers returned to work the clay, her whole body was the pliable element between them.

A few days later she saw her father Ay in the palace gardens and looked at him wide-eyed as a child and asked, "Father, can one's secret thoughts be seen outside?"

He answered that certain people seemed to be able to see secret thoughts—Wanre, for one. She laughed and exclaimed, "He sees nothing, he's blind with light!" and there was a strange new bitterness in her laughter, an edge to it, sharp as a sword.

"Then others will surely see," he said.

"Even the hidden things?" she asked.

"Even those," he answered, adding in his most philosophical manner, *"What does anyone hide anything for, my child, except to have it found?"*

He did not know why her eyes turned away in fear.

One afternoon Wanre called Smenkhare into the room of the blue and gold jackal couch. The boy saw him outlined against the huge gold disc of Aton on the wall, and watched the brilliant arms reach down and offer golden *ankhs* like kisses to his body. Terrified, he stood before him and waited while the narrow eyes devoured him as they always did.

"Today you are thirteen, Smenkhare, is that not so?"

"Yes, royal brother."

"Then as of today you will reside in special quarters in the palace. I imagine you are sick to death of the harem after all these years. I've arranged for private tutors to advance your education...."

The narrow eyes burned into him. "Do you wonder—why I do all this, Smenkhare?"

"No. Yes! Sometimes ... royal brother."

"Oh, don't call me *royal brother*! Why if all the brats my father sired addressed me so—!" He stopped short, seeing the hurt look on the boy's face. "No. Disregard me. Believe me, I didn't mean that as it sounded. Do you recall your mother?"

"Wanre, the lady Sitamon died giving birth to Tutankhaton. I was one year old at the time!"

He gave a short nervous laugh. "Excuse me, of course you wouldn't remember...." Then his face clouded and he ran his fingers down the golden arms of the sun. "And ... your father? Do you recall him?"

Smenkhare wondered why the king trembled when he said that.

"No. I saw him from a distance a few times. I was never presented to him, you know." He stiffened, and watched Wanre out of clear, proud eyes.

"Neither was I, officially. My—our father was a cruel man." The boy was startled to see what looked like tears in Wanre's eyes. But when he spoke again his voice was a rasping whisper. "Do you feel the blood of . . . I mean, do you feel *his* blood in your veins?"

"Why, I've never thought about it. I think I feel my own blood in my veins, royal bro—Wanre."

*"My beloved—tell me whose blood flows within you. . . ."*

*Why was he so upset?* "I feel—myself!" the boy shrugged.

"So, you're in a kind of darkness, and I must keep you there for a while. Look how strong and bright you are! It's as though you sprang from thighs other than his—you are the seed of the sun!" Then he leaned forward until his breath burned the boy's face. "Do you understand?"

"Wanre, I understand nothing."

He stiffened and drew away. His voice became once again impersonal and remote. "You will take up residence in your new quarters today. You will be tutored well. I'll call upon you again."

Smenkhare made his way softly towards the door. At the threshold he stopped and for an instant turned back, a puzzled frown on his face as though something had touched him and vanished—a burning kiss of gold on his mouth, the edge of a hawk's wing across his chest.

"No," he whispered, "not the blood of Amenhotep."

The king remained motionless. The only indication that he might have heard was the swift flinching of the muscles in his shoulder. But his back was turned, and the moment passed.

The king was about to confer upon his favourite pupil the titles of High Priest and Great Seer. The man singled out to receive this enormous honour was none other than Merire, the would-be assassin who had held a club over his head some years before in the shrine of Ra-Horakhte at Opet. Clever student that he was, Merire had let the king take him under his wing and instruct him in the finer points of the Teaching. He had a brilliant memory and was able to rhyme off all that was expected of him whenever he was asked— and often when he wasn't. In the beginning everyone thought that Wanre had an excellent sense of humour to convert a thwarted killer to High Priest. Later they began to wonder if he wasn't simply a poor judge of character.

One day he called Merire in to instruct him as to the revision of the official title of the god. The old title had to go; it was too complicated, and besides, it contained the word *Shu*, meaning "heat," but simple folk kept mixing it up with Shu, god of the atmosphere. He worked himself up into quite a pitch of excitement and asked Merire if he thought the people were still baffled by the god. Could the man on the streets of the Horizon grasp the true, utterly simple character of the Aton? Did he not, perhaps, regard the mere Disc as the god? Was he not, perhaps, confounded by lengthy titles? And Merire played up to him, infinitely more concerned about his forthcoming promotion than about the understanding of the people. "Aton instructs you, my king, and you instruct me in turn," he recited in sugary tones. "The words of Ra are before me for you teach me their essence."

"But I'm trying to clarify my *meaning*!" Wanre cried. "*Ra lives, Ruler of the Horizon, in His Name Ra the Father Who has returned to Aton.* That's so much simpler! No one can fail to understand it, even the foreigners. The secret power, the *centre*!"

For Merire himself, the new title was even more obscure than the old, but he hummed, "No one has seen the Aton save his son Akhenaton. Only he has seen within Ra, only he has seen the Invisible."

For the first time in his life Wanre was faced with the confusion he himself had created. The more he tried to simplify the Teaching, the more murky his meaning became. And now when he desired that his message be spread to all the nations of the world, he was being told that he alone was the Seer and the eyes of the devout were upon him, not the god. He could not blame them; he had made it so.

He began to fear. Parennufer had told him the people could only understand personal gods, friendly beings they could speak to, clutch to their breasts, wear about their necks. But the supreme Aton was remote to them, fearful and inaccessible in his majesty. They couldn't accustom themselves to worshipping what to them was the "royal god" in any of his forms. They couldn't conquer their terrible awe of Ra; he was lord and protector of all who lived—but he was not human, not even animal. Not close, but huge and remote.

In the past priests had been men of magic, and there was an air of mystery in the old temples which didn't exist in the house of the Aton with its flooding, blinding light. Parennufer had tried to urge him to revive more of the ancient ceremonies, but he had only smiled indulgently. He had had too much belief in Aton's becoming the god of the world to believe the evidence before his eyes. He had tolerated reality with the blind indulgence of a loving father towards a wayward child.

*"In the Teaching there are no real mysteries, only truths,"* the old tutor had told him. *"You are the mystery. I ask you then what will the Teaching be ... without the Teacher?"*

Now as Merire's voice droned on, he told himself he was surely going mad. He faced the final mockery of hearing his own words repeated to him in a context he had never intended. Now that he craved spontaneous understanding he met with blind faith. Yet in the beginning faith was all he had asked of men. A man reaped exactly what he sowed; Maat was Maat.

He told Merire to go home, and sat alone playing with the golden melancholy heads of the jackals until his gloom left him, shaking its wings like a great waterbird among the reeds. He went to the Butcher's Yard in the temple where the Overseer of the sacred cattle was inspecting a bull hair by hair, seeking out the single black strand which would mar its fitness for sacrifice. Behind, in an isolated pen, stood the Holy Bull of On which he had vowed to keep and bury in the Horizon; a garland of flowers caressed its thick neck, and heavy ropes held it fast, for lately it had been in bad temper.

The Overseer pronounced his beast pure and placed his seal around one of its horns. Seeing the king, he prostrated himself in the dirt of the cattle pen.

"Get up!" Wanre ordered. "Give me your ring, the one that bears the seal."

Bewildered, the Overseer took it off and handed it over.

"There will be no more sacrifices of cattle! It's barbaric, I can't stand the stench of this place." He looked into the slaughter yard, where the blood of countless beasts had dyed the dirt rusty red. "Let them go, all of them!" he cried.

And all the cattle which had been brought from the Land of the Papyrus for sacrifice to the Aton were released. They wandered about for days through the streets of the Horizon until the poor people gathered them up for their own use.

But when the Holy Bull of On saw his friends departing, he made a terrible stink and tossed his head so wildly that the garland of flowers fell into the dirt. Wanre went into the pen, showing no fear for the beast's threatening snorts, and draped one arm about the huge neck and whispered into the huge ear. "You can't go with them; you're good luck to me, you'll stay here forever like I will."

Perhaps the bull understood; at any rate the fierce rectangular body became quiet. Wanre gazed at the purple plaque of the Aton on a far wall and wondered when, if ever, the Holy Bull and he would die.

Despite Merire's uselessness, he was appointed High Priest and Great Seer and half the city turned out in the Royal Road beneath Wanre's balcony to see the honour bestowed. The parrot's success was an inspiration to all but a very few, for whom the spectacle of a hired killer becoming Great Seer was a disgusting shame.

"I give you the office, and you shall eat the food of your lord in the house of the Aton!" Wanre announced, and bent down and kissed Merire's bald head as the people tossed palm leaves and flowers up onto the balcony. Presently he went quite berserk with happiness and found himself kissing everyone in sight—including Ay, who bent his head obediently and felt the king's whisper tickle his ear.

"It might have been you, my beloved Unbeliever."

the sixth hour of the night

"When did I begin to fear?" the king asked himself. There was a point at which he began to experience the grave loss of confidence which struck all men when the fires of their youth burned less brightly. There was the snapping of some invisible thread, the slackening of a muscle he had never known existed until it ceased to perform. *When did he begin to fear? When he started giving too many gifts.*

"Parennufer," he asked the old man, "you know everything. Tell me, can I trust Ay?"

"Trust? He serves you well, he never complains."

He had been doing clay modelling in his spare time and was busy on a self-portrait which he half realized was a caricature of someone else's caricature. "*How* does he serve me? I like him, but I don't know why. He lacks passion—yes, *passion*." Long fingers applied a clay lip to a clay mouth. "He's capable yet unconcerned, brilliant yet bitter. He performs expertly but his heart is in nothing he does. He's like one of his own cursed horses. Tell me your thoughts, teacher, I need to hear them."

"Ay's clever," Parennufer ventured, "but his cleverness is a prison with bars, not a bird with wings. He can't be ruthless but on the other hand he can't love. Perhaps the two are interdependent. But he takes refuge from all such extremes in that silly bitterness of his, what else can he do?"

"In truth, teacher, does he love me? Does he serve me as a man serves a friend?"

"Can a king have friends, prince?"

"You are my friend."

"That's because I still regard you as the child I tutored. I believe—yes—I believe Ay 'loves' you, but he doesn't know it."

"Then what good is that? I kissed him on the head; I must have been mad. I know he loves the dead sage Ptah Hotep more than the Teaching."

"He doesn't love it because he doesn't love himself. Didn't I once teach you always to see men as they see themselves? You represent something to him, I'm sure—perhaps something beautiful and frightening, perhaps his own lost youth...."

"Yes, but then surely he'd also love another man who represented another part of his 'lost self.' He could love a ruthless man, a fiend. Tiy once told me he used to torture lizards for fun when he was a boy. Can I trust him?"

Parennufer pretended to be engrossed in the portrait. "He serves you faithfully," he murmured.

"But in future—?"

Parennufer studied his sandals. "Trust no one, prince."

Wanre's hands trailed dejectedly down the wet weeping clay.

"You've thrown the land into confusion, and I once told you Keme cannot accept any change easily. You must tread cautiously, I told you that too."

"Ay doesn't know the god. He never goes to the temple; he worships dead horses and sages."

"The man without passion is the man without a god."

"I want him to know the Aton, I want him to be *burned* once— just once!"

Parennufer gazed at him bewildered. "Why does it matter so much, Wanre—a single man, a single unbeliever?"

"He matters," came the reply. "Don't ask why... I only know *he* matters."

"So how will you go about making him *know the god*?"

"Why—I'll reward him for his services, I'll cover him in gold!"

"You mean," remarked Parennufer carefully, "you'll try to buy him?"

"Watch your tongue, old man!"

"Watch your *actions*, little prince."


Ay was lavishly decorated, and a few days afterwards found himself drinking wine with his king and talking about lettuce and thunderbolts.

"Then you are saying, Ay, that lettuce is in fact a stimulus to one's sexual prowess?" he asked, leaning back and playing with his blue throwstick.

They were both a little drunk.

"I was merely remarking that local—ah—the local..."

"I'm not sensitive today. The local *what*?"

"The local, er, god—of my hometown Ipu was said to consume lettuce for that purpose," Ay explained.

"So the Nameless One of whom you speak was similar to the Unspeakable One in that he was some sort of Thunderbolt One, am I right?" Wanre asked, his tone implying that the gods were already ancient history.

"Quite so. In fact, the very name of my hometown is written with the sign of the thunderbolt."

"What you are saying in fact is that the Thunderbolt One ate lettuce. How hilarious!" and he burst out into gales of laughter.

By mid afternoon they were both totally inebriate and had long since forgotten the purpose of their interview. Ay suggested a trip into the desert around the northern suburbs where they might come across several thunderbolts if they looked long enough. Would he like to make a search? He quickly added that *biya* iron might be extracted from them—very good for knives—to which the king replied he had no use for weapons. Nevertheless, he consented to be led on a search and they drove out to a place near the desert altars and left the chariots on the road which led to the northern tombs; a few attendants stayed behind and a handful of workmen followed them into the yellow sands. Presently Ay spotted a suspicious-looking tube protruding from the ground; they knelt over it like schoolboys on a treasure hunt. Ay told him that when the bolts fell they were still hot, and they burrowed at an angle into the soft sand, melting some of it around them. And when the sand hardened it formed small tubes like this one, marking the place of entry. He dug an arm elbow-deep into the sand, and made contact with something hard. Then he drew the bolt out—a small one, black and shapeless. He offered it to Wanre, but he drew back with fear or repugnance as though the thing were a cockroach or some other abomination. Presently though, he reached out one hesitant finger and touched it. Then in a soft pleading voice he asked, "Is *this* the stuff of which the vaults and gates of heaven are made?"

He told the workmen to continue searching for more bolts; as for him, he was going back to the palace. Ay walked with him back to the chariots, and when he mounted his, he stood for a moment clutching the reins in anger. "Up *there*, Ay," he said, looking up and squinting at the light, "is light and fire. You can't tell me the stars dwell beside such an ugly black mass as that stone was part of!"

His horses bounded forward but at the last moment Ay noticed something strange and cried out, "Wanre, stop!" He drew the beasts in and turned, puzzled. Ay pointed to the left wheel of the chariot. The linchpin had been loosened and in a few moments would have fallen out. Just when he reached top speed the entire wheel would have dropped away.

He stepped down and went over to Ay. There was fear in his brown eye, anger in the blue. He laid a hand on Ay's shoulder either from gratitude or from the need for support. "Be my eyes," he whispered. "Be my ears! I'm not surprised at this. I know there are some who wish me dead. But I don't know their names...."

"Charge every man who remained behind with the chariots!" cried Ay. "Charge them all!"

"No . . . I only want to *know* them. Find out who they are and tell me."

"Wanre," remarked Ay, "you trust me with this task but if I hadn't cried out, how would you know it wasn't me who loosened the linchpin?"

He smiled an odd, crooked smile. "I know it was not you," he said. Then the blue eye winked playfully. "I know who *you* are—and your time has not yet come."

Ay was told to spend the rest of the week overseeing the workmen who were hunting for the thunderbolts. They dug around day after day and gradually got over their fear of handling the stones (at first they recalled old tales of stars which fell from the sky, and of Horus and Set fighting each other by hurling the great bolts of fire across the heavens). At the end of the week Ay was thoroughly exhausted and hoped he might be rewarded for his labours by being made Master of Thunderbolts at least. A nice title, he thought.

He gathered a good collection and presented them to the king, who looked at them distastefully and asked to what use the iron might be put. Ay refrained from suggesting that they make one huge broad sword like the swords of the warriors of Kheta, and suggested instead that they make a number of small ceremonial knives for the Opening of the Mouth of the Dead. This didn't exactly delight Wanre either, for he recalled how the mouth of the sacred statue of Amon was opened each morning by means of small chisels and knives.

"But thunderbolt iron is another thing," Ay pressed. "What can better accomplish the ceremony of the Opening of the Mouth of the dead than the blasting, tearing power of the bolts of heaven? And my father," he added, "used to say that it was the children of Horus who opened the mouth with their fingers of *biya*. And this same iron also opens the gates of heaven for the dead to pass through...."

Wanre agreed to have the iron extracted and numerous small chisels made; these were stored in the treasury until he had use for them. And he did have, sooner than he thought.

After the matter was settled he looked at Ay a long time. "And who drew out the linchpin?" he whispered.

"The exact man I do not know. Who paid him, I do know," said Ay, wishing at that moment he could be miraculously transported to Men Nofer or some remote garrison a thousand miles away.

"And who paid?"

"An officer."

"Which?"

"It doesn't matter, they're all involved, every one. I have it from Rames who has it from Paatenemheb, who has it from someone else he refuses to name."

"My officers, all my officers ...!"

"Under May, your Chief Scribe of Recruits!" Ay blurted out.

"*May!* He was Overseer of the sacred beasts in the temple of Ra at On! *May*, whom I brought to my city, my beloved May—it's impossible!"

"It *is* May. Permit me to arrest and interrogate the officers."

"No! I've always walked near death and I won't stop now!" Wanre cried.

"Then let me arrest May!"

"No, I want to think, my head's going to blow off, I've got to think."

Had he really thought, he would have realized that the list of people hungry for his death ranged from fishmongers in No Amon to half the officers in his army. His bodyguard shot up around him like a small forest whenever he felt insecure, which was not often—for who, he asked, would be so foolish as to shoot an arrow at the sun?

For more than a year May walked free while the king, without letting him know what he knew, instructed him in the ways of love and peace. The results were: three attempts at sabotaging the royal chariot, one attempt at food poisoning (which was unsuccessful because he had a stomach like a horse), and one wild scheme to sink the royal barge. His affection for May increased daily. He always loved most those who came to destroy him.

The little princess Meketaton was the meekest and frailest of all the king's daughters, and she'd just learned how to rattle the sistrum in the temple at sunset and send the Aton to sleep with her small music. She was too nervous to go riding in the chariot with her older sister Meritaton, and the latter used to call her an ugly little baboon, and play cruel tricks on her, like dipping her arm into the red paint-pot until she wept. But she loved to paint, and one day she took her own little paintbox and went out into the garden to play with the colours. She sat alone on the ground, trying to paint each blade of grass a different shade. She was determined to finish the whole garden before sundown, but she fell asleep instead, her naked body languishing in the greenness, her silver toenails and small bracelets glistening in the grass. When she came back into the palace she was laughing, for she had stripes of red and yellow and blue all over her skin and she thought she looked very funny indeed. She ran to her father to show him, but halfway across the floor she screamed once, and fell down, and curled up like a little rabbit on the tiles.

He thought she was playing, and went and picked her up. But she didn't move. He froze, and stood with her in his arms for a full hour. The wet paint left little multi-coloured streaks on his white gown. When someone finally came they had to pry her away; his limbs were so stiff he keeled over backwards and smashed his head against the floor. He didn't awake for two days.

In Aton's temple, Meketaton's private shrine had been called the House of Rejoicing. He went there, and found its name a bitter joke. How often had he told his daughters that for him they were like the Imperishable Stars which shone low on the horizon and never set? But Meketaton had set. Had he forgotten that those stars were also the souls of the dead? He stood in the dead child's shrine, disbelieving death, disbelieving that at that moment she lay in her bath of death to be prepared for entombment in the Orient Cliffs. She who had slept like a gorgeous disarrayed flower in the grass.

He lit incense over her small altar and offered up a feeble prayer to the Aton to protect her *ka*. It did no good. Then in a trembling voice he found himself calling upon the old lords of the dead, the forbidden ones, to see to it that her spirit might shine forever in the night sky in the north, and all her little bracelets glitter there among the stars which never set.

How easily the names fell from his lips. How much more soothing they were than the name of the Aton. *Thoth, Anupew, Osiris...*

Then he locked himself up in a small room, giving orders to Parennufer to let no one inside, for he was jealous of his grief and had no wish to share it. He sat huddled in a chair, his head bent forward at an alarming angle as though the neck were broken or about to break. His hands clutched the arms of the chair, the knuckles drained of blood, sorrow staring insanely from the two caves of his eyes. Parennufer disturbed him now and again by offering him pears and grapes lest he starve himself to death. From time to time he would cry out a single word, *"Why?"* And Parennufer would answer, "Don't ask why, prince. She was always a feeble child. Whatever disease once wracked your body must have entered hers. But your other daughters are in health. Perhaps the Aton desired the child for Himself."

"*He is no Lord of Death!!*"

"*Maat, met...,*" sighed Parennufer. "*Truth* and *death*, how similar the two words sound. It's only a matter of pronunciation."

Wanre's teeth broke into the delicate skin of a grape and juice dribbled down his chin and the half-eaten triangle of fruit dropped to the floor. Parennufer gently wiped his face as he would a child's, while the mad eyes stared into space, seeing Meketaton laughing and tumbling and crawling all over him—one of his naked little daughters, one of his miracles. Then the eyes grew black and wild and saw the child giggling with joy and the next minute falling to the floor shrieking, foam on her small mouth, falling among painted gazelles and entering that sleep from which she never awoke.

"*Maat! Met!*" he cried. "*No* Lord of Truth, *No* Lord of Death!" and he reached out his hands as though to clutch something, and fell forward from the chair and slipped into a sudden sleep.

One day a few weeks later he stood leaning against the bedroom wall for support, lost among the god's golden arms. His whole body broke into an ugly laughter and a message fluttered to the floor. Nefertiti picked it up and read: *In the first month of harvesting in the twelfth year of your reign, I will journey with all my attendants and possessions, to take up permanent residence in the Horizon.* The letter bore the seal of the winged sphinx with the head of the Great Mother Tiy.

Nefertiti said nothing. Wanre laughed and laughed and collapsed among the golden arms of the sun. Later that night he came to her and laid his clothes by the steps which led to the royal bed, and she was afraid. His organ was erect and furious. He moved upon her, his anger a live thing, his body a borrowed thing—his sex a weapon, a charm. And seeking to open the deepest part of her, the part which only a child or the moon might open, he cried, "*I* am the Aton, *I* determine life!" She watched his face and for a moment she believed him, for this was no man upon her loins but one long flame, incarnate fire.

But the power to create life had left him. His physicians concluded that somehow the old ailments had found their way into his private parts. Or perhaps one of the demons of the night had assailed him, the one known as the Phallus-Eater. He believed the tears he shed for Meketaton had dried his body and her death had stolen the life from his loins. When the child was ready for her tomb he ordered an iron chisel to be taken from the treasury. Then with his own hands he performed upon his daughter the ancient ceremony of the Opening of the Mouth, that her *ka* might find passage through the small sweet lips forever, and the way be blasted open by the magic iron of the thunderbolt in the hand of her father. And the thunderbolt fell and the sweet mouth opened in death like the response to some desperate act of love.

the seventh hour of the night

Now it all began. The elaborate game lay before them. It was the twelfth year of his reign.

"Hounds," said Wanre.

"Jackals," said Ay.

"We must toss," said the king, "to see which of us is which. Your colour?"

"Black."

"Then I'm white as usual." He threw half a dozen ivory wands across the table. "Four black sides, two white. Proceed, Ay—today you are jackals and I'm hounds."

The elaborate game lay before them. The long, exquisitely carved playing pins stood upright in their slots; the ivory hounds and jackals faced each other across the board. Politely, ferociously. He had recently taken up the game to relieve the tension in his hands. Ay was his favourite opponent, and every afternoon they played until they were bleary. Hounds and jackals required little skill; it was, like all games, a distraction for the bored, or the tormented.

"Your jackals look particularly vicious today, Ay; their eyes gleam," he teased.

"And your hounds, my good god, appear equally ferocious."

"They look ferocious because they were carved ferocious!"

"But surely it's not their mere workmanship that makes them so formidable...?"

The room was silent save for the tense, soft clicking of the warring pins as they moved them from slot to slot, advancing, retreating, circling. He and Ay had an odd sort of silent rapport when they played; their thoughts were embodied in the ivory animals and when they removed each other's pieces from the board it was as though they removed parts of each other's minds. The king curved over the board like a cobra—there *was* something reptilian about him, Ay thought—the elongated body, the greenish pallor which often crept over his face.... And always behind him on the wall, the huge golden disc and arms of the Aton, protecting him from himself.

"My hound intercepts your jackal!"

"But, Wanre, my jackal avoids your hound—thus—and in avoiding it falls back on another...."

The soft click-click of the warring pins.

"I don't like this," Wanre announced as his opponent withdrew another hound from the board. Ay often wondered if he shouldn't let him win from time to time. Wanre was a dreadful player; he never seemed able to co-ordinate his pieces. He would move one piece, totally unaware of the alteration that one move would make in the overall game. Often the board would be in a state of chaos and his defences weak while he lovingly manipulated *one* hound back and forth. And when through neglect he lost another hound he would frown as though he did not understand, as though it were not a defeat but some sort of odd mistake.

Ay felt guilty every time he captured one of Wanre's hounds. He couldn't really enjoy a contest unless his opponent was as ruthless as himself. When the king invariably lost, Ay would tell him, "But perhaps you should have been jackals today!"

One by one the hounds were taken off the board and the jackals took over Wanre's territory. Outside the room a blind musician played on a huge harp like the kind the desert people had. They were alone in a waste of sand. Now only one hound remained and Wanre frantically manoeuvred it. He always played best at the end of the game when he knew he was trapped.

"This hound is a terror, I can't catch him!" cried Ay.

"This one I leave to the *last*," Wanre smiled.

When it was over his eyes strayed from the board and he watched something—another, greater game being played out somewhere above him. "Ay, I am alone in the light. I am a great bird flying in the high vaults of heaven. My tall eyes see the god. I am alone between the desert altars. How is it you can't join me? How revolting that I must try to teach you the unteachable...."

Over pomegranate wine Ay made bold and asked what was troubling him, and he answered the question with a host of his own. Were Tiy's quarters prepared? Were the inscriptions on the walls of her private sanctuary by the river completed? It was obvious that the Great Mother's decision to come to the Horizon had obsessed him for months and he met it with the curious mixture of apprehension and impatience with which a man met death, or a lover. Nefertiti had several times been jolted awake at night by his moans as he tossed about in his sleep murmuring, "There's the smell I remember, stink of a scavenger bird, salt smell of natron and death. I was born in her claws ... the dense wings on my face again, my nostrils prick with the stink of the vulture.... *Have no fear, prince, it is the Lady of Dread who assails you!*"

Wanre wandered over to the window and said, "Yesterday the barges came across the river from the west bank and delivered the first crops to the temple. It's the first month of the harvest."


A week later she came from the south, and with her came the winds of sand which darkened the skies for weeks and cast a thick dirty veil over the face of the god. People wondered why she chose to travel at such a time. It was a bad omen, for on the very morning of her arrival the light of the Aton dimmed and a fine powder settled in the streets and found its way under the thresholds of houses and into eyelids and hair. Akhenaton waited under an elaborate canopy by the shore, the streamers of his Blue Crown flying out behind him, the vulture on his brow watching. His hands held the flail and sceptre, his fingers gritty with sand.

Then the Great Mother rode in on the uneasy river, bringing the days of darkness in her wake.

Though no longer queen, she continued to wear her great crown with its double plumes; the crown of the great Cow Hathor which hugged the sun between its golden horns. The royal family sat facing her across tables piled high with roasted meat on skewers, pigeons and chickens, wine and fruit. Her daughter sat at her feet, the last child of Amenhotep, whom she had named Beketaton. The double plumes dominated the room as her attendant ran about tasting the various dishes and Beketaton threw green figs at Wanre's daughters. Storms of snorts and giggles broke out from the princesses, and Ankhespaaton heaved a pear back into the enemy camp.

"Don't throw fruit!" chided Nefertiti.

"She threw a fig in my face!" protested the child, who, like her sisters, hated the dark grandmother in the tall crown and the spoilt brat who was their aunt.

Tiy herself went on and on about how awful her trip had been and how a careless porter had dropped her favourite wig basket into the river. And Wanre stole long glances at her and thought, *She does not change. I change. The sphinxes do not move, Tiy does not move, she hovers above me like a vulture on the cliffs, she waits.* And Nefertiti sat back silently, feeling a long chill creep up her spine as though a viper slithered there whose head bore two golden horns.

He was severely weakened by the loss of his daughter. Tiy knew this and acted upon it; her timing was admirable. No sooner did she arrive in the Horizon than she began to deliver the tirade of admonitions and warnings which she had been rehearsing for some time. From morning to night she followed him around the palace telling him of the dire consequences which would eventually result from the erasure of the gods; the Lords of Heaven would not tolerate such an evil. They would have their revenge. The death of Meketaton, she insisted, was only the first punishment he would receive from the gods he had mocked. Graphically she described how death might one day claim the other princesses—one might tumble into the blue pool when Benremut wasn't looking and plummet to the bottom like a stone. Another might fall from the chariot and be crushed beneath its wheels; another might be the victim of some insidious disease....

He begged her to stop the torture for, unlike other men, he regarded words as real things. He *visualized* everything to the last detail; he did not merely imagine. But Tiy already knew this. She learned from the court physicians that he had become impotent, and skilfully used this new bit of information to further convince him that the gods were taking their revenge. And as for his wilful desecration of his father's name—the consequences would be too horrible to tell. The *ka* of Amenhotep endured; it was everywhere, it was even in the Horizon. Didn't he feel its presence, didn't he feel it watching?

He was ill. Unable to bear the noisy complaints—which, when added to the private noises inside his head, almost drove him mad—he agreed for the sake of peace and quiet to make a temporary halt to the chiselling. He fully intended to resume it later.

Tiy then demanded that he decorate her old steward who had served under Amenhotep; this would imply that he was honouring the house of his dead father, and he hated the thought. But Parennufer urged him to do it as a sentimental gesture—official sentiment, of course. "Where is my official sentiment?" he exploded. "In my kneecap perhaps, in my left ear, in the sole of my foot? Am I a wooden puppet like those the women carry at harvest festivals with strings attached to its legs and arms and penis, that I can be moved by *official sentiment?*"

But eventually he gave in, and the old man was decorated and made an old-fashioned speech through the spaces in his teeth. "Praitheth to thy *ka*, O Wanre, great Nile god of the whole land!" Everyone laughed at his quaintness, and Wanre compared the shapes of their laughter; his own was a small yellow bird singing from the full lips, it was several small yellow birds. Tiy's was shaped like a cluster of black grapes. The Vizier's was a small silver fish bubbling and needing air. Nefertiti's was a large pale blue flower. And when Ay laughed, he looked down his nose and went cross-eyed. As Aton lived! He had the most interesting laughter of all!—a whole parade of perfectly shaped, tiny red horses!

The Great Mother sat perfectly still in her best thinking position and she reminded him of an old veteran he'd seen when a boy, who'd been wounded in one of the Kush campaigns and who sat for days still as the summer air until they finally trepanned his skull. He was fully prepared to bore a hole in hers for keeping him waiting. Her favourite sculptor Auta whom she'd brought along with her luggage was busy chiselling that difficult old face. This at least was better than watching her have her hair arranged, a scene he'd witnessed at least a thousand times.

"They've been knocking at our doors too long," she said at last.
"Who?"

"Who do you think? The ambassadors, of course! Dozens of them seeking audience with you. Tutu always has to apologize to them, poor Tutu. They come bearing gifts and letters, and you're too distracted to see them. Shameful."

"Shameful," he echoed.

"Auta, don't chisel me when I'm distraught; I don't want to look distraught for eternity in limestone."

"Serpentine, Great Lady," the sculptor corrected her.

"Well, in that either. My son, look—the disintegration begins deep within the empire. The weakest parts go first—then, total collapse!"

"I've heard you say the same thing about women," he remarked drily. Then he could have bitten out his tongue, for she went grey with anger. He learned later that she'd been suffering for a year from her body, which had betrayed her as it betrayed all women. The blood of youth which once ran thick and fast on her moondays had stopped, and it was the end of her life. All year her handmaidens had tried to console her with precious oils and perfumes and unguents, expressing awe at her beauty and running their little brown hands over her face and body, but to no avail. She grew shrill and bitter. Every night she laid her heavy head on the headrest and stared across the room at her crown—the double plumes and the two great horns of the Cow glistening in the darkness, bearing the sun between them as the legs of a fertile women bore the fire of a man. Every night she tossed for hours before falling into troubled sleep.

"It's time for you to hold a Tribute Festival!" she announced. "Then you can see all the ambassadors at once. I'm arranging it for this winter. They've been insulted too long."

"What if I refuse?" he asked, watching Auta's hammer tapping the chisel, and drawing the line of the serpentine mouth up at the corners into a half-smile.

"You won't," she said.

The night before the eighth day of the second month of winter was the coldest he could remember. He sat up through half of it huddled in front of a brazier of burning logs, and when morning came he was scarcely ready to cope with the Tribute Festival. But by mid morning he and Nefertiti were seated on their thrones in the Hall of Foreign Tribute. By noon the city was utter chaos—crowds, horses, dancers, scribes, foreign ambassadors jostling each other in the streets, apologizing in a hundred different tongues, captive spies, groups of Beduwi with curved staffs, black Nehesu from the south, hordes of captured Amu desert people, language interpreters gone half mad translating a dozen speeches, war captives from Ashur, infantry parades with contingents of archers and Shardanese warriors . . . and in the middle of the din and disorder he kept exclaiming, *"What's he saying, I can't hear a thing!"* Gorgeous plumes on the heads of the Nehesu, monkeys and leopards and antelopes, chariots stuffed with vases and spices, ivory elephant tusks and black slaves and a million golden rings. And his voice murmuring, *"You separated mind and speech and skin, that we might distinguish man from man."*

A spokesman from Mitanni began talking frantically about someone called "Tadukhipa," and bewildered, he asked, "Who's Tadukhipa, who on earth is Tadukhipa?" Someone close by reminded him that she was his second wife, living for years in the Great Harem, lost among a thousand other foreign gifts. Two princesses stroked a gazelle in front of the throne and a nervous ambassador from Karaduniash made a lisping speech about how he hoped the *Sar* of *Misrii* would remain as friendly with the new king of the land as he'd been with Burnaburiash. It took him a moment to remember that the great Burnaburiash was dead.

Later he went into the temple and consecrated the gifts to Aton. He was nauseated from having seen the spoils of war; the sight of the captives with murder in their eyes had turned his stomach. He looked at the gifts piled high in the temple. Gifts? The nations that were left had merely paid their dues. Darkness closed in around the gold and silver, the leopard skins, the exquisite swords.

The next day Haremhab arrived unannounced and confronted him with a group of escaped princes from Retenu. The General was furious as he marched in, gleaming with necklaces and armbands which set off his bronze skin. He looked like a dangerous animal, weather-beaten and very intelligent, quite out of his element in the dainty immaculate reception hall.

"These foreigners," he cried, "have come from the north, and they don't know how they're going to live! Their countries are starving and they live like animals in the desert and their children perish. They have been broken, and their towns laid waste, and fire has been thrown into their grain. They come begging sanctuary in Keme, after the manner of your father's fathers since the beginning. I have told them that the Great of Strength"—here he paused sarcastically to set off the irony of the title—"will send his *mighty arm* in front of his army, and destroy the enemy and plunder their towns and cast fire into the Nine Bows, the vile and miserable Amu!"

The soft scratching of a scribe's pen was the only sound in the hall after Haremhab spoke.

"...and your army which was in Retenu has joined the enemy," he added, almost as an afterthought. "For years there were bribes, secret coalitions, and one by one they left their posts."

Akhenaton sat perfectly still with his arms crossed over his chest. His collarbone stood out as sharply as the handle of the royal flail. "I...thought I sent General Bikhuru some time ago to slay the Habiru who were plundering the Retenu towns...." he said weakly.

"Bikhuru blundered! He dispatched an army against Rib-Addi of Gubla because he thought the poor old man was a traitor. A horrible mistake. By the time the matter was cleared up, it was too late, and Gubla fell to the enemy, as I'm sure my Sun is aware!"

"What... finally happened to Rib-Addi?" asked Wanre, and Ay, who was watching the goings-on, remembered bitter wine in Gubla and an old man's hands forming pyramids in air.

"Rib-Addi, a loyal old fool who is now either dead or would be better off so? I don't know. Nobody does."

Wanre found himself unable to meet Haremhab's eyes. "Tell me," he put in, to break the tense silence in the hall, "about these mysterious Habiru."

The General gave him a wry smile. "My Sun, they are scarcely *mysterious*! They're a desert people, a dispossessed people, a mixture of many tribes. Some are landless citizens from heaven knows where. Some of them look like the wandering traders or metal-workers one sees sometimes in the Two Lands. Others resemble the tribes who dwell in the Land of the Papyrus. Others—who knows? The desert might hide an army—even a nation. Their name means 'donkey nomads' or 'dusty ones'—something like that. They pressed past the borders of Retenu, attacking in small groups, stinging and biting like flies, and the princes of the cities had to flee to the coast. Some used to be in Aziru's pay; others hired out as mercenaries anywhere. Some of the cities of Retenu united against your deputy Abdi-Khiba in Ursalim. Ursalim was reduced to rags. Remember his letter? *The lands of the king are lost and ruined, but you do not listen to me! All regents are lost, there remains not one. Though a man sees the facts, yet the two eyes of the king my lord do not see!*"

Hearing this, Wanre laid two trembling fingers across his left eye. *Does he mean I'm going blind?* he thought.

"You might recall," went on Haremhab, no longer attempting to soften the rancour in his voice, "another letter from him in which he begged that you send someone to fetch him and his two brothers so that they might die in the Two Lands beside their king. When Ursalim and Megiddo fell, the southern half of the empire was lost. Hazor and Gaza only recently succumbed. *Gaza*, my Sun—our most important base."

Another tense silence.

"I hear that a certain group of Habiru worship someone called El Shaddai, the Mighty, who dwells on a mountain," commented Haremhab, apropos of nothing. "He must be a very powerful god." He looked at the king guilelessly.

"I know *nothing* of our enemies' gods!" Wanre cried.

Later he agreed to dispatch another small army to Retenu, but refused to place Haremhab in command. "I need you in Keme," he said, and there was an audible snicker from one of the foreign princes in the background.

A day later when the air was cold and the wind rushed down the Royal Road making the banners on the temple gates flap wildly, he sat in the Court of Petitions, and listened for two hours to pleas from irate landowners and criminals, growing more and more depressed. He hated having to judge men, and usually let Nakht and the Kenbet Council make his decisions for him. He was weary and morose, and as the hours slipped by he slumped down farther and farther on his throne until he looked as though he were stretched out after a long exhausting race—royal legs sprawled in two directions, royal shoulders slouched in chilled weariness, a few limp flowers dangling from his fingers. But then a man was ushered into the court, another refugee from one of the sacked cities of Retenu. His face and hair were dirty from long weeks of travel, his body was cut and bruised by those who made it their business to "detain" foreign messengers. He fell at the king's feet and told him how vandals had looted his town, how the regent prince was taken into captivity, the women and children kidnapped and defiled. He begged for troops and archers, a few, a handful....

But Wanre remained in his curious slouch and stared at him with outraged disbelief. Presently he looked off into space and a smile played around the corners of his mouth. Beads of perspiration broke out on his brow. "You say your city weeps, messenger! Memorize now my reply to her: *O city of Retenu! The rays of my Father the Aton do not shine upon you less brightly than they do upon me! His beams unify the empire of the king and all men flourish beneath them! Why then, city, do you weep? Why then do you war upon one another? Lift up your eyes and gaze upon the Aton Who makes all nations one!*"

The messenger looked like someone jolted out of a nightmare. "*Milku*, my king, my city *burns!*"

"Have you ever," he sighed, "seen the summer flowers nodding their heads in the warmth of the sun?"

The man flailed his arms in exasperation. A guard stepped forward and whispered in his ear, "Tell him no more of the gory details, or he'll faint." But he shook off the guard's restraining arm and cried, "So then it is true! A blind man sits upon the throne of *Misri*!"

"That is impudence. Seize him," muttered Nakht weakly.

But Wanre's eyes grew moist and his hands trembled. "Leave him be, he's only misguided. Give him safe escort out of the Two Lands."

And when at last the Court of Petitions was empty save for himself and Nakht and a few guards, he covered his face with his hands and wept loudly.

"O my cities, O my people—why do you kill me when I am your life?"

A few days after the Tribute Festival Ay encountered a man in Nakht's office whose face was alarmingly familiar, although it was covered with dust and partly obscured by an enormous beard.

"He's been caught trying to make off across the eastern desert with a band of spies," said the Vizier. "He came in from Khor a week ago to petition the king."

Two or three guards were restraining the prisoner, who, when he saw Ay, leaned forward and asked, "Aren't you the messenger Ay?"

"My name is Ay, but I'm no messenger," he replied.

"Ah, but you *were*! In Amki. Don't you remember? You came bringing 'messages' and ended up fighting beside us."

"That was many years ago!" Ay cried. His reaction was involuntary and he didn't quite know what prompted it—disgust with the prisoner's appearance, or embarrassment at being recognized as the reluctant soldier who had joined in battle with the three princes of Amki.

"What are you doing *here*, then?" Ay asked.

"What, messenger, is anybody doing *anywhere* these days, I ask you? After I last saw you I fled down the coast and tried to build up another army, but it ended up smashing its way out of the path of Aziru. So here I am," he grunted.

Ay did not like the squinting eyes, the crooked smile.

"I suppose," he went on, "you've heard that our famed Aziru is now a devoted subject of Kheta. Perhaps he took a wise course. And you, messenger—I see *you've* fared well these last few years!" He looked Ay up and down as though his good health and well-fed appearance were obscene. "What happened to the message I gave you many years ago? *Send help*, it said, or something like that." Then he shot a mouthful of spit at Ay's feet. "For the message you never delivered!" he cried.

Ay clapped him over the left ear and sent him tumbling to the ground. One of the guards picked him up. He was laughing and his laughter echoed back and forth between the dainty walls of birds and flowers.

"Why in the name of heaven did you join the spies?" Ay cried. "Weren't you here on political asylum?" Then he saw the heavy jaws working again and he stepped back to avoid another deluge of spit.

"Asylum ceased to appeal to me," he sneered. "After taking my fill of this sweet little city, after being fed up to the guts trying to get an audience with *him*—my Lord, my Sun!—I decided I preferred war. Anybody's war. In anybody's pay."

"Treason!" exclaimed Nakht. "Oh, dear." Wringing his pale white hands.

Ay wanted to wring Nakht's neck, but instead he was seized with a fury he'd never known before. He lunged forward and grabbed the bearded prince. He hit him once, twice, he didn't know how many times. The guards finally restrained him and as he came out of the red cloud of anger he heard the Vizier's voice as though from a great distance. "Come, come, Ay—you're not the judge here!" And from an even greater distance the soft mocking voice of the man he longed to kill. "So your conscience is as stricken as that, messenger Ay!"

The words sobered him instantly. The man had read him better than he could read himself. He saw blood on the prince's cheek and realized that his fist had opened up an old jagged scar, a scar gained fighting more battles than *he'd* ever fought.

Nakht sentenced the man to lifetime labour in the quarries of Hat Nub where he could vent his fury on the giant blocks of alabaster. After he was led away Nakht remarked, "If there's anything I hate it's a spy without *taste*, a spy who works for just *anybody*," and he turned several rings around on several fingers. "And the city is just crawling with them. It's so uncouth! I can't tell the king, I can't possibly tell the king. That man was here on *asylum*...."

"There was a time," Ay said, enunciating his words very clearly, "when death was the punishment for the sort of treason we witnessed today."

"Times have changed," said Nakht, and lightly stepped away.

That night every time Ay made to mount the lovely creature who shared his bed, he saw the face of the prince before him, and his manhood wilted in her eager hands. Later in dreams he saw the prince with his nose cut off, scribbling Ay's name and obscene poetry all over the walls of Hat Nub. He wore Ay's clothes and his laughter travelled all the way from a misty morning on a battle plain through many years of time.


Haremhab stormed up and down the city complaining about everything from the worthlessness of the troops to the lack of leather for army sandals. On the day of his departure Ay was anxious to get to the barracks; there was a new supply shipment coming in, and he had an appointment with Ranofer regarding a decrease in army expense accounts. But Haremhab cornered him, Nakht and May and proceeded to lecture them on their general incompetence. Nakht wrung his delicate white hands; Ay studied his feet, and May became terribly interested in something going on in the sky.

"Nakht, aren't you responsible for army transport?"

"Yes, General."

"Then why in the name of Set is nothing ever *transported*!"

"I have no orders," Nakht sighed, "and if I spent all my time on army matters instead of judging criminals, where would I be?"

Haremhab's escort drew up beside his chariot; all their faces wore identical scowls, and his own face was taut with scorn. "Gentlemen, good day!" Then he addressed May, unconcerned that the others were listening. "I wish you luck," he said. "You know you have my unqualified support after you've succeeded in your plan. I'll rejoice with everyone else when it's over."

And in a moment he was gone.

"An extraordinary man, wouldn't you say, May?" asked Nakht. "What was he talking about, by the way?"

"About another 'extraordinary man,'" May replied, eyeing them carefully. "One we are better off without. You know who I mean, don't you, gentlemen?"

Nakht folded his nervous hands over each other, listening. May's questioning eyes darted around, seeking in their faces some acknowledgement of his words.

"Take care, May," Ay warned him. "You're saying more than you should."

May laughed. "It's no secret any more, is it? Haremhab know's my intentions—so do you, Ay. What about you, Nakht? Do you know what I intend?"

"I haven't the foggiest idea," Nakht replied, although his expression betrayed him. "I'm a delicate man myself . . . refined, one might say. People like me don't get involved in military matters."

"This is hardly a *military* matter, Nakht," put in May. "It's a matter involving that other *extraordinary man*—you resemble him, you know."

"Wanre is a weak man, in spite of being rather terrifying as well. I'm a *delicate* man—there's a difference!" cried the Vizier.

"You've spent too long running alongside the royal chariot," muttered May under his breath. "But you *do* know what I'm talking about."

"I said I haven't the foggiest idea," Nakht repeated, turned away, and left.

Ay stood a while with May and remarked in a low voice, "So, you've got Haremhab behind you. He's a professional soldier, you know . . . I mean a killer. He itches for the battlefield, he's hungry for blood."

"But wouldn't you say he has good reason to itch?" asked May. "Or have you become another of our soft, peace-loving troop captains?"

Ay looked off into the distance where the yellow clouds from the General's chariot still hung in the air. He was furious with May's insubordination, but he found himself murmuring, "I would, May, I would say he has reason."

"I've being trying to get you to commit yourself for months!" cried May. "Are you with me or not?"

"I'm not."

"You're a fool!" he cried, "You don't love the king, you don't worship his god—*what does he mean to you?*"

But the words hung unanswered in the air, for they formed a question Ay had too often asked himself.

A month later, on Tiy's orders, May and seven of the officers who were plotting Wanre's death were seized and thrown out of the city. The whole affair took place by night while the king slept. When he learned what had happened he went wild. What appalled him was not so much the fact that Tiy had taken control, but that he had been training May for the priesthood and overnight lost his most challenging pupil. He ordered his mother out of the city, but she had no intentions of going anywhere. If he wanted to use force on her, she said, he was free to try.

He tore his clothes in impotent frustration, went out to May's tomb in the cliffs, and had three men erase the inscriptions on the walls. May's public disgrace hung like a heavy chain around his neck.

"You conquer by love," he kept screaming at Tiy. "You conquer by *love!*"

**the eighth hour of the night**

Ay felt the thirteenth year would be unlucky from the start. One night he was having a glorious time star-gazing in his garden, a cold beer in one hand and a bunch of daisies in the other, when he was rudely interrupted. There he was, his head bent back and his eyes fastened on the starry Lord of the Chambers of the South, when a voice behind him whispered. "Stars again, brother? You should have been an astrologer!"

He turned to see Tiy standing in the courtyard; she passed out of the shadows into a small patch of light from one of the torches.

"Why aren't you asleep?" he asked, annoyed with her.

"Human beings need very little sleep. I rarely sleep, it's a waste of time. I hate wasting time."

"Just think," he said, "if you could only live fourteen hundred and sixty years you could save up a whole extra year out of the tag ends of the others!"

"I've no intentions of living fourteen hundred and sixty years."

"Maybe your son will live so long," he said, then gave a short embarrassed laugh.

"He's not a god, he's an idiot."

"An idiot who turned the tables on you and wouldn't let you rule from behind the throne! Rare idiot indeed!"

"You're drunk! Don't tell me *you're* a religious madman like the rest!"

Ay studied his fingernails and mumbled, "Maybe so, maybe not. You're mad because in the Horizon you're the Great Mother, but at the Southern Residence you were still treated like a queen, right?"

She shot him a dangerous glance, and to change the subject he swung an arm around the dark enclosures of the courtyard. "How do you like my garden?" he asked. The blaze of colours was silent by night but the heavy fragrance of the shadowy flowers filled the air and deep gurgling sounds issued from the sunken water tanks.

"Beautiful, what a *splendid* view of the stars!" she teased.

"I love night," said Ay. "When the spirits of the dead take their place in the heavens and one can admire the *akhu* of the great ones from a distance, without having to put up with them on earth. They're so calm, so civilized."

"You seem eager to join them," she remarked, dropping the cloak from her head to reveal the golden vulture on her brow. It gleamed in the dark; it disturbed his garden. "Still at your Underworld books and philosophical treatises, still reading *Am Duat* and thrilling over the demons? What does Wanre think of that?"

"He tolerates my literary tastes."

"You're a tottering old man!" she cried. "Where is your ambition? What's he done to you?"

"Nothing," he lied.

"I wish you'd *please* get off your rump and do something about Nakht! A feeble old fool! I demanded he put his pretty foot down for once on the matter of the punishment of spies and criminals. No one's been executed for treason since my son's been on the throne; he's got this childish horror of bloodshed, it's intolerable! And you sit counting stars!"

"I wasn't *counting* them, I was merely enjoying them."

"Ay, I'm telling you—slander Nakht, poison him, I don't care what, he's useless as a wart, and he's in your way!"

"And what is *my way*, Tiy?"

"The Viziership, of course!"

"I love stars because they don't argue in dark gardens, they don't think of becoming viziers, they don't do anything. I envy them, they're dead and yet they live forever...."

"You're in love with death."

"No. It amuses me. Long ago they used to pull apart the bones of the dead, wrench legs and arms from their sockets to prevent the dead from taking vengeance on the living. Now I imagine myself scattered east, west, north, and south—and my bones whimpering: *O head, come and join neck! Neck is northeast of Ipu! O feet! Legs are southwest of the Horizon—please join us! O fingers wherever you are!*"

"You *want* the Viziership."

"If Wanre wants me, he'll call on me."

"You forget he's as erratic as a desert hare. He changes his mind five times a day. He sees the infinite but he's blind to the present. He's charmed his officials out of their wits and made them see everything in terms of *shay*. You can't run a country on *fate*. Everybody looks frail and sickening, officials look like love-struck fools, they've got glazed eyes like sleepwalkers! It's disgusting! He lavishes gold on everyone . . . were you there when he decorated Parennufer? *Parennufer!* Crowds like a bird pond during the flood. Gold for useless old men, gold for a flimsy city built so badly it won't withstand the desert winds!"

He smelled deeply of the fragrance of the flowers and Tiy's dark form began to circle the garden. "Cities are like men," he murmured, "ephemeral. Who builds for eternity, who believes that when he dies he'll meet his everlasting *ka*? Only peasants, they believe everything."

"He talks of eternity," she cried, "but he can't think ahead an hour at a time. He's got no male heir but there's a harem the size of a small city which he's never used. His wives rot; not a single male child has been fathered by him."

"Some of them were his father's women. You know he won't touch them . . . it would be as bad as sleeping with you."

She ignored the last remark.

"I took charge of the harem; I offered him dark meat, light meat, he didn't respond. He has one woman—what kind of taste is that! What man eats the same meat for thirteen years?"

Ay felt his hands grow cold with anger. "My daughter is worth ten women, and to offer him those Mitannian pigs is like offering fish to a priest. He won't mix his blood with foreigners'.... Besides, it's the latest thing—loyalty to one's chief wife!"

"And do *you* follow this new custom?" she challenged.

"Ah, I'm a traditionalist at heart," he sighed.

She laughed loudly. "And a *foreigner* at heart too, my part-Kushian, part-Khorian brother! Listen—he's got *one* city, *one* woman, *one* god—"

"And, alas, *one mother*," Ay muttered.

"Nefertiti's the cause of it all, *she's*—"

"I forbid you to speak of her!"

*"She's in my way, Ay!"*

"If you harm a hair of her head I'll kill you," he said, and he meant it.

At the end of the courtyard there was a bowl full of burning oil which cast rays of bronze light that danced and intertwined on the surface of the water tank. Tiy moved back and forth like a dark furtive animal between the fire and the water. What a weird inversion of the feminine and the masculine she and her son presented, Ay thought. He couldn't see the game for his concentration on one piece, while she saw the game immediately but refused to recognize its parts. She was lost in generalities; he, in particulars. Then she fingered her severe geometric bracelets and said, "He's sleeping now. Why? Because he fears darkness!"

"We all fear it, we're all children," he countered.

"Do we? Do you and I fear anything? We move equally well in

light and dark, so our strength is doubled." Her voice sounded hollow, coming from somewhere in the blackness at the far reaches of the garden.

"Ay, my brother—*use* the darkness! Join me. Don't sit forever counting stars until your body shrivels up from cold and you go to join the *akhu* in the night sky...."

He didn't answer. He knew what she wanted, and it wasn't merely his loyalty or brotherly love.

She asked him the time and he told her it was the eighth hour of the night. A snake with a woman's head dwelled within that hour. It was fitting, he added, that she had visited him then.

But when the Great Mother left and the gates of the garden closed, he found himself shivering. The stars hung like bright threats above him.

Wanre sank into a deep depression and moved about like a rain cloud between the palace and the temple. Between him and Tiy something dark, almost tangible, had sprung up—like the carcass of a bird long dead, the corpse of an old dream. It was in his eyes when they shifted about nervously and avoided other eyes. It was in Tiy's eyes when they narrowed and widened at the oddest times. It was in everything, the walls of the palace, the floors. It was in the royal bed—an odour, a smell of salt. And Nefertiti, whose face had become dark and closed with pain since the death of her daughter, lay like a stricken thing under his body, whose demands increased as its power decreased. But all other times she felt him drawing away from her, lost in some secret part of himself, nervous and fearful of the slightest thing, living off his own wounds as a hyena lived off carrion. Behind him the plumes of Tiy's tall crown trailed him like spies. Her dark eyes were sharp and watchful, the eyes of a small ferreting animal which burrowed tunnels beneath the earth. She seemed always to be waiting for him to weaken, waiting to seize the right moment to work her will upon him, and often her eyes would turn to Nefertiti, bright with a secret triumph, and she would say, "My dear child, why don't you go into the garden and rest? My son and I have matters to discuss, matters into which—as you used to tell me—it's not *feminine* to inquire."

The people loved puns, and used to say that behind the Window of Appearances on the Great Bridge, Wanre *appeared* to be many things, and *apparently* all his forms were true. There was a small corridor behind the Window which he used as a resting-room, its walls painted with poppies and daisies and cornflowers. Sitting in it, he felt as though he were in some riotous garden suspended between heaven and earth. He often used to stop there in the high field of flowers and drink wine, and stretch his legs out on dark leather cushions studded with blue diamonds.

Once by night three people met in a weird collision in the sky— he and Tiy in the resting-room and Nefertiti, who had gone for a lonely walk on the bridge. Hearing voices ahead of her, she stopped to listen. Tiy's voice, hollow and compelling. "Are you really the Great Seer, my son? The cobra and the vulture on your brow are your Two Eyes—but has the prophecy come to pass and they no longer see?"

Outside, the city slept, caressed by an uneasy wind. North in the sandy spaces were the desert altars visited by jackals and snakes. Lean and hungry forms circled the holy places by night.

Nefertiti drew nearer. A row of flaming lamps lit the corridor within the bridge, but the king and his mother were mere shadows behind a dim blue veil which hung about the resting-room. Her husband's shadow was embraced by bright wings on the arms of his chair, and Tiy's shadow kept moving around it.

"Listen to the wind! It steals everything, it covers everything with sand.... In time it will obscure your city. How dark the night is! Haven't you ever feared it wouldn't end? I know your fears. There are legends of a night long ago when Ra didn't rise at His appointed time—and when at last He rose it was out of the seat of the *west*, and there were fires and floods and earthquakes, and the universe was upside down!"

He knew the legends; he didn't want to recall them. He begged her to stop the torment, and stared ahead into the darkening fields of poppies and cornflowers. Then there was silence in the high garden and Nefertiti saw him shudder with fear—a fear that began deep in his loins and radiated outward like the rings of water around a stone thrown into a pool. How often had she held him like a mother when that terror visited him! Now he was watching the floor where a dizzying design of parallel lines and triangles and small suns shifted, and blurred his sight.

"Some peasants," Tiy went on, "were recently seen conducting forbidden ceremonies at the desert altars; they laid on a pyre the fresh skin of a ram...."

"Impossible, impossible!"

"Your Vizier Nakht has a small statue of Amon concealed in his water closet, my son."

"I beg you, stop. There's no proof."

"I am your mother! I am the proof! Would I lie to you, I ask you, would I lie to you? You must act! The people will turn upon you, scorn you, mock everything you hold sacred, tear the golden arms of the Aton from his shrines and melt them down for bracelets or images of the Ram."

"No, no!"

"Of Min, of Khonsu, of Ptah. They'll parade them about the streets of the city and your temple will be defiled and your name and the name of your god will be a standing joke from here to Ursalim. You'll be laughed at in the camps of the Beduwi, mocked in the palaces of Amor, spat upon in the houses of Kush. And the belly of the empire will quiver and it will be said that a child sits on the throne of the Two Lands with toy temples and a toy god ... whom even his own family mocks in secret!"

"What do you mean, *even his own family?*" he gasped, and got up from the chair.

"I *hate* to be the one to tell you, my son. I know what a shock it will be for you. Your beautiful wife, I always loved her. Your honour hangs in delicate suspension now...."

His face turned chalk white. "Speak, woman, before I tear out your tongue!"

"Wanre, she is prostituting your god. I've known it for a long time. I found a casket full of forbidden charms and amulets in her room—among them was a small statue of Ptah. She's always favoured the doctrine of Men Nofer, even as a young girl. Now she worships him in secret; I know this, I have information."

He leaned against one wall sobbing, "I don't believe it, lies ... it's all lies!"

And Tiy went over to him, slowly, saying, "I know, I know ... better it were her body she sold, better she were a whore!" And when she saw him trembling she held out her dark arms and whispered, "Come burn, little bird, in your nest of fire...."

But he fell forward onto the dizzy floor crying, *"Have no fear, prince, it is the Lady of Dread who assails you!"* as an old musty image of a scavenger bird fell upon him.

Nefertiti heard the Great Mother soothing him, for there were sounds of heavy breathing, salt rustlings of a vulture's wings, pained flapping of a hawk. There was a weeping behind the veil, and a laughter. There were sighs, groans and choking noises, and the two royal ones sat upon the floor like children, or the fallen fragments of an empire. Then Nefertiti could stand it no longer, and burst into the room. "Wanre, she slanders me, don't believe her!" she cried. But Wanre's eyes were rolled up into their sockets and he saw nothing. She turned on Tiy then. "May your hole reek with a hundred abominations!" she hissed. "May your lies become hands to strangle you!" Then she covered her eyes so as not to look upon the foul black bird, which hovered over her husband. She spun around and her dark figure darted down the length of the corridor. Wildly, illogically, she thought of how the city was full of hands, golden ones and brown ones, hands of men and children, hands of the Aton. Then she remembered one pair of hands, industrious and thickly veined, and her feet led her where her mind alone would not have permitted her to go.

The sculptor Thutmose was sleeping on his small cot in his studio surrounded by faces of clay and plaster and stone. Suddenly something awakened him. There was a great wind that night. He balanced himself on one elbow and squinted his eyes in the darkness. Sounds outside, the shuffling of feet. Perhaps only a dog. No, some other noise, contained in the wind. The rapping of small knuckles on the gate in the outer court.

Loath to call his servants at that hour, he went outside and whispered into the wind, "Who is it?" And there was a long silence before he heard the single breathed word, *"I."*

When he opened the gate he might have fainted, but his legs supported him by an act of will. She was a dark figure in the half-light with a black cloak thrown around her body. She did not move, but waited, poised somewhere between heaven and earth, and above her the Woman of Night arched her body of stars. Drawn up to her full height she was slender, regal, more noble in her shame than in her pride, for he knew that shame on some women shone like silver chains. In the eerie light he understood; he saw for the first time the complete image of a queen.

*"Nefertiti, Beautiful Are the Beauties of the Aton, the Beautiful One has come."* He fell on his knees before her, whether by instinct

or sheer loss of strength, he couldn't tell. His mouth kissed the sandal beneath the cloak.

"Close the gates, we will be seen!"

Inside the house a hundred eyes of turquoise and black jasper watched as she took off the cloak and flung it defiantly to the ground. For him it was as though the whole black heavens had collapsed around him, for the cloak had been all that remained between subject and queen, between lie and truth.

"*Give me a form, find me, give me life,*" she whispered, and lay down on his narrow cot. He went to her and his hands drew apart the thin linen gown. Outside, the gates of the garden creaked and trembled.

His hands worked as they were trained to work; they searched her face and throat for the final shape, the flaw. They moved down the length of her taut body, over her breasts and thighs.

"*Give me a form, mould me,*" she breathed.

He wanted to speak but his mouth feared it might be foolish. He was afraid, but she drew him down. His mouth made a trail of small bites and kisses down her flesh, seeking, finding, until beneath him she was the pliable earth, the night, the Black Land, all that was dark and original and unformed.

Even then he was afraid, and his seed might have been trapped within him, had not her body carried him forward like the swell of a sea, and on the crest of one wave he groaned loudly and pulled the thin gold tiara from her head, his fist closing over the royal snake as though to strangle it as the hot blood of love was wrung from his loins.


Before dawn he hid his face in the dark night of her cloak to stop time and delay the Aton's rising. For a moment she let her fingers rest on his black curls. Then without a word she was gone.

He fell into an unreal sleep and woke later to see sunlight shining through the dust particles in the studio until a mist of golden powder hovered about the room. His right fist still kept its grip around the tiara he had wrenched from her head. From it rose the furious head of the royal cobra, rearing back to strike. *The power of immediate death*—that was the meaning of the royal serpent.

Ay's other daughter, Benremut, whom he lovingly called the Ugly One—it was a standing joke that he had sired a gazelle and a scorpion—was usually highly dissatisfied. She was the product of Ay's second marriage, and had for years been the nurse of the royal children, just as her own mother had been Nefertiti's nurse when Ay's first wife died giving birth. She would have gone about totally unnoticed, even shunned, were it not for her two dwarves, who lent her a kind of perverse distinction. She confided all her troubles to the grotesque duo, especially the one called Er Neheh. She loathed her job as Chief Governess of the royal daughters, almost as much as she loathed her half-sister the queen, and made very little secret of the fact. For years she had allowed her various complaints to solidify into pure bitterness—that being easier to handle than the multitude of hurts and disappointments. She was unmarried, and according to her father, that was the source of all her troubles. In his opinion unmarried women were disgusting creatures, for the sweet place between their thighs became in time a goblet of poison whose bitter waters seeped through the whole body and finally soured the heart. Benremut tried to imagine herself married—to the king, for instance. Ugh! To have to sleep with the freak! Those bloated thighs upon her in the night, that fearful face in her neck! She took comfort in the fact that such was the price Nefertiti had paid for becoming queen.

When she was not in public with her dwarves, she was in her bedroom brooding into several mirrors at once or pulling an ivory comb through her hair, guiding it like the teeth of some vicious animal which raked her scalp in search of delicious morsels. She had the world's most complicated bedroom; it was packed with an assortment of useless articles—old cosmetic jars whose contents had caked like mud-flats in the heat of summer, empty flasks, knick-knacks enough to make one's head swim, animal figurines, toothless combs, broken mirrors, heaps of unused textiles, punctured cushions with their feathers falling out (she stabbed them with needles in her tantrums), assorted rugs, empty *kohl* tubes, wigs lying helter-skelter like weird female war trophies, trinkets, baubles, pieces of glass....

And on a table just beside her bed she kept a very odd article whose value was rather hard to determine. It was a white fish carved in ivory, a nice fat little fish with smooth contours and a lovely thick-lipped mouth. Nothing else lay on the particular table. She told people she was sentimentally attached to it, it was lucky, and so on. A few, however, had their own theories about its purpose.

Ay rued the day he made her. She had his face, for one thing, and while his face was quite fine on him, he felt it was less flattering on a woman. However, her dwarves consoled her, and one morning Benremut was visited by her three-foot-high "vizier," who shivered and slobbered with agitation and was quite unable to speak. She asked what troubled her sweet freak, but he danced wildly about the room knocking over stools and footrests in his frenzy. She combed her hair so hard that sparks issued from it and she bristled with frustration when she shook her mirror in his direction and demanded he stop on pain of going without dinner that night. He cowered in a corner. "Speak up!" she said. And the dwarf's long arms dangled down between his gangly little legs. Deflated, he shook his head from side to side. "Speak, or I'll be angry with you, I'll take away your new collar—you wouldn't like that, would you?" Er Neheh raised his mournful liquid eyes to her, then bumbled his way across the floor until he stood beside her chair, his head on a level with her waist. From deep inside his throat came a gurgling and choking—"I saw, I saw—" and she sneered, "I'm glad you can *see*, not everyone can see! And *what* did you see, my vizier?"

And what had he seen? Ah, when she heard the name of her sister the queen, and what and where, and when, the last sparks from the comb bristled in the quiet air and she put down her mirror and leaned over her dwarf's head and patted the bald spot like a mother. Her eyes were wide and a smile played about her red mouth as she took from her jewel box a thick bracelet of gold.

"You've always liked this, haven't you, Er Neheh? Because it's got a carving of your dwarf-god Bes on it. Very well, it's yours." But as his thick fingers reached for it she drew it back sharply. "On one condition, my vizier, I give you this for your silence—do you understand?" He nodded ecstatically. "One word, though, and it comes back to me together with your arm. *Two* words and there will be *no Er Neheh* to wear it!"

Then Benremut sat alone, feeling fat with knowledge; she thought about something her father had once told her. "Knowledge," he'd said, *"is power. Knowledge unshared by others is power. Select well the one who will receive your knowledge, there is wealth in that."* She turned what she knew over and over in her mind like an uncut jewel, watching the light play upon it, revealing first this side, then another. Its possibilities were limitless. No good jeweller ever cut a gem without first spending hours discovering its natural planes.

Later that day she saw Nefertiti standing with Meritaton on the high terrace of the garden amid the little maze of irrigation channels. Unable to resist the temptation, she went to her and heaved a long sigh. "Ah, Nefertiti, what a night it was! The wind, I never heard it howl so in my life! Did you hear it?"

"The wind, no, I can't say I heard the wind ... I must have slept quite soundly."

Benremut smiled. "Truly, sister, I never heard it roar so. I trembled in bed! Why, one of the servants told me this morning that the place where it blew strongest was to the north of the palace. Isn't that odd? They say it fairly roared around the north end, close to where the sculptors have their studios—imagine! And the *corner house* was almost blown down."

Only Benremut could have translated the swift expression that came over Nefertiti's face as one of terror. Then the queen laughed. "Strange indeed, Benremut, that the wind should suddenly choose to blow more in one place than another!" She watched her half-sister's face closely.

"Yes, it's probably some kind of joke," said Benremut, and bowed with an exaggerated politeness.

After she had gone Nefertiti stood with her daughter and gazed down at the shadowy *tekhen*. *The wind, and all night the creaking of the gate.* She draped an arm over Meritaton's narrow shoulders as though it were the girl, not herself, who needed protection then. And the two of them looked down, watching the sharp blade of shadow cut across the grass.

Not long after, Benremut told her father what she knew. She'd rehearsed the words a thousand times in her mind, savouring them. "On the night of the great wind, my dwarf Er Neheh saw Nefertiti leaving the house of the sculptor Thutmose just before dawn."

It took all of Ay's self-control to refrain from thrashing her black and blue. "How long have you known?" he shouted. "Have you kept it to yourself?"

"Oh, Father, there I was with all that *knowledge* weighing down on me, alone with it, trying to decide whether to tell anyone or not. I was in an agony of indecision. I suffered! Then I decided to tell you; after all, she's your daughter."

"She is also the queen," Ay reminded her. "Did you consider that?"

"Oh, I've always *considered* it. In fact, it was because of that that I kept it a secret a whole week."

Ay marvelled at the two girls he had sired—one a beauty, the other a nightmare. Someone had once told him they were the two extremes of himself. "How you must have gloated over it!" he cried. "Keeping it hidden, bringing it out every so often to play with like a new toy!"

"But a valuable toy, you must admit. Your precious Nefertiti sleeping like a common whore with—"

*"Daughter of Set!"*

"But that only makes *you* the demon, Father!"

"I've got to think," he mumbled, pacing up and down the floor and reminding himself of Tiy in her distracted moments.

Benremut crossed her legs daintily and popped a grape into her mouth.

"Who else knows?" he demanded.

"My little vizier, but he's not talking."

"I don't trust you, the tongue in your mouth is a snake in its hole."

"I don't blame you. I'm probably not trustworthy. You reared me on stories of your damned old demons—Shadow-Eater and Bone-Breaker and Stinking-Face and Knife-Eyed.... Should I be a good little girl after such an upbringing?"

"I gave you a good liberal education," he said. "I want you to swear to me you've told no one."

"Will you remember your little Benremut when the time comes?"

"When *what* time comes?"

"When you sit on the throne of the Two Lands and I am the royal heiress, of course."

"Do you think I want the crown, silly fool?"

"To have it is simpler than you imagine. Tiy is your sister, and she's the queen."

"Nefertiti is queen!"

*"Not after this she isn't."*

Ay clutched his head to stop it from blowing off.

"Knowledge is power, Father, but this is a wild animal; you'll have to keep it on a leash to stop it from clawing you and everyone else...."

Ay sank into a couch and watched the flames from the brazier rise higher and higher. After a while he calmed down, thinking things weren't so bad because no one else knew. But then Benremut laughed and said something which he heard from a great distance.

"I'm sorry, I lied. This morning I told Tiy."

He was scarcely aware of his open hand when it slapped her mouth.


That night Wanre combed the palace looking for his wife, but she seemed to have disappeared. It was only when the first rays of the god cut through the night and he went out to the terraces of the garden that he saw her standing in a trance. She was waiting, quietly; she had passed the whole freezing night without moving.

"Nefruaton, what have you done to me?" he whispered.

And looking up, her voice a cold monotone, she replied, "I waited all night for the sun, and now you have come."

He crossed the terrace and fell at her feet, his head in the dark wet morning grass, his body given over to great sobs. He felt no anger—only the pained incomprehension of a child who could not admit the reality of error, who believed suffering to be some gross mistake which would surely right itself. But the minutes passed and no miracle came; the nightmare did not end.

"My god was in you, He was in us, *we were one!*" he wept into the earth at her feet.

"My Sun, don't fall at my feet, it is I who should fall at yours!"

He got up and wiped the strands of wet grass from his clothes. He told her she would go into exile in the North Palace and the people could interpret her departure as they wished. While she was away, he would pray and await the blessed voice of the god who would in time reveal to him the reason for this strange "mistake." Then he caught her wrist in a painful grip and asked, "Who does Thutmose worship?"

"No one, Wanre. His hands."

Before she left she saw him in the temple, pouring holy water upon the altar. It was as though the sacred fluid of his own body was running out and he was giving up the last drop of himself in a horrible meaningless sacrifice. Close by him stood the Great Mother. He embraced his wife and a libation of tears fell on her neck, and the temple singers sang, *"Nefertiti who sends the Aton to rest with a sweet voice, Nefertiti whose two beautiful hands hold the sistrums.... May she live and flourish forevermore."*

Tiy smiled a dark smile of triumph as the three of them descended the white ramp.

Ay begged Nefertiti to open her heart and tell him what had driven her to her indiscretion. She replied with a coarse joke about how, if a woman wished to fall, there was always a man to fall upon her. Her attitude infuriated him and he tried to wring the truth from her. "Did Wanre ill-treat you?" he asked.

"No," she said. "Come to me in the North Palace in a few months and I'll tell you a riddle."

"I don't want riddles!" he shouted, but she was silent.

The day she left, Wanre saw the skies darkened once again by the sand winds. The same dirty veil which had formed when Tiy had first sailed into the Horizon formed again over the face of the Aton. The day stood out in his memory for years after, sharp as a tomb relief. The day of her exile. No one thought of it in such strong terms; it was generally assumed she was going on a prolonged vacation to the North Palace for reasons of her health, for what other purpose could the pleasure palace serve, with its pools and aviaries? Only a few knew the truth. She took the boy Tutankhaton with her, whom she had always favoured as heir to the throne, her daughter Ankhespaaton to whom he was betrothed, and the three younger daughters. Only the eldest child Meritaton remained behind, frightened, sensing something.

He remembered the scene so well he loathed the accuracy of his memory. She held onto the thin rail of the chariot, the wind in her gown (there had always been wind in her gown), her head held high and proud, though he detected a slight quivering about the mouth.

When she left the palace walls she looked back only once, and her gaze was as penetrating as the gaze of a wild bird. Perhaps she knew she would never return. It was such a short distance to the North Palace—a mere day's outing, yet it might as well have been a sea journey.

He looked out one night into the empty garden and a line from the writings of the sage PtahHotep ran through his mind. *"A thousand men are undone for the enjoyment of one moment like a dream."*


Not long afterwards, Thutmose called his friend Hatiay into his studio to watch him finish Nefertiti's portrait. He painted in the last bit of colour on the lips. He inlaid the right eye. Hatiay's sleek greyhound snuffled around the studio, knocking over things, but Thutmose was unconcerned. He was just about to insert the second crystal eye into the wax when he stopped suddenly, remembering something. He ran his fingers over the finished eye, the unfinished eye, and then very slowly and deliberately put down his tools.

"*The flaw,*" he said. "There it is. Leave it."

His friend asked him what he meant, but Thutmose only smiled. Then a fiendish humour possessed him and he recited an old magical spell which peasants used to place beside their dead to ensure the Ferryman's consent to ferry the dead across the great river. "*Thou uncircumcised one,*" he laughed, "*leave the road free for me. I am the Great Male looking for the Great Female!*"

His friend stared at him as though he had gone quite mad. Thutmose apologized for himself and asked Hatiay to leave him alone. A few moments later he stood on a chair and fastened a thick noose about his neck. "One eye watching, the other eye blind," he whispered. "Nefer Nefruaton, I have attained the unattainable."

The beautiful flawed face watched him as he kicked the chair out from under him and, after one great jerk, hung suspended in mid-air.

That same afternoon a child peered into his window and saw the corpse. Someone sent word back to the palace, and Wanre hurried out alone to Thutmose's house, where he found the police chief Mahu with a handful of men kicking open the front gate of the villa. He ran with them down the halls until they reached the door of the studio, where Mahu applied his huge shoulder once, twice, until it gave way. They almost fell inside the room, and at the same moment a cloud of golden dust rose into the air, so strong was the light.

In front of them a pair of naked feet dangled, slowly turning this way and that.

"Cut him down!" cried Mahu, and the body of the sculptor was carefully lowered to the floor. The rope with which he'd hung himself had cut deeply into his throat. His eyes stared at Wanre in the mad mockery of death; they held his gaze longer than any man had ever been able to hold it. *"Maat, Met, Truth and Death, how similar the two words sound,"* Parennufer had said.

"I wonder why on earth he had to punish himself?" Mahu was muttering, but Wanre wasn't listening. He was staring at a shelf in one corner of the room. Upon it was the bust of his wife, dazzlingly beautiful, one-eyed, flawed. He went over to it and ran his fingers down the cheek, the curved neck, the still mouth. He seemed to hear her whisper, *"Here* is my self, my Sun!" For a moment he felt he would faint. She could not be in two places at once, she could not be more than one person at once, no one could.

He saw the second eye lying on the shelf beside her, and wanted to pick it up and insert it, but dared not.

After the body was taken away he ordered the entrance to the villa bricked up. It was never reopened, for he forbade anyone to enter, terrified someone might see her there. The treasures were never removed, and just before the last window was blocked, sunlight shone through the dust particles in the air, and time itself hung suspended in a million small golden worlds above her head. Then, amid a hundred eyes of turquoise and black jasper, one crystal eye watched the golden dust gather, year after year after year.

For the rest of the thirteenth year Tiy shaded her son from pain, from the sun, from himself. He lost his taste for playing hounds and jackals, although once or twice he invited Ay to a listless game of Senet. He was so distracted, however, that he couldn't even concentrate on one piece, let alone the whole board. Tiy would stand over them and deliver her nightly lecture on the state of his health, referring to him constantly in the third person, for he wasn't really there. "He hasn't slept for nights, he's thin and shrunken. Ay, don't you agree he's thin and shrunken? The headaches have come back and the vomiting and that *awful* noise in his head. I haven't seen him like this since he was a boy. He's not sick, he says. Just depressed. Poor dear. I wish he'd eat, food always helps. He chides me for my concern, I tell him he's careless about his *health*. Poor baby. Look, his chest is caving in again and he's going to fall into one of his dreadful glooms. I can't bear it. Oh, look, Ay's just captured another piece!"

When she became insupportable he would summon the boy Smenkhare and place a sad arm around his shoulders and ask him what he had learned that day. This made Tiy furious. He started to call the boy *Nefer Nefruaton,* and in the summer palace of Meru Aton he erased the name of Nefertiti.

the ninth hour of the night

The fourteenth year was a year of death. Three died, their deaths as violent and strange as the storms of rain that sometimes crashed through the narrow wadis in the cliffs.

The first was the architect Hatiay, most beloved of all Wanre's artists ... the man who designed the city.

He gave his king a monthly report on the progress of the northern suburb, and the news was grim. "Due to the failure of certain noblemen to take up residence in the estates laid out for them," he read, "the architectural plans for the suburb are not proceeding as scheduled. Of the three hundred houses, only a fraction are occupied and the central area is almost completely unpopulated. Also, due to the wadi which runs from the desert to the river, a large area is flooded two months out of every year. Also, the poor are building their hovels over the rubbish pits and obstructing the workers. Also, since many of the noblemen who ordered estates built have decided to remain in the old capital, the contractors will be forced to—"

"Enough!" interrupted the king. "If the owners of the villas want to stay *there*, that's their loss, isn't it? *Isn't it?*"

Hatiay went on. "The waste is appalling. Many of the private wells on the empty estates are not in use—countless poor are forced to live close to the river for water, which shouldn't be necessary...."

And Wanre said, as Hatiay had known he would, that the poor would be allowed to use the wells of the rich, and meanwhile the gorgeous villas could go to ruin for all he cared, but as he spoke his eyes travelled north and saw the exquisite chapels and private altars yellowed by the piss of dogs, and rubbish piling up around the sun-shrines in the gardens.

Hatiay went home and did nothing for a full month but sit with his greyhound on the roof of his magnificent house in the northern suburb, drink wine, and talk to himself and the dog for hours on end. He erased Akhenaton's name from the lintel at the gates of his house, leaving only the names of Nefertiti and the Aton. One night he invited his artist friend Bek over for an evening of (as he put it) "unparalleled entertainment," and Bek found him on the roof, gazing out over the tops of the villas of the northern suburb.

"Bek, do you realize this city is a lie?" he asked.

His friend shuffled about uneasily. "You've scratched out the name of the king from your gates, I saw it coming in. Why?"

"The king is a lie."

"And when did you come to this conclusion?"

"Quite recently. I'm not the only one. The northern city and suburb are crawling with rumours. Haven't you heard? People are asking what Nefertiti's doing in the North Palace. They think she fell out of the king's favour by embracing false gods. They're dividing into two camps—one with her, the other with him. The city is broken in half; there's a stink in the air. I smell it, I sit here with my dog and smell it."

"You smell something because you sit in the company of an animal, my friend," sighed Bek.

"Don't insult my dog! Me you can insult, him, no. He's more intelligent than all of us put together." He patted the beast on the head. "You know, when Wanre erased the queen's name in Meru

Aton I straight away erased his from my gates. Then I bumped into It Neter Ay somewhere in the palace and asked him what protest *he* made. He couldn't support the accusation in my eyes, for he just turned away. *So blood is not thicker than water for you, eh?* I called after him."

Bek and Hatiay stared out in silence over the northern suburb. Far off were the walls of Nefertiti's palace, too far to see, yet that was all they saw.

"She sleeps out there. The Beautiful One," he said. "Thutmose was my friend, I knew him well."

Bek pretended not to understand what he meant, but Hatiay would have none of it. "Oh come, Bek! You don't think I'm so naive as to think she simply embraced false gods! All right, I know it's a palace secret . . . but as I say, I knew Thutmose well. Did you ever see the portrait? Ah, you did—I can tell by your eyes! *The flaw,* I heard him say, *leave it.*"

"Flaw, what flaw?" Bek asked. "I saw it in a very early stage, there were a hundred flaws then. . . ."

"No, I mean the final one. The great mistake, the imperfection which makes all things real. The king, the city. . . ."

Bek was getting nervous. He felt he was on the verge of some horrible argument with his friend, and asked for some wine to change the subject.

Hatiay laughed, and lightly began talking about his various misadventures with courtesans, as he summoned his servant girl to pour the wine. "One was a foreign girl," he chatted. "She smelled of all kinds of alien herbs and oils. She didn't know that hair was unfashionable, so I gave her money and told her to have it all removed; I think she understood what I meant. Anyway, she taught me to say *Hello* and *Goodbye* in her tongue and I in turn taught her some spicy and inappropriate greetings in mine! I wonder how she fared after that in the streets chirping what she thought were 'friendly' greetings to the young men. But can you imagine what she did to me? I had a severe blow to my pride when once I greeted a visiting ambassador with what I thought was 'Hello,' and he turned and smacked me in the face! What did that imp teach *me*?"

Bek thought that his friend's mood was uncommonly light, but listened on.

"And another time, Bek, I ended up in the bed of a particularly fat creature who talked the whole time I was on her about an orange grove back home in her beloved somewhere or other. I was so exhausted I fell asleep on top of her before I finished, and only awoke when she gave a great animal heave and turned me onto the floor. I got to my feet crying, *Earthquake, earthquake!* and she threw a huge wig basket at my head and sent me out into the night. Then I made a vow to stay away from whores, you see, and stick to my own servants. I even entertained the outrageous idea of sleeping with only one of them. It is, after all, the latest fashion—one god, one woman, one Wanre...."

Hatiay looked at the stopper on the great wine jug beside his couch. "Year something or other, Amenhotep. A very bad year. Nevertheless, a very good wine." As the lovely servant girl tipped the jug and poured some of the wine for Bek, Hatiay patted his dog fondly and gazed quizzically at his friend. "You'll go on forever, won't you, Bek—creating beautiful images and portraits and sculptures for Wanre.... When you die the Lords of Heaven will no doubt commission you to do their portraits, and you'll spend eternity in some celestial studio with your clay and your paints...."

"It's a delight to be an artist in these times," Bek replied. "You know that. I love my work. I used to be a mere copier, drawing the trite designs of my predecessors, until Wanre showed me how to free my spirit and draw and paint and sculpt in Truth!"

"You still believe the *Truth* business, eh?" sighed Hatiay. "Well, I don't. I have an errand for you, my friend. When you go back to him, tell him the northern city and suburb are very unhappy. Tell him his former servant Hatiay who loved him—yes, who *loved* him—has gone to meet his *ka*. Tell him his *ka* wants to design other cities, elsewhere...."

Open-mouthed, Bek watched him summon the servant girl and lower her by the arm to the divan. "You will lie with me," he ordered. "You will do it well, when you feel me reaching my end you will hasten me—do you understand?"

"Hatiay, what on earth—"

"It's none of your business. You can turn your back if you like. But this is my last request—stay and witness the innocence of the girl. Take care of my dog, will you?"

Then without further preliminaries he mounted the servant girl. Bek's stomach turned over with fear and unbelief and he was rooted to the spot. As he and the greyhound stared out into the night sky Hatiay took her. Bek heard their breathing, and it was the breathing of a dying city. At one point he heard Hatiay whisper hoarsely, *"Not now, little fool—move away, move away!"*

The stars were descending like dagger tips to the earth. Then there was a shriek. Bek wheeled around, and Hatiay was balanced on his knees and hands over the girl, his face turned up to heaven like that of a great dog braying at the moon. His cry had been the cry of ecstasy; it was also the cry of death. As his seed fell, so his blood. Blood ran down his belly, dripped onto the frozen body of the girl beneath him.

"I didn't do it!" she shrieked. "He grabbed his knife at the last minute and did it himself!" and she rolled out from under him and a moment later his limp body sagged onto the divan.

Bek took her away and returned to the palace. He summoned the police. He told the king. His mind was a whirlpool and he remembered little of what had happened, his only clear recollection being that during the whole scene the greyhound had sat on its haunches, motionless, staring at stars. He took the sad beast home to his villa and tried to care for it, but it died within a week of its master.

Hatiay had been right about the split of loyalty among the citizens of the Horizon. After his death the people of the north city and suburb, disgruntled and confused, decided that he too had embraced forbidden gods and been cast out of the king's favour. The number of devout worshippers of the Aton dwindled and artisans seized the opportunity to get rich by making little caricatures of the king—one was a toy chariot drawn by monkeys with a driver who had a long idiotic face. Little amulets, trinkets and charms began to appear slowly in the city, and some adventurous souls even began manufacturing cheap pendants in the images of Amon or Ptah. These were sold and circulated furtively in the northern city. In the marketplace people swore by the lesser deities—"By Bast, pay me what you owe, you thief!" How much easier it was to swear by the old gods! How, after all, might a man swear by the very Sun, Giver of Life and Supreme God of the Universe, that he had been cheated in a sale of chickpeas?

Soon the north city and suburb split from the main city and the Teaching, and the people turned their eyes towards the queen, whom they believed was in exile for leading a welcome rebellion against the worship of the Aton. An incredible ceremony took place one night in the streets; some drunkards put together a makeshift image of an obscene god with the face and feet of a pig, wearing the crown of Osiris, and paraded the abomination through the streets crying, "O Dwarf! Monkey-Face! Fall, O flames! Woe, fire! Hail—Baboon!" Then they set fire to the disgusting effigy and danced and got more drunk around the flames.

Those surrounding the king went out of their way to demonstrate their loyalty to him in a hundred little significant acts. Ay made a point of letting himself be seen in the temple, praying loudly and clumsily in a chapel, or lustrating himself rigorously in one of the sacred pools. It was only by night when he wrote pleading letters to his daughter begging her to tell him what had led to her downfall, knowing full well he'd get no answer, that an old sickening guilt would creep up his spine. His wife refused to let him sleep with her, demanding to know why he hadn't gone into exile with his own flesh and blood. She aggravated him in a dozen other ways until life became a torment, and he twice moved out of his villa to take up residence in the army barracks—only to move back home again, preferring her cold silence to the chilling loneliness he felt among the men. Afraid to be alone with his thoughts, he submerged himself in philosophy.

*Be not light, for you are weighty. Speak not falsehood, for you are the balances. Swerve not, for you are a correct sum. Lo, you are one with the balances!*

But his contemplative spirit was crushed when his unhappy wife told him he was just like the title of that book—*an eloquent peasant*. He started advising the young soldiers never to marry unless they wished to become wretched vegetables who preferred their hell to their freedom.

When some months had passed and he still hadn't heard from his daughter, he decided he was not a correct sum, nor was he one with the balances. A day came when the scales rocked like boats in a whirlpool and Maat was no more.

His private messenger, who was really a spy—such a secret one, though, that he himself scarcely knew who he was—told him that Nefertiti spent her days behind the walls of the North Palace and saw no one. She had a pet gazelle and had been seen with it when she went out on the first day of each month to the desert altars. On those occasions she had been accompanied by a single guard. She hadn't been known to communicate with anyone.

Ay rode out north, alone on New Year's day. The breath of Set, the sickening south wind whose damp heat turned men into criminals and women into shrews, had begun to blow slow and foul. The Nile started to bloat and swell and a myriad insects slept within their eggs, waiting to be born and flourish in the tumid summer heat. Sweat ran into his eyes and his hands shook with nausea as he came upon the desert altars, standing like ruins of a small ancient city. He waited half the morning and was just about to leave when a dust cloud in the distance announced her arrival. The ill wind sang between the dunes, and gradually he made out her small chariot. When she stepped down she looked like some young desert girl lost from her tribe.

"Nefruaton," he whispered, from his place behind an altar. She came beside him and greeted him in a voice dull and heavy as the air.

"For months I've asked after you, why didn't you write?" he cried.

"I don't write lately, it tires my eyes," she answered in the same flat tone.

"Don't mock me, I've only come to see you."

"It is forbidden."

"No one saw me come. Is there no way I can restore you to favour?" he cried. "Tell me everything. . . . Who led you to this disgrace?"

But she laughed at him lightly and said, "Don't you realize, Father, that your sister is in favour now? There was never room for the two of us."

"Tiy," he said, throwing off the name as a bothersome triviality, "is getting old. She's respected because of her age."

Again the laughter, mocking this time. "*Only* because of her age? Are you blind too, like everyone else in the palace? Do you not know what she plans?—to reduce Wanre to a shivering idiot, a child, a fool. . . ."

He felt a chill in his spine. His horse hopped and danced in the sand which boiled beneath its hooves. "What do you mean?"

"Perhaps I shouldn't say more."

"What do you *mean*?"

"She works on him secretly, from the inside; she strikes at places no one else can see—his doubts, his darkest fears, she knows where they lie...." Nefertiti went forward and patted the horse, letting her delicate fingers trail down the long sleek head. "Let me ask you a riddle," she said. "What is the beast that draws its breast over the mouth of the king when he is a child? And extends its wings around him when he dies?"

"The vulture!" replied Ay. "The Divine Mother. Why these silly questions?"

"That's what he fears, Father. That's what will destroy him."

They stood apart in silence a long time, then Nefertiti turned to leave.

"Wait—you've told me nothing!" he cried.

She turned back once and whispered, "She slandered me, Father; *she* told Wanre I embraced forbidden gods...."

Stung by a fly, the horse shied back. *"No!"* Ay cried.

"Oh yes, Father, *yes*."

He mounted the horse and bolted away from her, wild with impatience to get back to the palace. His hair and eyes were full of sand and he felt at war with the obscene breath of Set. It was an insane ride; he kept spurring the beast on, then reining it in until it was frantic. He screamed all the while to the yellow sands and the cliffs, "Monstrous, monstrous! What the god commands is that which happens, therefore live in the midst of *quiet*! Establish wisdom by QUIET SPEECH!" he roared, and once or twice he thought he heard the stone cliffs roar back.

It was night when he crossed the corridor to Tiy's private apartments. Hearing voices inside, he stopped and peered through a slit between the great panels of the door. Tiy was sitting on her sumptuous bed talking to her son, whose back was turned to her as he

215

gazed out the night window towards the river. When he turned around his face was pale as death.

"You would like to be immortal, wouldn't you?" she was saying. And slowly she uncrossed her strong brown legs and whispered, "But would you dare?"

Something hung in the air between them, a nameless shapeless dark like the dark of a vulture's wings. Wanre passed a hand over his brow to wipe away the sweat; his body swayed with dizziness, nausea.

"You believe yourself to be your own creator, don't you?" she said, searching his eyes. "You think you created yourself from your own seed, like Ra."

"Thus did the Lord of Heaven create Himself!" he cried. "But no man has done likewise, not even Pharaoh!"

Ay felt the palms of his hands sweat, trembled from head to foot, and leaned against the door for support. Nefertiti had been right; how well Tiy knew where to find the child within the man! How long had she held the child in her talons?

"Ah, but you *think* of yourself as Ra!" she pressed. "Bull of His mother, the Self-Created, the great bird enveloping Himself in His own flames and springing forth reborn from the ashes! Don't you? Weren't you always determined to prove yourself *fatherless*?"

He sat on a couch, exhausted, his face in his hands. She watched him a long while, then her voice changed and her tone became suddenly airy and light. "You must forgive me, my darling! Women are strange creatures!" And she laughed gaily, a metallic tinkle no one had heard for a long time. "They move about in a constant flurry, you know. Once every lunar month their minds take leave of them—sometimes never to return! They're so easily swayed, poor things—so like clay in the hands of an artist.... Oh, excuse me! I meant to say, so vulnerable to flattery. Why even I, my dear, am still like clay in the hands of a flatterer. You won't mind if I loosen my dress a little, it's so dreadfully stifling in here. Yes, as I was saying ... those common artists, such worthless peasants they are. They lack morals, the lot of them. You were wrong to encourage them to experiment with new arts, my son. Why I remember once that *my* sculptor, Auta... well, never mind....

"Ah, that's better; it's good to feel the air on my skin. Tell me, do you still think I'm a handsome woman, my son? No, seriously. I wonder if I'm still, shall we say, desirable? You don't know! What do you mean you don't know! Oh don't fade away again! I was merely asking you if you found me attractive. Now your poor mother is pleading with you to flatter her—how can she survive without it? Oh dear, I can't bear it when you *fade away* like that. Try to stay awake, I want to distract you from your griefs and worries. Now, what were we saying?"

Ay tried to bring himself to consider the idea Tiy was intimating behind each careful word. It was an abomination, a travesty of nature, the very thought of which made the heart pall. It was an overturning of the universe, and Maat.

"Ah yes. Well, I know my breasts aren't as firm as they once were, but they do have a kind of heavy grace. They swing, like broad palm leaves in a breeze.... Neferkheprure, where are you going? You're not leaving!"

Ay barely had time to hide behind a pillar as the door opened and Wanre slipped out. Quickly, silently, he went down the corridor, and then all was silent. Ay returned to the door, and saw Tiy's hand reach up to snuff out the last light in the room. He waited, ten minutes, half an hour, his brow pouring with sweat. Then he gently pushed the door open and stepped inside the room.

At first he saw nothing. Then, silver moonbeams allowed him to make out the shapes in the room. He saw Tiy lying in the bed, face up. He prowled around her, hands behind his back, feigning interest in a dozen dim trivial objects, sniffing them out. He felt as though he were inspecting a stable.

She had not seen him; she had sunk into one of her rare deep sleeps. "Do you wonder why I'm here?" he asked, looking towards the bed where she lay, heavy and highly perfumed, held together by strange arts, her skin stealing the sheen of youth by means of a hundred exotic oils and lotions. Beneath the layer of scent was a smell of sweat, unmistakable. Like a hunter, he imagined he smelled fear.

"If there was ever anyone in this filthy place who lived in Truth," he whispered, "it was my daughter!"

He approached the bed.

"She alone had the right to wear white robes in the temple and stand innocent beneath the god; she harboured none of the thousand evils you carried into the holy places!"

Tiy had begun to stir in her sleep. Slowly her eyes opened. He stood directly above her and she stared at him, dazed. His eyes fell upon the plaque of the Disc behind the bed, and then a great cry welled up from deep within him.

"Living in Truth! *Ankh em Maat!*"

It was the sound of the last word that guided his hands towards her neck where they dug into the soft flesh, searching for the pulsing cord that was their prey. She made no sound save one almost funny little sigh like that of a child. Then she was dead.

He drew back and tore off his gloves. His eyes fastened on the metal plaque of the Aton with its yearning arms. Wanre's glorious and unreal god. An impulse made him go and touch the disc with his naked fingers. A shock went through him; he remembered something. At the same moment he was aware of someone behind him. He knew, even before he spun around, that it was the king.

He had stepped out of the shadow of the doorway where he must have been for some time. They stared wordlessly at each other for what seemed like hours. Ay realized suddenly, with a sharp pain, that he loved him, that he always had. Wanre's eyes were feverishly bright, then they changed into a dark calm and then to something almost like humility. His face seemed to be at rest for the first time in many years. It was as though the vulture no longer gripped the child; in death her talons had relaxed, dropping to earth the man.

"How long were you in the doorway?" Ay asked.

"Many years, It Neter."

"What did you see?"

"Everything."

Wanre's eyes searched him for a long time, then he revised his answer slowly, deliberately. "*Nothing.* The Great Mother Tiy died in her sleep." Then he went over to the bed, and for a moment his legs gave way and he crumbled and dropped to the floor, and buried his head in the sweet-smelling sheets. But the moment passed, and he got up and went near to Ay, and Ay was afraid he would touch him and he'd feel again the shock of flesh against metal.

"I give you my silence, It Neter," he breathed. "I will not reveal what I saw tonight. But I do this in return for something else . . . something you must promise to give me in the future. I will give you one last command one day, and you must obey it. Let us be each other's balances. Swear it!"

Ay nodded, scarcely able to breathe.

"*Swear it*, by whatever is holy to you!"

"By Maat I swear it."

Wanre smiled sadly. "*You* force me to respect you. How strange that the oath of an unbeliever rings so true." He looked again to the body of Tiy; great red welts had appeared on her neck. "*Why?*" he asked.

"Nefertiti was innocent; Tiy poisoned you against her. . . . She worshipped no other gods in secret, as you thought."

Wanre's eyes grew wild and he covered his face with his hands. "I'll go to the temple," he moaned. "I'll ask my Father to forgive me, I'll ask Him to speak to me. But sometimes He is silent, Ay, *silent as death*, and I am alone!"

Ay put a hand on the king's forearm, where the names of the god were strapped to his flesh. "Wanre, *you* are the temple," he whispered. In saying that, he had made a confession of love which would haunt him to the end of his days, and he was not sorry. For a moment he found himself considering something he had never framed in words before—the fact that Wanre had always confided to him his innermost *fears*, not his thoughts. He wondered what relevance that had to the present moment.

"Father of the Horse, *Father*," Wanre whispered. Then for some reason he took Ay's knife and went over to the bed and cut off a lock of Tiy's black hair, and gave it to him without a word.

Foul Set still breathed on the river, its breath full of noxious evils and crimes. Tiy's death brought the flood and a myriad insects and the tumid summer in its wake.

Her body was sent back to the old capital, for she had never expressed any wish to be buried in the Horizon. A golden shrine protected her coffin, one which Wanre had had made for her in his early years on the throne. She rested, surrounded by the dead Lords of the Two Lands in the great valley between the western cliffs. Hathor's shrine was upon those peaks, and the demon called the Lover of Silence dwelt close by. Ay was sure she would be happy there.

The land trembled from somewhere deep within. One night Wanre dreamed he saw a dwarf, and Parennufer told him sadly that such a dream could only mean that his life was to be severed in half.

One day Wanre summoned Ay and told him simply, "In the name of heaven, ride out to the North Palace and bring her back!"

Ay ran to his chariot.

But several hours later Wanre and Meritaton were standing on the top terrace of the garden, and they saw Ay staggering towards them like a drunkard, his eyes glazed and his breathing tortured. Then all in one breath he spoke.

"My Sun, the Great Wife Nefertiti, Living and Flourishing forevermore, Nefer Nefruaton, Beautiful Are the Beauties of the Aton—is dead. She hung herself this morning from a golden cord."

And then the only sound was the single piercing shriek of the princess Meritaton—a shriek so shrill it made the garden faint. All the flowers the king ever held in his hands died in that moment and the grass turned black and cold.

Akhenaton fell without a sound beside the *tekhen*.

She was buried in the royal tombs in the Orient Cliffs; a great scarab was placed over her heart. A single prayer to the Aton lay in the coffin with her, for there was no longer any Underworld or Judgment. Her *ba* was to float and fly through the bright streets of the Horizon forever.

the tenth hour of the night

In the tenth hour of the night, according to the ancient books, there are four lakes and in them three kinds of men—the Swimmers, the Floaters and the Submerged. In the fifteenth regnal year few were swimmers battling the currents of events; most were floaters riding the waters and waiting to see which way they would be led, and many were already drowned. The king, though, was a submerged swimmer, for he always swam, no matter how the depths dragged him down. He swam underwater like a fish and his movements were hidden from sight.

When Tiy died it had been like the passing of a thundercloud, but the death of Nefertiti shook the land to its foundations. She had been the shadow which lingered behind him, giving depth to his Teaching and form to his chaos. Her presence had somehow made everything real. Now, without her, both he and his god stood suddenly stark and sterile, living yet not alive, brilliant yet two-dimensional and flat as tomb reliefs. The people stubbornly believed that she had suffered and died in an attempt to turn him back to the old gods. At last their anger turned directly against him—not only in the north city as before, but everywhere in the land.

One night a well-to-do merchant gathered some of his close friends for a party, and at the height of the festivities he got some paint and a big brush and painted a grotesque red phallus on the Aton's disc where once the sacred cobra had been. Only a few years before he had reverently called in the same group of friends to watch the artists cut the image of the god. His wife was appalled, and almost fainted dead away. A close comrade took him by the shoulder and whispered, "This is blasphemy, you know!" But the merchant cried, "Why should a man nowadays worry about the consequences of blasphemy, my friends? Didn't our king tell us that the Aton was pure love, devoid of the anger and revenge of the other gods?"

A few of the more drunken members of the party saw the point immediately, and the jokes went on all night.

The public court of the Great Temple grew emptier day by day, the altar stood naked in the sunlight, and Wanre turned in upon himself like a cat licking its wounds and in the process creating new ones.

"All are against me!" he shrieked. "But it is just, for I am the lowest and vilest of men, and my head deserves to be dragged through the dirt. But no! I am the temple, I am defiled by bats and scorpions and snakes. Is there nothing pure left in the land?"

It was the second month of the harvest and across the river the peasants were gathering in their wheat and barley, and the vines were bursting with fat black grapes. "I want to run down the flower path and dive into the river. But the weight of my crown would sink me!"

Then he brought his face close to Parennufer's and whispered, "The flood is coming, can't you feel it? The tongue of the river is licking its way forward in the Netherworld, over dark midnight flowers and fruits. Like the tongue of a snake." Then abruptly he drew back. "There are two honest men in my court. I am one of them. *You* would never lie to me, would you?"

Parennufer fell down and kissed the thongs of his sandals as his answer.

He began to accuse everyone of plotting to defame or dethrone him. Tutu felt the lash of his tongue, so did Nakht, and even the young Smenkhare. A cook was imprisoned two weeks for having inadvertently prepared a tasty dish once popular during the feast days of Opet. The only one he never accused was Ay; he kept making vague references to some strange role he was to play in future. (*"I know who you are, Ay, and your time has not yet come!"*) Ay would shrug his shoulders and make some equally cryptic remark about astrology.

Eventually he grew weary of his own anguish and decided to convert despair, for the last time, into action. It was time for another purge—to close more temples, harass more priests, and suppress more gods. Now he turned his attention to the lesser deities, and attempted to close all the temples which had continued to eke out a precarious existence for some years without support. The furthermost shrines of Khnum or the lion-goddess Sekhmet in the small towns needed but a feather to knock them over. His Chisellers, now increased in number, marched into the humblest provincial chapels of the cat-goddess Bast, and defaced the walls, the names and images, the very word "god." But it was an impossible project; to see it to its end would have been tantamount to counting the grains of sand in the desert, for how might anyone destroy every picture, statue, charm or amulet made in the image of any god since the beginning of time? Yet that was his wish. Only a few gods were left unmolested—those whose histories were so vast that they had become a part of the meaning of Ra or of Pharaoh himself. Horus, whose head bore the sun's disc. Maat, who could not be erased for she was part of one of his own names. He got around that problem by ordering that the name be spelled differently—without her *image* in the middle.

The temple lands lay fallow and the statues of countless gods gathered dust in their shrines. But no less desolate were the altars of the Aton in the desert, and no less silent was the temple of his own god. Now, at the morning services there was a mere handful of worshippers, mostly women with their children who came out of habit, and because the day was long for them while their husbands worked. And at dusk, when he went into the temple for the evening ceremonies, he often walked through the public court and down into the middle court and down again into the inner courts—utterly alone, save for the blind singers who would sing forever, for to them it was all the same.

People were starting to get suspicious about the doings of Tutu the Eggheaded One; the Chief Mouthpiece of the Land was behaving most oddly, even for him. "Is he talking to his cat again?" Wanre asked, and his informer said no, not exactly. "Well, what?" Well ... he was talking to *himself* quite a lot and being very strange and furtive about certain letters he kept locked up in a cabinet in his office. At day's end he would pull them out, laugh uproariously, scrawl a few things on the papyrus, and replace them.

One morning Wanre went to visit him in the private office behind the vast complex of libraries and training schools; he found him sitting alone at his desk—the secret lord of an empire of scribes, his cat in one corner, the dust that never seemed to vanish all over the tablets and shelves. He looked utterly distracted, and kept picking things up and putting them down like a listless child bored with his toys.

"Tutu, are you quite all right?" asked the king. Immediately Tutu shot him a dangerous, hurt look, then picked up a tablet from the desk and began to read in a loud singsong, *"Thou shalt be my husband and I thy wife. I will give thee dominion in the great Underworld; I shall give unto thine hands the tablet of wisdom. Thou shalt be lord, and I, queen!"*

Seeing the surprise on the king's face, he began to laugh. "It's not a letter, my Sun—it's one of those silly tales from Karaduniash. Storytellers were always such dolts. It loses something in the translation, don't you think?" Without waiting for an answer he picked up another tablet. "Now here's one—it almost makes me weep. *O why has Ea allowed mankind to see the unbeautiful things of heaven and earth?"*

"Tutu, is it possible you are overworked? Don't you think a long rest is in order?" he ventured.

"A month ago, my Sun—I decided I was going mad. I'm an old man. I served under two kings, and I served well. I've seen more nations crumble than there are flies on a cow's snout. I am a loyal old dolt! What have I gained from my years of service—nothing!"

Wanre could think of no reply to this unprecedented outburst.

"... Clever *little* men, I'm surrounded by their names; they gain kingdoms by their wiles, not by their loyalty. Did Aziru—my Lord, my Sun—grow strong on his loyalty? No, by heaven—on vice and thievery! Now he's a sworn servant of Kheta. He's a hero! Why, years ago he invited me to grow rich on Amorite gold...."

"You didn't report this to me!" Wanre stiffened.

"My Sun ... there are many things I didn't *report* to you. We're surrounded by hypocrites and scheming opportunists! Sometimes their names rise up in the air and whirl around my head and mock me...."

Wanre felt Tutu was on the verge of hysteria, and tried to quieten him, but the little Mouthpiece started laughing once again. "I served you well, my Sun—you don't know the half of it! You can't give me back one hour of the million hours I spent in the dusty bloody library of the empire checking tribute inventories, grovelling like a hound, snuffling through the corridors and aisles that never end. Look at this place—it's a maze where a man loses his head!"

Sunlight shone through the window on the clay tablets and scrolls.

"*Gold, gold through which the blood shines....* That's how they described precious jewels. *Send me ten ornaments of gold through which the blood shines,* they wrote. Money, the blood of the empire ... jewels ... war ... blood."

Outside the window the sound of a cart creaking down the street, the sound of donkey bells. On the desk, ink-pots and pallets, soot and gum and water, lumps of red ochre, half-written letters.

"My Sun, I have a game I play with myself these days. Oh, don't be alarmed, I'm merely in my second childhood!"

"And what is your game, dear Tutu?"

He motioned to a cabinet behind the desk. "I've been writing belated letters to Aziru—eight years late, in fact!—accepting his bribes! Isn't that hilarious? Wait—here's one, I'll read it to you. *Aziru my brother, I who was once your countryman and friend have read your words for many years, in which you proclaim your loyalty to Pharaoh. I have heeded these words even though they are not to be believed in the place where I am. Yet I have abstained from mentioning slanders against you to the king.* Oh, I can't stand my own wit! Of course I mentioned the slanders, but the point is no one heeded them until it was too late, right? *Yes, by refraining from speaking these words I have done a great service to the loyal Aziru. Now I say this: because of this great service I request the following gifts: gold, ingots, turquoise, silver, iron swords, rings from the fingers of captured princes, hair from their heads, cut-off hands....*"

With a cry Wanre reached out and grabbed the letter, and Tutu burst out into gales of laughter as high and shrill as a girl's. "I'm only joking!" he cried. "If I were writing to Aziru would I write in the language of the Two Lands?" Then he doubled over with his mirth. "I've sickened myself with my own lies! Look, my skin is brown and brittle as old papyrus. When I die, my Sun, will you file me on one of the library shelves mistaking me for a scroll—and label and catalogue me like all the others? I can see it now, the cabinet will read: *Tutu, Foreign Minister, body of, to be bound, shelf 48.*"

Now he could scarcely speak coherently but managed to blurt out the last few sentences of his mock letter, which he thought were marvellously funny. *"And if these things are not received by Tutu thy brother then your countryman will, be assured, with great haste report to the king of the abominable treacheries of the loyal Aziru over many years of time!"*

Finally the laughter subsided and tears rolled down his face. "By the way, my Sun—people are very interested in that cabinet of letters. They say I'm behaving oddly, don't they, don't they? Do you think I'm behaving oddly, my Lord Wanre, do you?"

Tutu stared into the cool shadows of the Records Office, seeing once again the drama of the empire play itself out. The shadows on the walls were armies, the sound of carts outside on the street were the clashing of bronze and iron swords; the wailing of alley cats was the wailing of deposed princes, the shrieks of raped women, the screams of orphaned children.

*"Beauty, beams and love,"* he murmured. "In trying to avoid bloodshed you have spilled more blood than the mightiest general! An empire without bloodshed, you thought.... One might as well imagine a childbirth without pain. But the Aton, as we all know, is a *beneficial* god!"

The king started to say something, stiffened, then closed his mouth.

"Do you notice a slight note of hysteria in me?" asked Tutu, who then broke out once again into his insane laughing gurgle.

Wanre looked down with pity at the Chief Mouthpiece of the Land, crumpled up and half mad in his chair. He saw a cloud pass over the sun and darken the shelves of imperial correspondence.

"I'm struggling to be *perfect*!" he cried one day. "Don't you understand that, you nitwitted priest? What do I want with ceremonies and charms and holy oil—trinkets, everything's become trinkets!" And to prove it, he swept his arm in a wide arc through space as though clearing some invisible cluttered altar before his eyes. "*Turning round and round and round,* like the ox at the well, he thinks he's going straight and getting somewhere because his eyes are covered, he doesn't *know* he's turning round and round and round!"

Merire and the others looked on, bewildered.

"I'm *suffering*! Does no one in my kingdom know what that means?"

"The lame, the leprous, the poor, the blind," droned the courageous Parennufer, but the king didn't hear him.

"I'm alone! I've always suspected it. Now I know for sure! Alone, *alone*!" And though the faithful old teacher stretched a warm hand towards him, he jerked away, refusing to believe that he was not what he claimed to be, for he wanted his pain. He savoured every drop of it; he invited more. "Is that not right? Am I not alone?" he cried, casting wild eyes around the room, challenging someone to prove him wrong.

"Quite so!" said Parennufer.

"There! Mark his words, *he* said so, *he* knows! Now you all know, but what does it matter if you all know? If I'm alone anyway, who cares then but me? Ahhh . . ." he cried and, overcome with his own words, flung himself on the floor and curled up in the position of a child in the womb, kicking his heels up in a holy rage to get out of the prison he had carefully built around himself.

"Wanre," suggested Parennufer, leaning over him cautiously, not sure whether to treat him as a helpless child or a cobra coiled to spring, "a little wine perhaps? From last year's vineyards . . . the sweet red kind you love so much?"

But by the time he reached the end of his offer the king had rolled over on his back and was staring in deep melancholy at the ceiling. Then very slowly he got up, cast surprised glances at the four standing anxiously around him, and asked in the mildest of voices, "Well, my friends, what are you all hanging around for? Haven't I told you the god is love? Haven't I instructed you that we're all brothers? Come, it's time for the evening prayers. Come, the god is setting. . . ."

And then, completely forgetting his former state, he bade them all join hands like children, and in the most amiable of moods led them out into the courtyard in the red-gold light of sunset.

He fell ill; his eyes were failing him and his limbs were wracked with the inexplicable pains he had had as a child. Since the death of Nefertiti his position on the throne had become shaky, and he was compelled to solidify his royal claims by marrying the royal heiress. However, he took his second daughter Ankhespaaton as his bride, which puzzled those who did not know the plans he had for the eldest daughter, Meritaton. Now anyone who had harboured hopes that the boy Tutankhaton would become the husband of Ankhespaaton was sorely disappointed—Ay most of all, for it had been Nefertiti's wish. After her death he'd taken the boy under his wing. He hated him, but felt it was the least he could do; becoming his guardian was one way of atoning for the unendurable guilt he felt for his daughter's death. But the boy was a wretched child, a little Amenhotep who had all of his father's more disagreeable attributes. He was smug, petulant, saucy, and wholly uncomfortable to have around. Ay would have liked to rewrite *Am Duat* and add his name to the list of demons of the Underworld.

Most of the people at court passionately hoped that Wanre would enter into a co-regency with a younger ruler. A large part of the population favoured Tutankhaton as that ruler, mainly because he had been Nefertiti's favourite. Ay himself couldn't help but think of what a grand position he would occupy if Tutankhaton ever took the throne. He would become Vizier at last—priest of his beloved Maat.

Sniffing the winds of change and opportunity in the air, many of the high officials at court grew suddenly lyrical, if not utterly rhapsodical, in their praise of Wanre. *May Aton bestow upon him many years of peace. Let him sojourn here until the swan turns black and the raven white, until the hills arise and depart! Grant unto him all that his heart loves, like the multitude of sands on the dunes, like the scales of fish in the streams or the hairs of the cattle!* they wrote on their tombs.

Meanwhile he spent hours in the company of Smenkhare, kissing and fondling him and calling him his Beloved. Some said he was merely lonely and his mind was failing; others looked on distressed and furious, and still others postulated that he was pursuing the strange, repugnant appetites of his father and had acquired a taste for young boys.

A few secretly challenged his right to rule, for his second marriage had only been a temporary measure—and a fairly ineffective one at that. A handful of officials met quietly by night to discuss the possibility of a dethronement.

But then the blow came. He announced the forthcoming marriage of Smenkhare with the royal heiress Meritaton—and following it, the coronation of Smenkhare as co-ruler on the throne of the Two Lands. The court was stunned by the speed with which he intended to raise the boy to power; he had given no one time to think or interfere, although there were some who had suspected all along that such would be his plan. The majority of those surrounding him couldn't help but respect the self-assertion he had shown. It was a return to the confidence and speed with which he used to act.

Ay was profoundly disappointed, and Tutankhaton became impossible, frequently going into tantrums, and Ay was obliged to read him stories of Stinking-Face the Demon to console him. He found the boy obnoxious; he had fat cheeks like a baby and used to pick up Ay's best lamps and smash them on the floor. Most of the time Ay would have loved to join him; he was furious with Wanre, for he felt he had been completely overlooked.

the eleventh hour of the night

M*y hidden appearances and My secret radiance cause your life, O you who advance to your shadows,*" said Ra to His enemies in the eleventh hour of the night.

A coronation hall for Smenkhare was thrown together with great haste as an addition to the palace. Badly levelled, it was constructed on piles of debris and looked as though it should have been an elaborate desert dwelling, to be torn down and hauled away in the morning. But it *appeared* beautiful, with its pillared hall, the centre of which was open to the sky like a temple. And despite the faulty construction of the floors and walls, much care was taken in the columns. They were made of wood, a rarity in those days, and covered with gilded plaster. The hall along the outer galleries was painted with intricate designs of intertwined vines, which represented the co-regency.

But few cared much what the vines represented, for the court was in an ugly mood on the day of Smenkhare's coronation. They watched in stony silence as the king anointed his Beloved, embraced and kissed him, and said, "By the grace of my Father the Aton, I anoint Smenkhare with lotus oil, and he shall be known henceforth as Djeser Kheperu Ankheprure, Holy of Forms, Living in the Creations of Ra. I take him, Beloved of the Sun and seed of His body, to rule beside me on the throne of the Two Lands."

No one had heard the expression "Beloved of the Sun and seed of His body" before. A few wondered what it meant; Wanre had emphasized the words quite strongly. His voice spread through the pillared court, smooth and fragrant as the holy oil. He savoured the words and dwelled on them one by one, reluctant to allow the lovely names of his Beloved to fall from his mouth and disappear.

There was a triumphant smile on the boy's face, and some who watched the ceremony inwardly remarked that it was almost the same expression of relief and victory that Akhenaton himself had worn sixteen years before in the temple of Opet.

Then came the most solemn part of the ritual, when the hall of pillars had to be absolutely silent, and everyone fell to his knees softly and bowed his head as the invisible hawk of Horus descended from the blue vaults of heaven to rest like a blessing on the head of the new king. In that awesome moment Wanre heard the faint flashing and rustling of the sacred wings as Smenkhare became living Horus. And amid the holy-sounding silence the two kings sat on their separate thrones, inviolate, two yet one.

A moment came when he could bear his curiosity no longer, and stealthily raised his head just a little. In the same instant the boy raised his, and their eyes met with secret, poignant understanding. Wanre blanched, and sweat broke out on his brow, for at that moment Smenkhare's eyes were his own eyes, and in the dreadful silence which never seemed to end, he wondered what would be the fate of the young Ankheprure. Then he bowed his head again, driven almost to tears by the sound of those beating, invisible wings.

Afterwards they were never apart. They ate together, worshipped together, held audience together, did everything in fact but sleep together—although some seriously wondered about that too. Their union was rich and strong—but it did not bind the city as he had hoped. Many of the wealthy citizens who had lived only a year or so in their villas bricked up their doors against thieves and returned to the old capital. He cried out that they were treating his city as some kind of trifling summer residence, and Parennufer told him that the climate in the Horizon was enough to sicken anyone.

"Climate, what *climate*?" he roared, and straight away disguised himself as a merchant and went into the marketplace to see for himself. But he was soon sorry he went, for there among the eggplants and fruit stalls he heard himself being called a baboon, a madman, a criminal. He was being accused of having every conceivable perversion. People were saying openly that he had driven his wife to suicide, and that his god was the god of a madman—the product of a disordered mind. One eloquent fellow was delivering a satirical parody of the Teaching. "It's a circle with a hole in the middle, you see, but the hole is the thing, not the circle; no one can see it because it's a hole, that's the secret!"

In his rage Wanre knocked over a table full of statues and charms; then, frightened by the faces which turned to stare at him, he ran and disappeared into the crowds. He stayed in bed for a week afterwards in a sleep so profound that no one dared awaken him.

Ankhespaaton bore her father a child so weak and sickly that everyone wondered if she would ever be able to stand up, walk or talk. On the night he had created her, he had called on the god to give him aid, and for a brief moment life had flowed once more through his loins. But the result was a travesty of life. The baby—he shuddered whenever he saw her—lay like something neither dead nor alive, her pale eyes trying to focus on some intangible thing which dwelt in the ceiling, her little mouth making tiny weak wails which broke his heart. She kept throwing up her white hands, no bigger than the paws of a rabbit, as though trying to surrender her unasked-for body to death. The vapid eyes stared, tiny blue liquid circles which seemed to be asking why they had ever been made to see.

Wanre whispered that his death and the death of his god were near. Smenkhare went to him a hundred times and urged him to save himself in the only way left—by relaxing his censure of the gods and bringing about a final settlement with the House of Amon. During the first year of the co-regency the issue flared up again and again like the sheets of flames from the oil lamps. Time, Smenkhare warned, was running out. One had only to count the number of vacant villas in the city to know the truth.

At first Wanre argued, and swore that Smenkhare was the traitor rumour had him to be. It took him many months to understand the boy's purpose. Then one day Smenkhare spoke, and he never questioned him again.

"For love of you I must press this issue until you agree!" he cried. "Where else in the world is there a man with the power of a god? Who is behind Baal of Gubla, Nergal of Ashur, Arinni of Kheta? No one. They are names. You are spirit! You will make yourself and your god felt throughout the world, I feel it, it will be! But we must let the people worship as they choose. Why did anyone ever love your god? Because they first loved *you*. But now you can't name a single district in the Two Lands which hasn't suffered for your reforms. They turn against the Aton because of you, Wanre. You can keep the god supreme by leniency, by demonstrating that you are as tolerant and beneficial as He. By forbidding worship of other gods you merely made them appealing, don't you see? The reins *must* be loosened, otherwise I tell you there will be total destruction!"

He groaned and cried he would never reconcile himself with the swine of Opet, but Smenkhare put an arm around his shoulders and gazed deep into his eyes and the king saw in him a reflection of himself when he was a boy, when all he knew was love.

"Hear me," Smenkhare whispered. "Who is the force within the Aton, the mysterious inner spirit you speak of and no one understands? It is *you*!" he cried, and his fingers dug into Wanre's shoulders to hold him quiet as he went on. "Listen, if we permit the temples to reopen and the priests to take up their duties once more, the people will have a choice. I swear they will choose your god. You will reign supreme, you will be released from the danger which has threatened you for years...."

Wanre looked the other way.

"If you are destroyed, I promise you the Aton will go down with you. You will set in the Horizon together—two slain suns, and the sky will be red with your blood!"


Later he sat in the small room overlooking the terraces of the garden. It was the painting room where his little daughters made havoc with the colours; there were still dabs and splotches of paint on the floors, some delicate fishbones strewn about, and some limestone shards with funny pictures. One of the girls had drawn a bright orange hippopotamus and a picture of Benremut, green, with fangs. He stared at the grass outside, thinking. When had he first noticed *it*? *It* was creeping upon him slyly as a jackal, striking sometimes and then retreating to its lair for the final attack. There were a hundred signs. His memory was failing him and the noise in his head had grown louder, his bones became slow and stupid and his muscles didn't respond. But finally—*his eyes*.

*"In one year I'll be blind, blind as a shrewmouse,"* he whispered into the darkness. He had not consulted the doctors; he thought if his suspicions were left unconfirmed, the symptoms might disappear. He was becoming unable to distinguish the gradations from light to dark, the gorgeous receding degrees of the dusk, the stages of the dawn.

*The sun of him who knows Thee not will set, O Amon....*

It was twilight, but he was suspended between pure day and pure night, unable to see the shades between.

*The forecourt of him who assails Thee shall be in darkness but the whole earth shall be in light.*

The noises in his skull were a babble of cruel children; his inner voice pounded in his head amid the clamour of those hundred other tongues.

Is it Nefertiti there in the garden, watching the shadows? No, it's only a slim tree. But the shadows are playing; are they shadows? No, children, many small girls giggling on the terraces. My children. I see their gold earrings like little suns, I see their silver fingernails like little moons in the grass. Meketaton is laughing with her sisters, now she falls to the grass with foam at her mouth, her silver fingers writhing like glow-worms in the black garden. No, there is no one in the garden! A guard or two. Some trees. Some flowers. Look now, Tiy emerges. I see you, Mother, your legs wide as pillars in the temple, your hands on your hips like a peasant woman. What a fantastic place! *Blind, blind as a shrewmouse in one year.* O king look now while you still can see. The forms in the garden take shape and move. Nefer Nefruaton living in beauty forever and ever with a golden noose around her neck. Beloved, why do you hang there from that dreadful tree? Come inside, I tell you the night is falling. Lift Meketaton from the dark grass and stop this hideous game!

Tiy, legs apart, relieving herself against the tree trunk like a peasant. There is a Nile between her legs and she puts out the fiery sun on the ground.

Come unto me my gold my silver my wife my daughter, it is cold....

Where is the Aton? Is the god in the garden? Yes, fallen in the black grass, small and red as blood. The Disc has fallen and melted there. O Ra my Father, rise! No one knows You save Your son Akhenaton! The Eye of Ra has fallen....

*Blind as a shrewmouse in one year.* Look now while you still can see. List the things in the garden: one *tekhen*, many trees, two guards, the fallen Eye of Ra, the woman with the golden noose, the girlchild with foam on her lips, Tiy's legs. What else? It Neter Ay with the red leather gloves I got for him. Now the gloves are travelling alone through the black grass. Look—they're lifting up the fallen sun, the little moons! They are gathering everything up—the trees, the garden, the woman, the child, the palace.... They're coming this way!


Smenkhare had been standing silent behind him for a long time. Then he went in front and gazed into his face.

"Your eyes!" he cried.

"I do my best thinking with my eyes half closed, you know that. Well, Smenkhare, best-beloved! Go back to the old capital and make our peace. But go quickly, before I change my mind."

He tore off from his collar one of the golden rectangles which bore the name of the god, and hooked it onto Smenkhare's collar where it hung heavy, burning, against the brown skin.

"Wear it everywhere, when you confront the priests, when you reopen the temples. Let its light blind them!"

But even as he spoke his own face was in shadow.

Just before Smenkhare and Meritaton left, Parennufer talked to the young queen in a hallway. "Child," he said, "does your father expect a miracle that he sends you two children to restore all he has destroyed?" Meritaton stiffened with indignation and replied that her husband was not a child, but a ruler of stature, and few ever considered his age when they confronted him. Parennufer smiled sadly and said he feared for them both.

She remembered his words when later they arrived in the old capital and met a chilling silence and a reception so hostile it filled her with terror. Not one flower was thrown; not one child squealed or laughed to see them. Smenkhare whispered to her, "Would anyone have believed that Pharaoh would one day enter this city amid such a *silence?*"

An icy cold crept over the two young rulers, although the day was stifling hot. The city seemed desolate, although it had once been the capital of Keme. The few old dignitaries who came to the shore to greet them were fossils, relics from the old house of Amenhotep. They nervously wrung their hands and apologized for the thousand details which had been overlooked; then they conducted them to the palace.

Before getting into the litter Smenkhare found himself staring at a man who stood alone, not far off. He in turn cast long, unreadable glances back, but made no move to come forward. Smenkhare turned to his private scribe and aide, Pawah, and asked who the man was.

After a moment's hesitation, Pawah whispered fearfully, "My Lord, I believe it is Amenemhet."

And as the litter bore them silently away, Smenkhare realized that the lean dark figure who bad come alone to the quay to stare was the First Prophet of Amon. For years the dispossessed priests of the forbidden god had met secretly, held consultations, and maintained their natural hierarchy. Now that he, Smenkhare, had come back to the old capital, the First Prophet had come out of the darkness and shown himself. The small black eyes, Smenkhare had noticed, kept blinking in the light.

the twelfth hour of the night

In the twelfth hour there are goddesses holding many eyes. The Snake enters his tail and comes forth through his mouth. It is the final hour of the night.

Some time after Smenkhare reached the old capital, he sent his first long report back to Wanre, and Parennufer had to read it to him, for his eyes were too weak to distinguish one letter from another. He lay back on cushions, dangling a few dead flowers from his fingers, and bade his old friend begin.

"The good king Smenkhare reports that his immediate project is the building of his own mortuary temple. It will provide for—"

"Provide for what? Go on!"

"Provide for small offerings to Amon. The scribe Pawah will be elevated to the post of Temple Scribe of the Offerings. Meanwhile, he goes on, he and the queen are setting an example to the citizens by making small daily offerings in a few of the small shrines which he has reopened. The people, it seems, are pleased by these gestures...."

All the little flowers fell to the floor, and he sighed once and sank back into the cushions to lose himself among their softness. If he dwelled too long on the thought of Smenkhare offering in those disgusting shrines, he would go utterly mad.

Parennufer read on.

"Smenkhare pledges again that, as previously agreed, he will for the moment ignore the Great Temple. As for the First Prophet Amenemhet—"

"Don't speak his name aloud!"

"As for *that priest*, he will not be granted audience until such time as all the conditions of the agreement are met; until such time as the House of Amon agrees to bow to the will of Pharaoh in future, to give over two-thirds of the profits from its land to the house of Aton at all times, and to forfeit forever the right to hold the coronation of future kings within its precincts."

At this point Wanre began to complain bitterly about the necessity of Smenkhare's making a public display of serving the gods, and about how difficult it must have been for him to pretend to such devotion. Parennufer's tongue slipped, and he pointed out how easy it was to pretend in such matters. Wanre turned on him, his mouth curled down in a bitter smile. "By that you are implying that my people also *pretended* to worship my god, aren't you? No, save your protests!" he cried, as the tutor tried to cover up his error. "From your mouth I can take all kinds of truths which from others would shatter me to bits. You exclaim! Since my eyes are failing me, old man, I see things more clearly than ever before. . . . Isn't it strange?"

Parennufer mumbled a passage from one of the ancient legends of Ra. *"Remain seated on Thy throne; the fear of Thee is yet great, if only Thine eyes be turned upon those who blaspheme Thee."*

"Who blasphemes me?" came the cry.

"Everyone. They're all about you," he replied recklessly. "One who blasphemes you might be here beside you now."

At this Wanre fell into silence, and Parennufer thought with a shudder how easy it would be for his enemies to trick him now into believing anything. Now with Smenkhare gone, and only he and Ay remaining in his trust—to what ends might he not be led?

The High Priest Merire was sick of being a lump, of existing without an immediate aim, and bored to death with the Horizon. *The fool's life is like death; he dies, living every day,* so the saying went.

He decided to enlighten himself personally on what was actually happening in the old capital, for he sensed that Smenkhare's letters were glossing over the true situation. So he wrote a hasty note to an old colleague of his in the college of Amon—someone who was eternally indebted to him for being helped out of a nasty scrape some years before. He garbed his words in harmless clothes, knowing that his sly friend would read their hidden meaning.

*Your fond friend Merire greets you after many years. How are the fortunes of my brother? Does he prosper as usual? I prosper here in the Horizon whence some time ago the "beautiful boat" set sail for your city. I am most interested in knowing where that boat is harboured and the condition in which it now rests. Your fond friend sends a gift to demonstrate his undying affection—a collar of gold worked by the best artisan in the land.*

He sent the note off by a secret messenger, and an answer was not long in coming.

*Dear Merire, eternal companion and most generous friend. Your fond brother thanks you for the lovely gift, although he regrets there is a better artisan in the city where he dwells. However, the beautiful boat arrived, and very few people here admire its workmanship. Most admire it not at all and claim it is too clumsy. While it might sail well on the Nile it will never navigate on the open seas, as the builder thought. Some, so I have heard, think that to speedily sink it to the bottom of the river would be better than maintaining the high cost of its upkeep. It is said in my city that the Great Boat, of which this is but a smaller model, now sits in dry dock and cannot sail at all. Is this so, my friend? Please send me two more beautiful gold collars. Meanwhile I send you a turquoise ring and some cups of copper.*

(Turquoise and copper, the thief!) Merire was furious, but he finally sent his informer so many gold collars that he lost his entire set—a set given to him by Wanre. But it was well worth the trouble, for he learned that the enemies of Smenkhare were growing daily and there was very little chance that he would wake to many more dawns. Thus far his friend had done all the talking, but if he started asking *him* for news of Akhenaton's health or any other palace secrets, he'd demand his collars back, one by one. However, the correspondence stopped rather abruptly, for Merire feared it would be found out.

Wanre ceased his games of Senet, for his eyes could no longer see the board. The left one went first as he always expected it would. He couldn't sleep, for the old moving bands of light travelled back and forth in his skull, and he lay awake for hours, watching them, watching them.

People grew nervous in his presence. When he'd been at the height of power no one had feared him, in the real sense of the word. But now, his eyes failing and the city crumbling and the lustre of the god dimming, they feared him much. Now that he could scarcely see, he *saw*.

As his condition grew worse he summoned various people to come and read him the hymns of the temple. Most often he summoned Ay, and the Master of Horse protested loudly that he didn't have a good enough voice for that sort of thing, and besides, he couldn't do justice to the holy words. But for some perverse reason which he could never understand, it pleased Wanre more to hear the prayers read by an unbeliever than by a devout worshipper. So Ay mumbled the lines under his breath, and one night Wanre interrupted him in the middle of a sentence and cried aloud:

*"Lo my name is abhorred
More than the stink of birds
On a summer day
When the skies are hot!"*

Ay recognized the words as part of an old story about a man weary of his soul. It scared him to hear Wanre recite them; it reminded him too much of himself. A bitter humour had crept into the king's speech, an awful sadness with sharp edges.

Now whenever he made an appearance at the Great Window there were no crowds to greet him. He looked down into the bleak streets; a few people passed, pointed to the Window, and then, no longer curious, walked away. A year before, he might have wept at that. Now he laughed.

It was a long while before he consented to have his physician examine his eyes.

"Would you say, roughly speaking, Penthu, that your king is going blind?"

"My Sun, I dare not say," answered the nervous doctor. "But when I hold this strong light before your eyes, the orbs do not respond in the same manner in which other eyes respond to such an experiment...."

"In other words, you would say, roughly speaking, that your king is going *blind!*"

"My Lord Akhenaton, I dare not say."

"Parennufer, would *you* say I am going blind? No—don't tell me, I don't want to hear it from you! Thoth, come and spit on my eyes and heal them!"

Parennufer gasped; it was the first time in eight years that anyone had heard him utter the name of another god.

One day he saw a snake lurking in the grass beneath a tree, and above it in a high branch a little pigeon. He saw the bird transfixed by the snake's stare and gradually, softly, fall down, branch by branch, into his jaws.

For some months Smenkhare refused to grant audience to the High Priest Amenemhet. Pawah warned him of the danger in this, saying that until the people saw some signs of reconciliation between the royal house and the House of Amon there would be no peace in anyone's heart. It made no difference that he granted a hearing to the High Priest of Ptah and gave him his blessing; or that he permitted countless smaller shrines and temples to be reopened. As long as he ignored the First Prophet of Amon, all his efforts were in vain. People rumoured that Smenkhare was afraid of him, and gradually he came to realize that in keeping his promise to Wanre he might in fact be doing him more harm than if he broke it and saw Amenemhet.

The High Priest was a cunning man; he made a public display of his "poverty" and went about complaining that the lands and fields and the god of Opet were as destitute as he.

Smenkhare lay awake nights thinking of the sly panther who prowled around his gates. The few times he did sleep, it was only to have nightmares which made him cry out in pain and anger. Finally no choice remained but to receive Amenemhet. He made sure it was a very formal reception with no hint of intimacy. He surrounded himself with a host of scribes and aides, calculating that the coolness and over-formality would dampen Amenemhet's spirits and demonstrate his exact position with the royal house. But it took more than formality to intimidate a man like Amenemhet. He strode into the audience hall, taking in the whole situation at a glance, fully aware of the embarrassment it was intended to cause him, and spoke. "The humble servant of the good Smenkhare wishes to speak on the matter of the Great Temple of Opet."

Smenkhare let a few moments pass, then, feigning surprise, looked up and bade him continue. He did not reveal by word or expression that he had been shocked and insulted by Amenemhet's omission of the word "king."

The High Priest in turn let pass an even longer and more impolite silence before going on. "I rejoiced when I heard of your coming, for many years ago the great gates of our temple were shut, and I was told that now he who rules from the Horizon intends to open them once more and breathe new life into the sanctuaries of Amon."

Smenkhare thanked him for his words, and softly proceeded to outline the first main stipulation which Akhenaton had set, before a settlement with the House of Amon could be brought about. "Agree then, that in future you and your colleagues will bow to the will of the king and give over two-thirds of the profits from the land of Opet to the house of Aton at all times."

"And *what* profits, my Lord? We will *have* nothing to give!"

"You will give, then, two-thirds of your *poverty!*" Smenkhare cried.

Amenemhet stared at the golden name of the Aton which blazed from Smenkhare's naked chest beneath the pectoral ornament of a vulture.

"My Lord, in the past the Great Temple *received* gifts from the royal house; she did not *give* them!"

"But she will give them now if she wishes to exist side by side with the temples of the Aton," said Smenkhare. "This is the command of my royal brother Akhenaton, and this is how it must be. You know the conditions of this agreement; they have been laid out detail by detail. You are also aware of the second main stipulation . . ." he paused a moment, ". . . that the House of Amon relinquish its rights of holding the coronations of the future kings of the Two Lands at Opet. My royal brother has decreed that all future kings be blessed in the house of Aton."

Amenemhet let a sly smile play around the corners of his mouth. "*You*, my Lord Smenkhare, were 'crowned' in the Horizon, were you not?"

Smenkhare said nothing.

Then the High Priest let his gaze insolently circle about the room. "I would like to announce this day," he cried aloud, "that the servants of Amon do not recognize your 'coronation,' and therefore do not recognize your *right* to hold the flail and sceptre of the Two Lands!"

The hall fell into a shocked silence. Smenkhare's face went dead white. *"You will leave now, Seer!"*

"How well you resemble your royal brother who rules from the Horizon," Amenemhet sneered. "It is an unfortunate resemblance."

*"You will leave now, Seer!"*

Amenemhet turned, but not before putting in one last remark.

"The mirror shall be shattered, and both the image and its poor reflection shall perish—my Lord, *my Sun*!"

Akhenaton was in the temple smashing the head of a snake. He'd had a huge image of Apop made out of gum and papyrus, and the monster was placed on the white ramp leading to the altar. In ancient times the priests of Ra had assisted the god in his journey through darkness by fashioning such a snake and beating it to a pulp in the hour before dawn. Now Apop lay in his temple, a huge grey mass, and he attacked it with a large stick and recited the ancient curses. It did not matter to him that it was already day, and the god shone in the skies and needed no help to rise. He raised his club over the reptile's head and brought it down flat. Then he trampled it under his feet and spat upon it and screamed:

*He's fallen in flame,*
*A knife is in his head*
*His ear is cut off*
*His name is no more on earth.*
*I order him stricken with wounds*
*I annihilate his bones,*
*I destroy his soul every day.*
*I cut the vertebrae of his neck asunder*
*Opening with my knife*
*Separating his flesh...*
*I make him as though he had never been,*
*His name is no more*
*His children are not*
*His egg cannot grow*
*Nor is his seed raised*
*His soul and body are no more*
*Nor his spirit nor his shadow nor his magic!*

Servants rushed forward to carry the boat of Ra over the dead body of Apop. Their king, meanwhile, was weeping.

The next day he repeated the ceremony, this time with even more venom. He danced about on the white ramp and cursed at the top of his voice until the snake was a shapeless hunk beneath his sandals.

"I have conquered darkness!" he screamed.

"But my lord Akhenaton," ventured a priest, "it is *day*."

"That," said he, "is not the point."

Parennufer had to read Smenkhare's next letter aloud, and he stumbled about, afraid to reveal its contents. Then the dark slits of Wanre's eyes fastened upon him and he gritted his teeth and read. Smenkhare had granted audience to Amenemhet; it had followed hard upon the pressure of public opinion. Nothing had been accomplished by it. Wanre lay like a great shapeless lump upon the couch and groaned, "Now, surely, my sun begins to set!"

Parennufer wanted to cry, "The white ramp leads nowhere, don't you see! The white highway to the sun is full of snakes! Do you hear me, it leads *nowhere*! Come down from your holy grape-trampling, it's too late for magic!" But he felt too sorry to speak.

A month passed without further news; then the land was suddenly alive with rumours, and a shadow of horror and disgust cast itself over everyone. Some unknown desecrators had opened the sepulchre of Tiy in the Western Valley and thrown its contents outside onto the sands. The magnificent coffin was stolen, and the body was thrown onto a burning pyre and destroyed for eternity. The great golden shrine which had enclosed her coffin was defaced and cast into a dirty abandoned tomb nearby. It had borne the images of Tiy and her son making burnt offerings to the god. Wanre's image had been scratched out with some sharp instrument like a knife.

No act was more horrible than the destruction of the human body. Tiy was wiped out, erased, expunged, and now her son was the shadow of a shadow—his father an invisible god and his mother a pile of ashes in the sand.

*Her shapeless ka will endure*, he thought, but his thoughts were full of panic. *The form, the body is a mere boundary line drawn around the force!* he insisted, but inside him the last threads of reason broke. He continued his weird, lame dance of death over the body of the snake as though the empty ritual would somehow correct everything. The city crumbled around him; hundreds more citizens left and clouds of dirty dust hung over the desert altars. He danced and danced and one day took his old tutor aside and asked, "Have you ever noticed, Parennufer, while some men spend their lives finding out who they are, others spend it forgetting who they *were?*" And the horrible slits of his eyes saw nothing, yet saw everything, and he told him that he was dreaming in cycles of nightmares again, as he did when he was a child. Vipers emerged from his loins, their heads flailing about and darting fire. A purple horse with eyes of stars charged through his sleep and thrust a sharp hoof into his belly. And Parennufer told him the snake's tongues were the tongues of the generations of the future darting fire and venom at his memory, for a man's future lay within his loins. He could not interpret the purple horse.

Then, quite suddenly, Wanre was totally blind. The physicians heard him let out one long wail when the last shreds of sight left him. He fell on the floor praying loudly, his weight so great that no one—not even the palace guards—could lift him.

But the next day he insisted that his blindness was not going to stop him from performing the temple services. He had himself carried into the temple, where he piled the altar high with invisible shapes of things, for the sun he could not see, in the temple he could not see. He lavished gifts on the god, for nothing remained but to appease His "anger," as all gods at all times in the past had to be appeased. In doing this he knew he was reducing the Lord of Life to a mere selfish deity like the others, who had to be bought off, feared, bargained with.

One night he lay in boiling fever and talked loudly to himself and recognized no one, either by their voices or the shapes of their faces between his thin hands. He thrashed about, and the physicians recited ancient spells to coax out the spirit of the disease.

*"Flow forth, poison, flow to the ground! Horus commands thee, he destroys thee, he spits on thee! Thou canst not rise, but fallest down, thou art feeble...."*

But on hearing the words Wanre thought they referred to him rather than the disease within him, and he cursed the doctors in a language used by street boys.

"Find *someone* he'll recognize!" insisted Penthu, so they brought in little Ankhespaaton, then Parennufer, then the other little daughters who huddled in a circle and shook and wailed—but it was no use. They brought in the Vizier Nakht and the High Priest Merire, the personal servants and butlers and even the cooks.

Then they brought in Ay. He asked everyone to leave the room, and went over to Wanre and stared down into the sightless eyes like abandoned shafts of wells where the water of Nun, the Great Nowhere, churned.

"Who are you?" Wanre asked. "They brought me a hundred nameless shapes and voices. Who are you?"

"My Sun, I'm It Neter Ay."

"I know of no such man. Identify yourself more clearly."

"Father of the god, Master of Horse, your friend."

"I have no friend. And what ridiculous title is that—Father of the Horse? Are you a purple horse who sires purple beasts? Answer—or I'll call the guards!"

"Let me ask you first," Ay said, "to identify *yourself*."

There was a long silence. No one had thought to take such an approach.

"I? *I?* I'm ... the wind between the desert altars. I am Khepri of the morning, I am Lord of the Disc, I am Ra."

"But then you are so many things at once? How can I give you my meagre titles when yours are so abundant?"

"Voices, voices, they keep bringing me voices. What hour of the night is it? Name this hour! Come. Father of the Horse, consult your stars and name this hour!"

*"This is the last hour of the night."*

"Then it is a good hour. Is Ra in danger in this hour?"

"No. All the demons are destroyed and the great Snake is dead."

"Who are you, Father of the Horse?"

"I am your enemy," Ay said. The words were unplanned.

"Enemy. I have many enemies, that doesn't mean anything. Which enemy? Political, religious, private?"

"All of those, and more."

"All? Then you're a surprising creature. I think I should know you, I should know someone of such stature."

"You know me well. I am your enemy who loves you."

"I have no enemy who *loves* me! Name yourself!"

"It Neter Ay, who loves and hates you. Call me Set, call me Apop, call me anything you like."

Ay felt himself trembling from head to foot, for his own tongue scared him. He asked Wanre again who he was and he answered, *"I am son of myself, I am Ra. I was wounded by a serpent I couldn't see. It's not fire and it's not water, but I'm hotter than fire and colder than water!"*

Ay recalled the ancient tale of how Isis made a snake to poison Ra, in order to learn his secret name. Taking the voice of Isis, Ay asked, *"What is it, Divine Father? Behold, a worm has done Thee this wrong! Tell me Thy name, Divine Father, for he whose name is spoken shall live."*

Wanre smiled and replied, *"I am He who created heaven and earth and piled up the mountains and made all living things."*

But the fever didn't depart and Ay begged him again to reveal his true name, for sometimes in extremity such a confession could release the soul and cure the body. But Wanre cried aloud, *"Let no man know your secret name!"*

"Then," said Ay to the blind eyes, "I can't help you, Nameless One." And when the king began to shudder violently, he held up a bracelet of gold before his eyes and asked, "Can you see the light?"

"Father of the Horse, there is no more light. The sun and moon are dead. My Eyes abandoned me—both the vulture who protected me, and the cobra who defended me—they wandered away like the Eye of Ra for they had a life of their own."

*"His majesty has grown old,"* sighed Ay, *"and His bones are of silver, and His flesh is of gold, and His hair is pure lapis lazuli."* As he spoke, Wanre's white hand reached up to touch his face, but Ay shuddered and drew back; he still feared Wanre's touch.

Outside in the hallway he shook his head and told the doctors that no one could bring him out of the fever now, save Wanre alone. Penthu whispered, "His present state mustn't be revealed, do you understand? We who saw him tonight will keep it to ourselves, do you agree?"

Ay agreed and everyone agreed and they went their separate ways. The High Priest Merire looked extremely impatient and was the first to leave, but no one gave it much thought. They might have, had they known that he went directly home and wrote out an urgent note to his former colleague in the old capital—a note which simply read:

*"His sun is setting, his forecourt is in darkness. Ask Amenemhet what to do about the younger."*

It was easier for a man to draw a hood over the face of Ra than it was for Pharaoh to hide himself. But a day came when he was lost—gone from his bed, gone from the palace, and it was as though the earth itself had swallowed him up. The cries of the confounded guards resounded through the halls and the cries of the people resounded through the streets. Servants ran everywhere in the palace, past the great pillars and up and down the terraced gardens. The Medjay sent out their entire force to comb the city; police overran the temple, peering into the shrines and abandoned slaughter yards. Children ran along the riverbanks, and a mounted force set out along the margin of the desert.

He couldn't have gone far—his body was too weak, his eyes too blind. Private citizens searched through the alleyways, each one imagining it was his destiny to find the Lord of Glorious Appearings lying with foam on his mouth on some grimy dark doorstep, or at the bottom of a well.

No one had seen him leave. Where then, where?

If the sands had been able to speak they would have said that during the night, when it was cold, someone had walked upon them, someone with golden sandals had walked upon them, going east. Or had the Orient Cliffs been able to speak they would have said that in the depths of the night a tall figure staggered towards them, wearing the White Crown of the Upper Land, the wind blowing against his naked flesh. And he had laughed like a child when he reached the great wadi which cut through the rocks and he had looked back to the city and sneered—*"My rampart of a million cubits, my witness of eternity!"*

All day the search went on, and it was not until evening that one of the tomb guards came across his body at the far end of the gorge. Were it not for the White Crown which lay beside him there would have been no way of knowing it was he, for jackals had chewed the body beyond recognition. The famous form he had worn so bravely was a heap of mangled, shapeless flesh. The embalmers scarcely knew how to preserve it for eternity.

No one thought to wonder how he had reached the Orient Cliffs alone. No one investigated fresh marks left by the wheels of a chariot on the desert road, or scattered bits of a woman's clothing on the sand, or a pair of red leather gloves flung loosely on the ground. They chose to believe that he had, miraculously, found his own way by foot into the desert, and in the royal wadi succumbed to the jackals. But jackals rarely, if ever, attacked a living thing.

That most ignoble and horrible death was taken as a final sign that the gods had exacted their ultimate revenge by decreeing that he be torn to shreds in the depths of the night. His own god had not saved him; therefore the Aton was powerless. There were whispered tales of how he was not really dead, of how he still wandered about the fringes of the Horizon. Peasants told wild stories of seeing him pass through their fields by night. Wanderers feared to go near the boundary stones, for it was said that his *ka* hovered about them, disembodied, alone and furious. Still others claimed that he, like Osiris, had been scattered in a hundred directions—his head flung to the south, his legs left in the north, his genitals lost somewhere in the ancient watercourse between the cliffs.

Smenkhare went into the temple of Ra-Horakhte which Wanre had built in the first years of his reign. For him it was the only familiar place in the vast strangeness of No Amon, and on this particular morning it seemed unbearably beautiful. The statues of Akhenaton gazed down on him, smiling. In the sanctuary the altar of the sun was bathed in morning light. He raised his hands to the light as Wanre had taught him and stretched them higher and higher until he could feel his tendons strain and crack. He threw back his head to reveal his face to the god. The golden rectangle bearing the name of the Aton blazed from his chest. He had worn it everywhere, but its light had blinded no one.

Wanre was in the light, on the altar, beneath his feet. The warmth gave him strength and he believed he could still conquer anything. Then he heard a voice behind him and he wheeled around.

*"The sun of him who knows Thee not has set, O Amon!"*

The side chapels were bathed in lime-green shadows and from where he stood the light blinded his eyes and he couldn't locate the origin of the voice.

*"The forecourt of him who assails Thee is in darkness!"*

He called out for the temple servant but no one came. "Who are you, speaker?" he cried. "Come forth and show yourself!"

He was answered by a sound of gentle mocking laughter from the shadows.

*"His sun has set—and yours!"*

The altar was bright with fruits and flowers and fresh bread. The hands of the Aton reached down to accept the sacred gifts.

It was only an instant between the sound of shuffling feet behind him and the sudden smashing blow of the club, which split his skull once lengthwise and twice widthwise in little zigzag lines.

Then his blood became a red libation and mingled with the gifts on the altar, and the long arms of the Aton reached and gathered up the final offering of his flesh together with all the other holy offerings—flowers, fruit, bread, blood, everything.

# THE SECRET PAPYRUS OF AY:
## Circa 1337 B.C.

I who write am Kheperkheprure It Neter Ay, and when four years ago I mounted the throne of the Two Lands I called myself *Ir Maat* in a wild attempt to convince myself and everyone else that my life was a perfect example of justice and harmony. So men hail me now as the "Lover of Truth"—but I am neither, as I know well. The name follows me about year after year in the same manner as an old shoe or glove which one hesitates to throw out even when it casts up enough stink to make the wearer faint.

    I rose from the dust of Ipu to the seat of Pharaoh. Why then have I never captured that elusive goddess who is Truth? Have I not looked well enough or listened well enough, or can't she be seen for her very size? (There's a place just south of the Upper Land where a mighty waterfall renders all the inhabitants stone deaf from its din; so am I beside the deafening thunder of my memories.) But now an image flashes across my mind—an image of the Unspeakable One, standing high above me in his chariot, his face surrounded by sun. He speaks and I cannot tell if he is angry or merely amused. "O Ay," he says, "most incorrigible of men—it's not that you failed to find the answer. Father of the Horse, you never could ask the *question!*"

## King of Egypt, King of Dreams

There is not a single scribe in the palace whom I can trust to write this tale, so my own hands hold the brush and palette beneath the alabaster lamp which I keep lit day and night. (There's a design drawn *inside* which only shows up when the lamp is lit.) My companions are three wine jars bearing the seals of Amenhotep, their juice the juice of vineyards which flourished thirty years ago.

There are times, like right now, when I could swear someone is laughing at me, but the laughter I hear is only the barking of dogs outside the palace walls. The land is full of dogs, dogs and jackals, and the sound of hounds is always at the back of my mind when I think of him. Hounds, twenty of them fighting over some bitch in an alleyway. Jackals, four of them entering the mouth of a gorge....

He has been dead some thirteen years. Now I'm not a superstitious man, but that might be significant for me. Something in me lived and died in him, and I moved about for years beneath his shadow...but why do I say "shadow" when he was in fact the child of light? The land lived in a kind of eclipse when he reigned, though he sang day and night to the sun. But it was a shadow, so black that only a great form standing beneath a great light might have cast it, and even now its dark fingers stretch across the floor and touch my sandals. I knew him well (if indeed one can know the light well, or the darkness) and people still look at me as though trying to catch a glimpse of him through me. Impossible! At this very moment the land dares not utter his name, and women beat their children if they catch them snickering it like an off-colour joke behind the garden gates or between the secret reeds. Something came and went with him, a hot wind through the Two Lands, a wind of change which never blew before and perhaps will never blow again. Even the Breath of Set is not so foul, so compelling.

So, it is death to utter his name. But I, It Neter Ay, Lord of the Two Lands, utter it here in the night, softly, to myself, to him. And it is a prayer or a curse, I don't know which.

*Akhenaton.*

I understand that when one writes his memoirs he should begin with some sort of confession. I confess now—to have it done with—that I've never experienced anything remotely holy in my life. I never understood the passion which causes grown men to moan like lovers at the feet of stone images, or even beneath the sun. I care little for the gods, and if I have ever prostrated myself it was only to kneel and enter the heaven between a woman's white legs—not the heaven of the gods between the turquoise sycamores of the sky. Only once did I see an image which made my blood boil and my eyes cloud. It was carved on a pillar in a shrine at Opet. The king Sesostris and the god Ptah were shown in close embrace, their lean waists encircled by each other's hands, their calm and passionate eyes staring into one another's like those of lovers after the act of love. I made the mistake of mentioning my feelings about it to Wanre, asking, "Is it thus, so subtly, that the man merges with the god?" Then I remember I laughed, embarrassed, and he told me my laughter betrayed me. Just the other day I was looking at an old drawing of Thoth; I noticed how the artists had drawn the headdress over the neck to hide the joining of the human body with the bird's head and I thought—is it thus, so subtly, that the beast merges with the man?

I'm sick of holy things. But I'm lying. I remember long ago I had a long look at the young son of Amenhotep; it was just before we were leaving for the festival of Opet, and I had been standing close to his litter for some time before he noticed my presence. (I had a way of creeping up on people which usually caused me more embarrassment than it did them.) It was one of the rare times I had seen my nephew the prince, and I took advantage of the situation to study him long and hard. The look he gave me in return convinced me that he saw me as Set, the evil uncle of the young Horus, who meant to destroy him. But did I imagine later, when I leaned forward to adjust something and my hand accidentally brushed his—that awful piercing shock which went through my flesh? I have noticed similar phenomena from time to time; as, for instance, when you rub your hand across a piece of silk and then touch the edge of a sword. But then it disturbed me deeply. I've always had very sensitive hands. He must have felt it too, for he drew his hand back with a start, then smiled, a little embarrassed. The sky was blood-red and violet.

In those early years, in my bad moments, I used to ponder over the fact that I owed most of my success to the fact that I was Tiy's brother (borrowing her greatness, basking, shall we say, in her reflected glory). I was a rather important but inconspicuous person, and pondering this, my bad moments usually became worse. I was less than delighted when Tiy reminded me, as she so often did, that otherwise I'd have been a dismal failure in life. Nor did it exactly delight me to know that I'd inherited most of my military titles from the tall white-haired foreigner who was my father. Oh, I worked hard enough at my military career, climbing from army clerk to recruit scribe, then to Chief of Bowmen, Troop Captain and Master of Horse—but it had been known all along that these would be my positions, for I was to function under Wanre in the same capacities my father had under Amenhotep. I was thankful, though, that I never had to inherit his priestly post as supervisor of the sacred cattle of Min in the town of Ipu where I was born. What would I have done in that horrid little provincial temple, I, smelling of horses and leather and reeking with impiety?

Despite my high rank I never felt I'd proven my worth to my own satisfaction. My early years spent as a student scribe copying the ancient books and writing the wisdom of the sages in the common tongue had planted in me an everlasting love for philosophy, and sometimes I longed for nothing more than to spend my days in quiet meditation of the follies of men and the hopelessness of all causes and all gods—save the goddess of Truth and Order, Maat. But Tiy always played with me, goading me on to this or that achievement, yanking me in like a puppet on strings whenever I wished to escape her. I had a thousand frustrated ambitions, and often wished to heaven I'd been no more than a bum in the marketplace, earning my bread and beer by reciting poetry—simplifying life as the happy ignorant workers in the turquoise mines of Sin simplified the writing of our language.

To make matters worse, I was afflicted with that queer disease known as divided loyalties. I was *not* treacherous, as everybody seemed to think. I merely reacted differently to different people. With the king I was one man; with Tiy, another, and so on. I remember being vaguely frightened by the idea that perhaps, after all, everything depends on where one stands. With Wanre I felt obliged at times to point out the logic of Tiy's ideas; but with Tiy I found myself again and again hotly defending her son! How I burned with desire to discuss these new ideas with him! Maybe, I mused, he could incorporate them into the Teaching—thus: *Each man is many men beneath the Aton and he changes according to which ray strikes him at any time.* But then again, maybe this didn't happen to all men, maybe it was only I who changed. I felt all my life like one of those wooden wedges which men hammer into the cleavage of a rock and then soak with water until its swelling bursts the rock asunder.

When Tiy arranged for her son to marry my daughter Nefertiti she cleverly forged a link to the throne through me. I was human, and becoming father-in-law to Pharaoh caused mighty vistas to open out before me; my imagination ran wild as a greyhound let off the leash. I assumed then the honoured title "It Neter," *"Father of the god"*—a title which in ancient times referred to the king's actual father, but later designated that man whose son or daughter married into the royal house. I saw myself at the right hand of the king, advising him in firm yet honeyed tones how to cope with this or that dilemma, just as my own father had once advised Amenhotep and Thutmose before him. I imagined myself eventually becoming Vizier... and limitless vistas beyond that. *It Neter*, I kept repeating to myself in an intoxicated singsong. *It Neter Ay.* When I think of it now, I was a child even in middle age; what foolish things delighted me!

Tiy always knew how ardently I coveted the Viziership; she knew me well. Pharaoh's Vizier is Priest of Maat, the embodiment of order in the realm. I wondered how a man such as I might fare as the chief administrator of justice. The many arms of my conscience branched out like the seven arms of the Nile in the Land of the Papyrus, and sometimes one great stream of thought would break away like the great Canal which runs to the Eastern Sea, and the flow of myself would be weak and misdirected. Time has divided me even more, and today part of me flows in the river of the Water of Ra, and part in the river of the Water of Ptah, and the rest I feel trickling away through unknown channels which never reach the sea.

I was always my own mystery, unable to make a single movement, however trifling or grand, which wasn't at once thrust up against the judging council of my own mind and questioned as to its final value. I needed no Osiris or forty-two judging gods at my death to weigh my heart in the balances, for at least forty-two times a day I weighed myself. My life was always a string of inner queries, but I found peace in my paradoxes. Indeed, if anyone could have provided me with answers to the questions I asked, I would have rejected them anyway, in favour of the questions. I sought no answers, though I pretended to—enlarging my library of philosophical literature, for instance, until the shelves overflowed—for I regarded answers as spiritual stagnation. The disappointment of something *reached*. My love for Maat was perhaps more of a nostalgia than anything else. Childhood, the pure unequivocal desert around my hometown, the simplicity of a life long since lost. . . .

So, I thought, would the many arms of my conscience hinder me from administering fair justice to other men? Or couldn't the most disorderly man deal out order better than the feeble judge with the one-track mind whose *neatness* he confused with Truth? Order is surely born of chaos. Now I know why I always distrusted the pure, the singular man. He is a river with no branches. He flows into the sea. He is a lie.

Akhenaton was a lie. I heard that Hatiay said that on the night he killed himself. At the time I wasn't sure what he meant, but I am now. It is a lie to assume there is only light, only goodness. Behind the tales of creation and the doings of the gods are strange and dark meanings which perhaps only the gods themselves can fathom. If ever the weird stories of the creation and life of the universe could somehow be made *real*, they could destroy that universe; if ever a bull were to enter his mother and be reborn from her loins it would be an abomination. Thus the holy and the obscene exist side by side; beneath Heaven is the *Duat*, and beneath the bright heart of a man is the dark underworld of his soul. But Wanre never permitted himself to reveal that underworld full of the creeping crawling things like violence or bitterness which all men must contain. He distorted those evils and let them build up within him until they emerged in grotesque, insane disguises. He couldn't bring himself to imagine human suffering—but let a flower be trodden on or a useless alley cat be mistreated by children and he'd be depressed for hours. Once I spoke to him about my childhood in Ipu, and how I used to find rocks outside the town in which were embedded little spiral-shaped creatures with frail spines and odd, twisted shapes. They seemed to me like tiny ancient beasts doomed to spend all eternity trapped in the stone. Can you imagine—he almost wept at the cruelty of such a fate, and talked of nothing else for days! I imagined him climbing and sobbing all over the rocks of Ipu, trying to claw the silly beasts out of their prisons, while entire cities starved and burned around him. When I was a boy, I used to pull lizards out by their tails from under the rocks, then string them up by their tails on my mother's clothesline and, as they swung languidly in the breeze, pummel them one by one with stones. I certainly never wept about *that*.

Perhaps his sickness was his violence redirected against himself. Perhaps that's why he used to fall to the ground and thrash and foam—like the time we drove to the House of Amon and he had his battle with MeryPtah, then walked slowly out of the temple gates, gave a single shriek, and fell, his mouth bubbling with white froth. I remember it well; I ran forward and turned him over onto his back and pinned him to the ground, my knees digging into his thighs, one hand clutching his wrists together in a kind of horrible embrace—a distortion of the position a man takes over a woman. The other hand shoved between his teeth. He thrashed about beneath me in painful ecstasy—a victim of such pleasures and agonies as I couldn't imagine—a victim of himself, of the demon fighting to be born out of his head, of the bands of light which penetrated his skull. It was a private war to watch him; his flesh was a battlefield of armies I could not name. After a long time he relaxed and went limp; he gave up a great sigh and gazed at me like a child, as though trying to remember something. His hands moved in my fist, turning. "You hold me to the ground . . . why? Whom have I harmed?" The eyes pleaded with me for an answer, and all I could say was, "Yourself." And a moment later we raced away, the exhausted horses grateful to put space between us and the House of Amon.

I am reminded of the tale of the ancient struggle between the two royal beasts, the bull and the falcon. The falcon lost an eye, and the bull his testes, no less. But many beasts ruled within Akhenaton—snakes, vultures, falcons, bulls—and much more was lost than an eye or a mere pair of balls when the royal beasts fought within him.

I must confess I admired the newness of the Horizon, and never gave much thought as to whether or not it would last. Isn't everything ephemeral finally? And sleeping, I had many dreams of glory, not that I needed them, for I was perhaps the most titled nobleman in the city; I'd been made Chancellor and Chief Companion of the King, Acting Scribe, Bearer of the Fan, and so on. The last couple of titles were mere formalities, and I never bore the fan for Wanre, although no doubt I was free to do so if one day I were so inspired.

He kept *giving* me things—titles, gold ... why? I know why but I won't admit it, I'll never admit it. He was so patient with me, so impossible. When he tried to interest me in the priesthood I pleaded lack of time. Most of the court officials were at least part-time priests and they looked askance at my blunt refusal to take up temple duties. But *he* kept saying he would wait for his beloved Unbeliever to believe.... He knew this only served to make me feel more bound to him, he *knew*.

I remember how I used to wander around my villa, which bored me to tears even though it was one of the finest houses in the city, with a pillared hall and a beautiful garden with water tanks sunk deep beneath the pavement and alabaster lamps which I kept lit all night. A servant used to bring me beer which I sucked up pensively through a long straw while I watched and envied the ignorant fish in the sunken pools. My wife called me Fish-Eye when I got drunk; she claimed I acquired their dazed, watery stare. Strange, now that I think of it, that her name was *Tey* ... but when one is as old as I such coincidences become suddenly significant. At any rate, she was an amazingly discreet woman, sparing in her speech—a quality which I deeply respected. I think I married her because of her silence alone (how I love silence!), as well as her other obvious attributes which, alas, faded with time. I often used to watch her adjusting the perfume-cone on her wig before a party, and I thought the thing was an absurd beehive. But as she struggled to balance it she'd explain how fashionable it was, how the perfume melted when she nodded her head and a shower of fragrance filled the air. Once I was literally attacked by her perfume-cone and a "shower of fragrance" filled my face, my drink, escaped into the cake I was eating and which, not to appear rude, I continued to eat, and I got sick afterwards.

I recall one night in particular when I was going to take a shower, and I felt something deadly grip me as I crossed the floor. A sudden nostalgia, a horrid fear coming from deep in my belly. I realized I was aging. I tried to forget it, for I was a happy man—I must have been, I kept telling myself that. In my tomb I was having these honest and humble words inscribed: *I was eminent, possessing character, successful, contented of disposition, kindly, following his Majesty as he commanded, and the end thereof was an old age in peace.*

Suddenly it hit me. The *end* thereof! I could scarcely remember the beginning!

In my shower room I picked up a bronze mirror and studied my face—the receding forehead and large nose, the protruding cheekbones, big lips and deep jaw. The features were totally unfamiliar to me—a brooding, intelligent face looked out at me, a face from nowhere, the dark face of someone called Ay. *I am a happy man*, I told myself as I settled down beneath the perfumed shower and let its waters, like the Nile, annihilate me. But later when a servant oiled and massaged my weary limbs the mirror revealed more disturbing things—the two deep lines running from the sides of my nose to the corners of my mouth, sunken eyes, the face of a reluctant fanatic who had not yet found anything to be fanatical about, the face of a reluctant believer—in what? That remained to be seen. I had wasted time seeking an ideal, knowing the more one sought the less one found; this was the way I wanted it to be, for I dreaded the idea of one day stumbling upon Truth, however much I fancied the word.

Later the same night I drank frothy beer beneath a shady tree, feeling light-headed and seeming to float away on the froth of my thoughts. I was a pondering a saying of PtahHotep.

## Gwendolyn MacEwen

*Make your popularity a permanent monument to yourself. The good behaviour of the righteous is more acceptable than the ox sacrificed by the sinner.*

Beautiful words, those. Only in intelligence lies the harmonious silence which brings restraint in life. Maat is harmony; anything which is not harmonious is not Maat; anything which disturbs the restrained silence of the thoughtful man is not Maat.

A messenger entered the garden gates bearing a message from Wanre—an invitation to dine with him that evening. That wasn't Maat, it was a definite disturbance of my inner peace. But I was intensely curious. I remember, though, how ill at ease I was through that naked, private little banquet as he smiled at me from behind a leg of duck. We ate in silence, our only communication a sort of silly flirtation like that of adolescents, and the meat in my mouth was dry as paper. When at last he spoke it was to tell me he meant to reward one of his favourites, and I said I'd be delighted to organize another parade for the occasion. Oh, no, he said, he'd get Ranofer to do it, leaving me steaming in silence. Only when I was ready to leave did he cock his head to one side in amusement and whisper, "Be sure to attend, Ay—otherwise I'll have no one to give all that gold to!"

I didn't know whether to be delighted or outraged. If I accepted (and I had to), what would he expect from me in the future? Was he buying me? For what? After giving the matter some deep consideration I decided that while gold might be a disturbance of Maat, it was nevertheless a lovely one. So I chastised myself by reading more philosophy, feeling very pious all the while. *If you become great—after you were small, and accumulate possessions after you were formerly poor—do not be proud because of your wealth! It has come to you as a gift of the god.*

Then came my day of decoration, and crowds gathered below Wanre's balcony heaving and shoving so rudely that the police had to form a tight-knit circle to hold them back. My wife and I were carried on a litter through a sea of bodies and I caught fragments of absurd conversations, like, "Who's all the rejoicing for, anyway?" "For It Neter Ay and his wife! They're being made people of gold!" Recognizing us, the people closed in, laughing and trying to tear our clothes; somehow we managed to reach the open area beneath the balcony and I heard a sentry hiss voluptuously under his breath—"See, these are the beauties of the age!"

I looked up to see Wanre and his family leaning over the balcony—three nude brown princesses; the youngest, tiny as wishes, clambered over his neck and arms. He was gathering rows and rows of golden collars and bracelets, thin flat pieces which he could throw like discs. I lifted up my arms to receive them, and suddenly I realized how similar it was to adore and to beseech. Who was more naked that day, he the giver, or I the receiver? Then as the crowd let up one great shout he threw his blessings down to me one upon the other, and the discs whizzed and spun through the air like a river of falling, spinning suns. I tried to catch them on my arms but missed nine times out of ten, till I felt like a drunken juggler, and Wanre laughed and laughed as the gold eluded me.

Then—two birds came flying at me, and it took a moment for me to realize that they were a pair of brand new leather gloves. Someone must have told him Haremhab had taken mine. How thoughtful of him ... but how odd.

Meanwhile, a servant faithfully ran about picking up the discs and hanging them from my neck until their weight almost choked me. I felt particularly ridiculous and rich, and, for a moment, guilty—but the moment passed (gold made all things pass), and I decided I felt absurd because I'd been cajoled into wearing one of those damned perfume-cones on my head. Some of my friends broke through the crowd and fell upon me laughing and shaking both my hands at once; then they lifted my wife and me up onto their shoulders and paraded us about, as flowers and palm leaves fell on our heads and Wanre's high-pitched laughter cascaded from the balcony. All the little princesses were laughing too—I don't know why.

That night I got roaring drunk and pranced around the banquet hall making, probably, a perfect ass out of myself in front of everyone. The king watched me, no longer laughing, and I heard him ask Parennufer if he thought I was pleased with my honours. The old man answered that of course gold pleased any man. This must have depressed him for he groaned, "Gold! That's only the symbol, the token! Under the Aton everyone is gold, does Ay know this? Of course he knows it, he must—I am his king, I am his friend!"

The festivities continued all night and it was dawn before I found myself delivered like a sack of cauliflower at the gates of my villa, the heavy collars still around my neck. But I'd worn them so long I'd almost forgotten their weight.

It's a strange thing about those gloves. I always loved to have my hands covered (I have terribly sensitive hands), and when Haremhab took my old gloves I felt positively naked and vulnerable for months. The things had been with me in Amki; they were full of blood-stains, wine-stains, and even the marks of Wanre's teeth from the time I shoved my hand into his mouth. Without them I was lost. But the new red pair Wanre gave me were incredible. He'd had them specially made by the best foreign tanner in the city. Taking them off and putting them on was no casual task, for I made a kind of ritual out of it, reverently unlacing the strips and lingering over each glove as it was removed. They gave my days new meaning and I almost arranged my activities around them. I took them off only to eat, bathe and sleep, and these mundane events gained new significance for they became occasions for the repetition of the ritual.... I even looked forward to mealtimes—a fact which my wife interpreted as a renewal of my otherwise lagging appetite—but in fact my culinary enthusiasm was based on the expectation of the slow, almost sensual taking-off ceremony. And when I slept, the things lay beside my headrest; I was terrified of losing them.

I wonder why I'm going on about this. Perhaps because one night I had nightmares that Wanre handed me a pair of something I thought were gloves—but turned out to be a new set of *hands*. Perhaps because I wore those hands, those gloves, when I murdered Tiy, and later took them off and touched the metal Disc on the wall and got a shock like the one I'd had years before at Opet. Perhaps because I wore them later ... in the gorge....

Things would have gone differently if he had never allowed Tiy to take up residence in the Horizon. Had I been him I'd have told her straight, "Tiy, the time is not yet ripe. Hathor, you old cow, don't dare come to my city, don't dare interfere!" Of course I never liked my sister. She was beautiful, but at times from certain angles it was the cheap beauty of a whore. Strip her naked, I used to say (and I knew what she looked like naked), remove her crown and jewels, and you'd have a brooding half-negro slave picked up for a not-bad price at a trading station in Kush. *That* was Tiy. I often wondered about how she satisfied herself in those years after her husband's death; then I learned she had been nicely provided with several young black slaves, all deaf and dumb, but otherwise in fine condition.

Ah, she was enough to give one nightmares. Everything a woman shouldn't be, she was. I remember a day when we walked together to the riverbank and I listened to her weary speech of how she wished she were a peasant's wife, her hands covered with the fertile mud left behind by the river, or basking in a raft of plants and pots. She had reminded me of a great weary dying plant as she spoke of the beautiful vineyards across the Nile (*The deep dark smell of them, Ay!*) ... and for a moment I thought that perhaps she was beginning to soften in her age, and mellow. I thought that perhaps under her ridiculous coiffure was a simple, tired old woman, no longer formidable or proud. We sat among the plants and she laughed and reminded me of the times when as children she and I used to play secret games with each other's bodies. (*Oh, don't frown like that, my brother—children always do such things!*) Then, still laughing, she reminded me of another time, years later in the palace of Amenhotep when we had slept together a little drunkenly, stupidly, and then forgotten about it afterwards.

She did not understand. I did not want to be reminded of that night. Couldn't she see what it meant to me? Didn't she know I was a haunted man?

I used to construct in my imagination wild images of her death. Her blood making a small river within the Nile, her polluted body sliding under the waiting waters, sinking beneath the murky mass of plants. The flood giving the dead weight momentum and carrying it down to the primordial waters of Nun below the earth. Or the flood receding and leaving the Great Mother high and dry in the fields along with the red and black muck that was its gift. The peasants coming at the end of the month of Hathor to sow their seeds and finding her lying in a mud-bath, dead, but fertile as the mud, fertile in the final sense, fertile in her own decay.

One night not long after she came to the Horizon I got thoroughly drunk and started thinking seriously of becoming a temple timekeeper. In my intoxication the idea appealed to me enormously. Imagine, I could spend my days and nights consulting the sacred books, studying the movements of the great and small stars, gazing for hours at Red Horus and the Star of Evening, mapping out the heavenly pictures—the Leg of Beef, the Running Man, the Dragon, the Scorpion, the Ram. What bliss! I'd trace every ten days the rising of a new decan; I'd follow the hours of the night by marking the passage of Sar. I'd be the Watcher of the Night! Then I'd place Wanre as a landmark and he and I would form a north-south axis and I'd announce, "My Sun, when Sar rises about your left ear it will be the seventh hour; when Septet shines above your right eye it will be the ninth." Then in my drunkenness I called to the starry gods of the seventh hour, "O you who are Maat in your flesh, who have magical powers, who are united with your stars, who rise up for Ra...."

But they didn't answer. I knew I was in for a disgusting hangover the next day, but I sat on the edge of a water tank and gazed down at the reflection of the flames from the brazier, thinking them the drunken dancers of my thoughts. I thought of the old legend of how Ra once made Hathor drunk on a ghastly mixture of blood and beer to stop her from destroying the world. I wondered if I could cook up a similar concoction for Tiy.

Now I remember her standing in my garden between the midnight flowers which cast up their dark perfume in a mockery of sweetness. I heard her saying, her voice a seductive murmur, *"Come and join me, Ay, at the far end of the garden."* But I shut my ears. Many years had passed since that one dark night in the palace of Amenhotep when my sister had lain in my arms as my wife.

All the things that Tiy wasn't, Nefertiti was. I pluck from my heart an image of her standing hand in hand with her ungainly young husband, her eyes wide with love, and surprise, and life. They were always—both of them—such alarming children, staring wide-eyed at the green and golden world of their dreams, standing naked in the light of their god. Even when their hands dropped, they were children. They had that frightful innocence which scared me more than the sight of an army. And she was always silently at his side, never trying to impose her character on him or the world outside. For her the flow of life was from the outside in. She allowed all things to enter her, she shaped and reformed the world inside herself—a dying breed of female.

Tiy had ruled, but my daughter never desired to barter the grace of her sex to gain the unnatural respect given to a woman like Hatshepsut, or my sister. People forget such glory and remember only the indignity it casts upon the woman. Nefertiti commanded another kind of respect and her power was enormous, born from the core of quiet within her, yet she herself never knew its size.

Wanre mistook her devotion to life for a religious fervour as strong as his. The innocent, devastating adoration she had for all things inspired his hymns to the supreme god of the world. But her lustrous face in the temple was the face of *human* love. Her eyes were large and pale ... woman's love is large and pale, covering vast seas of life. It can't be focused on a single object as can the love of a man. It can't take on the narrow piercing nature of a beam of light whose intensity takes effect on the world. Rather its nature is flat and broad like a great sheet of water which borrows and reflects a thousand beams at once. But wasn't it this very quality that allowed him to glimpse the vast universal reality of the god? The final form of his religion took shape around *her* largeness of sight, *her* innocence.

But why do I speak of my dead, my noble daughter? Her stone bust sits on a flimsy shelf in the house of Thutmose in the Horizon, surrounded by chisels and drills, fish-hooks, and all kinds of tools. One eye stares across the silent room waiting for the other eye—a piece of dead crystal lying beside it. The dust of the endless morning has long since settled into the floor, and the beautiful head is alone in the golden dark, now, and for infinite time to come. Tonight I long to see it, to send men to the carcass of the city and have them smash down the doors and take it away. But I cannot disturb her. I may be the only man left who knows she is there....

After she died I saw her *ba* many times—a flicker of movement in the air, something white and shot with light at the corner of my vision, something silent as the light is silent. And a white dove who was as she, Thrice Beautiful, came many times to sit on my windowsill in the hour after dawn; but when I used to reach to touch it it flew away, the red sun painting blood on its fragile wings.

I hardened. I became a tube of hardened sand left by the passage of a thunderbolt. I sank into myself, I was hollowed out, I was more dead than all the corpses since the beginning of time. Even now I cannot permit myself to remember her without a flashing pain that jerks my blood back into unwilling life.

Now I come to it. A tale so horrible my fingers can hardly hold this brush as I write. I'm cross-eyed from gazing at the letters taking shape under my hand; my belly's protesting the wine I've drunk, but I must write how he died, and relieve myself of the weight.

It was the night of the full moon and I was sitting in my garden again, trying to locate the constellation of the Ram, when a servant announced that someone was at my gates—a woman who refused to come inside or give her name. I couldn't imagine what female would have business at my villa so late, and it was with intense curiosity that I went and looked outside. A tall slender thing with a black wig, clad in several shapeless garments, stood a few feet from me, its back turned. As I neared her, a bitch in one of the lanes let up a tremendous wail, and the whole pack of neighbourhood dogs clamoured into the lane to fight. Their noise sent shivers through my spine. I could never bear the sound of dogs.

The woman turned to face me and I found myself clutching a knob of the gate for support. Under the heavy black wig was the face of the king.

"*Ay my father*, Father of the Horse, Father of the god, come with me...." he said.

Then he guided himself down the lane by running his hands along the stone walls. There was nothing to do but obey him, and I went after him and found myself trailing my own fingers along the walls as though my eyes were as blind as his. I joined him at the far end of the villa, and we stood together staring bleakly at nothing. The star Sar was just over his left shoulder. I wondered what hour of the night it was.

"Get your chariot," he told me, his teeth clattering from the cold. "Get it and take me beyond my city."

"But Wanre..." I started to protest.

*"Obey me!"*

It took me some time to prepare the horses, and I was afraid that someone might hear the commotion in the stable. But no one woke, the villa slept, and at last I had the chariot ready in the lane. We made off very quietly through the dark streets of the Horizon until we came to the edge of the city. We continued east, through winding paths and across little fields. Then the fields stopped and the desert began. The horses hesitated on the fringe.

"Continue!" he ordered.

"But on what road?"

"The road that leads to the great wadi and the tombs," he replied. "Due east." His voice had become deep and hollow, and the hand that clutched the rail of the chariot was white as death.

We made our way deeper into the desert and soon the Orient Cliffs loomed up before us with the great dark gash between them which was the royal wadi. He bade me stop, and took off the black wig from his head, throwing it carelessly onto the sand. Then he produced from beneath his many robes the White Crown and placed it on his head.

"You see what resourcefulness, what..." he mumbled, and lowered himself down from the chariot and began to stumble towards the moonlit cliffs. His feet made zigzag marks in the cool sand.

"Where are you going!" I cried.

"Due east—to the wadi... and from there, farther east—to the Rising!"

"I'm coming with you," I called after him, and jumped down onto the sand.

He wheeled around and pointed a long finger in my direction. "I warn you now, It Neter Ay! You may follow me but I shall give you the one last command we spoke of years ago."

I stood paralysed for a few moments and watched him zigzag away until he was a white speck in the blackness. *What command?* I asked myself. Would he have me open my daughter's tomb? Then I cursed myself for an idiot, and began to go after him. The horses were confused at seeing me go, but they didn't stray from their spot.

At first I kept a good distance behind him, but gradually I followed him up by a matter of yards. He was removing his robes one by one, and there was a little trail of them behind us. He talked to himself most of the time, saying, "What a beautiful day!" although it was deadest night, and many times he looked up into the skies where the moon shone round and full and whispered *"Aton,"* raising his arms to the god and bathing himself in the sunlight which was not there.

The cliffs were black, the colour of death and of rebirth. His sense of direction was uncanny, for somehow he managed to make a perfect zigzag due east and now we were approaching the stark mouth of the wadi. Once, many generations before, water had run through that dark cleavage in the rock, for the Nile like man has changed its position many times. In times of rainfall the place is a death trap, for the water creates a pounding deluge which instantly drowns anyone within it. Lions once roamed about those rocks, and on that awful night I seemed to hear their ancient, ghostly roaring.

On either side of the wadi were the tombs cut for himself and his family. Nefertiti was there, and Meketaton as well. He entered the gorge, crashing into loose stones and stumbling every which way. Then he was feeling his way with his hands, which were bloody from a dozen cuts, deeper and deeper into the ancient watercourse, stopping every now and then to lift his hands to the sun which was not there and flinging off the last of his robes until he was stark naked as the stone. He wept, he laughed, he called aloud the names of Smenkhare and Meritaton and the names echoed back and forth against the rock walls.

I crashed once against a pile of loose gravel and he turned around and cried, "Who's there?"

"It is I, Apop, Snake of the Night, Slayer of the Sun!" I cried.

"Apop?" came the voice. "I bashed you to death in the temple a hundred times!"

Then he sat down on a rock panting and bleeding, his white skin gleaming, his White Crown gleaming in the moonlight. I thought of how, at that very moment, the silver light was playing about the great thighs and faces of the statues in the parade grounds and silvering the gates of the temple, and lending unreal light to the desert altars....

I approached him and stood above the place where he sat. We were but twenty yards away from the tombs of Nefertiti and the child; I do not know if he was aware of it. His sightless eyes looked up at me and he said, *"When I was sinking to rest in the Chamber of my Eye, I saw..."*

And a strange smile came over his face.

"It Neter Ay!" he concluded. "Come, Lover of Maat, come judge me! Come and right the balances."

And it was as though I heard him say, *"I have carried you around with me all these years like a secret. I have elected you to bring me the gift of my death. That is your destiny and you must fulfill it. Haven't you felt it singing within you since the moment at the Festival of Opet when I was a boy and you touched my hand and drew back with a shock?"*

I felt myself sinking into a trance, and scarcely aware of my own voice I asked him, "What beast's blood flows in your veins? A serpent's blood—a dove's?"

And still smiling he answered, *"Father, yours."*

A thrill shot through me, sensual and secret as the touch before an act of love. He remained motionless below me like a dove held in the gaze of a waiting snake, fascinated by his own deepest fear, yearning towards the yawning jaws.

"My mother the sky stretches out her arms to me," he whispered. "I will become Ra and journey through the great starry cow.... Ay, look at the stars! See them for me!" And then the poor eyes closed, as though to block out even the last shadows of the world they once saw, and he breathed, "Kill me, my beloved Unbeliever, *do it now!*"

I drew near to him, guiltily, passionately, preparing a deed which was part pain, part love—the proportions of those parts being such that no man could count them. Do not lovers turn into antagonists during their act, tearing each other's flesh for love? Do not the barriers between love and hate break down then and all truths become one?

"My Sun Akhenaton!" I cried, and I lunged forward with my knife, my whole body following the thrust of the blade until my weight fell upon him like a rock.

He made no sound as the bronze entered deep into his belly. I lay upon him, feeling the life flow out of him, feeling his heartbeat against my own become fainter and fainter ... until it stopped.

*Pharaoh is dead; the sky weeps, the stars shake, the servants of heaven flee.... He rises up as a god who lives on his fathers and possesses his mothers....*

I arose and looked around. The moonlight shed its ghastly silver film over everything, and the great rocks of the gorge shivered, transitory and unreal, lost in a dream of being. From the lips of the gorge came the barking of jackals, and the walls of the wadi tossed their hideous noise back and forth.

I ran from the place. I did not look back. When I reached the opening I saw the dark shapes of the dogs circling the edge of the desert, passing back and forth between the cliffs and the sand. Jackals, who draw the boat of Ra, jackals, who guide the dead through hell....

Now two of them were entering the lips of the gorge, on the trail of fresh blood. They barked sharply several times more and the noise receded far back into the wadi.

Then two more jackals joined the first two, and the four of them entered the mouth of the gorge.

Had I not fled, I might have had the presence of mind to drag the body onto a ledge where it might have been safe from the teeth of the dogs. But I couldn't contain my deed, and like a madman I raced back to the chariot, passing the bits of clothing he had cast off onto the dark sands. They lay there like parts of his body. At one point I tore off the cursed red gloves I wore (he *knew* red was the colour of evil!) and tossed them onto the ground, so that my hands would lie scattered as his body lay scattered in the dark desert. I spent the rest of the night in the barracks shivering and tossing about with alternating chills and fevers. When he was found, I didn't shave my beard or body for seventy days, and a forest grew up around my face, concealing me.

I took command of the city in the chaotic weeks that followed. Total disorder overcame Maat; there was looting and pillaging everywhere. Hoodlums broke into the great temple and smashed his statues, piling up the pieces in heaps outside the walls. Bands of marauders made off across the desert with gold stripped from the walls of the shrines; they sliced off the golden hands of the god and ran away, their pouches filled with little pieces of the sun. I executed the looters who were captured; I had them killed in public as an example to the rest of the citizens.

I knew that as time wore on, chaos would continue with greater energy, and now the royal tombs in the wadi were not safe to house my daughter and her child. I supervised the secret removal of their bodies to a spot where they were reburied. When Wanre's mangled body was ready for entombment, I had it transported to the same place. They will never be found, this I swear. The secret of the place where they rest will die with me as it died with those who dug the new tombs.

Only one course remained open for us—to abandon the Horizon and move the court back to the old capital. With Wanre gone the city could no longer stand; it seemed to crumble, almost of its own accord. We began the speedy preparations for our departure. Tutu, who had become increasingly insane, managed nonetheless to pack all the imperial correspondence into big wooden chests and bury them—I will not write where—to be safe from the pillagers whose moment was the present and who had no respect for the words of the past. Then Tutu went quietly and utterly mad and spent his last years in complete silence. He was not dumb, for the physicians found nothing wrong with the cords in his throat which controlled his speech. He chose, simply, not to speak, and no one ever heard the voice of the Chief Mouthpiece again.

Parennufer's hollow face and severe accusing eyes almost drove me out of my mind. He alone reflected in those last chaotic days; he became my conscience. The mere presence of that dignified, offended old teacher was enough to put me in even greater confusion. He went about his business, of which there was very little left, in painful silence, his head held high like a young man's, an expression on his face which was almost a sneer. He held himself aloof from everyone, his only friend being the steward Any who was even more ancient than he, and who could also cast his memory back to the days of Amenhotep and Thutmose. They often sat together and drank fruit extract for hours, nodding quietly like two dry leaves in the wind. One remarked on the weather, and the other replied with a profound dip of the head—so profound that both knew the weather was not the topic in question. Three kings had died, but they lived on. Once I heard them muttering to each other, their voices very weary and brittle.

"I always believed," Parennufer was saying, "that in extreme old age, dear friend, a man should take to philosophy. What a wealth of knowledge he should have gleaned from the years! Behind him are kings, armies, cities, generations ... surely he might dazzle his young listeners with his wisdom! But it's not so, not at all. You and I don't even dazzle each other anymore!" He took a long slow sip from the fruit juice and went on. "*We* have seen, *we* know. But we won't live much longer, old friend. What is there left for us to do? What extravagant, dazzling actions are left for us? Well, *I* know what I'm about to do!"

"And what are you about to do?" Any asked, trying his best to appear curious.

"Never mind, you'll hear of it later," said Parennufer.

And they finished their drinks in profound silence.

And what he did he did well, but it didn't dazzle anyone. He stumbled into my quarters one night (I was residing in the palace for the time being) and confronted me with shrill peals of laughter like the horrible cackling noises old women make. I thought for a moment a witch was in my room, but on seeing him I asked if he was in his right senses. I saw that he was severely ill, for between the shrieks he clutched his stomach and supported himself against a table.

"I'll send for Penthu!" I cried, and made for the door.

"Don't bother!" he laughed. "I'm an old man and Penthu's worse than the poison he destroys. I have already, as you can see, poisoned myself. Oh, don't look so grim! I merely felt lonely as I was drinking the stuff and decided to come and die here in your apartments. I trust you don't mind?"

He stretched himself out on a couch, his feeble body trembling with awful sobs and laughter. My resentment at his intrusion was greater than my anxiety for his health and I blurted out, "Can't you go and die somewhere else?" Then I was horrified by my own callousness and went over to him and stood impotently above the couch, wringing my hands and asking if he "needed anything." I was amazed to realize that he had me by the tail and that this incredibly gruesome stunt was an awful joke on *me*. He was gasping for breath but managed to moan, "They say that old men become children before they die. Tonight I'm a child and I'll do as I please! I wanted to perish in your apartment—don't ask me why—it was a whim, it seemed like a good sound idea. Besides, I wanted to put you to some inconvenience!" Another fit of coughing and giggling followed. *"Say your say!"* I told him, and he answered, "I say you're a swine, It Neter Ay. I pity you and anyone else who's left alive in these days. *He's dead!* How does that strike you, Unbeliever whom he loved more than the rest of us?"

Now a whisper was all he had left for a voice, and the small frail body trembled, disappearing into vapid puffs of breath. "I loved his folly, I loved his god. Was I a nostalgic, stupid old fool for that? He was a child; only children question the inner meaning of things which have long since sunk deep into a part of ourselves which sleeps and doesn't care . . . such a terrifying *mature* child. . . . O little prince, what sad thoughts on such a happy day! How beautiful you made even Death! Now your teacher is dying, and he asks for something simple . . . *a draught of water at the swirl of a stream* . . . do you hear me?"

And with that he fell back and died.

I punished the slave girl who had procured the poison for him; I punished the deaf and dumb servant who had first taken the message to her. I punished half of the cooks in the kitchen for no reason at all. Then, not realizing the connection, I punished myself by not eating for four days. I told myself my abstinence was due to a sour stomach from some bad beef I'd eaten on the night of Parennufer's suicide. My heart, such as it was, went out to him.

Before we left the Horizon I went on horseback to the desert altars and rode round and round them as though they were the dark altars of my memories. I wondered if Wanre had ever doubted (as I've always doubted) if there's anything that can give form and order to this life. Isn't the greatest adoration born of the greatest doubt? Are not Priest and Unbeliever, finally, of the same spirit? I was more a caricature of myself than he; I was a kind of fox, playing the double pipes.

An impulse drew me eastward towards the craggy, compelling shapes of the cliffs. I rode as far as the mouth of the royal wadi, but a queer creeping sensation played about the back of my neck and I dared not enter. He was everywhere. In the midday haze I thought I saw a huge dead ibis floating in the air between the cliff walls. I tried to look at the Aton, but I saw only Wanre's face bathed in an awful white. Then laughter fell from the heights of the canyon and resounded through the tunnels of stone—gentle, devastating laughter. I turned back to the city and the same sensation crept up the back of my neck. Now as I write I feel it again. He has followed me forth from those cliffs, his blind white eyes burning holes in my back, his unreal self keeping pace with me, his holy body moving behind me in the bright light of day forever.

Tutankhaton, first in line for the throne, was given a hasty coronation in the Horizon before we left. He was a little less obnoxious after passing his puberty, and had acquired a handsome but vapid face which never quite lost its infantile chubbiness. Given time, I was sure he might one day become a man. Back at the old capital, the servants of Amon, who had speedily reorganized themselves and taken up residence once again at Opet, demanded his re-coronation within the precincts of their temple. Young, and lacking real power, Tutankhaton could in no way oppose them. The powers which arose from behind the throne would rule.

I was the main power. I was appointed at last Vizier of the Realm, the very instrument of Maat. My duties were to advise the young king as to the restoration of the old forms of worship and the old relationships between the royal house and the temple. No other course was feasible, and I considered myself fortunate that I hadn't been done away with, for I was the oldest surviving member of the despised line of Yuyu. My lack of enthusiasm for Wanre's god over the years seemed sufficient proof to everyone that I was not liable to attempt a continuance of his worship. I was, in fact, looked upon as a sort of saviour, a man with sound judgment who could somehow, miraculously, produce order out of chaos. It still amuses me that I had gained such a reputation for sanity.

Tutankhaton, married to the little widow Ankhespaaton, was re-crowned with haste, for we all wanted to be lost in feverish activity and not have to reflect on recent events. We were suddenly too busy to discuss the painful questions that plagued us; fan bearers were too busy swooshing their fans; peasants were too busy tilling their fields. The coronation was clumsy, and Tutankhamon sat on the throne holding the emblems of state with a kind of silly pride as though they were presents someone gave him for his birthday. After the ceremony I encountered Haremhab, who had been appointed Commander in Chief.

"It's really up to us now, isn't it, Ay?" he asked, squinting at me and smiling humourlessly.

"It is indeed, Commander," I sighed.

"I see their names have finally been changed. Tutankh*amon*, Ankhesen*amon*. A good idea. A simple matter, but important. Everything in moderation, wouldn't you say? Keme is like a pregnant woman right now; startle her and she might abort again. We don't want that, do we?"

"We don't indeed," I said.

Then we exchanged one long glance which told us that we understood each other completely and trusted each other not in the least.

I was Vizier to Tutankhamon for nine long years; the temples were once again subsidized by the throne, and peace reigned in the land. Then Tutankhamon died one day after overexerting himself in a hunt and I buried him together with his countless possessions—some of which, like the gold shrine for his coffin, he'd confiscated from his dead brother Smenkhare.

Then I married the royal widow Ankhesenamon, my own granddaughter, for the child was once again the royal heiress for the third time in her brief life. She was a spirited little thing, and desperately tried to avoid marriage with me, whom she termed "her servant." She even sent off a letter to the king of Kheta—he was camped at Karukamesh at the time—asking him for his son in marriage! He was understandably suspicious, for such a request was unprecedented, and let a lot of time slip by before finally sending one of his sons to the Two Lands. The young prince, however, was murdered on the way. What an alliance that would have been! The empire of Kheta now sprawls like a great, fat hippopotamus over half of our former provinces in the north; nowadays the king of Kheta is far more concerned with the rising power of Ashur than he is with us.

I mounted the throne and ruled these last four years. Now as I write, my tomb and temple await me at the westerly branch of the Valley; they will not wait much longer. Commander Haremhab has made a spectacular rise to fame in the last few years and it's certain he'll succeed me. He's so sure of himself that whenever he writes me a letter, which is not often, he deliberately misspells my name— *"Aai, the ass."* He calls himself Beloved of Ptah and Beloved of Amon, so it seems he'll please everybody. The people call him "Mighty Arms, Dictator, Father of the Two Lands, General of Generals, Hereditary Prince," and so on. He has the army behind him plus the unqualified support of the House of Amon. Whereas

I've become lean and feeble, he's gained healthy fat around his middle and looks sickeningly prosperous. Maybe next month, maybe tomorrow, he'll march down from Men Nofer—I'll be dead, thank heaven—and the oracle of Amon will proclaim him king at the Opet Festival. Then he will have to marry the royal heiress—my beastly daughter Benremut, who is now, incredibly enough, High Priestess in Opet. One of the most outrageous developments in the last ten years was her appointment as Divine Consort of the god. I remember years ago when Haremhab was in the Horizon, Benremut was particularly stricken with him and made every effort to gain his attention. At one point the general turned to me and said bluntly, "Keep that scorpion of yours away from me!" Now, all these years later Haremhab will have to marry that "scorpion" to realize his ambitions, *and* consummate the marriage, *and* listen to her prattling for the rest of his life. That more than compensates for his ambition. Everything balances out. Truth is Fair. Right is Right. Maat is Maat.

This fourth year on the throne will be my last, I feel it in my bones. Few will care, I think. No one ever even makes fun of me, I know when I'm not liked. There'll be no magnificent mourning when I lie in my bath of brine. Times have changed. There's a very fine red granite sarcophagus waiting for me—amazing how many sets of funerary furniture I've accumulated over the years, one for every death I've died—and it is the colour of old blood. It has four goddesses guarding the corners, and all I ask of death is that I might bed one of them—Nebhet, perhaps, who is always weeping. Each of my days falls like a tear and when I weep I am my own water clock. Time is flowing from me, yet I look forward to the eternal sleep. *No man takes his goods with him and no man returns who has gone there*, the saying goes, but for me it holds no terror. I have nothing to take and nothing to return to, except maybe the light from this feeble lamp, but even now the flame splutters, dying to die. And the blinding rays of Ra Himself which once struck *his* hands, *his* eyes, *his* loins, are now only sliding streams of yellow tears.

Who will remember him? The tribes in the Land of the Papyrus who copied his hymns, the last few zealots with their secret society in the capital who are found one by one knifed in the back in the marketplace? I have not persecuted these last few followers; but the servants of Amon will not tolerate the merest mention of the Criminal and his god. Thirteen years have passed and still they sing their song of triumph over him—*The sun of him who knew Thee not has set, O Amon.*

My sun, mine too will set. Only last year I made some additions to the small shrine of Ra-Horakhte across the river, the first temple he ever built, the last place Smenkhare ever saw. I did it because I wanted him to see, to forgive—though I loathe the word—me, his greatest non-disciple, his most loyal unbeliever. However, I didn't endear myself to anyone by that move, and I doubt not that in the future my name will also be struck off the list of kings as the name of one too closely associated with the Criminal. But then Truth is Fair. Right is Right. Maat is Maat.


I yearn at last towards my heavenly *ka*. I've become strangely lame in spirit, and nothing can move me—words, songs, truth. The closest I ever came in my life to the ecstasy a man feels towards a god was at the moment my knife sank into the flesh of my Sun. Have I missed something real and imposing as the pyramids? Had I found it, would it have been as meaningless? For a time another river flowed, strong as the Nile, whose source lay in the secret springs of a future world. Wanre was the great clash of foam sent up when the two rivers of past and future met head on. Now the foam dribbles away and the thirsty sands of Keme suck it up as in time they will suck up everything. All is contradiction, nothing is real. Wanre who lived in Truth overthrew Maat.

I've been carried off on the currents of my tale and sailed farther downstream than I had a mind to. But all I have written came from the heart of a dying man. Men do not lie, days before they go to meet their *ka*, lest they wish their very hearts to speak out against them at the Judgment. The great scarab they place over the heart of a corpse will silence the lies of the past, but all I have written here is Truth.

The alabaster lamp beside me burns like living flesh. It is the end of the night, but there is yet another night. The great Ra speaks to the gods of the Duat saying:

*"Open your hidden doors that I may look upon you and throw aside your darkness, and that wind may come to your nostrils and you may not be destroyed and overcome by your own stink or choked by your own dung.*

*"Grant me your help, that I may travel on the following of my Eye and journey forward with those who go to my place in the East."*

If I prayed now I would pray for the power to follow my own Eye through darkness towards dawn. Or perhaps I would pray as *he* taught me.

*"May I be allowed to go out from the Underworld in the morning to see the Aton as it rises, may my two eyes be opened to see the sun, may my name be remembered and established upon earth, may I be permitted to attend the king and queen every day in the palace, entering it in favour and leaving it in love."*

The papyrus of the princess Meritaton lies next to mine on the table; it was written twelve years ago as she was slowly starving herself to death. How feeble some of the characters are, how delicate is the hand. She never intended it to be seen and planned to destroy it, but her end came more quickly upon her than she had planned. I found her lying over the papyrus, dead. I saved the writings all these years—she wouldn't have thought me capable of such an act. I'll send her papyrus and mine—two scrolls worth all the gold in this room—to be buried in the City of the Horizon like two embalmed housecats, side by side. My messenger, who's a marvellous keeper of secrets (he has to be, for he knows if anything goes wrong I'll have him knifed in the back) will bury them beneath the Orient Cliffs. I'll draw him a map of the exact spot. I'll tell him to swear by whatever is holy to him that he'll stop nowhere on his journey and talk to no one. I'll tell him to stand for a moment or two beneath the great boundary stone and repeat three times, *"I have forgotten."*

These writings will go where I dare not go—back to where the winds will cover their tale with many generations of sand, even as they have in a few short years covered the city. The very name of the place is anathema now, and it's no more than an obscene carcass, a haunt for owls and jackals. After we abandoned it the pillagers kept going back, so I ordered layers of cement to be poured over some of the ruins. Peasants still spread tales of how the city is full of crawling evils, and how the *ka* of the great Criminal moves forever round and round the broken walls. In the night I hear it sigh like a wounded animal, yet it is many miles upstream. The desert altars sigh as the sand caresses them, the Great Palace creaks and moans, and the temple is full of lizards and snakes who worship their own invisible gods.

Will these words make the city go to sleep at last, will they still the breathing and creaking, will they make *him* sleep in me at last? I don't want his long face visiting my dreams any longer; I don't want those narrow eyes fixed upon me for eternity. I don't want to hear him as I've heard him every night for the last thirteen years, whispering *Father*.

It cannot be. It is impossible. I have told myself a thousand times it is impossible. Tiy would have told me, after that dark night in the palace of Amenhotep, if—No, I do not want to think about it. After all, I was Father of everything—Father of the Horse, Father of the God, Father of the Thrice Beautiful. And right now I am Father of the whole land. It was only because I was his beloved Unbeliever that he chose me to bring him the gift of his death—wasn't it, wasn't it?

A curse upon any man who finds these writings and reads what is written herein.

But did I not once ask my daughter, *"What does anyone hide anything for, my child, except to have it found?"*

# THE PAPYRUS OF MERITATON:
## Circa 1549 B.C.

Give me the hands that hold your soul
And I will receive your soul and never die.
Call upon me by name forever and ever
And never shall it sound without reply.

No, Smenkhare, I told no one where I buried you. Would the Nile ever reveal its source? Often from out of the dark deserts of my sleep I cry *"Ifnai, Ifnai, he is mine!"* for in death you are mine as in my own death I am yours.

It is easy to die, easier than I ever would have thought. I simply do not eat; I let my body consume itself bit by bit and burn itself out like a candle. They cannot deny me this privilege; I am a royal person and my last command is to be allowed to die. Oh, there are some who try to talk me out of it—my sister Ankhesenamon, who is queen, and my grandfather, the Vizier Ay. He comes almost every day and pleads with me, but I spit on him, this "Priest of Maat." His face is dark and sullen like the bottom of a pool; his eyes are slanted and his mouth curls downward in a perpetual sneer. I sense there is blood on his hands, but I don't know whose. Sometimes I think it is our father's blood. Today I slapped his mouth (I hate his mouth) and he left my room with his head hanging, like a sick dog.

Tutankhamon struts about his palace in a robe studded with little golden rosettes, playing at his newest game of being king. The Horizon is no more and the royal house dwells once again in the city of Amon. After his coronation the little beast took his revenge upon you, and permitted the priests to close down your mortuary temple and forbid you the privileges of a royal burial. He, like them, did not acknowledge that you were ever king. The servants of Amon confiscated all you possessed; they seized the three golden shrines that were to house your coffin, the little golden coffins for your vital organs, the chairs and couches, the *ka-house* for your statue—everything. They ground out your name from the furnishings and one day they will be used for the tomb of Tutankhamon. May it be soon! May he meet his death in some disgusting ignoble manner that will make people snicker and laugh!

Meanwhile your body lies in the dankest, filthiest hole in the Valley of the West; even a peasant would shun it as his final house, but in your meagre death, Smenkhare, you are more of a king than the spoiled boy who now sits on the throne.

I feel I am eight years old again, and I am falling, falling onto the magical floor in the palace of the Horizon. My big turquoise ball rolls across the pavement, over the animals and birds, the painted cranes standing one-legged in their painted marshes. It rolls over the flat papyrus thickets, the herons and flamingos and kingfishers and ducks. How I loved that floor—the green zigzags on the plaster, the tall reeds and flat faces of the captives of Khor! I used to sit in the different squares and make fantasies about the occupants. One day I was in the papyrus thicket square, which in itself was not very exciting, but it reminded me of the times my nurse Benremut took me to the riverbank to play among the waterplants, dozing there and having horrible dreams of the ovens of Hell, the lakes of Fire, the Swallowers. Dreams of crocodiles surfacing from the water with the hands of Horus between their teeth—the most honourable death was to fall into the Nile and be devoured by a crocodile—dreams of Isis hovering in the air like a hawk over the corpse of Osiris, taking his seed. I didn't know what that last part meant, but it sounded wonderful, and after all, I couldn't understand all the legends Benremut told me. Father said

I had to forget those awful tales, for they had no part in the Teaching. He told Benremut to shut her mouth, which was hard on her, for her mouth was all she had, really. She was never quite the same afterwards; she'd sit all day stringing collars and cursing when she dropped the beads. She'd learned the curses from Ay, who was always willing to share his vocabulary with anybody who was interested.

She couldn't care less about the floor. I couldn't understand how anybody could just walk over it to get somewhere, without getting lost in it, or lying flat out upon it like I did. Flat out, my toes stretching far as the foot of the flamingo, my fingers reaching back to poke out the eye of the Khorian.

I was the Beloved of Aton, and I wore long strands of jewels in my ears and a wide collar of flowers and nothing else. My fingernails were bright silver, and all the hair was shaven from my head except for one sidelock held by a turquoise ring. This drew attention to my long narrow head. All my sisters had long heads too, like our father; he permitted us to wear no headdresses to disguise the elongation of our skulls. It was not an abnormality, he said, but a sign.

I was small and tubular and unripe, and my body was for me a kind of toy, a lithe nut-brown thing with no dark places, no secrets.

The big turquoise ball went plop into the pond and I lay back imagining that I was painted onto the floor. Father would come and be unable to find me; he'd walk all over me and I'd just scream with laughter. Then he'd look down and see that his princess no longer lived in the world of men. They'd bring me my food and I'd still have to continue my writing lessons, but it would all be so much more tolerable. How silly everyone would look— giving advice to the floor, scolding it, taking orders from it! I laughed out loud and Benremut looked up dully. Like her father Ay, she had no sense of humour. She never smiled. She laughed a lot, but that's different.

Then I looked up and saw you standing in the doorway. You were brown and lean and you wore the pleated linen tunic of a young aristocrat. You were confident but not arrogant; you seemed overly serious, always brooding over some secret problem. But you were only eleven then, and the sidelock hadn't yet been shaven from your head. Your eyes were wonderfully clear and large, your features small but well-shaped. And your teeth, when I could see them on the rare occasions of your laughter, were even and white. You were so restrained and controlled, but there were always parts of your body which betrayed you—a flickering muscle in the cheek, a hand clenching and unclenching. Your left eye, more candid and clear than your right....

You stood for a moment absorbed in something, then wandered over to me and sat down on the Khorian's left foot. A small live bird was pulsating in your palm and you held it out to me. "I caught it this morning in the marshes, do you want to hold it?" you asked. I answered, "I'm a floor, and a floor can't hold anything!" but then I felt rather silly and accepted the tiny throbbing bundle of white feathers. You showed me your new throwstick, painted bright blue and decorated with flowers and *Wedjet* eyes. "The king your father gave it to me, it's the same kind as his!" you said proudly. "When I throw it, it's so well glazed that it catches the light and flies like a shiny blue hawk against the sky!" You fondled the weapon and I watched you, proud that you chose to speak to me about such remote boy's business.

"I just clipped this bird on the wing, enough for it to fall," you said, and while its warm vibrant belly nestled in my palm I told you about my father's aviary which was going to be built in the North Palace with hundreds of little niches for nests and long drinking troughs. I asked if you intended giving him the bird, and you replied very emphatically that you'd catch a rare one for him—one he could never find himself. At that moment you reminded me of someone I knew very well, so well that it was impossible to recall.

You looked down at my body. "You have no breasts," you said.

Now I had often watched how grown-up ladies behaved with men, and I replied with what I thought was the proper mixture of coyness and sophistication. True, I was only eight, but in Keme one learns such things very early. "In three years my breasts will start growing, I was told they would. But if you speak to me again about breasts I'll tell Benremut. You may come back in three years and see them, though—if you like." Then I turned sideways and pressed my fists down between my legs in what I thought was an attitude of mature indignation. "You don't have any either!" I cried.

"But I don't want any."

"You have *something else*, and I know all about it."

"And that's another thing you don't have!"

"I don't need one—so there!"

"Well, you look pretty funny without it," you said, staring down at the naked little hump between my legs.

I took the bird and placed it there, to cover my nakedness, but you gently removed it from my lap and held it by the feet while it fluttered and tested its wings.

"When you have breasts," you whispered, "I will come and touch them."

I started to protest but when I saw your mouth pulled back in a wide flashing grin, I forgot what I was going to say and gazed fascinated at the most beautiful teeth I had ever seen. Nevertheless, I vowed to tell my father of your impertinence.

"Keep the bird," you said, "and in three years it will fly away free." You forced it back into my hands, got up from the floor, and passed out through the gates. The blue throwstick still flashed in your hands, catching the afternoon rays of the Aton on its glaze. I stayed a while longer and tried to renew my games, but soon lost interest and found myself musing on how the north harem where you lived was almost exactly opposite my quarters in the royal estate, across the Royal Road. And from the top terrace of my father's garden, where all the trees were, it would be very easy to see.


Then suddenly I was ten, and I watched Father's artisans make my set of coffins. Strange to be a child and look dispassionately upon one's own house of death. Foreigners think that we in the Two Lands love death, but how wrong they are! We hate it and dread it and we furnish ourselves for the great journey well in advance. It is life we love, jealously, painfully, and wish to continue it forever.

They were grinding up lumps of red ochre into a paint crimson as blood. There were three coffins—each to be contained in the other, like three generations, I think; past, present and future. The middle one was made of wood and covered with great sheets of gold foil inlaid with a feather pattern of turquoise and carnelian stones. A long strip of gold ran from the chest to the feet, awaiting the insertion of the signs which would identify me. I watched them lay the gold mask over the wooden face and I stood transfixed with its beauty and wished my own face could be pure gold.

Then I felt something behind me, and turned to see you watching me, your head cocked at a studious angle, your eyes slightly squinting. "I am thirteen today," you announced, and stared at the coffin with its great wings of jewels. You walked around it, your face clouded with some strange trouble.

"What's wrong, don't you like it?" I asked.

"I don't know, don't ask. I think I saw a name on the golden strip."

"*My* name will be on it, and my father's, and the name of the Aton."

"Those were not the names I saw," you said.

We walked down the long path from the palace to the river and the way was lined with shrubs and palms. Father's barge floated on the green water held by mooring stakes to the shore; its dozens of oars languished in the river like tongues, its masts were straight as young men's spines, white sails shivered high above the bright red cabin. Around it were sycamore skiffs, single-sailed boats, a few freight ships waiting to carry out their cargos of coloured glass which the Horizon manufactured. Fishermen, their faces brown as ancient papyrus, sat mending nets by the shore.

"You still have no breasts, Beloved."

"Next year I will. This year I have buds and they hurt me."

"I bet you can't run, then. I've seen girls your age running and they look like they're going to fall apart."

"I can run!" I cried, and to prove it I darted down to the riverbank and collapsed beneath a palm. You sat beside me and drew up your knees to your chin and rocked back and forth. We spoke of the seasons and you told me your favourite month was this one, Hathor, because it was your birthday, because the river receded and the air cooled and the peasants sowed their crops. I told you mine was the first month of the flood, and you replied that that was how it should be, for the river in its inundation was like a woman, while the river receding lean and calm was more like a man. I didn't see the point, but I nodded wisely and told you about the time I found a foreign coin left behind by the Nile; I had washed the mud from it and shown it to my father. But he had thrown it back into the Nile, for there was an image on it which displeased him.

Once again an expression came over your face which reminded me of someone I knew very well.

"What are all your other names?" I asked.

"Names! I have a hundred names!" and then you recited something:

*In the Great House and in the House of Fire*
*On the dark night of the counting of all the years,*
*On the dark night when months and years are numbered,*
*O let my name be given back to me!*

I asked you what it meant but you said you really didn't know. You found it written in one of the ancient books in the Baou Ra. "But the books in the Baou Ra libraries are forbidden!" I cried.

"Not to me they aren't," you murmured, and your expression told me the matter was closed.

We watched the green heaving river for a long time. The great Nile with its seven mouths, its living pulse, its green death. We argued about its source, for I believed it was born in the Underworld, but you scoffed and called me a child. You had known that was untrue, since the tender age of seven, and since then had lacked all such illusions. You several times got into fistfights with your young friends over it.

"All right, then, where *is* the source?" I asked.

"What do you mean, where is the source? I don't know *that*. I only know it's *a secret of movement, a darkness in daytime.* Wanre told me that."

You were silent a long while, then said suddenly, "Would you like to live long?"

"Father says the Aton determines the length of life. And you?"

"Short, like the wind. I want to burn and die like a thunderbolt, like a flame."

The living river was west; the hollow tombs in the cliffs were east. Between life and death we sat, between the water and the stone we sat, children who did not know the meaning of our own words. We went back to the palace and parted at the gates.

"I understand nothing," you said, and I burst into a fit of nervous laughter (I'd been laughing a lot lately; it had something to do with having hurting buds of breasts and being almost eleven). Then I ran away and left you standing alone. Now when I think of you I do not remember you as a king, but as a boy on his thirteenth birthday saying, *"I understand nothing."* And I did not even know the nothing which you didn't understand.

I remember the day I wore a necklace of glass fish and grasshoppers joined by small glass suns, and a palm-leaf basket laughing with flowers hung from my arm. The air was a web of gold as we walked through the gardens of the summer palace of Meru Aton. Ahead of us was my private shrine, surrounded by tiny canals and water-plants, and I told you that yesterday I'd offered a goose and five ripe melons to the god. You trailed along with me beside the gurgling musical canals and said that my father's world was a miniature garden like this one, and that he must begin to look outside, or the weeds would eat their way into his world and destroy it.

"That's monstrous!" I cried. "If you were king, what would *you* do?"

"I'd preserve the garden," you said, "I'd make terms with the weeds!"

Just then I spotted a rabbit and went bounding after it behind a bush. I got down on my belly and tried to poke my arm through the little thicket where I saw it disappear, but it got away. I felt you drop softly beside me then.

"Princess, you have breasts. Let me touch them!"

"But Benremut—"

"Is busy watching her reflection in the water...."

Shyly you placed your hand on one breast, then on another. You touched a glass fish on my collar and said you wished you were a fish plunging and dipping into mysterious rivers or swimming about in secret enchanted pools. Just then your finger caught on one of the grasshopper's sharp glass feet and you winced with pain. A drop of blood appeared at the tip. I rolled over and over on the grass laughing at you, but suddenly your young body was flat upon me and your mouth covered my mouth. For a moment I did not breathe or move; then I pushed you away. "She's coming!" I whispered. And we had just enough time to get up from the grass before Benremut reached us.

That night, alone, I caressed the small glass fish. I wanted to touch that secret part of you I'd never seen but only felt when you were upon me, that strong hard part between your legs which was made to dive and swim in dark unknown rivers. Recently my mother had told me I should expect something very soon. She had wept, and I had asked myself, why was Nefertiti weeping, she who was so beautiful, no one in the whole kingdom was half so beautiful, why did my mother weep?

And a week after you fell upon me beneath the bushes of Meru Aton, the red wetness between my thighs told me I had become a woman. The kiss must have made it begin in me, your hard body must have drawn it out.

A month before you became my husband we couldn't encounter each other without stammering and blushing, for the memory of that afternoon in the summer palace loomed up before us golden and red. Now you were eighteen, and I, fifteen. Tiy was dead. My beautiful mother Nefertiti was dead. We were no more children. We knew more was to come for us than a kiss in the bushes or a cut finger from the edge of a glass grasshopper. What would it be like? I asked myself a thousand times but my imagination called up only the most hazy pictures. Behind the haze, though, my blood coursed strong as the Nile in flood, and my blood knew. It would be a new and secret form of night. The Lord of the Atmosphere holds heaven and earth apart, but when Nut descends to lie with Geb, everything becomes dark as it was in the beginning.

On our wedding night after the feasts and dances were over, we were alone in our vast apartments. Two great eunuchs stood in the hall outside our door, guarding, not our privacy as I then thought, but our very lives. I turned upon you, forgetting everything but the gnawing doubts in my mind, and demanded to know your plans once you were on the throne. Were the ugly rumours true? Would you tear down all that Father had built? Would you use him like the others had? I was white with anger, but you remained very quiet, letting me circle around you, listening and not listening.

"Sister..." you said.

"I don't want any romantic words from you!" I cried. But I saw that flashing smile on your face, the one I'd seen years ago when you brought me a bird you'd caught in the marshes.

"Let me tell you something..." you began, but I strode across the room, carefully avoiding the sumptuous bed strewn with flowers and sprinkled with a dozen different scents.

"Don't come any nearer... upstart!" I cried, and you followed me with your hand held out, smiling still, making a game of my anger. Then I trembled, for something delicate was moving within me, something raw and untouched.

"I'm not going to destroy the king," you said. "I'm going to restore him. What do you think he and I have been talking about these last four years? Now...look in my eyes, Beloved of Aton, and tell me who I remind you of...."

I looked and my hand flew to my mouth in surprise. The same narrow eyes, the same features, only softer, saner than his. Why had I not seen it before?

"Now you know why I call you *sister*. Once he asked me whose blood flowed in my veins, and was it the blood of Amenhotep. And I said, *No*, feeling at that moment something touch me soft and sharp as a wish. *No*, I said... and I whispered, *Royal brother, yours!* but his back was turned. Look, my mother Sitamon was his sister, and he lay with her—I know this, for he told me—when he was a boy no older than I. He doesn't really know if I am his... but he's watched me all these years. He called me the Child of the Aton, he called me his Beloved. Today he called me *his son*."

"Who else knows?" I asked, my voice so soft I could scarcely hear it.

"No one. He says it would mean my death to have it known."

Now I looked at you and whispered *"brother,"* and the word was not strange on my tongue; it was as though I had spoken it inwardly a thousand times. We stared at each other and saw nothing but the shadow of the king our father who had made us one. Your flesh was my flesh; your mouth, my mouth. The great wings of the royal hawk thrashed the air between us. You took my hand in yours and placed it over your hard sex as once many years before you gave me the white wild bird you caught, to hold, to feel its shape and pulse, that I might not fear it.

"I don't want to hurt you, sister...."

"It will only be the first moment."

Then we were sinking into the vast bed of linen and flowers, into a private garden, into the magical painted floor of the palace to lose ourselves among the birds and lotuses. And we were lost among the magic squares, we were children lost in the bushes of Meru Aton, we were man and woman lost in the great bed which had become the world.

And I murmured from the depths of the garden, "Come down, my brother, come down." And you came and roughly ripped the collar of beads and flowers from my throat and threw it across the room where it fell in a hundred pieces. We watched each other's faces and smiled; we were on the verge of laughter, triumphant silver laughter of children no more children. Our eyes never closed, not once, as the profound flowers pulled us down and down. And when our bodies came together it was heaven descending upon earth and creating night. My loins rose and called you in, and the pain was a moment felt and forgotten like the pain the glass grasshopper once gave your finger. My body obeyed some instinct it never knew it possessed. It swam, it danced. It arched up once, and again—and the movement surprised you and you gasped, and the gates of your loins opened. And as the sweet salt seed burst from your sex another instinct made me open my mouth wide with a cry or a laugh—

"O my brother, yes, *yes!*"

The next morning your soul, like a new alien body, throbbed within mine. And across the room was a sea of beads from my broken collar.

The day we left the Horizon the quays were crowded with vessels flying bright ribbons and streamers; hundreds of masts rose from the river and the shores were lined with silent citizens waving limp flowers and palm leaves. From the west gate of the palace a long line of porters and officials came to follow us down the flowered path to the river. It was the same path we had walked as children, but now we were the co-rulers of Keme. Would we ever walk down that path again?

The silence of the crowds on the shoreline filled me with fear and the faces of the officials were drawn and tense. Father waited for us, motionless beneath a red and blue canopy, clutching the royal emblems to his breast as though he feared someone would take them away if he held them less tightly. Then you and he faced each other for the last time, and your eyes searched one another's eyes for a reassurance neither could give. There was nothing to say. You wore the Blue Crown, the helmet of war, the crown he had worn in his youth.

And when I embraced him his body felt like some great shivering plant that the merest wind could destroy.

The great boats pulled away from the shore and formed a long procession in the river. But the silence on the banks was the silence of a funeral, and I felt we were sailing upstream towards the Valley of Death in a blaze of boats, and that we were already dead.

I looked back and saw that the red and blue canopy had become a purple splash in the distance. I imagined him under it, still clutching the royal emblems, his knuckles dead white from the strain, a small river of blood running down his wrist. I screamed with fear and ran into the cabin, and you came and hid your head in my breast and whispered, "I know, I feel it too. Time closing in on us, *myriads of years*, a string of endless suns hanging about our necks. We are the land. Last night I was strong, I dreamed I was Horus the Avenger, plucking out my eye to save my father. I whispered, *I come to thee, Father, arise for me. I gather thy bones, I make thee whole* ... but today I am weak. I feel him there, downstream. I feel we will not see him again!"

"Say no more!" I cried, and held you to me. We clung to each other because we were more than ourselves; we were *him*, we were his body, his blood, and in our embrace we held him together, and in our separation he fell apart. And only when we loved was he made whole.

For most of the journey we stayed in the cabin. Neither of us wanted to look at the river.


Do you remember the incredible old hag who came in front of our procession in the city of Amon, who stood before our litter and refused to give way? She traced a circle in the sand with one naked hideous foot and mumbled something under her breath. One of the guards stepped forward to remove her, but on seeing her face he winced and moved away. She screeched like an owl and came up beside you and bent her head down to yours and whispered something in your ear. I never learned what she said, you would never tell me... but the power of her words could be seen in the sudden pallor which drained your face. You drew back, your mouth taut; your hand flew to the insignia of the god which hung from your collar. The hag laughed and disappeared into the crowd.

And our scribe Pawah identified her. *"That,"* he said, "was the Divine Consort of Amon in the days of Amenhotep. That bundle of rags was once the High Priestess of Opet!"

I trembled with cold. I had heard that her power had been great. That gruesome witch with the filthy breath had once lain with the god Amenhotep as the earthly wife of Amon, and had wielded as much influence as the High Priest himself. It was said that hers was the voice of the oracle which had first cursed our father when he was a child. Today she had cursed you. I begged you to tell me what she had said, but your lips tightened, and the chill in my bones sank deeper.

And when we entered the gates of the palace of Amenhotep you remarked that it looked like the dry bones of a desert bird picked clean by vultures. I could not bring myself to believe that I had been born within those walls. The peaks of the West rose up beyond them, and it was as though we had already entered the land of death.

In those horrible months at the old capital there was one thing which frightened me more than the chaos which surrounded us. I did not conceive. Your seed did not take root in me. The simplest peasant could lie with his woman once in the fields and she'd become fertile, but though we lay together a hundred times I was empty. Was that the curse the witch placed upon you? I wept into the hollow place between your shoulder and collarbone and cried that the gods were taking their revenge on our father by making us sterile. You tried to soothe me with silly jokes and puns (*remyet, romyet*, man was made from the tears of the Creator)—but even as you did your own body trembled and we made love in furious, frightened defiance of whatever perverse force choked the life in our loins. I took to wearing a knotted cord around my neck as a charm—the kind that peasants use—made of small cowrie shells which looked like the vulva of a woman.

Then one night I dreamed I saw you slain on the altar of the sun, and the next morning I feared for you and took Pawah with me and went into the temple of Ra-Horakhte. I found you as in the dream, fallen across the altar. The gates of heaven broke and the great vaults collapsed around me. The universe burst in my head and the body of Nut with its flesh of stars was soaked red with your blood. Your face was turned down, as though in the shame of your own death, and you were one with the sacrifices. The Blue Crown lay at your feet. I bent over you and called your name.

Pawah went into the dark recesses of the shrine and sought out a servant and asked, *"Who did it?"* And the fool answered with a smirk, "Ask not who is guilty, but who is *innocent* these days, O scribe of Ankheprure!" Then your gentle Pawah struck the man across the mouth.

And when we went to take you away, my brother, the altar of the sun burned with its offerings and you lay among the bloody flowers and the bread.

The same day word came of the death of our father. I do not remember anything about the weeks that followed. I think perhaps I became Isis and kept watch over your body for endless days.

By the time your body was ready for burial Tutankhamon was already on the throne and your belongings had been seized. There was only one place to bury you—the filthy hole where the desecrators had thrown the shrine of Tiy. I cringed to think that such a foul place would be your house of death, but there was nowhere else.

We gathered together all we could find—cast-off bits of things in the palace, discarded pieces of furniture made for others. I felt as though I was combing the world for those miserable trinkets which would accompany you on your journey. Then the meagre furnishings assumed gigantic proportions in my imagination. I listed in my mind again and again the articles which would surround you, as though the repetition of the list would somehow increase their number. Even now it soothes me to remember them:

—Four magical bricks bearing the name our father bore when he first took the throne. We feared to insert your name in place of his, lest they crumble to dust.

—Four alabaster jars made for me when I was a girl, to contain my vital organs when I died. They had my portrait on the lids, and the irises of the eyes were black jasper. I had glass cobras added to the brows, and my name ground away from the surface of the jars.

—One small trinket box containing an inner box full of broken, useless things—small vases and playing wands and pendants of ibises, and a little silver goose head....

—And one of the coffins Father had made for me in the City of the Horizon. (Remember the day you stood behind me watching the artists work upon it? You saw a name and it made you afraid; now I know it was your own name you saw.) It was the middle coffin in the set of three, and we changed it from that of a princess to that of a king. It was as though my own body was being reworked to accommodate your death. My golden hands holding *ankhs* became your hands clutching the royal emblems—a crook and a flail of blue glass beads on rods of bronze. The gold mask which was my face became your face; a blue beard was added, and a green and gold cobra on the brow. The words on the strips which were to have run down my body were changed from feminine to royal male, and down the length of the coffin from chest to foot the brilliant red and blue letters were adjusted to spell your name: *Beloved of the King of the Upper and Lower Land who lives in Truth, Lord of the Two Lands, the goodly child of the living Aton, who lives forever and ever, Smenkhare.*

It took the workers from twilight to dawn to drag the poor furnishings down the stairs into the shabby hole and arrange your house of death. We paid them well, but they never knew who they were burying. When first we led them through the dark Valley they were quiet, but when they saw where we were going they let up shrieks and groans and vowed they would approach no closer the dirty little tomb where the desecrators had thrown Tiy's shrine. A serpent dwelled within it, they said, with eyes that could paralyse a man and render him mad and impotent for the rest of his days.

Then with one great sweeping gesture Pawah lifted the sheet from your coffin and pointed to the royal cobra on the brow whose eyes gleamed in the moonlight. "There is yet another serpent whose gaze can paralyse a man!" he cried. And as they shrank back in fear he shouted, "Choose!" They chose, and continued their work.

But during the night it required more gold to hold them to their task, for one of them kept scaring his companions out of their wits by pointing to moving shadows on the tomb walls or claiming that the coffin lid had burst open of its own accord, or by stepping over the collapsed walls of Tiy's shrine with his feet making a noise like that of a barking dog against the thin metal. The night was filled with their prayers to Amon and Ptah and Hathor until they had called down the entire colony of the gods to protect them in their deed. Once one of the men, who was very drunk, fell down trembling and begged to be allowed to go home, but at that very moment the others accidentally banged the coffin against the shrine, and he took it as a sign of royal anger. Green-faced and gasping, he went about his work.

When it was over, I stood alone in the tomb, aware for the first time of the peeling plaster and the reeking dampness of the walls. An old leak near the door had been cemented over once in the past, but now it opened again, and a trickle of water crawled along the floor towards the lion-headed bier which supported your coffin. One drop per hour, maybe more, maybe less, would flow beneath your body. One drop per hour for eternity . . . enough to rot the bier, the coffin and all its contents! There was no time now to shift you to the eastern wall. How many years until those drops attack the wood of the bier, then soak through and soften the linen strips which bind you . . . and then seep into your flesh?

I put my fist to my mouth to stop the scream. I removed the white sheet from the coffin and in the half-light from the torches I saw something else. There was a thin line of shadow along the side where the lid had slipped open from rough handling. That child's coffin was too small for a man... and some of the gilt plating had been knocked off from the foot-end when it had lurched and bumped down the stairs of the shaft.

I heard an argument going on outside; the burial crew was threatening to return home without sealing up the tomb unless their payment was doubled. Pawah's angry words echoed down the shaft. "Scum! Drunkards and death-mongers! You've been paid enough. Scavengers—you would turn around and break open this same tomb tomorrow if there was enough wealth in it. But I warn you, this place is doubly cursed!"

There was a silence and I heard Pawah lower his voice and invent a last cunning story to scare them off. "Do you know who you've buried this night?" he asked. And into the uncomprehending silence which followed he flung the words, "You've buried the bones of Tiy, who was a commoner like yourselves and whose body was destroyed on the pyres of the desecrators!"

They fell at the mouth of the tomb blubbering with horror. Not one of them would reveal the whereabouts of the place, not now.

I stood over you. All the torches had flickered out save one, and its light played upon your golden mask, your hands. I suddenly remembered that of the three coffins—past, present and future—this was the middle one, the present. Only it had survived, for the past was destroyed and the future unsown. Inside it you lay with one of my collars about your neck and three of my bracelets on each of your arms. Your fingers were capped with little caps of gold; once your living fingers upon me had been warm as the sun. And you were crowned, for days before I had torn the golden vulture from your chest and twisted it round and round and placed it on your head.

You lay in the attitude of a woman as we had arranged you—left arm across the chest, right arm straight down with the hand against the thigh, to mislead anyone who might one day find you and think you were the Beloved of the Criminal.

I knelt at your feet and read the prayer which was cut into the gold foil:

*I breathe the sweet air from your mouth*
*And gaze upon your beauty every day.*
*To hear your voice like the north wind*
*Is all I pray,*
*For love will give life to my bones.*

*Give me the hands that hold your soul*
*And I will receive your soul and never die.*
*Call upon me by name forever and ever*
*And never shall it sound without reply.*

Then I heard myself crying *"Smenkhare!"*, the syllables bursting upon the foul air of the tomb, their sweetness for a moment erasing the salt smell of death. *"Smenkhare, Smenkhare!"* ... remembering the time when as children we had run laughing to the river-bank, our feet tangled in flowers and river-plants, the kiss in the bushes of Meru Aton, the drop of blood on your finger from the glass ornament. I had laughed then, to see your blood. And in my mind an old song:

*O fair boy, come to your house,*
*I am your sister whom you love,*
*You cannot leave me*
*My brother, my brother!*

... The bed of ebony and straw, our bodies straining the woven cord beneath us, my necklace of cowrie shells clattering and protesting in our dance of love....

"The dawn!" Pawah shouted from the top of the shaft.

I did not answer, for there was one thing left to do. Now I was unreal, yet fully real. It did not seem strange to me when I found myself hovering over you like Isis hovered over Osiris in the form of a hawk. Nor when I felt myself lying along you, the length of my body along the full length of the gold and turquoise and carnelian letters, the brilliant signs which spelled your name. Then the name was burned into my own flesh from breast to foot. My arms were the wings of death embracing you, and it seemed my loins received your last gift, the seed of your death.

Then I stepped over Tiy's shrine which still lay unhinged at the entrance. Banged up and beaten, it bore the titles of that fearful woman who was my grandmother. On the panel she and Father were making burnt offerings to the god; his image had been obliterated, yet the marks of its obliteration were deeper than the outlines of her body.

I went up the filthy stairs out of the tomb, and stepped out of the foul dampness of your eternal house and into the slanting rays of dawn. The workers re-sealed the tomb with the seal of the nine captives beneath the jackal, the symbol of the priestly college of Amon-Ra. The seal of the past had been broken only once, and then restored.

The rays of the Aton were remote, virginal. The power of the god was in its rawest form. Things were merely being *lit* by it, not drawn towards it. Was this the horror that my father had felt, was this his private fear—the *remoteness* of the god? There was nothing beneficial now in those awful rays, nor did it seem to me there was anything simple about dark and light—for this cold impersonal dawn was for me another kind of darkness, a new and secret form of night.

My life is as worthless now as a grain of chaff or a single bead. But I don't fear death. You lie within my own coffin, and it is like the shell of my body containing you forever. You are caressed by my great wings of red and blue and gold. My end is upon me, but it is my victory. *Smenkhare!* I possess your secret name; did you not grant me your eternal soul when you told it to me? O my brother, your breath is locked forever in my ears where once the name was whispered, and I defy eternity to take from me what is mine! ... I have just remembered something. Before I left your tomb I pulled a single cowrie shell from my collar and placed it in the dirt at your feet. Your *ba* will see it glittering there forever like a small brilliant vulva, the entrance and the exit of life. You will remember the curled and swirling passages of our love. *You will call upon me by name and never*

# AUTHOR'S NOTES:
## Historical background and family relationships

The line between history and fiction becomes precariously thin when dealing with a period some three and a half thousand years ago. In the process of conjecture, the historian is no less involved than the writer of historical fiction; while the former must account for history's frustrating silences, the latter must try to fill in those silences for his narrative purposes. Thus, while the names, places and major events in this book are based upon facts gathered from the archaeological findings during the excavations of Akhenaton's city, from the translation of the famous Tel-El-Amarna tablets, and from the researches of numerous scholars, the exact placement in time of certain political events may be open to question. For example, some of the campaigns of the Hittite king Shubiluliama are difficult to date. A. Goetze, in an article in the *Cambridge Ancient History* series, places the date of the *Amki* battles and the activities of the partisan Itakama very late in Akhenaton's reign. James Henry Breasted, however, writing earlier in the century, places an *Amki* battle before the fall of Tunip, and I have drawn from his account of the battle, rather than from that of Goetze. Similarly, the exact dates of the fall of certain coastal cities are difficult to determine, as is the exact time of the downfall of Tushratta.

The time and manner in which some of the figures in this tale meet their deaths is often, of necessity, conjectural. The blood relationships between certain of the figures is also often based upon surmise rather than fact. The issue of Nefertiti's parentage, for example, has not yet been closed; nor have scholars agreed on the origins of Ay and Smenkhare. The ultimate fates of Nefertiti, Tiy and Akhenaton himself are as yet not known, for their bodies have never been found, and later generations did their best to make life difficult for future writers by erasing all they could of the memory of the cursed royal house.

For the reader who is already familiar with the Tel-El-Amarna period, a word regarding my own arrangement of the much-disputed jigsaw of family relationships seems not out of place. That Ay might have been Tiy's brother is not established; it is a surmise based upon the similarity of his titles to those of Yuyu; in ancient Egypt the son of a successful man followed very much in his sire's footsteps. The similarity of names (Tuyu—Tiy and Yuyu—Ay) is another clue. Ay's supposed role of priest or High Priest is strongly disputed by the absence of any such title on the carvings in his tomb at Tel-El-Amarna. He is referred to as a "priest of Maat" but that was the title of a Vizier.

That Ay may have been the father of Nefertiti is another surmise; Cyril Aldred, in an article published in the *Journal of Egyptian Archaeology*, notes that the title *It Neter* may have referred to the father-in-law of the ruling king. However, Nefertiti is nowhere mentioned to be Ay's daughter (or anyone's, for that matter). I have chosen to regard her as such, as this seems somewhat closer to the truth than the other hypotheses—that she was a daughter of Tiy and Amenhotep, hence Akhenaton's sister (again disputed by the lack of inscriptions to that effect), or that she was the Mitannian princess Tadukhipa (which seems unlikely since the Egyptian throne rarely chose a foreigner as the king's chief consort as long as there were Egyptian ladies available). The right to rule was carried down through the female line of the royal house, normally through Pharaoh's own daughters, but in Amenhotep's marriage to Tiy we have already seen a breach of custom, so the fact that Nefertiti was not *Pharaoh's* daughter might be overlooked.

That Smenkhare is presented in this tale as Akhenaton's son may bring a frown to the brows of those readers who are aware of the fifty-year-old controversy which has surrounded the body of a young man found in the "tomb of Queen Tiy" at Thebes. First thought to be Akhenaton himself, due to the long skull, gynacoid bone structure, and generally effeminate appearance, the body was later labelled as that of Smenkhare, successor to the throne, brother or half-brother to Tutankhamon. My taking him to be Akhenaton's son is not supported by any evidence other than the tremendous physical similarities and the rather doubtful appellation "Beloved of Wanre." However, so much mystery surrounds Smenkhare (as it does the other figures in Akhenaton's circle) that almost any hypothesis regarding his origin is as yet open to question.

Finally, to place another piece in this fascinating and infinitely frustrating jigsaw—Akhenaton himself was nowhere mentioned to be the son of Amenhotep III, although he was Tiy's child (*that* is written!).

His physical deformities, some of which were shared by other members of the royal house (Smenkhare and Akhenaton's six daughters) are also ambiguous. The long skull, which to some suggests a hydrocephalic condition, was not uncommon in Old Kingdom Egypt, judging from bodies found in tombs of that early period. Dr. A. T. Sandison, writing in the *Journal of Egyptian Archaeology*, points to an endocrine disorder as the cause of the abnormalities in the trunk and limbs. However, Akhenaton had numerous daughters, which rules out the possibility that he may have had an endocrine disease resulting in eunuchoidism (despite the Karnak statue with its undraped, effeminate torso). Upon examination of the mummy of Smenkhare, it was found that the main features pointed to the possibility of secondary hypogonadism; in such a condition, sterility is inevitable.

*Regarding the ambiguity of Egyptian myths and gods*

In ancient Egypt gods were often combined to form dual-deities; for the Egyptian, the aspects of one god could easily be incorporated into another with no apparent contradiction. Examples of this are Ra-Horakhte, Amon-Ra, Ra-Atum, and, even in Akhenaton's monotheism, Horus-Aton. The main cult centres of the predominant gods each claimed their own version of the Creation; hence in the Memphite creed Ptah became the father of Atum. In the Osirian creed centred at Abydos, Osiris assumed a universal role above and beyond his original role of god of vegetation. As a result of these incorporations and interminglings of gods, there arose many paradoxical but *coexistent* accounts of Creation. One such account stated boldly that Ra arose out of the lotus created by eight original gods and then proceeded to create *all things*, divine and human!

As Veronica Ions states in her book *Egyptian Mythology*, "The search for new symbols went on constantly; each one was considered to represent one facet of the truth and did not necessarily entail rejection of previously held concepts.... [T]he modern reader must constantly bear in mind that the Egyptian myths ... cannot be considered as fixed stories."

*Akhenaton and Atonism*

A glance at some of the scholarly studies of Akhenaton reveals the vast differences of opinion scholars hold. Freud hypothesized that Akhenaton and his monotheistic creed were the forces behind the later Mosaic faith. Immanuel Velikovsky sees in Akhenaton the original Oedipus whose city was the Egyptian, rather than the Greek, Thebes. We are confronted with the "co-regency" and the "non-co-regency" schools which argue the issue of whether or not the young Amenhotep IV ruled beside his aging father before abandoning Thebes. Breasted believed Akhenaton to be the "first individual in history"; others see him as a mere fanatical upstart. Some scholars regard Atonism as a brilliant and original creation, while others recognize in it a simplification of the ancient worship of Ra.

In ancient Heliopolis (On) Aton was the designation of the sun's disc, but Akhenaton's deity was "Lord of all that the Disc surrounds." No doubt the difficulty of expressing something so foreign to the Egyptian mind as an *intangible* power gave rise to the clumsy and misleading holy epithets of the Aton. Akhenaton's god signified more than it did in the days of Heliopolis—the invisible Being who manifested Himself within the Disc was the one god, and the actual object of worship was the mysterious power emanating from the physical sun.

Akhenaton himself was neither saint nor sinner; no doubt like all great reformers he was a combination of both. He created a religion but lost an empire through neglect; it is little wonder, then, that scholarly opinion is sharply divided. As always, the truth should rest somewhere between the apparent extremes, yet I doubt it is the task of either historian or writer to establish that kind of truth. In the present book I have tried to find a midway point between the major theories of historians and my own view of Akhenaton himself. We know how he lived, but not how he died. We know of Nefertiti's exile, but not its cause; we know of a tomb made for Queen Tiy, but we are still in doubt as to its contents, and so on.

Anatole France said, "History is not a science; it is an art, and one succeeds in it only by imagination." Such a remark is especially apt when one is dealing with the remote Amarna period and the ambiguous solar priest himself.

G. MacEwen.

# A GLOSSARY OF ANCIENT NAMES AND TERMS

Wherever possible I have used the ancient Egyptian names for festivals, places, gods and persons, in preference to the Classical or modern names—except in those instances where long usage has rendered the derived form more familiar and in some cases almost indispensable (i.e., *Isis, Osiris, Horus*, etc.). In Egyptian place-names, however, I have avoided the Classical *Thebes, Heliopolis, Memphis*, etc., and have used the ancient Egyptian name in as close an English transliteration as possible. Countries have their ancient names and many of the foreign cities are readily identifiable—*Karukamesh*, Carcemish; *Ursalim*, Jerusalem; *Dumaska*, Damascus; and so on.

Following is a list of certain ancient names and terms used in the book whose meanings might well be further elaborated upon for the interested reader.

*Akhu* Disembodied spirits of the deceased, able to assume many forms. Those of noble birth were often considered to appear as stars.

*Am Duat* The ancient writings which described the nightly voyage of Ra through the Underworld.

*Amor* A kingdom on the upper Orontes River in what is now Syria.

*Amu* Asiatics in general, enemies of Pharaoh.

*Amuru* Literally "Westerners," northwestern Semites of the land of Amor.

*Ankh* The symbol of life, later the *crux ansata*. Sometimes termed "the key to the Nile." Grammatically it refers to "Life" or "living," and often formed parts of names, e.g., *Ankh em Maat*, Living in Truth.

*Anupew* Anubis, jackal-headed god of the Underworld.

*Apop* The cosmic Snake Apophis, associated with evil, darkness, night.

*Ashur* Assyria.

*Ba* Half-bird, half-human creature, soul of the deceased which hovered about the tomb area.

*Baou-Ra* A sacred library or collection of ancient writings containing religious or scientific wisdom.

*Ben-Ben* The sacred pyramidical stone, symbolic of the point of land where Ra as a bird first alighted at Creation; also symbolic of the slanting rays of the sun. The origin of obelisk and pyramid structures.

*Benu Bird* The sacred bird of Ra, depicted as a hawk with the head of a heron; the hieroglyphic spelling of *benu* included a heron. The *benu* was identified by the Greeks with the phoenix.

*Biya* Iron extracted from meteorites which was thought to have magical powers. Although the Hittites were working iron in Akhenaton's time, the metal was relatively unknown in Egypt.

*Djed Pillar* A pillar used in sacred festivals to represent the regenerative power of Osiris. Its symbolic origin is not known, but it would seem to be, among other things, an elaboration of the phallic motif in ancient art.

*Duat* The Egyptian Underworld.

*Habiru* The much-discussed invaders of Palestine, probably a semi-nomadic Semitic people of the same basic stock as the later Hebrews.

*Heb Sed Jubilee* A ceremony wherein Pharaoh publicly renewed his youth by demonstrating his vigour. A sort of anniversary as well, marking the end of a certain regnal term. A modern parallel might be found in Mao's swimming of the Yangtse River.

*Horakhte* Literally "Horus of the Horizon"—an aspect of the god Horus which became associated with Ra as Ra-Horakhte.

*Horus Eye* In the battle between Horus and Seth, Horus's eye is torn and scattered and later restored by Thoth. In another segment of the same myth, Horus revives his dead father Osiris by plucking out his eye for him to eat—thus any offering to a god became the "Horus Eye." The famed "Eye of Osiris" was thought to have magical powers of warding off evil. (see also *Wedjet Eye*)

*Ka* The transcendental self or spiritual twin of a man which was shaped in heaven as the physical body was shaped on earth. Hence to die was to "meet one's *ka*." The *ka* itself would seem to have had two aspects, in that, after a man's death, his *ka* was simultaneously in heaven and close to the tomb.

*Karaduniash* The powerful kingdom between the Tigris and Euphrates rivers. Babylonia.

*Keme* Literally "The Black Land." Egypt is geographically dual-natured, due to the desert and the cultivated strip along the Nile. In ancient times it was called the Black Land, or the Red Land to denote either area. The former designation was the more popular.

*Khepri* The Creator in the form of a scarab or dung-beetle which rolls balls of dung or mud in front of it in which it lays its eggs. Hence one form of Ra the Creator was the winged scarab with the sun's disc between its feelers. Grammatically *khepher* referred to "creation"; hence certain names—*Ankheprure* (*Ankh Kheperu Ra*), Living in the Creations of Ra; *Nefer Kheprure*, Beautiful Are the Creations of Ra.

*Kheta* The land of the Hittites.

*Khor*  Syria. Sometimes referring to the territories of Syria and Palestine in general.

*Kush*  Ethiopia and the Sudan, under Egyptian sovereignty.

*Land of the Papyrus*  The Delta.

*Medjay*  Wandering tribesmen from the eastern desert of Egypt, employed as police or mercenaries.

*Merkebet*  Electrum, silver-gold alloy, popular in the ancient world.

*Misrii*  "Egypt" in the Semitic tongues. To the modern Arab, "Misra."

*Milku*  "King" in the Canaanitic tongues.

*Mitanni*  The powerful kingdom south of Kheta which played a heavy role in the politics of the 18th Dynasty.

*Naharin*  Northernmost Egyptian frontier province on the southern border of Mitanni. According to some scholars, Naharin *was* Mitanni.

*Nehesu*  Negroes from Ethiopia and the Sudan.

*Nine Bows*  A term designating the enemies of Pharaoh in general.

*No Amon*  The City of Amon, Thebes.

*Opet Isut*  "The Southern Sanctuary," Luxor.

*Opet Risut*  "The Northern Sanctuary," Karnak.

*Retenu*  Palestine.

*Sa Gaz Mesh*  A term used to denote wanderers, pillagers or cut-throats. Sometimes associated with the Habiru.

*Sar*  "King" in the Akkadian tongue. Also the name of a certain star.

*Septet*  The dog-star, Sirius, on which the ancient Egyptians based their yearly calendar.

*Set*  Seth, evil uncle of Horus who fought him after Osiris's death. The "Cain" of Egyptian mythology.

*Sin*  The Sinai.

*Tekhen*  Obelisk or gnomon, a rudimentary type of sundial, essentially a *ben-ben* with a tall base. Sometimes enlarged to monumental proportions, as "Cleopatra's Needle."

*The Two Lands*  Egypt, Upper and Lower. Originally two separate lands eventually united by King Narmer. Pharaoh's double crown and the two royal symbols worn in front of it (the cobra for Lower Egypt and the vulture for Upper Egypt) represented the union of the Two Lands.

*Wedjet Eye* Originally the left eye of Ra or Atum, which was finally placed on the god's brow to rule the world as the divine eye in the form of the *uraeus*. Associated with the ancient cobra goddess Wedjet or Buto, it symbolized royal power on the brow of Pharaoh. *Wedjet* eyes were frequently used as symbols of protection or power on amulets or in tombs. One of the most salient features of the Egyptian religion in general is not only the creation but the *preservation* of the life of the gods, often accomplished by a re-absorption or restoration of their divine or bodily substance (see *Horus Eye*); thus the *Wedjet* was also the "intact eye."

# Afterword

Gwen had a wonderful imagination even at a very young age. As children, one of our favourite outings was to the Royal Ontario Museum in Toronto. The dinosaurs and totem poles were awe-inspiring, but even more exciting was the Egyptian exhibit. There was jewellery and artefacts from a time we couldn't quite fathom and the Mummy with its cloth deteriorated and yellowed, a little frightening, was something we were drawn to visit again and again. I believe these outings were the beginning of Gwen's absorption with Egyptian history and culture; perhaps also the beginning of an idea which would someday become *King of Egypt, King of Dreams*.

Gwen first visited Egypt in 1962 just prior to the breakdown of her marriage to Milton Acorn. The trip had been planned and anticipated for some time and it was a stimulating experience for her: digging in the ruins, collecting small treasures and recording the sounds of the open marketplace.

In 1965 Gwen received a grant from the Canada Council enabling her to begin research on her next novel. Her personal life was now much more settled; she eventually left her house on Ward's Island, resided for a time in the Sunnyside area of Toronto and in the late 1960s moved to my home and became a live-in aunt.

This was a move that was extremely popular with her nieces and nephews. Gwen's intention was to help me out as I was now going through a difficult time as a single mother. But a house full of youngsters was not the ideal environment for a serious author. Gwen found a small apartment nearby where she could write with no interruption and still be close to the family.

At the end of the 1960s Gwen met Nikos Tsingos; she had found the love of her life. My children thought he was wonderful, as did I. Gwen adored him. This was an extremely happy period for Gwen—life was good again—a perfect time for the completion and publication of her second novel.

Carol Wilson
Barrie, Ontario, 2004

# Suggested Reading

Literary critics have been less interested in MacEwen's fiction than in her poetry. Among the small number of sustained engagements with *King of Egypt, King of Dreams* are Jan Bartley's two monographs, *Invocations: The Poetry and Prose of Gwendolyn MacEwen* (1983) and *Gwendolyn MacEwen and Her Works* (1984), Jane Kilpatrick's unpublished *The Conscious Gods: A Critical Study of the Novels of Gwendolyn MacEwen* (1972; can be accessed at the University of Toronto's Scarborough College Library), and Rosemary Sullivan's biography *Shadowmaker: The Life of Gwendolyn MacEwen* (1995). An article by Maria Luz González, "El Camino arquetipico del héroe: el mago y el sumo sacerdote en las novelas de Gwendolyn MacEwen," in *Revista Canaria de Estudios Ingleses*, 1999, 39: 307-21, is also of interest.